KU-273-503

the collectors

ALSO BY DAVID BALDACCI

Absolute Power

Total Control

The Winner

The Simple Truth

Saving Faith

Wish You Well

Last Man Standing

The Christmas Train

Split Second

Hour Game

The Camel Club

David Baldacci

the collectors

MACMILLAN

First published 2006 by Warner Books, USA

This edition published 2006 by Macmillan
an imprint of Pan Macmillan Ltd
Pan Macmillan, 20 New Wharf Road, London N1 9RR
Basingstoke and Oxford
Associated companies throughout the world
www.macmillan.com

ISBN-13: 978-1-4050-8984-5 (HB)
ISBN-10: 1-4050-8984-9
ISBN-13: 978-1-4050-9011-7 (TPB)
ISBN-10: 1-4050-9011-1

Copyright © 2006 by Columbus Rose, Ltd

The right of David Baldacci to be identified as the
author of this work has been asserted by him in accordance
with the Copyright, Designs and Patents Act 1988.

This book is a work of fiction. Names, characters, places,
and incidents are the product of the author's imagination or
are used fictitiously. Any resemblance to actual events, locales,
or persons, living or dead, is coincidental.

All rights reserved. No part of this publication may be
reproduced, stored in or introduced into a retrieval system, or
transmitted, in any form, or by any means (electronic, mechanical,
photocopying, recording or otherwise) without the prior written
permission of the publisher. Any person who does any unauthorized
act in relation to this publication may be liable to criminal
prosecution and civil claims for damages.

5 7 9 8 6

A CIP catalogue record for this book is available from
the British Library.

Printed and bound in Great Britain by
Mackays of Chatham plc, Chatham, Kent

Visit www.panmacmillan.com to read more about all our books and to buy
them. You will also find features, author interviews and news of any author
events, and you can sign up for e-newsletters so that you're always first to hear
about our new releases.

To Art and Lynette,
with much love and respect.

And to the memory of
Jewell English.

the collectors

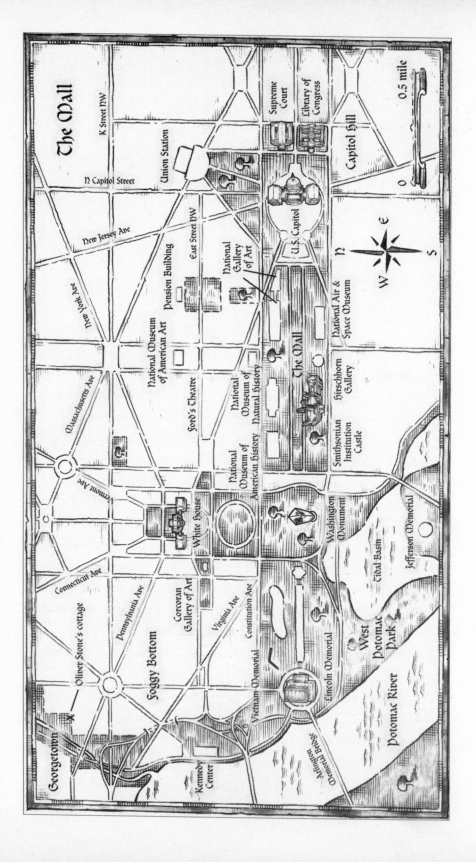

CHAPTER

1

ROGER SEAGRAVES WALKED OUT of the U.S. Capitol after an interesting meeting that, surprisingly, had had little to do with politics. That evening he sat alone in the living room of his modest suburban home after arriving at an important decision. He had to kill someone, and that someone was a very significant target. Instead of a daunting proposition, Seagraves saw it as a worthy challenge.

The next morning Seagraves drove to his office in northern Virginia. Sitting at his desk in a space that was small and cluttered, and looked exactly the same as other work spaces up and down the corridor, he mentally assembled the critical pieces of his task. Seagraves finally concluded that he would do the deed himself, unwilling to trust it to a third party. He'd killed before, many times in fact; the only difference now was he wouldn't be doing it for his government. This one was all for him.

He spent the next two days in careful, decisive preparation efficiently conducted around his day job. The three imperatives of his mission were embedded in every action he performed: (1) keep it simple; (2) provide for every contingency; and (3) never panic no matter how much your plan goes awry, which it occasionally did. However, if there were a fourth rule, it would have to be: exploit the fact that most people are fools when it comes to things that actually matter, like their own survival. He had never suffered from that shortcoming.

Roger Seagraves was forty-two, single and childless. A wife and brats would certainly have complicated his unorthodox lifestyle. In his previous career with the federal government he'd adopted false identities and traveled across the world. Fortunately, changing identities was stunningly easy to do in the computer age. A few clicks of the Dell, a server somewhere in India hummed, and from one's fancy laser printer out popped a new you with all the official bells, whistles and available credit.

Seagraves could actually buy all that he needed on an Internet site that required a carefully guarded password. It was akin to a Macy's department store for criminals, sometimes dubbed by its felonious clientele as "EvilBay." There one could purchase everything from first-rate ID packs and stolen credit card numbers to the services of professional hit men, or sterilized weapons if you were inclined to commit the murder yourself. He usually obtained the necessary materials from a dealer who had a 99 percent approval rating from his customers *and* a money-back guarantee. Even killers liked to go with quality.

Roger Seagraves was tall, well built and handsome with thick blond wavy hair; on the surface he seemed carefree in his ways and possessed an infectious grin. Virtually every woman in his vicinity copped a second look, as did some envious men. He often used this to his advantage. When you had to kill or deceive, you used whatever tools you had as effectively as possible. His government had taught him that too. Though he still technically labored for the United States, he also worked for himself. His "official" pension plan fell far short of giving him the quality retirement he felt he deserved after so many years of risking his life for the red, white and blue. For him, though, it had been mostly *red*.

On the third afternoon after his enlightening visit to the Capitol Seagraves subtly modified his features and put on several layers of clothing. When it grew dark, he drove a van up into the expensive fringes of northwest D.C. where the embassies and private mansions all had paranoid guards patrolling their compounds.

He parked in a small courtyard behind a building across the street from a very exclusive club housed in an imposing brick Georgian that catered to wealthy *and* politically obsessed persons, of whom Washington had more than any city on earth. These folks loved to gather over passable food and average wine and talk polls, policies and patronage to their hearts' content.

Seagraves wore a blue jumper suit with "Service" stenciled on the back. The key he'd made earlier fit the simple lock of the vacant building that was awaiting extensive renovation. His toolbox in hand, he took the steps two at a time until he reached the top floor and entered a room facing the street. He flashed a penlight around the empty space, noting the single window. He'd left it unlocked and well oiled on an earlier visit.

He opened his toolbox and quickly assembled his sniper rifle. Next he attached the suppressor can to the muzzle, chambered a single round—he was nothing if not confident—crept forward and drew up the window a bare two inches, just enough to allow the can to fit in the opening. He checked his watch and looked up and down the street from his lofty perch without much worry of being spotted, since the building he was in was completely dark. In addition, his rifle had no optics signature and sported Camoflex technology, meaning it changed color to match its background.

Oh, what the human race had learned from the humble moth.

When the limo and lead security car pulled up to the club, he drew his bead on the head of one of the men who got out of the stretch, but he didn't fire. It wasn't time yet. The club member walked inside followed by his security men sporting ear fobs and thick necks sticking out of starched collars. He watched the stretch and the security car pull off.

Seagraves checked his watch again: two hours to go. He continued to scan the street below as town cars and cabs dropped off serious-faced women outfitted not in carats of De Beers and yards of Versace, but in smart off-the-rack business suits and tasteful costume jewelry, with their social and political antennae set on high. The serious-faced men accompanying them were hunkered down in pinstripes, bland ties and what seemed to be bad attitudes.

It won't get any better, gents, trust me.

One hundred and twenty minutes dragged by, and his gaze had never once left the club's brick façade. Through the large front windows he could see the efficient swirl of folks who cradled their drinks and murmured in low, conspiratorial tones.

Okay, it was time for business.

He gave the street another quick scan. Not a soul was looking his way. Over his career he'd found they never were. Seagraves waited patiently until the target walked through his crosshairs for the last time, then his gloved finger edged to the trigger. He didn't particularly like firing through a windowpane, though it wouldn't interfere with the flight of the ordnance he was using.

Thwap! This was followed instantly by a tinkle of glass and the heavy thud of a pudgy dead man hitting a highly polished oak floor. The Honorable Robert Bradley had felt no pain at all with the impact. The bullet had killed his brain before it could tell his mouth to start screaming. *Not a bad way to go, actually.*

Seagraves calmly laid down the rifle and peeled off his jumpsuit, exposing the D.C. police uniform underneath. He put on a matching hat he'd brought with him and marched down the stairs to the rear door. When he exited the building, he could hear the screams from across the street. Only nineteen seconds had passed since the shot; he knew because he'd counted the ticks off in his head. He now moved rapidly down the street as he continued to time the action in his head. The next moment he heard the powerful whine of the car engine as the carefully choreographed scene was played out. Now he began to run all out, pulling his pistol as he did so. He had five seconds to get there. He turned the corner in time to almost be hit by the sedan as it raced by him. At the last instant he leaped to the side, rolled and came up in the middle of the road.

People across the street shouted at him, pointing at the car. He turned, gripped his gun with both hands and fired at the sedan. The blanks in his gun sounded sweet, just like the real thing. He placed five shots and then sprinted hard down the asphalt for half a block and slid into what appeared to be an unmarked police cruiser parked there; it raced after the fast-disappearing sedan, its siren blaring and grille lights flashing.

The car it was "chasing" turned left at the next intersection, then right, and headed down an alley, stopping in the middle. The driver in the car jumped out, ran to the lime-green VW Beetle parked in front of his in the alley and drove off.

Once out of sight of the club, the other car's grille lights and siren stopped as it peeled away from the hunt and headed in the opposite direction. The man next to Seagraves never once looked at him as he climbed into the backseat and stripped off the police uniform. Underneath the cop clothes he wore a tight-fitting one-piece jogging outfit; black sneakers were already on his feet. In the floorboard of the car was a muzzled six-month-old black Lab. The car whipped down a side street and turned left at the next corner, stopping beside a park deserted at this late hour. The back door opened, Seagraves climbed out and the car sped off.

Seagraves held the leash tightly as he and his "pet" commenced their "nightly" jog. When they turned right at the next corner, four police cruisers flew past the pair. Not one face in the cop convoy even glanced at him.

A minute later, in another part of the city, a fireball raced into the sky. It was the rented and fortunately empty town house of the dead man. Initially, it would be blamed on a gas leak that had ignited. Yet combined with the murder of Bob Bradley, the federal authorities would seek out other explanations, though they wouldn't come easily.

After running for three blocks Seagraves abandoned his pet, a waiting car was climbed into and he was back at his home less than an hour later. Meanwhile, the United States government would have to find another Speaker of the House to replace the recently deceased Robert "Bob" Bradley. *That shouldn't be too hard,* Seagraves mused as he drove to work the next day after reading of Bradley's murder in the morning newspaper. *After all, the damn town is full of bloody politicians. Bloody politicians? That's an apt description.* He pulled his car to the security gate, displayed his ID badge and was waved through by the armed guard there who knew him well.

He strode through the front door of the sprawling building in Langley, Virginia, passed through additional security gauntlets and then headed to his eight-by-ten-foot cluttered cookie-cutter office. He was currently a midlevel bureaucrat whose main work consisted of being a liaison between his agency and the incompetent and brainless on Capitol Hill who'd somehow been voted into office. It was not nearly as taxing as his old job here, and represented a bone thrown his way for meritorious service. Now, unlike decades ago, the CIA let its "special" employees come in from the cold once they'd reached the age where re-flexes slowed a bit and enthusiasm for the work diminished.

As Seagraves looked over some tedious paperwork, he real-ized how much he'd missed the killing. He supposed people who had once murdered for a living never really got over that bloodlust. At least last night had given him a bit of the old glory back.

That was one problem out of the way, but another one would probably soon take its place. Yet Roger Seagraves was a creative troubleshooter. It was just his nature.

CHAPTER

2

GREAT BELCHES OF BLACK
smoke—probably packed with enough carcinogens to vanquish
an unsuspecting generation or two—were propelled from ancient brick factory stacks into a sky already dark with rain
clouds. In an alleyway of this industrial town that was dying an
irreversible death due to penny wages paid in far more polluted
cities in China, a small crowd had gathered around one man.
This was not a crime scene with a dead body, or a street Shakespeare honing his acting chops, or even a big-lunged preacher
hawking Jesus and redemption for a modest contribution to the
cause. This man was known in the trade as a "broad tosser," and
he was doing his best to relieve the crowd of its money in a game
of chance called three-card monte.

The "shills" supporting the tosser were adequate as they won
staged betting rounds at timed intervals to keep the marks hopeful for their own streak of luck. The "wall man," or lookout, was
a bit lethargic. At least the woman watching them from across
the street deduced this from his body language and listless eyes.
She didn't know the "muscle" that was also part of this con
team, yet he didn't look overly tough, just doughy and slow.
The two "ropers" were young and energetic and, as their title

implied, it was their job to keep a steady supply of innocents coming to play a card game they would never win.

She moved closer, watching as the enthusiastic crowd alternately clapped and groaned as bets were won and lost. She'd started her career as a shill for one of the country's best tossers. That particular con could run a table in virtually any city and walk away an hour later with at least two grand in his pocket, the marks having no idea they'd been the victim of anything more than poor luck. This tosser was excellent and for good reason: He'd been trained by the same man as she. To her informed eye he was using the double-card queen-up-front technique that would substitute the back card for the queen at the critical moment of delivery, for this was the entire key to the game.

The simple object of three-card monte, like the shell game it was based on, was to pick the queen from the trio on the table after the tosser had mixed them around with blurring speed. That was impossible to do if the lady wasn't even on the table at the time the guess was made. Then a second before the queen's "correct" position was revealed, the tosser would smoothly replace one of the cards with the queen and show the group where it had supposedly been all the time. This simple "short con" had lifted money from marquises and marines and everything in between for as long as playing cards had been around.

The woman slipped behind a Dumpster, made eye contact with someone in the crowd and put on a pair of large tinted sunglasses. A moment later the wall man's attention was completely distracted by a cute miniskirted bettor. She'd bent straight over in front of him to pick up some dropped cash and gave the lookout a nice view of her firm butt and the red thong that made little attempt to cover it. The wall man no doubt thought he'd gotten incredibly lucky. However, just as with three-card monte, there was no luck involved. The woman had earlier paid the miniskirt to perform the "drop and bend" when she signaled her by putting on the shades. This simple distraction technique had worked on men ever since women had started wearing clothes.

Four quick strides and the lady was right in their midst, moving with a swagger and energy that parted the crowd immediately as the stunned lookout watched helplessly.

"Okay," she barked, holding up her creds. "I want to see some ID from you," she snapped, pointing a long finger at the tosser, a short, pudgy middle-aged man with a small black beard, bright green eyes and a pair of the nimblest hands in the country. He studied her from under his ball cap, even as he slowly reached in his coat and pulled out his wallet.

"All right, folks, party's over," she said, opening her jacket so they could see the silver badge attached to her belt. Many of the people gathered there began to back away. The intruder was in her mid-thirties, tall and broad-shouldered with a sleek pair of hips and long red hair, and dressed in black jeans, green turtle-neck and a short leather jacket. A long muscle in her neck flexed when she spoke. A small, dull red scar the shape of a fishhook was perched under her right eye but remained hidden by the sunglasses. "I said party's over. Pick up your cash and disappear," she said in a voice notched an octave lower.

She'd already noted that the bets left on the table had vanished the moment she started speaking. And she knew exactly where they'd gone. The tosser *was* good, reacting to the situation instantly and taking control of the only thing that mattered: the money. The crowd fled without bothering to argue about their missing cash.

The muscle took a hesitant step toward the intruder but then froze as her gaze cut into him.

"Don't even think about it, because they just love fat boys like

you in the federal swamp." She looked him up and down lasciv-
iously. "They get a lot more meat for their dime." The muscle's
lip began to tremble even as he fell back and tried to fade into
the wall.

She marched up to him. "Uh-uh, big boy. When I said clear
out, I meant you too."

The muscle nervously glanced at the other man, who said,
"Get out of it. I'll look you up later."

After the man had fled, she checked the tosser's ID, smirking
as she handed it back to him and then made him stand against
the wall for a pat-down. She picked up a card from the table
and turned it around so he could see the black queen. "Looks
like I win."

The tosser stared unfazed at the card. "Since when do the feds
care about a harmless game of chance?"

She put the card back on the table. "Good thing your marks
didn't know how 'chancy' this game of chance really was. Maybe
I should go and enlighten some of the bigger guys who might
like to come back and beat the crap out of you."

He looked down at the black queen. "Like you said, you won.
Why don't you name your payoff?" He took a roll of cash from
his fanny pack.

In response she took out her creds, slipped the badge off her
belt and dropped both on the table. He glanced down at them.

"Go ahead," she said casually. "I have no secrets."

He picked them up. The "creds" didn't authenticate her as a
law enforcement officer. Behind the plastic shield was a membership card for the Costco Warehouse Club. The badge was tin
and engraved with a brand of German beer.

His eyes widened as she slipped off her sunglasses and recognition instantly came. "Annabelle?"

Annabelle Conroy said, "Leo, what the hell are you doing cooking monte with a bunch of losers in this crappy excuse for a town?"

Leo Richter shrugged but his grin was wide. "Times are tough. And the guys are okay, a little green, but learning. And monte's never let any of us down, has it?" He waved the wad of bills before stuffing them back in his fanny pack. "Little dicey pretending to be a cop," he scolded mildly.

"I never *said* I was a cop, people just assumed. That's why we have a career, Leo, because, if you have enough balls, people assume. But while we're talking about it, trying to *bribe* a cop?"

"In my humble experience it works more often than not," Leo said, fishing a cigarette out of a pack in his shirt pocket and offering her one. She declined.

"How much you making on this gig?" she asked matter-of-factly.

Leo glanced at her suspiciously as he lit his Winston, took a drag and blew smoke out his nostrils, neatly matching at least in miniature the fetid clouds coming out of the smokestacks overhead. "The pie's split up enough as it is. I've got employees to take care of."

"Employees! Don't tell me you're issuing W-2s now?" Before he could answer, she added, "Monte's not on my radar, Leo. So how much? I'm asking for a reason, a good one." She folded her arms across her chest and leaned back against the wall waiting.

He shrugged. "We usually work five locations on a rotation, about six hours a day. Clear three or four thou on a good one. Lotta union boys 'round here. Those guys are always itching to lose their cash. But we'll be moving on soon. Another round of factory layoffs coming, and we don't want people remembering our faces too well. It's not like I have to tell you the drill. I get the sixty split of the net, but expenses are high these days. Saved up about thirty Gs. I'm looking to double that before winter. It'll hold me for a while."

"But *just* a while, knowing you." Annabelle Conroy picked up her beer badge and Costco card. "Interested in some *real* money?"

"The last time you asked me that I got shot at."

"*We* got shot at because *you* got greedy."

Neither one was smiling now.

"What's the deal?" Leo asked.

"I'll tell you after we run a couple shorts. I need some seed for the long."

"A long con! Who does that anymore?"

She cocked her head and stared down at him. In her high-heeled boots she was five-eleven. "I do. I never stopped, in fact."

He noted her long red hair. "Weren't you a brunet the last time I saw you?"

"I'm anything I need to be."

A grin eased across his face. "Same old Annabelle."

Her gaze hardened slightly. "No, not the same old. Better. You in?"

"What's the risk level?"

"High, but so's the reward."

A car alarm erupted with eardrum-shattering decibels. Neither of them even flinched. Cons at their level that lost their cool under any circumstances became either guests of the penal system or dead.

Leo finally blinked. "Okay, I'm in. What now?"

"Now we line up a couple other people."

"We rolling all-star on this?" His eyes glittered at the prospect.

"Long con deserves nothing but the best." She picked up the black queen. "I'll take my payment in dinner tonight for pulling the lady out of your 'magic' deck."

"Afraid there aren't many restaurants worth eating at around here."

"Not here. We're flying to L.A. in three hours."

"L.A. in three hours! I'm not even packed. And I don't have a ticket."

"It's in your left jacket pocket. I snaked it there when I was feeling you up." She eyed his flabby midsection and raised an eyebrow. "You've put on weight, Leo."

She turned and strode off as Leo checked his pocket and found the plane ticket. He grabbed his cards and raced after her, leaving the card table where it was.

Monte was on vacation for a while. The long con was calling.

CHAPTER

3

OVER DINNER THAT NIGHT IN L.A. Annabelle laid out parts of her plan to Leo, including the two players she was looking to bring on.

"Sounds good, but what about the long con? You haven't told me about that."

"One step at a time," she answered, fingering a wineglass, her gaze wandering around the swanky dining room automatically searching for potential marks.

Take a breath, find a chump. She flicked her dyed-red hair out of her face and made momentary eye contact with a guy three tables down. This jerk had been ogling and overtly signaling Annabelle in her little black dress for the last hour while his humiliated date sat silently fuming. Now he slowly licked his lips and winked at her.

Uh-uh, slick, you couldn't even come close to handling it.

Leo interrupted this thought. "Look, Annabelle, I'm not going to screw you. Hell, I came all this way."

"Right, you came all this way on *my* dime."

"We're partners, you can tell me. It goes no further."

Her gaze drifted over him as she finished her cabernet. "Leo, don't bother. Even you're not that good of a liar."

A waiter came by and handed her a card. "From the gentleman over there," he said, pointing to the man who'd been ogling her.

Annabelle took the card. It said that the man was a talent agent. He'd also helpfully written on the back of the card a specific sex act he'd like to perform on her.

Okay, Mr. Talent Agent. You asked for it.

On the way out she stopped at a table with five stout guys in pinstripe suits. She said something and they all laughed. She gave one of them a pat on the head and another, a man of about forty with gray temples and thick shoulders, a peck on the cheek. They all laughed at something else Annabelle said. Then she sat down and talked with them for a few minutes. Leo looked at her curiously as Annabelle left the table and walked past him toward the exit.

As she passed the talent agent's table, he said, "Hey, baby, call me. I mean it. You are so hot, I'm on fire!"

Annabelle swiped a glass of water off the tray of a passing waiter and said, "Well, then let's cool you off, stud." She dumped the water in the guy's lap. He jumped up.

"Damn it! You're gonna pay for that, you crazy bitch."

His date covered her mouth to hide her laughter.

Before the man could reach out to grab her, Annabelle shot out a hand and clutched his wrist. "You see those boys over there?" She nodded at the five suits that sat staring at the man hostilely. One of them cracked his knuckles. Another slid his hand inside his suit jacket and kept it there.

Annabelle said smoothly, "I'm sure you saw me talking to them, since you've been staring at me all night. They're the Moscarelli family. And the one on the end there is my ex, Joey Junior. Now, even though I'm no longer technically in the family, you never really leave the Moscarelli clan."

"Moscarelli?" the man said defiantly. "Who the hell are they?"

"They were the number three organized crime family in Vegas before the FBI ran them and everybody else out. Now they've gone back to doing what they do best: controlling the garbage unions in the Big Apple and Newark." She squeezed his arm. "So if you have a problem with your wet pants, I'm sure Joey will take care of it."

"You think I'm buying that crap?" the guy shot back.

"Well, if you don't believe me, go over there and talk to him about it."

The man looked over at the table again. Joey Junior was holding a steak knife in his beefy hand while one of the other men was attempting to keep him in his seat.

Annabelle gripped the man's arm tighter. "Or do you want me to have Joey come over here with some of his friends? Don't worry; he's out on parole right now, so he can't bust you up really bad without ticking off the feds."

"No. No!" the alarmed man said as he tore his gaze from murderous Joey Junior and his steak knife. He added quietly, "I mean, it's no big deal. Just a little water." He sat back down and dabbed at his soaked crotch with a napkin.

Annabelle turned to his date. The woman was trying and failing to hold back her giggles. "You think it's funny, sweetie?" Annabelle said. "This is a case of where we're all laughing *at* you, not with you. So why don't you try finding some self-respect, or little shits like him are the only slime you'll be waking up next to until you're so old nobody will give a crap anymore. Including you."

The lady stopped laughing.

On the way out of the restaurant Leo said, "Wow, and here I was wasting my time reading Dale Carnegie when all I needed to do was hang around you."

"Give it a rest, Leo."

"Okay, okay, but the Moscarelli family? Come on. Who were they really?"

"Five accountants from Cincinnati probably looking to get laid tonight."

"You're lucky they seemed pretty tough."

"It wasn't luck. I said I was practicing a scene from a movie with a friend of mine in public. I told them it happens all the time in L.A. I asked them to help out, that they were to look like the mob; you know, to give us the right atmosphere to deliver our lines. I told them if they did well enough, they might even get a part in the film. It's probably the most excitement they've ever had."

"Yeah, but how'd you know that jerk would collar you on the way out?"

"Oh, I don't know, Leo, maybe it was that *tent pole* in his pants. Or did you think I just threw the water in his crotch for the hell of it?"

The next day Annabelle and Leo cruised down Wilshire Boulevard in Beverly Hills in a rented dark blue Lincoln. Leo intently eyed the shops they were passing. "How'd you get a lead on him?"

"Usual sources. He's young and doesn't have much street experience, but his specialty is why I'm here."

Annabelle pulled into a parking place and pointed to a storefront up ahead. "Okay, that's where gadget boy screws the retail consumer."

"What's he like?"

"Very metrosexual."

Leo looked at her quizzically. "*Metrosexual?* What the hell's that? New kind of gay freak?"

"You really need to get out more, Leo, *and* work on your PC skills."

A minute later Annabelle led Leo into a high-end clothing boutique. Inside the store, they were greeted by a lean, good-looking young man dressed all in chic black with slicked-back blond hair and a day's worth of fashionable stubble on his face.

"You here all by yourself today?" she asked him, looking around at the other well-heeled customers in the store. They'd have to be wealthy, she knew, since the shoes here *started* at a thousand bucks a pair, entitling the lucky owner to stumble around on four-inch golf tees until her Achilles snapped.

He nodded. "But I enjoy working the store. I'm very service-oriented."

"I'm sure you are," Annabelle said under her breath.

After waiting until the other customers had left the shop, Annabelle put the Closed sign on the front door. Leo brought a woman's blouse to the cash register while Annabelle wandered around behind the checkout area. Leo handed over his credit card, but it slipped out of the clerk's hand and the man bent down to retrieve it. When he straightened up, he found Annabelle standing right behind him.

"That's a really neat toy you have there," she said, eyeing the tiny machine the clerk had just swiped Leo's card through.

"Ma'am, you're not allowed behind the counter," he said, frowning.

Annabelle ignored this comment. "Did you build it yourself?"

The clerk said firmly, "It's an antifraud machine. It confirms that the card is valid. It checks encryption codes embedded in the plastic. We've had a lot of stolen credit cards come in here, so the owner instructed us to start using it. I try to do it as unobtrusively as possible so no one gets embarrassed. I'm sure you can understand."

"Oh, I completely understand." Annabelle reached by the clerk and slid out the device. "What this does, *Tony,* is read the name and account number, and the embedded verification code on the magnetic stripe so you can forge the card."

"Or more likely sell the numbers to a card ring that'll do it," Leo added. "That way you don't have to get your *metrosexual* hands really dirty."

Tony looked at both of them. "How do you know my name? You cops?"

"Oh, much better than that," Annabelle said, putting her arm around his slender shoulders. "We're people just like you."

Two hours later Annabelle and Leo were walking down the pier in Santa Monica. It was a bright cloudless day, and the ocean breeze delivered waves of deliciously warm air. Leo wiped his forehead with a handkerchief, took off his jacket and carried it over his arm.

"Damn, I'd forgotten how nice it was out here."

"Beautiful weather and the best marks in the world," Annabelle said. "That's why we're here. Because where the best marks are . . ."

"Are where the best cons are," Leo finished for her.

She nodded. "Okay, that's him, Freddy Driscoll, crown prince of bad paper."

Leo stared ahead, squinting against the sun, and read the small sign over the outdoor kiosk. "Designer Heaven?"

"That's right. Do it like I said."

"What other way is there to do it but like *you* said?" Leo grumbled.

They reached the merchandise display where jeans, designer bags, watches and other accessories were neatly arranged. The older man next to the kiosk greeted them politely. He was small and plump with a pleasant face; tufts of white hair stuck out from underneath the straw hat he wore.

"Wow, these are great prices," Leo commented as he looked over the items.

The man beamed proudly. "I don't have the overhead of the fancy stores, just the sun, sand and ocean."

They looked through the merchandise, selected a few items, and Annabelle handed the man a hundred-dollar bill in payment.

He took it from her, put on a pair of thick glasses, held the bill up at a certain angle and then quickly handed it back. "Sorry, ma'am, I'm afraid that's a forgery."

"You're right, it is," she said casually. "But I thought it was fair to pay for fake goods with fake money."

The man didn't even blink; he just smiled at her benignly.

Annabelle examined the bill in the same way the man had. "The problem is that not even the best forger can really duplicate Franklin's hologram when you hold the bill at this angle, because you'd need a two-hundred-million-dollar printing mill to get it right. There's only one of them in the States, and no forger has access to it."

Leo piped in, "So you take a grease pen and do a nifty sketch of old Benny. That gives anyone smart enough to check the paper a little flash and the illusion that he saw the h-gram when he really didn't."

"But *you* knew the difference," Annabelle pointed out. "Because you used to make this paper about as well as anyone." She held up a pair of jeans. "But from now on, I'd tell your supplier to take the time to stamp the brand name on the zipper like the real manufacturers do." She put the jeans down and picked up a handbag. "And double-stitch the strap. That's a dead giveaway too."

Leo held up a watch that was for sale. "And real Rolexes sweep smoothly, they don't tick."

The man said, "I'm really shocked that I've been the victim of counterfeit merchandise. I saw a police officer just a few minutes ago farther down on the pier. I'll go and get him. Please don't leave; he'll want your full statements."

Annabelle gripped his arm with her long, supple fingers. "Don't waste your cover story on us," she said. "Let's talk."

"What about?" he asked warily.

"Two shorts and then a long," Leo answered, making the old man's eyes light up.

CHAPTER

4

ROGER SEAGRAVES LOOKED across the conference table at the mouse of a man and his pitiful comb-over consisting of a dozen strands of greasy black hair that vainly attempted to cover a wide, flaky scalp. The man was skinny in the shoulders and legs and fat in the belly and butt. Though still in his forties, he probably would've been hard-pressed to jog more than twenty yards without collapsing. Lifting a grocery bag would no doubt have taxed the limits of his upper body strength. He could be a poster boy for the physical degradation of the entire male race in the twenty-first century, Seagraves thought. It irked him because physical fitness had always played paramount importance in his life.

He ran five miles every day, finishing before the sun was fully up. He could still do one-handed push-ups and bench-press twice his own weight. He could hold his breath underwater for four minutes and sometimes worked out with the high school football team near his home in western Fairfax County. No man in his forties could keep up with seventeen-year-old boys, but he was never that far behind them either. In his previous career these skills had all served one purpose: keeping him alive.

His attention turned back to the man across the table from

him. Every time he saw the creature a part of him wanted to place a round in the man's forehead and put him out of his lethargic misery. But no sane person killed his golden goose or, in this case, golden mouse. Seagraves may have found his partner physically lacking, but he needed the man nonetheless.

The creature's name was Albert Trent. The man had a brain under the wretched body, Seagraves had to give him that. An important element of their plan, perhaps the most important detail, had, in fact, been Trent's idea. It was for this reason more than any other that Seagraves had agreed to partner with him.

The two men spoke for some time about the upcoming testimony of CIA representatives to the House Permanent Select Committee on Intelligence, of which Albert Trent was a prominent staff member. Next they covered key bits of intelligence gathering undertaken by the folks at Langley and other agencies in the U.S. government's vast arsenal of spooks. These folks spied on you from outer space, through your phone, fax, e-mail and sometimes right over your shoulder.

Finished, the two men sat back and drank down their lukewarm coffee. Seagraves had yet to find a bureaucrat who could make a decent cup of coffee. Maybe it was the water they had up here.

"The wind's really picking up outside," Trent said, his eyes on the briefing book in front of him. He smoothed his red tie over his flab and rubbed his nose.

Seagraves glanced out the window. Okay, now it was code time, just in case someone was listening in. These days nowhere was safe from prying ears, least of all Capitol Hill. "Front's coming in, I saw on the news. Might get some rain later, but then again, maybe not."

"I heard a thunderstorm was possible."

Seagraves perked up at this. A thunderstorm reference always got his attention. Speaker of the House Bob Bradley had been such a thunderstorm. He was now lying in a plot of dirt back in his native Kansas with a bunch of wilted flowers on top of him.

Seagraves chuckled. "You know what they say about the weather: Everyone talks about it, but no one does a damn thing about it."

Trent laughed too. "Everything looks good here. We appreciate Central Intelligence's cooperation as always."

"Didn't you know? The 'C' stands for cooperation."

"We still set for the DDO's testimony on Friday?" he asked, referring to the CIA's deputy director of operations.

"Yep. And behind closed doors we can be very candid."

Trent nodded. "The new committee chairman knows how to play by the rules. They already took a roll call vote to close the hearing."

"We're at war with terrorists, so it's a whole new ball game. Enemies of this country are everywhere. We have to act accordingly. Kill them before they get us."

"Absolutely," Trent agreed. "It's a new age, a new kind of fight. And perfectly legal."

"Goes without saying." Seagraves stifled a yawn. If anyone *was* listening, he hoped they'd enjoyed the patriotic crap. He'd long since stopped caring about his country—or any other country, for that matter. He was now solely into caring about himself: the Independent State of Roger Seagraves. And he had the skills, nerve and access to things of enormous value to do something about it. "Okay, unless there's anything else, I'll be hitting the road. Traffic will be a bitch this time of day."

"When isn't it?" Trent tapped the briefing book as he said this.

Seagraves glanced at the book he'd given the other man even as he picked up a file Trent had pushed across to him. The file contained some detailed requests for information and clarification regarding certain surveillance practices of the intelligence agency. The massive briefing book he'd left for Trent held nothing more exciting than the usual dull-as-dirt overly complicated analysis his agency routinely fed the oversight committee. It was a masterpiece of how to say absolutely nothing in the most confusing way possible in a million words or more.

However, if one read between the proverbial lines, as Seagraves knew that Trent would do that very evening, the briefing book's pages also revealed something else: the names of four very active American undercover agents and their current locations overseas, all in coded form. The right to the delivery of these names and addresses had already been sold to a well-financed terrorist organization that would knock on these people's doors in three countries in the Middle East and blow their heads off. Two million dollars a name in U.S. dollars had already been wired to an account that no American bank regulator would ever audit. Now it was Trent's job to move the stolen names on down the food chain.

Business was booming for Seagraves. As the number of America's global enemies continued to pile up, he was selling secrets to Muslim terrorists, communists in South America, dictators in Asia and even members of the European Union.

"Happy reading," Trent said, referring to the file he'd just given him. It was here that the encrypted identity of the "thunderstorm" would be revealed to Seagraves along with all the whys and wherefores.

At his home later that night Seagraves stared at the name and began plotting the mission in his usual methodical way. Only this time it would take something far more subtle than a rifle and scope. Here Trent came through like a gem with a piece of intelligence on the target that simplified things greatly. Seagraves knew just whom to call.

CHAPTER

5

Punctually at six-thirty on a clear, cool morning in Washington, D.C., the front door of Jonathan DeHaven's three-story home opened, and out he stepped dressed in a gray tweed jacket, pale blue tie and black slacks. A tall, spare man in his mid-fifties with a carefully combed head of silver hair, DeHaven inhaled the refreshing air and spent a few moments gazing at the row of magnificent old mansions that lined his street.

DeHaven was far from the wealthiest person in his neighborhood, where the *average* price of a towering brick structure would set the purchaser back several million dollars. Luckily, he'd inherited his place from parents savvy enough to be early investors in the choicest D.C. real estate. Although much of their estate had gone to charity, the DeHavens' only child had also been left a sizable amount to supplement his government salary and indulge certain whims.

Even though this windfall had allowed DeHaven to pursue his life without worrying about earning money by any means possible, this was not true of other dwellers on Good Fellow Street. In fact, one of his neighbors was a merchant of death—

though DeHaven supposed the politically correct term was "de-fense contractor."

The man, Cornelius Behan—he liked to be called CB—lived in a palatial space that cobbled *two* original dwellings into a fifteen-thousand-square-foot behemoth. DeHaven had heard rumors that this had been accomplished in the strictly controlled historical area by well-timed bribes. This conglomerate not only boasted a four-person elevator but also had separate servant's quarters with actual servants living in them.

Behan also brought an assortment of ridiculously beautiful women to his manse at odd hours, though he did have the decency to wait until his wife was out of town, often on one of her shopping sprees in Europe. DeHaven trusted that the wronged woman enjoyed her own dalliances while across the Atlantic. This summoned up an image of the elegantly attractive lady being mounted by a young French lover while perched nude on an enormous Louis XVI dining table with "Bolero" playing in the background. *And bravo for you,* DeHaven thought.

He cast aside thoughts of his neighbors' peccadilloes and set off to work with a lively bounce in his step. Jonathan DeHaven was the immensely proud director of the Rare Books and Special Collections Division at the Library of Congress, arguably the finest rare books collection in the world. Well, the French, Italians and Brits might debate the point, but the obviously biased DeHaven knew that the American version was the best.

He walked about a quarter mile along a series of rumpled brick sidewalks, with a precise tread learned from his mother, who'd meticulously marched every step of her long life. On the day before she died DeHaven was not completely sure his famously imperious mother wouldn't simply skip the funeral and stalk right up to heaven demanding to be let in so she could commence running things. At one corner he boarded a crowded

Metro bus, where he shared a seat with a young man covered in drywall dust, a battered ice cooler wedged between his feet. Twenty-five minutes later the bus dropped DeHaven off at a busy intersection.

He crossed the street to a small café, where he had his morning cup of tea and a croissant and read the *New York Times.* The headlines, as usual, were very depressing. Wars, hurricanes, a possible flu pandemic, terrorism, it was enough to make you crawl in your house and nail the doors shut. One story dealt with a probe into irregularities in the defense-contracting arena. There were allegations of bribery and corruption between politicians and weapons manufacturers. *What a shock!* A dollars-for-influence scandal had already brought down the former Speaker of the House. And then his successor, Robert Bradley, had been brutally murdered at the Federalist Club. The crime was still unsolved, although a domestic terrorist group, heretofore unknown, calling itself Americans Against 1984—a reference to Orwell's masterpiece of fascism—had claimed responsibility for the crime. The police investigation was not going well, at least according to the media.

DeHaven occasionally glanced out the café window at government workers striding with great purpose down the street ready to take on the world, or at least a nebbish senator or two. It really was the most unusual place, he thought. Here you had epic crusaders dancing alongside sleazy profiteers coupled with more than a fair sampling of idiots and intellectuals, with the former, unfortunately, usually holding higher positions of power. It was the only city in the United States that could declare war, raise your federal income tax or reduce your Social Security benefits. The decisions reached in these few square miles of monuments and mockeries made legions of people either furious or euphoric, and those sides kept switching depending on who was in control of the government at any given time. And the fights, spins and conspiracies concocted and then carried out to hold or regain power consumed every ounce of energy that enormously bright and talented people could give it. The swirling, ever-changing mosaic had too many frenetically moving parts for any outsider to even come close to comprehending what was really going on. It was like a lethal kindergarten that never ended.

A few minutes later DeHaven trotted up the broad steps of the massively domed Library of Congress' Jefferson Building. He signed for the alarmed door keys from the library police and headed up to the second floor, quickly making his way to room LJ239. Located here were the Rare Books reading room and the honeycombed series of vaults that kept secure many of the nation's paper treasures. These bibliophilic riches included an original printed copy of the Declaration of Independence that the Founding Fathers had labored over in Philadelphia on the march to freedom from England. *What would they think of the place now?*

He unlocked the massive outer doors of the reading room and swung them back against the inside walls. Then he performed the complicated keypad procedure allowing him to enter the room. DeHaven was always the first person to arrive here each day. While his typical duties kept him away from the reading room, DeHaven had a symbiotic relationship with old books that would be inexplicable to a layperson and yet a bond immediately understandable to a bibliophile of even modest addiction.

The reading room was not open on the weekends, which allowed DeHaven to ride his bike, collect rare books for his personal collection and play the piano. It was a skill he'd learned under the rigorous tutelage of his father, whose ambition to be a concert pianist had been rudely crushed by the reality that he wasn't quite good enough. Unfortunately, neither was his son. And yet ever since his father's death, DeHaven had actually enjoyed playing. Despite sometimes bristling under their strict code of conduct, he had almost always obeyed his parents.

In fact, he had really only performed one act that had gone against their wishes, yet it was quite a large transgression. He'd married a woman nearly twenty years younger than him, a lady quite apart from his station in life, or so his mother had informed him over and over until she'd badgered him into having the marriage annulled a year later. However, no mother should be able to force her son to leave the woman he loved, even with the threat of cutting him off financially. His mother had stooped as low as telling him she would also sell all of her rare books, which she had promised to leave to him. Yet he should have been able to stand up to her, tell her to back the hell off. He thought this now, of course, far too late. If only he had possessed a backbone years ago.

DeHaven sighed wistfully as he unbuttoned the front of his jacket and smoothed down his tie. It had quite possibly been the happiest twelve months of his life. He had never met a person like her before, and he was certain he wouldn't again. *Yet I just let her go because my mother bullied me into it.* He'd written the woman for years afterward, apologizing any way he could. He sent her money, jewelry and exotic items from his trips around the world, but he never asked her to come back. No, he'd never done that, had he? She wrote him back a few times, but then his packages and letters started being returned unopened. After his mother died, he considered trying to find her, but finally decided it was too late. In truth, he didn't deserve her anymore.

He took a deep breath, put the door keys in his pocket and gazed around the reading room. Patterned after the Georgian splendor of Independence Hall, the space had an immediate calming effect. DeHaven particularly loved the copper domed lamps that sat on all the tables. He ran his hand over one lovingly, and the sense of failure in losing the only woman who'd ever given him complete happiness began to fade.

DeHaven walked across the room and pulled out his security card. He waved it in front of the computer access pad, nodded to the surveillance camera bolted into the wall above the door and walked into the vault. Coming here each morning was a daily ritual; it helped to recharge his batteries, reinforce the notion that it really was all about the books.

He spent some time in the hallowed grounds of the Jefferson Room leafing through a copy of the work of Tacitus, a Roman that the third U.S. president much admired. Next he used his keys to enter the Lessing J. Rosenwald Vault, where incunabula and codex donated by Rosenwald, the former head of Sears, Roebuck, sat next to each other on metal shelves in a room that, at great cost, was climate-controlled 24/7. Though the library operated on a very tight budget, a constant temperature of sixty degrees with a relative humidity of 68 percent could allow a rare book to survive for at least several more centuries.

For DeHaven it was well worth the extra money to a federal budget that had always allocated more to war than it ever did to peaceful purposes. For a fraction of the cost of one missile he could purchase on the open market every work the library needed to round out its rare books collection. Yet politicians believed that missiles kept you safe, whereas actually books did, and for a simple reason. Ignorance caused wars, and people who read widely were seldom ignorant. Perhaps it was an overly simplistic philosophy, but DeHaven was sticking to it.

As he looked over the books on the shelves DeHaven reflected on his own book collection housed in a special vault in the basement of his home. It wasn't a great collection but a very satisfactory one. Everyone should collect something, DeHaven felt; it just made you feel more alive and connected to the world.

After checking on a couple books that had just come back from the conservation department, he headed up the stairs to the vaults that stretched over the reading room. It was here that an early collection of American medical books was kept. And on the mezzanine level just above, a large array of children's books were housed. He stopped to affectionately pat the head of a small bust of a man that had sat on a small table in a corner for as long as anyone could remember.

A moment later Jonathan DeHaven collapsed into a chair and commenced dying. It was not a pleasant or painless death, as evidenced by the convulsions and silent screams as life was squeezed from his body. By the time it was over a mere thirty seconds later he was stretched out on the floor a full twenty feet from where he'd started. He seemed to stare at a collection of stories that had girls in tea dresses and sun hats on the covers.

He died without knowing what had killed him. His body had not betrayed him; he was in perfect health. No one had done him blunt injury, and no poison had touched his lips; he was, in fact, completely alone.

And yet dead Jonathan DeHaven was.

About twenty-five miles away Roger Seagraves' phone rang at his home. It was the weather report: sunny and clear for the foreseeable future. Seagraves finished his breakfast, grabbed his briefcase and headed to work. He loved it when the day started on a positive note.

CHAPTER

6

CALEB SHAW ENTERED THE Rare Books reading room and strolled to his desk against the wall at the back, where he deposited his knapsack and bike helmet. He took a moment to undo the strap around his ankle that kept chain grease off his pant leg, and then settled down in his chair. He had a lot to do this morning. The previous day a prominent American scholar had requested over six hundred books to prepare a complex bibliography, and it was Caleb's job as a research specialist to gather them together. He'd already looked the works up in the library's directory; now came the laborious task of plucking them off the shelves.

He smoothed down his rumpled gray hair and loosened his belt a bit. Caleb had a slightly built frame, but as of late he'd experienced an uncomfortable weight gain around his waist. He hoped that riding his bike to work would adequately address this problem. He avoided anything approaching a sensible diet, immensely enjoying his wine and rich food. Caleb was also proud of the fact that he'd never seen the inside of a gym after his graduation from high school.

He walked to the vault entrance, placed his card over the security pad and pulled the door open. Caleb was a little surprised not to have seen Jonathan DeHaven when he came in. The man was always here before anyone else, and the door to the reading room *had* been unlocked. Yet Caleb assumed the director was either in his office or perhaps in the vaults.

"Jonathan?" he called out, but received no answer. He glanced at the list in his hand. This task would easily take him the entire day, if not longer. He grabbed a book cart from against one of the walls and set about his work, methodically going through each of the vaults containing books he needed. A half hour later he came back out of the vault to get another list he needed as a woman he worked with entered the reading room.

He exchanged pleasantries with her and went back into the vault. It was very cool inside, and he remembered that yesterday he'd left his sweater on the vault's fourth floor. He was about to take the elevator up when he gazed down at his middle-age spread and decided on the stairs instead, actually running up the last few steps. He passed by the medical collection, took another flight of steps up and reached the mezzanine. He strode across the main walkway to the place where he'd left his sweater.

When he saw the body of Jonathan DeHaven lying on the floor, Caleb Shaw gasped once, choked and then fainted.

The tall, wiry man walked out of the plain cottage and into the small cemetery where he worked as caretaker. There was a lot of work to be done in making sure that the homes of the dead were maintained properly. Ironically, he himself "officially" resided in a grave at Arlington National Cemetery, and most of his former mates in the government would have been surprised to learn that he was still alive. In fact, it still surprised him that he wasn't dead. The agency where he'd worked had tried its best to murder him for no reason other than his no longer wanting to kill for his government.

He saw the creature's movement from the corner of his eye and checked to make sure no one was watching from the nearby apartment building. Then with a fluid motion he slipped the knife from the sheath on his belt and turned. Creeping forward, he aimed and let the blade fly. He watched as the copperhead writhed, the knife pinning it to the ground through the snake's head. The damn thing had almost bitten him twice over the last week while hiding in the high grass. After it was dead, he pulled the knife free, wiped it off and disposed of the serpent in a trash can.

While he didn't often use his old skills, they sometimes came in handy. Thankfully, though, the days where he would lie in wait for a target to enter his killing range were long in the past. Yet his present life had certainly been impacted by the past, starting with his name.

He had not used his real identity, John Carr, in over thirty years. He'd been known for decades now as Oliver Stone. He had changed his name partly to foil attempts by his old agency to track him down and partly as an act of defiance against a government that he felt was less than honest with its citizens. For decades he'd maintained a small tent in Lafayette Park across from the White House where he was one of a handful of "permanent protesters." The sign next to his tent read simply "I want the truth." In pursuit of this goal he headed up a small, informal watchdog organization called the Camel Club that had as its purpose keeping the American government accountable to its people. And he had been known to harbor a few conspiracy theories from time to time.

The other members of the club, Milton Farb, Reuben Rhodes and Caleb Shaw, held no positions of power and wielded no influence; and yet they kept their eyes and ears open. It was remarkable what could be accomplished when one was steadfastly observant and then acted on those observations with both courage and ingenuity.

He gazed at the sky that promised rain later. A wind from an approaching front rustled his close-cropped white hair, which used to be down to his shoulders, along with a thick, disheveled beard that had once covered his chest. Now the most he sported was a couple days' worth of growth before shaving it off. Both hair and beard had been altered to keep him alive during the Camel Club's last adventure.

Stone threw some weeds into a garbage pail and then spent some time shoring up an old tombstone that marked the resting place of a prominent African American preacher who'd lost his life in the fight for freedom. Odd, thought Stone, that one had to fight for freedom in the freest land on earth. As he gazed around Mt. Zion Cemetery, once a stop on the underground railroad shepherding slaves to freedom, he could only marvel at the remarkable persons that lay in the ground here.

As he worked, he was listening to the news on a portable radio he'd set on the ground beside him. The news anchor had just launched into a story about the overseas deaths of four State Department liaisons in Iraq, India and Pakistan in separate incidents.

State Department liaisons? Stone knew what that meant. U.S. intelligence operatives had gotten their cover blown and been murdered. The official spin would hide that fact from the public; it always did. Yet Stone prided himself on keeping on top of current geopolitical events. As part of his salary the church that employed him provided three daily newspapers. He cut out many articles and pasted them in his journals. At the same time, he used his experience to discern the truth behind the spin.

His ringing cell phone disturbed these thoughts. He answered, listened briefly and asked no questions. Then he started to run. His friend and fellow Camel Club member Caleb Shaw was in the hospital, and another man who worked at the Library of Congress lay dead. In his haste Stone forgot to lock the gates as he rushed through them.

The dead would have no doubt understood that the living took priority.

CHAPTER

7

CALEB SHAW LAY IN A HOSPITAL bed slowly shaking his head. Around him were the other members of the Camel Club. Reuben Rhodes was nearly sixty years old, over six foot four with the build of a football lineman. He had curly black hair that touched his shoulders and brooding eyes and an unkempt beard that made him appear quite mad at times; which, on occasion, was nearer the truth than not. Milton Farb was five-eleven and thin with longish hair and a cherubic, unlined face that made him look much younger than his forty-nine years.

Reuben was a much-decorated Vietnam War vet and former Defense Intelligence Agency employee, who currently worked at a loading dock after his military career had been derailed by booze, pills and his outrage over the war that he'd indiscreetly vented. He dried out with the help of Oliver Stone, who'd happened upon him at Arlington National Cemetery where Reuben had been unceremoniously lying stoned under a maple tree.

Milton had been a child prodigy of boundless intellectual ability. His parents had worked in a traveling carnival where their son's mental prowess was exploited in a freak show atmosphere. Despite that, he had gone to college and been employed at the National Institutes of Health. However, suffering from obsessive-compulsive disorder and other destructive mental ailments, his world had eventually come crashing down around him. He became destitute and fell into such debilitated mental shape that a court ordered him institutionalized.

Again Oliver Stone came to the rescue. He'd worked as an orderly at the psychiatric hospital where Milton had been a patient. Recognizing the man's remarkable abilities, which included a pure photographic memory, Stone managed to get a sedated Milton on *Jeopardy!* where he defeated all comers and earned a small fortune. Years of dedicated counseling and drug therapies had allowed him to live quite normally. He now had a lucrative business designing Web sites for corporations.

Stone leaned his six-foot-two-inch body against a wall, his arms crossed in front of him as he looked down at his friend in the bed.

Possessing twin doctorates in political science and eighteenth-century literature, Caleb Shaw had worked at the Library of Congress' Rare Books reading room for over a decade. Unmarried and childless, the library, aside from his friends, constituted the passion of his life.

Caleb had run into some hard times as well. He'd lost an older brother in Vietnam, and his parents had died tragically in a plane crash over fifteen years ago. Stone had met Caleb at the depths of his despair, when the librarian had seemingly lost his desire to keep going. Stone befriended him, introduced him to a bookstore owner in desperate need of help, and Caleb was gradually drawn out of his depression by his love of books. *I seem to collect hopeless cases,* Stone thought to himself. *Though I used to be one myself.* Indeed, Stone owed as much to his friends as they did to him, if not more. But for Caleb, Reuben and Milton, Stone knew, he wouldn't have survived either. After years of performing only destructive acts, Stone had spent the last thirty years of his life seeking a measure of personal redemption. By his count, he still had a long way to go.

Stone's musings were interrupted by the entrance of Alex Ford, a veteran Secret Service agent who'd played an instrumental role in helping the Camel Club in the past and been named an honorary member of the club for his heroics.

Ford stayed for half an hour and was relieved to find that Caleb would be okay.

He said, "Take care of yourself, Caleb. And call me if you need anything."

"How are things at WFO?" Stone asked him, referring to the Service's Washington Field Office.

"Way too busy. The criminal elements have kicked it into overdrive."

"Well, I hope you've recovered fully from our little adventure."

"I don't call a potential global apocalypse a little adventure. And I don't think I'll ever fully recover."

After Alex Ford had left, Caleb turned to the others. "It was truly horrible," he said. "There he was just lying on the floor."

"And you fainted?" Stone asked, his gaze fixed on his friend.

"I must have. I remember turning the corner, looking for my sweater, and there he was. God, I almost stumbled over him. I saw his eyes. My mind went blank. My chest tightened. I felt so cold. I thought I was having a heart attack. And then I just passed out."

Reuben put a hand on Caleb's shoulder. "A lot of people would've fainted."

Milton piped in, "The National Psychiatric Foundation reports that finding a dead body ranks as the second most traumatic event a human being can experience."

Reuben raised his eyebrows at this comment. He said, "What's the number one traumatic experience? Finding your spouse in bed with a monkey holding a can of expired Cheez Whiz?"

"Did you know DeHaven well?" Stone asked Caleb.

"Yes. It's tragic, really. He was in excellent shape. He'd just had a complete cardio workup at Hopkins. But I guess anyone can have a heart attack."

"Is that what it was, a heart attack?" Stone said.

Caleb looked uncertain. "What else could it be? Or a stroke perhaps?"

"Statistically speaking, it was probably a heart attack," Milton added. "It's the leading cause of so-called instant death in this country. In fact, any of us could drop at any moment and be dead before we hit the floor."

"Damn, Milton," Reuben retorted, "do you have to be so bloody cheerful?"

"Until the autopsy results come back we can only speculate," Stone pointed out. "But you didn't see anyone else in the vault area, did you?"

Caleb stared up at his friend. "No."

"But you passed out pretty quickly, so you wouldn't have necessarily noticed anyone else around on the fourth floor?"

"Oliver, you can't get in the vault without using your pass card. And there's a camera right there at the main door."

Stone looked thoughtful. "First, the Speaker of the House is murdered, and now the director of the Rare Books Division dies under somewhat mysterious circumstances."

Reuben eyed him warily. "I doubt terrorists are targeting book peddlers these days, so don't work this into another grand conspiracy with the fate of the world in the balance. I can only take one Armageddon per month, thank you very much."

Stone's eyes twinkled. "We'll table the issue for now until we know more."

"I can give you a ride home, Caleb," Reuben said. "I have my motorcycle."

Reuben's pride was his fully restored 1928 Indian motorcycle with the very rare left-hand sidecar.

"I don't think I'm up to that, Reuben." Caleb paused and added, "Frankly, that contraption of yours terrifies me."

A nurse bustled in, took the patient's vitals and stuck a temperature reader in Caleb's left ear.

"Can I go home soon?" he asked.

She took the reader out and looked at it. "You're almost up to normal. And yes, I think the doctor is preparing the discharge orders now."

As arrangements were made for Caleb's release, Stone drew Reuben aside.

"Let's keep an eye on Caleb for a while."

"Why? You think he's really hurt?"

"I don't want him to *get* hurt."

"The guy died from a coronary, Oliver. It happens every day."

"But probably not for someone who'd just been given a clean bill of health by Johns Hopkins."

"Okay, so he popped a blood vessel or fell and cracked his skull. You heard Caleb: The guy was all alone in there."

"As far as Caleb knows, he was, but he couldn't possibly know for sure."

"But the security camera and the pass card," Reuben protested.

"All good points, and they may very well confirm that Jonathan DeHaven was alone when he died. But that still doesn't prove he wasn't killed."

"Come on, who'd have a grudge against a librarian?" Reuben asked.

"Everyone has enemies. The only difference is for some people you just have to look harder to find them."

CHAPTER

8

"How's it check out?" Leo Richter said into his phone headset as he punched in some numbers on the keypad. He sat in his car in front of a drive-through ATM in Beverly Hills. In a van parked across the street Tony Wallace, until recently a felonious boutique store clerk, examined the video feed on the screen in front of him. "Sweet. I've got a perfect frame of your fingers inputting the PIN. And I've got a tight shot of the face of the card going in. With the zoom and the freeze I can read everything on it."

The night before, they had switched the metal box containing bank brochures that was bolted to the side of the ATM with a box of Tony's manufacture. He'd earlier stolen a box from another ATM and built an exact replica in the garage of the rental house Annabelle had them staying at. Inside the fake brochure box, Tony had placed a battery-powered video camera with wireless feed pointed at the keypad and card slot for the ATM. The camera could send the picture up to two hundred meters away, well within range of the van.

As a backup they'd also placed a skimmer Tony had built over the ATM's card slot. It was such a perfect replica that not even Annabelle could find fault with it. This device captured all the numbers on the cards, including the embedded verification code on the magnetic stripe, and fed them wirelessly to a receiver in the van.

Annabelle was sitting next to Tony. Across from her was Freddy Driscoll, who'd been plying his trade selling fake Gucci and Rolexes on the Santa Monica pier until he'd run into Annabelle and Leo. Freddy was manning another video camera aimed out the heavily tinted side window of the van.

"I've got a clear shot of the cars and license plates going through," he reported.

"Okay, Leo," Annabelle said into her headset. "Move out of the way and let the real money through."

"You know," Tony said, "we don't really need the camera at the ATM because we've got the card skimmer. It's redundant."

"Transmission from the skimmer gets garbled sometimes," Annabelle said, staring at the TV screen in front of her. "And you miss one number, the card's useless. Plus, the camera gives us info the skimmer doesn't. We're only doing this once. No mistakes."

Over the next two days they sat in the van as the ATM camera and skimmer captured debit and credit card information. Annabelle methodically matched this information with the cars and their license plates going through the ATM lane, loading it all on a laptop in a spreadsheet format. Annabelle was also prioritizing.

She said, "Bugatti Veyrons, Saleens, Paganis, Koenigseggs, Maybachs, Porsche Carrera GTs and Mercedes SLR McLarens get five stars. The Bugatti sells for one and a quarter million, and the others sell for between four and seven hundred thousand. Rolls-Royces, Bentleys and Aston Martins get four stars. Jags, BMWs, regular Mercedes get three stars."

Leo jokingly said, "What about Saturns, Kias and Yugos?"

At the end of the two days they regrouped at the rental house.

"We go quality over quantity," Annabelle said. "Thirty cards. That's all we need."

Leo read through the spreadsheet. "Perfect, because we've got twenty-one five stars and nine four stars all matched to their card numbers."

"Only in L.A. would you see *two* Bugatti Veyrons going through the same ATM," Tony commented. "A thousand horsepower, top speed of two-fifty and gas over three bucks a gallon. I mean, where do they get that kind of money?"

"Same way we do, they rip people off," Leo answered. "Only the law says the way they do it is legal for some reason."

"I fought the law and the law won," Tony crooned. He eyed Annabelle and Leo. "You two ever done any time?"

Leo started shuffling a deck of cards. "He's a real funny guy, isn't he?"

"Hey, how come you took down their license plate numbers too?" Tony asked.

"You never know when it might come in handy," Annabelle answered vaguely.

She looked at Freddy, who was going over some equipment he'd arranged on a large table in the adjoining room. This included a stack of blank credit cards and a thermal dye printer.

"You have everything you need?" she asked.

He nodded, looking over his tools with satisfaction while running a hand through his cottony hair. "Annabelle, you run a first-class operation."

Three days later Freddy had built thirty counterfeit cards, complete with colored graphics and a magnetic stripe encoded with the verification code on the back and embossed with the victim's name and account number on the front. The finishing touch had been the hologram, a security measure banks have been using since the early 1980s. The only way to tell the difference was that real holograms are embedded in the card while the fake clung to the surface, something an ATM wouldn't be able to distinguish.

"You can buy all the credit card numbers you want off the Internet," Tony pointed out. "That's where the real pros go."

Annabelle replied, "And I guarantee you that none of those 'quick' cards belong to anyone who owns a Bugatti, other than by luck."

Leo quit shuffling his cards and lit a cigarette. "It was probably a pro who told you that, kid, so you wouldn't start doing it the smart way and competing with him. Sizing the mark up right is Con 101."

Tony said, "Damn! Have I been that stupid?"

"Yes, you have," Annabelle said. "Okay, here's the plan." She perched on the arm of a chair. "I've rented cars for all of us under fake ID packs. The three of you each take eight cards, and I'll take six, which makes our total thirty cards. You'll individually hit forty ATMs in the metro area and perform two transactions at each. You'll alternate the cards you use at every ATM, so at the end you'll have accessed each account ten times.

"I've got lists of all the ATMs. And I've plotted it out for each of you. They're all drive-through, and there's hardly any distance between them. And we're all in disguise because of the ATM cameras. I've got outfits for everybody."

"But there're limits on how much you can take out of an account in a day," Freddy said. "To protect against stolen cards."

Annabelle said, "With the marks we're going against, it's a certainty they have elevated withdrawal limits. People who drive seven-hundred-thousand-dollar cars don't like three-hundred-dollar limits on their ATM accounts. My contacts on the bank side tell me the usual initial bump-up is to twenty-five hundred. But aside from that, the counterfeit cards give us access to all of the mark's accounts, savings, checking. If we make a deposit from savings into checking to more than cover the amount of the withdrawal, then in the machine's mind that'll net out as a plus and override the ATM withdrawal limit, whatever it happens to be."

"So if we deposit, say, five thousand from savings into checking and withdraw four thousand, it won't even register as a net withdrawal from checking," Leo added.

"Yes."

"Are you sure?" Tony asked.

"I did a dry run last month with ten of the major banks, and it worked every time. It's a software glitch they haven't focused on yet. Until they do, well, it's a nice payday."

Leo smiled and started shuffling his cards again. "After this gig, you can bet they'll focus on it."

"Why not do eight transactions at each ATM, one for each card?" Tony suggested. "That way we don't have to hit so many banks."

"Because it might look a little suspicious if you're feeding eight cards into the slot while people are waiting behind you," Annabelle said in an impatient tone. "With two cards, it just looks like there was a glitch and you're feeding the card back in."

"Ah, the criminal youth, so wanton *and* clueless," Leo muttered.

She handed them all three-ring notebooks. "Inside these are the PINs for each card, and the exact amounts at each ATM you'll transfer for deposit and then withdraw for each account. After we finish, the notebooks get burned." She rose, went to a closet and threw them duffel bags. "Your disguises are in there, and then use the bags to carry the money." She sat back down. "I've allowed you ten minutes at each bank. We stay in contact with each other at all times. If anything looks weird at one location, skip it and go on to the next one."

Freddy looked at the dollar amounts listed in his notebook. "But what if the people don't have the funds to cover the deposit? I mean, even rich people are sometimes short of funds."

"They have the cash. I've already checked that," Annabelle said.

"How?" Tony asked.

"I called their bank, said I was a vendor and asked if they had enough money in their savings to cover a fifty-thousand-dollar account payable that they owed."

"And they just told you?" Tony said.

"They always tell you, kid," Leo answered. "You just have to know how to ask."

Annabelle said, "And over the last two days I've visited all the marks' homes. Each one, to my eye, was worth at least five million. There were *two* Saleens at one of the mansions. The dollars will be there."

"You visited their homes?" Tony said.

"Like the lady told you, license plates come in handy," Leo remarked.

"The total take will be nine hundred thousand, an average of thirty grand a card," Annabelle continued. "The banks we're hitting all net out their ATM accounts on twelve-a.m. cycles. We'll be finished long before that happens." She looked over at Tony. "And just in case someone gets the urge to cut and run, the next short con is going to double what we make off this one."

"Hey," Tony said in an offended tone, pushing a hand through his styled hair. "This is fun stuff."

"It's only fun if you don't get caught," Annabelle pointed out.

"So have you ever been caught?" Tony asked again.

In response, Annabelle said to Tony, "Why don't you read over your binder? That way you make no mistakes."

"It's just ATM stuff. I'll be okay."

"It wasn't a request," she said stiffly, and then walked out of the room.

"You heard her, kid," Leo said, not trying very hard to hide his grin.

Tony muttered something under his breath and stalked out of the room.

"She keeps things close to the vest, doesn't she?" Freddy remarked.

"Would you want to work with a con who didn't?" Leo countered.

"Who is she?"

"Annabelle," Leo answered.

"I know that, but what's her last name? I'm surprised I haven't crossed her path before. The high-stakes con world is pretty small."

"If she'd wanted you to know, she would've told you herself."

Freddy said, "Come on, Leo, you know all about us. And I've been around the block. It goes no further."

Leo considered this and then in a low voice said, "Okay, you gotta swear to take it to your grave. And if you tell her I told, I'll deny it and then I'll kill you. I mean it." He paused as Freddy promised.

"Her name's Annabelle Conroy," Leo said.

"Paddy Conroy?" Freddy said at once. "Now, *him* I've heard of. I assume they're related."

Leo nodded, keeping his voice low. "His daughter. But that was a well-kept secret. Most people never knew Paddy even had a kid. He passed Annabelle off as his wife sometimes. Pretty weird, but that was Paddy for you."

"I never had the pleasure of working with the man," Freddy added.

"Yeah, well, I had the *pleasure* of working with ol' Paddy Conroy. He was one of the best cons of his generation. And also one of the biggest assholes." Leo glanced in the direction that Annabelle and Tony had left the room, and his voice sank even lower. "You saw that scar under her right eye? Well, her old man did that. She got that for blowing a claim con when they were cheating the Vegas casinos at roulette. She was all of fifteen but looked twenty-one. Cost the old man three grand, and she got a hell of a beating for it. And it wasn't the only time, I can tell you that."

"Damn," Freddy said. "His own daughter?"

Leo nodded. "Annabelle never talks about any of it. I heard from another source."

"So you were working with them back then?"

"Oh, yeah, Paddy and his wife, Tammy. They had some good stuff going on back then. Paddy taught me the three-card monte routine. Only Annabelle's a better con than her old man ever thought of being."

"How come?" Freddy asked.

"Because she has the one quality Paddy never had. Fairness. She got it from her mother. Tammy Conroy was a straight-up piece of work, at least for a con."

"Fairness? Strange quality for people like us," Freddy remarked.

Leo said, "Paddy always led his teams with fear. His daughter does it with prep and competence. And she'll never ever screw you. I can't count the times Paddy blew town with the entire haul. That's why he ended up working alone. Nobody would touch his action anymore. Hell, even Tammy finally ditched him, so I heard."

Freddy remained silent for a bit, apparently letting all this sink in. "Any word on the long con?"

Leo shook his head. "It's her game to call. I just work here."

As Freddy and Leo headed into the kitchen to get some coffee, Tony peered around the other doorway. He'd left his notebook in the room and had come back in time to hear the entire conversation. He smiled. Tony loved knowing things people didn't think he knew.

CHAPTER

9

THE SCAM NETTED $910,000 because Tony had gotten greedy at one of the ATMs.

"What's the poor schmuck gonna have to do, trade in his Pagani?" he said snidely.

"Don't ever do that again," Annabelle said firmly as they sat over breakfast in a new rental house five miles from the first one, which had been thoroughly cleaned in case the police paid it a visit. All the Hertz cars used to steal from the thirty accounts had been turned back in. The disguises that had been worn were in several Dumpsters scattered around town. The money was in four different safe-deposit boxes that Annabelle had leased. The film footage and computer files had been erased and the notebooks destroyed.

"What's an extra ten grand?" Tony complained. "Hell, we could've taken 'em for a lot more than what we did."

Annabelle pushed a finger hard against his chest. "It's not about the money. When I lay out a plan, you follow it. Otherwise, you can't be trusted. And if you can't be trusted, you can't be on my team. Don't make me sorry I picked you, Tony." She stared the young man down and then turned to the others.

"Okay, let's go over the second short." Then she eyed Tony

again. "And this one is a face-to-face con. If you don't follow instructions and play the mark just right, your ass is going to the can, because the margin of error is zero."

Tony sat back, not looking nearly as enthusiastic.

She said, "You know, Tony, there's nothing better than seeing a mark eye-to-eye and taking a measure of him *and* yourself."

"I'm cool."

"Are you sure? Because if it's a problem, I need to know right now."

He glanced nervously at the others. "I got no problems."

"Good. We're heading to San Fran."

"What's there?" Freddy asked.

"The mailman," Annabelle replied.

They made the six-hour drive to San Francisco in two cars, Leo and Annabelle in one, Tony and Freddy in the other. They cut a two-week lease on a corporate condo on the outskirts of the city with a partial view of the Golden Gate. For the next four days they took turns pulling surveillance on an office complex in a posh suburb of the city. They were watching the pickups from the outdoor mailboxes that were filled to overflowing on most days, with packs of mail stacked next to the stuffed container. On each of those four days the mail carrier arrived within a quarter-hour window, between five and five-fifteen.

On the fifth day, at precisely four-thirty, Leo, dressed as a mail carrier, drove up to the box in a postal truck that Annabelle had gotten from a contact of hers an hour's drive south. This gent specialized in providing everything from armored cars to ambulances for less-than-honest purposes. From a car she was parked in across from the mailbox Annabelle watched Leo approach in the truck. Tony and Freddy were posted at the entrance to the complex. They'd alert Leo through his ear fob in

case the real mailman showed up early. Leo would only be taking the mail stacked outside the box, since he didn't have a key
to unlock the box. He could've picked the lock quite easily, but
Annabelle had vetoed that as unnecessary and potentially dangerous in case anyone saw him do it.

She'd said, "What's lying on the ground or sticking out of the
box will be plenty."

As Leo stacked the mail inside his truck, Annabelle's voice
came through his earpiece.

"You've got what looks to be a secretary running at you with
some mail."

"Roger that," Leo said quietly. He turned and faced the
woman, who looked disappointed.

"Oh, where's Charlie?" she said.

Charlie, the regular mailman, was tall and good-looking.

"I'm just helping Charlie out because there's so much mail,"
Leo said politely. "That's why I'm here a little early." He looked
at the stack of letters in her hands, and he held out his mail sack.
"You can just dump that right in here."

"Thanks. Payroll's gotta go out tonight. That's what's in the
letters."

"Really? Well, I'll take super-good care of them, then." He
smiled and went back to collecting the stacks as the woman returned to her office.

Back at the condo they searched through the haul quickly, divid-
ing up the usable from the irrelevant. The letters that were of no
use Annabelle had Tony take down to the corner mailbox and
post. The others were pored over by Annabelle and Freddy.

When Tony came back, he said, "You guys cut loose a bunch
of payroll checks. What's that about?"

"Payroll and accounts receivable checks are useless to us,"

Freddy said with the confidence of the expert he was. "They have laser locks binding the toner ink to the paper and secure number fonts so you can't alter the dollar amounts."

"That never made any sense to me," Leo said. "Those are checks going out to people they *know*."

Freddy held up a check. "This *is* what we want: a refund check."

Tony said, "But they're being sent to complete strangers."

"That's what doesn't make sense, kid," Leo said. "You put security stuff on checks sent out to people who work for you or you do business with. And you got zilch on checks going out to who the hell knows."

Annabelle added, "I picked that office complex because it houses regional offices for a number of Fortune 100 companies. Thousands of checks flow out of those places every day, and those accounts are loaded with money."

Five hours later Freddy had assembled eighty checks. "These are pretty clean. No artificial watermarks, warning bands or detection boxes." He carried the checks over to a small workshop he had set up in one room of the house. With the others' help he placed Scotch tape over the signature line, front and back of each check, placed them in a large baking pan and poured nail polish remover over the paper. The acetone in the polish remover quickly dissolved everything on the checks that wasn't written in base ink. After they'd taken the tape off the signature lines, all that was left were essentially eighty blank checks signed by the company's CEO or CFO.

"Somebody ran a bad check on my account once," Leo said.

"What'd you do?" Tony asked.

"Tracked the bastard down. He was an amateur, doing it more for kicks, but it still pissed me off. So I did a change of address on him, diverted all his bills, and the guy ended up being dunned by creditors for a couple of years. I mean, you got to leave this stuff to the professionals." Leo shrugged. "Hell, I could've ripped him off big-time, assumed his ID, the whole nine yards."

"So why didn't you?" Tony asked.

"I've got a heart!" Leo growled.

Freddy said, "After we dry out the checks, I'll redo the Federal Reserve routing numbers."

"What's that?" Tony asked.

"Are you sure you're a con?" Leo asked in a bemused tone.

Tony exclaimed, "My tools are computers and the Internet, not nail polish. I'm a twenty-first-century con. I'm paperless."

"Whoopee for you!" Leo shot back.

Annabelle held up one of the checks. "This is the Federal Reserve routing number," she said, pointing to the first two digits in a string of numbers on the bottom of the check. "That tells the bank the check was deposited at the clearinghouse the check's supposed to go to. The New York clearinghouse number is zero-two. San Fran's is twelve. A New York–based company using checks issued by a New York bank usually has New York's routing number on its checks, for example. Since we'll be passing the checks here, Freddy will switch the routing numbers on all the checks to New York. That way it takes longer for the company to get the paper back and realize it's a bad check."

Annabelle added, "And more importantly, these are all big companies that keep their accounts payable books by zero cash management methods. So the odds are very good that even with a bad check in the mix they won't turn up a relatively insignificant transaction until they get their end-of-the-month statements. Today's the fifth; that means we have about a month before they discover anything wrong. By then we're long gone."

"But what if the bank teller looks at the check and sees that the routing number is wrong?" Tony asked.

"I guess you never saw that TV program, did you?" Leo asked. "The one where investigative reporters zip into a bank with a check that had written across it, 'Don't cash me, I'm a forged check, you effing moron.' And the effing moron still cashed it."

Annabelle added, "I've never heard of a clerk spotting the wrong routing number on a check. Unless you give the teller a reason to suspect you, they won't spot it."

After the checks had dried out, Freddy scanned them onto his laptop. Six hours later he stacked eighty checks on the table totaling $2.1 million.

Annabelle ran her finger down the perforated edge of one of the checks, a usual indicator that the check itself was legit, even if the amounts and payee on it weren't. She glanced at the others. "Now comes the human side of the con. Passing the bad paper."

"My favorite part," Leo said eagerly as he finished a ham sandwich and washed it down with a large swallow of beer.

10

THEY'D DECIDED THAT ANNA-
belle and Leo would pass the first series of altered checks while
Tony watched Leo to see how it was done for real. Annabelle,
Leo and Tony each had a series of complete ID packs that
Freddy had made for them. These packs either matched the indi-
vidual payee on the check or contained credentials showing they
worked for the company the check was made out to. Annabelle
had instructed Leo and Tony to only carry one set of ID at a
time. In case they were stopped, it would be difficult to talk
their way out of a jam if they had eight aliases in their pockets.

A number of the checks were made out to individuals, none
for over $10,000, since that would require IRS notification. Be-
cause of that limit, they would have to move far too many personal checks to reach the $2.1 million mark to be practicable.
Thus, the rest of the payees on the checks were businesses that
Annabelle had set up accounts for at various banks. Company
checks could be made out for over $10,000 without triggering
interest from the IRS. But the hitch was no bank will cash a
company check. The full amount has to be deposited. For that
reason, over a period of months Annabelle had been depositing
funds into and out of these accounts, to establish a track record.

She well knew that banks tended to get antsy when freshly minted accounts all of a sudden started to throw off lots of cash—that just screamed money laundering.

Over a two-day period Annabelle and Leo had grilled Tony on every conceivable obstacle he would face when passing the bad checks. They took turns playing the roles of tellers, managers, security guards and bank customers. Tony was a fast learner, and at the end of the two days they pronounced him ready to take his baby steps as a bad-check passer after he had watched Leo perform a few times for real.

The first ten passes went very smoothly. Annabelle was a redhead at one, a blonde at another and a brunet at a third. The back of the van had been set up as a changing area with a small makeup table and mirror. After several passes she and Leo would hop in the van and alter their look on the way to the next bank. At some places she wore glasses, at another a scarf around her head, at another pants, sweatshirt and a ball cap. With the right makeup, clothing, padding and hair she could significantly change her appearance and age. She wore only flats, since her five-foot-nine-inch height was less noteworthy than one of six feet with heels on. And while she never looked at it, Annabelle was always conscious of the bank surveillance camera taking her glossy.

Leo was, in turn, a businessman, a company gofer, a retiree and a lawyer, among others.

Annabelle's practiced delivery with the tellers was smooth, without a trace of apprehension. She immediately put the clerk at ease, talking about the person's clothes or hair or how much she loved the beautiful city by the Bay, even with the gloomy weather.

With the eleventh teller she confided, "I've had this consulting business for four years, and this is the biggest payment I've ever gotten. I worked my butt off for it."

"Congratulations," the female clerk said as she worked on the transaction. "Forty thousand dollars *is* a big payment." The woman seemed to be scrutinizing the check and Annabelle's perfectly forged identification and corporate papers a bit too much.

Annabelle noted the woman wasn't wearing a wedding band but had worn one recently, because the skin was lighter where the ring would've been.

"My ex left me for a younger woman and cleaned out our accounts," Annabelle said bitterly. "I've had to build my whole life back. It hasn't been easy. But I wasn't going to let him have the satisfaction, you know? I'll take the damn alimony because I *earned* that. But he's not controlling my life."

The woman's demeanor changed, and she said in a low whisper, "I know *exactly* what you mean," she said as she completed the deposit. "Twelve years of marriage, and my ex decides to trade me in for a new model too."

"I wish we could just give them a pill that would train them right, you know?"

"Oh, I want to give my ex a pill, all right. A *cyanide* pill," the clerk said.

Annabelle glanced at the docs on the counter and said casually, "I suppose there'll be a hold on the funds, won't there? It's just that I have some vendors to pay. I wish I could get to keep the whole amount, but my profit margins are only about ten percent, if I'm lucky."

The clerk hesitated. "Well, normally, there would be with a check this size." She looked at Annabelle, smiled and eyed her computer. "But the account the check's drawn on has plenty of money to cover it. And there have been no problems in your company account. So I'll make the funds immediately available."

"That's great, I really appreciate it."

"We girls have to stick together."

"Yes, we do," Annabelle said as she turned and walked out with her deposit slip showing her "company" to be $40,000 richer.

Meanwhile, Leo raced through his group of checks, usually not spending more than ten minutes at each bank. Speed was the key here, he knew. Speed without sloppiness, however. His method was typically to crack a joke, usually at his own expense, to break the ice with the teller.

"I wish that money was going into my personal account," he told one clerk in his guise as a company gofer. "Then I could make my rent payment. Is there anyplace in this damn town that doesn't want your firstborn for a security deposit on a one-bedroom?"

"Not that I've ever heard of," the teller answered sympathetically.

Leo went on, "I mean, I don't even have a freaking one-bedroom. All I've got is a one-sleeper-sofa apartment."

"You're lucky. On what the bank pays I'm still living with my parents."

"Yeah, but I've got about thirty years on you. With the way I'm going, by the time you're running this place, *I'll* be living with *my* parents."

The teller laughed and handed Leo a deposit receipt for $38,000. "Don't spend it all in one place," the young man chided.

"Not to worry," Leo replied, tucking the paper in his pocket and walking off whistling.

By later that afternoon they'd passed seventy-seven of the eighty checks, with Tony moving ten of them and growing more confident with each one.

"This is easy," Tony declared in the van as he changed clothes along with Leo. Annabelle was behind a sheet strung up across part of the van doing the same thing. Tony added, "Those idiots just stand there and take every line you feed them. They never even look at the paper. I don't know why anybody bothers robbing banks anymore."

Annabelle poked her head over the top of the sheet. "We've got three more checks. We'll each take one."

"And watch your head when you get out of the van, Tony," Leo said.

"Watch my head, what are you talking about?"

"I mean, it's so big right now, it might not fit through the doors."

"Why the hell do you keep giving me a hard time, Leo?"

"He's giving you a hard time, Tony, because passing altered checks isn't easy," Annabelle said.

"Well, it is for me."

Leo said, "That's because Annabelle in her infinite wisdom gave you the easiest ones to pass."

Tony whirled around to look at her. "Is that true?"

"Yes," she said bluntly, her bare shoulders showing above the top of the sheet.

"I can take care of myself," Tony shot back. "You don't have to baby me."

"I'm not doing it for you," Annabelle answered. "If you go down, you'll take us with you." Her eyes glittered at him for an instant and then relaxed. "Besides, it makes no sense to throw a talented con in over his head. That can do a lot more harm than good."

She ducked down behind the sheet. With a little light coming in from the van's tinted windows, the sheet was somewhat transparent. Tony stared at Annabelle's silhouette as she shed her clothes and put others on.

Leo jabbed him in the ribs and growled, "Have some respect, kid."

Tony turned slowly to look at him. "Damn," he said quietly.

"What, you've never seen a beautiful woman undress before?"

"No. I mean, *yes,* I have." He looked down at his hands.

"What's wrong with you?" Leo asked.

Tony looked up. "I think she just called me a talented con."

CHAPTER

11

IT WAS THE LAST PASS. TONY was standing in front of the teller, a cute young Asian woman with shoulder-length black hair, flawless skin and walnut cheekbones. Clearly intrigued, Tony leaned closer and rested his arm on the counter.

"You lived here long?" he asked her.

"A few months; I moved here from Seattle."

"Same sort of weather," Tony said.

"Yes," the woman answered, smiling as she worked away.

"I just moved here from Vegas," Tony said. "Now, that's a fun town."

"I've never been."

"Oh, man, it's a blast. You've gotta go. And like they say, what happens in Vegas stays in Vegas." He looked at her expectantly. "I'd love to show you around."

She looked at him disapprovingly. "I don't even know you."

"Okay, we don't have to start with Vegas. Maybe we just start with lunch."

She said defiantly, "How do you know I don't have a boyfriend?"

"As gorgeous as you are, you probably do. But that means I have to work all that much harder to make you forget him."

The woman blushed and looked down, but now she was smiling again. "You're crazy." She hit some keys on her computer. "Okay, can I see some ID?"

"Only if you promise you won't say no when I officially ask you out."

She took the ID from him and let her finger graze his. He gave her another smile.

She glanced at the ID and looked puzzled. "I thought you said you just moved here from Vegas?"

"That's right."

"But your ID says Arizona." She turned it around to show him. "And that really doesn't look like you."

Oh, crap! He'd pulled the wrong ID from his pocket. Despite Annabelle instructing him to only take one ID pack at a time, he'd stubbornly carried them all. In the photo his hair was blond and he had a small goatee and was wearing Ben Franklin eyeglasses.

"I lived in Arizona but worked in Vegas, it was cheaper," he said quickly. "And I decided to change my style, new color, contact lenses. You know."

As soon as he delivered these lame lines, he knew it was over.

The teller stared at the check, and her look became even more suspicious. "This is a California bank check and a California company, but the routing number is for New York. Why's that?"

"Routing numbers? I don't know anything about that," Tony said, his voice now quavering. From her expression Tony knew the woman had already pronounced him guilty of bank fraud. She glanced in the direction of the security guard and placed the check and Tony's fake ID down on the counter in front of her. "I'm going to have to call my manager over," the teller began.

"What is going on here?" a low voice said sharply. "Excuse

me." The woman pushed Tony out of the way and confronted the teller. She was tall and plump with blond hair and dark roots. Her glasses were slim designer models hanging on a chain, and she was dressed in a purple blouse and black slacks.

She spoke quietly but firmly to the young woman behind the counter. "I've been standing here for ten minutes while you two play cutie-pie with each other. Is that the kind of service this bank provides? Why don't we get your manager over here and see?"

The clerk took a step back, her eyes wide. "Ma'am, I'm sorry, I was just—"

"I know what you were *just* doing," the woman interrupted. "I could hear it, everyone in the bank could hear you two flirting and discussing your love life."

The clerk's face reddened. "Ma'am, we were doing no such thing."

The woman put her hands on the counter and leaned forward. "Oh, really, so when you were talking about boyfriends and Vegas and he was telling you how gorgeous you were, that was what, official bank business? Do you do that with all your customers? Would you like to talk to me about who I sleep with?"

"Ma'am, please, I—"

"Forget it. I'm done with this place." The woman turned and stalked out.

Tony was already gone. Leo had steered him out a few seconds after the woman had appeared.

Annabelle joined them in the back of the van a minute later.

She called out to the driver, "Let's roll, Freddy." The van immediately pulled away from the curb.

She wrenched off the blond wig and put the glasses in her pocket. Next she took off her coat and stripped away the padding around her middle. She tossed Tony's ID to him. He caught it, shamefaced, and then exclaimed, "Omigod, they have the check—"

He stopped talking as Annabelle held up the check, neatly folded.

"I'm sorry, Annabelle, I'm really sorry."

She leaned close to him. "Little piece of advice, Tony. Don't ever hit on the mark, especially when you're pretending to be someone else."

Leo added, "It was a good thing we decided to back you up on that one."

"Why did you?" Tony asked glumly.

Annabelle answered. "Because you walked out of the van way too cocky. Cocky kills cons. That's another good rule to remember."

"I can go to another bank and pass it," Tony said quickly.

"No," she said. "We have enough for the long con. And it's not worth the risk."

Tony started to protest but then slumped back and said nothing.

Leo and Annabelle exchanged glances, each of them letting out a sigh of relief.

Two days later, at the rental condo, Leo knocked on Annabelle's bedroom door.

"Yeah?" she called out.

"Got a minute?"

He sat on her bed while she put some clothes in a carry-on bag.

"Three mil," he said reverently. "You know, you called 'em shorts, but to most cons those were longs. Things of beauty, Annabelle."

"Any con with decent skills could've done them. I just upped the ante a little."

"A little? Three million cut four ways isn't *little.*"

She glanced sharply at him.

"I know, I know," he said quickly. "You get a bigger share because it's your game. But still, my share could last me a few years living high on the hog. Maybe even take a real vacation."

"Not yet. We have the long con, Leo. That was the deal."

"Right, but just think about it."

She dropped a stack of clothes in her bag. "I *have* thought about it. The long con is next."

Leo stood, fingering an unlit cigarette. "Okay, but what about the kid?"

"What about him?"

"You said we were going all-star on this. Now, I've got no problem with Freddy, his stuff is first-rate. But the kid almost cost us everything. If you hadn't been there—"

"If I hadn't been there, he would've thought of something."

"Bullcrap. That teller had him made all the way. He gave her the wrong freaking ID. Talk about your bonehead moves."

"You've never made a mistake on a con, Leo? Let me think for a second. Oh, how about Phoenix? Or Jackson Hole?"

"Yeah, but it wasn't on a multimillion-dollar scam, Annabelle. I didn't have that handed to me on a damn platter when I was still in diapers like Tony."

"Jealousy doesn't score you any points, Leo. And Tony can hold his own."

"Maybe he can and maybe he can't. The thing is I damn sure don't want to be there to find out that he *can't*."

"You let me worry about that."

Leo threw up his hands. "Great, you worry about that for all of us."

"Good, I'm glad we have that settled."

Leo prowled the room, his hands stuffed in his pockets.

"Is there anything else?" she asked.

"Yeah, what's the long con?"

"I'll tell you when you need to know. And right now you don't need to know."

Leo sat down on the bed. "I'm not the CIA. I'm a con. I don't trust anybody." He eyed her bag. "And if you don't want to tell me, then I'm not going wherever the hell it is you're going."

"You knew the deal going in, Leo. You quit now, you get zip. Two shorts and a long. That was the arrangement."

"Yeah, well, part of the deal wasn't babysitting some punk who almost landed us in prison either, so maybe we need to renegotiate the deal, lady."

She stared at him contemptuously. "What, you're shaking me down after all these years? I gave you the best action you've ever had."

"I don't want more money. I want the long con. Or I'm not going!"

Annabelle stopped packing while she considered this. "If I tell you *where* we're going, will that be good enough?"

"Depends on where it is."

"Atlantic City."

All the blood seemed to drain from Leo's face. "Are you out of your damn mind? What, the last time wasn't bad enough?"

"That was a long time ago, Leo."

He snapped, "It'll never be long ago enough for me! Why don't we do something easier like hitting the mob?"

"At-lan-tic Ci-ty," she hissed, forming five words out of two.

"Why, because of your old man?"

She didn't answer him.

Leo stood and pointed a finger at her. "You're certifiable, Annabelle. If you think I'm walking into that hellhole with you again because you got something to prove, you don't know Leo Richter."

"The plane leaves at seven a.m."

Leo stood there nervously, watching her pack, for a couple more minutes.

"Are we at least flying first-class?" he finally said.

"Yes. Why?"

"Because if it's my last flight, I'd like to go out in style."

"Whatever floats your boat, Leo."

He walked out the door while Annabelle kept right on packing.

CHAPTER

12

CALEB SHAW WAS IN THE RARE
Books reading room working. There were several patron requests to see some material from the Rosenwald Vault; that required a supervisor's approval. Then he spent a good deal of
time on the phone consulting with a university professor writ-
ing a book on Jefferson's private library, which he sold to the nation after the British had burned the city during the War of 1812,
forming the basis for the present-day Library of Congress. After
that, Jewell English, an elderly woman and a regular in the reading room, asked to see an issue of Beadle's *Dime Novels.* She was
very interested in the Beadles series and had a nice collection,
she'd told Caleb. A slender woman with powdery white hair
and a ready smile, Caleb assumed she was also lonely. Her husband had died ten years ago, she'd confided in Caleb, and her
family was scattered around the country. It was for this reason
he engaged her in conversation whenever she came in.

"You're fortunate indeed, Jewell," Caleb said. "It just came
back from the conservation department. It needed some TLC."
He retrieved the book, chatted with her for a few minutes over
the untimely death of Jonathan DeHaven and then returned to
his desk. He watched for a few moments as the elderly woman

slowly put on her thick glasses and looked through the old volume, copying down notes on a few pieces of paper she'd brought with her. For obvious reasons only pencils and loose-leaf paper were allowed in here, and patrons had to allow their bags to be checked before they left the room.

As the door of the reading room opened, Caleb glanced over at the woman entering. She was from the administrative department. He rose to greet her.

"Hi, Caleb, I've got a note here for you from Kevin."

Kevin Philips was the acting director, having taken De-Haven's place after his death.

"Kevin? Why didn't he just call or e-mail?"

"I think he tried, but either the line was busy or you didn't answer. And for some reason he didn't want to e-mail."

"Well, I have been pretty busy today."

"I think it's fairly urgent." She handed him the envelope and left. Caleb carried it back to his desk and promptly tripped over the bent-up edge of his chair mat, knocked his glasses off his desk and then accidentally stepped on them, crunching the lenses.

"Oh, good grief, how clumsy can I get." He looked down at the envelope as he picked up his destroyed spectacles. Well, he couldn't read it now. Without his glasses he couldn't read a damn thing. And it was urgent, the woman had said.

"You've tripped over that mat several times before, Caleb," Jewell reminded him helpfully.

"Thanks for the observation," he said between clenched teeth. He suddenly looked over at her. "Jewell, can I borrow your glasses for a minute so I can read this note?"

"I'm as blind as a bat. They may not work for you."

"Don't worry; I'm as blind as a bat too, at least when it comes to reading."

"Why don't I just read the note for you?"

"Um, no. I mean, it might be, you know."

She clapped her hands together and whispered, "You mean it might be classified? How thrilling."

He glanced down at the note as Jewell handed him her glasses. He put them on, sat at his desk and read through it. Kevin Philips was asking Caleb to come right away to the division's administrative offices located on a secure floor of the building. He'd never been summoned to the admin offices before, at least not in this way. He slowly folded the note up and put it in his pocket.

"Thanks, Jewell, I think you and I have the same prescription, they worked fine." He handed the glasses back to her, steeled himself and headed off.

In the administrative office he found Kevin Philips sitting with a man in a dark suit. The man was introduced to Caleb as Jonathan DeHaven's attorney.

"Under the term of Mr. DeHaven's will you've been appointed the literary executor of his book collection, Mr. Shaw," the attorney said, pulling out a piece of paper and handing it to Caleb. He also gave him two keys and a slip of paper.

"The large key is to Mr. DeHaven's home. The smaller key is to the vault at his home where the books are kept. The first number on the paper is the pass code to the alarm system at Mr. DeHaven's house. The second number is the combination to the vault. It's protected by both key and combo locks."

Caleb looked dumbly at the articles he'd been handed. "His literary executor?"

Philips spoke up. "Yes, Caleb. As I understand it, you helped him acquire some volumes for his collection."

"Yes, I did," Caleb acknowledged. "He had enough money and informed taste to build a very good collection."

"Well, he apparently thought a lot of your assistance," the attorney said. "Under the terms of the will you are to be given full and unfettered access to his book collection. Your instructions are to properly inventory the collection, have it appraised, carve it up as you see fit and sell it, with the proceeds going to several charities identified in the will."

"He wanted me to dispose of his books? What about his family?"

"My firm has represented the DeHaven family for many years. He has no living relatives," the attorney answered. "I remember one of the retired partners telling me that he was married once, years ago. Apparently, it didn't last long." He paused, seeming to search his memory. "Annulled actually, I think he said. It was before my time with the firm. Anyway, there were no children, so no one to make a claim. You're to be paid a percentage of the sales price of the collection."

Philips added, "That might come to a fair amount of money."

"I'd do it for free," Caleb said quickly.

The attorney chuckled. "I'll just pretend I didn't hear that. It might be more work than you think. So you accept the commission?"

Caleb hesitated and then said, "Yes, I'll do it. For Jonathan."

"Good. Sign right here to acknowledge your acceptance and receipt of the keys and codes." He slid a one-page document toward Caleb, which he signed with a little difficulty, not having his glasses.

The attorney ended by saying, "Well, it's all there waiting for you."

Caleb returned to his office and stared down at the keys. A few minutes later he made up his mind. He called Milton, Reuben and then Stone. He didn't want to go to Jonathan's house alone, he told them. They all agreed to accompany him that night.

CHAPTER

13

That evening Reuben and Stone drove to DeHaven's house on the Indian motorcycle, the tall Stone crammed into the sidecar. Caleb and Milton pulled up right behind them in Caleb's ancient and sagging pewter-gray Chevy Nova with a finicky tailpipe. Caleb was wearing his backup pair of glasses; he assumed he'd be reading a lot tonight.

"Nice digs," Reuben said as he tugged off his helmet and goggles and looked at the massive house. "Pretty ritzy for a government salary."

"Jonathan came from money," Caleb answered.

"Must be nice," Reuben said. "All I ever came from was trouble. And that's also where I always seem to be headed with you mates."

Caleb unlocked the front door, turned off the alarm system, and they all stepped inside. He said, "I've been in the vault before. We can take the elevator down to the basement level."

"Elevator!" Milton exclaimed. "I don't like elevators."

"Then you can walk down the stairs," Caleb advised, pointing to the left. "They're over there."

Reuben looked around at the antique furniture, tasteful artwork on the walls and sculptures in classically styled presentation niches. He rubbed the toe of his boot on the beautiful Oriental rug in the living room. "Do they need a house sitter until everything's settled?"

Caleb said, "That would be a no."

They rode the elevator down and met Milton in a small anteroom.

The vault door was a monster, two-foot-thick steel with a computerized keypad and a slit for the special security key. The key and combo had to be inputted at the same time, Caleb told them. "Jonathan let me go in the vault with him on several occasions."

The door slid open on silent powered hinges, and they went inside. The space was about ten feet wide, nine feet high, and looked to be about thirty feet long. As soon as they walked in the vault, specialized low lighting came on, enabling them to see reasonably well.

"It's fire- and bombproof. And it's also temperature-and-humidity-controlled," Caleb explained. "That's a must with rare books, particularly in basements, where those levels can fluctuate drastically."

The vault was lined with shelves. And on the shelves were books, pamphlets and other articles that, even to the untrained eye, looked rare and valuable.

"Can we touch anything?" Milton asked

"Better let me do it," Caleb answered. "Some of these items are very fragile. Many of them haven't seen natural light for over a hundred years."

"Damn," Reuben exclaimed, running his finger lightly along the spine of one of the books. "Like a little prison and they're serving their life sentences."

"That's a very unfair way to look at it, Reuben," Caleb said in a scolding tone. "It protects the books so other generations can one day enjoy them. Jonathan went to great expense to house his collection with exquisite care."

"What sort of collection did he have?" Stone asked. He was eyeing one very old tome whose cover appeared to be carved from oak.

Caleb carefully slid out the book Stone was referring to. "Jonathan had a good collection, but not a great one; he'd be the first to admit that. All the great collectors had an almost limitless amount of money, but, more than that, they all had a vision for what sort of collection they wanted and they pursued it with a single-mindedness that could only be called an obsession. It's referred to as bibliomania, the world's 'gentlest' obsession. All the great collectors had it."

He glanced around the room. "There are some must-haves for the best collections that Jonathan simply would never be able to own."

"Like what?" Stone asked.

"Shakespeare's Folios. The First Folio would be the obvious one, of course. It contains nine hundred pages with thirty-six of the plays. None of the Bard's original manuscripts have survived, so the Folios are incredibly desirable. A First Folio sold a few years ago in England for three and a half million pounds."

Milton let out a low whistle and shook his head. "About six thousand dollars a page."

Caleb continued, "Then there are the obvious acquisitions: William Blake, Newton's *Principia Mathematica,* something from Caxton, the earliest English printer. J. P. Morgan had over sixty Caxtons in his collection, if I remember correctly. A 1457 *Mainz Psalter, The Book of St. Albans,* and, of course, a Guten-

berg Bible. There are only three known mint-condition Guten-
bergs printed on vellum in the world. The Library of Congress
has one. They're priceless."

Caleb ran his gaze down one shelf. "Jonathan has the 1472
edition of Dante's *Divine Comedy,* which would be welcome in
any first-rate collection. He also has Poe's *Tamerlane,* which is
exceedingly rare and difficult to obtain. One sold some time ago
for nearly two hundred thousand dollars. Poe's reputation has
made a nice rebound lately, so today it would fetch a much
higher price. The collection includes a worthy selection of incunabula, mostly German, but some Italian, and a solid set of
first editions of more contemporary novels, many of them auto-
graphed. He was very strong in Americana and has a large sampling of personal writings from Washington, Adams, Jefferson,
Franklin, Madison, Hamilton, Lincoln and others. As I said, it's
a very nice collection, but not a great one."

"What's that?" Reuben asked, pointing to a dimly lit corner in
the back of the vault.

They all crowded around the object. It was a small portrait of
a man in medieval dress.

"I don't remember seeing that before," Caleb said.

"And why have a painting hanging in a vault?" Milton added.

"And only *one* painting," Stone commented. "Not much of a
collection." He was examining the portrait from various angles
before placing his fingers on one edge of the painting's frame
and pulling. It swung open on a set of hinges, revealing the door
of a small combination lock safe built into the wall.

"A safe within a safe," Stone said. "Try the combination the
lawyer gave you for the main vault, Caleb."

Caleb did so but it didn't work. He tried various other numbers without success.

Stone remarked, "People typically use a combination they won't forget so they won't have to write it down. It could be numbers, letters or both."

"Why give Caleb the key and pass code to the main vault but not give him the one to the inner safe?" Milton asked.

"Maybe he figured Caleb would know it somehow," Reuben commented.

Stone nodded. "I agree with Reuben. Think, Caleb. It might have something to do with the Rare Books reading room."

"Why?" Milton asked.

"Because *this* was DeHaven's rare books reading room of sorts."

Caleb looked thoughtful. "Well, Jonathan did open the room every day, about an hour before anyone else arrived. That was done with special alarmed keys, and he also had to input a security code to open the doors. But I don't have that code."

"Something simpler than that perhaps. So simple it's staring you in the face."

Caleb suddenly snapped his fingers. "Of course. Staring me in the face every day of my life." His fingers punched in a code on the safe's digital pad, and the door clicked open.

"What number did you use?" Stone asked.

"LJ239. It's the room number of the Rare Books reading room. I look at it every day when I go to work."

Inside the safe was one article. Caleb carefully drew out the box and slowly opened it.

Reuben said, "That thing's in pretty ragged shape."

It was a book, the cover was black and torn and the binding was starting to come apart. Caleb carefully opened it and turned to the first page. Then he turned another and then another.

He finally gave a sharp intake of breath. "Oh, my God!"

Stone said, "Caleb, what is it?"

Caleb's hands were shaking. He spoke slowly, his voice trembling. "I think, I mean I believe this is a first-edition *Bay Psalm Book.*"

"Is it rare?" Stone asked.

Caleb looked at him wide-eyed. "It's the oldest surviving object printed in what is now the United States, Oliver. There are only eleven *Psalm Book*s in existence in the entire world, and only five of them are complete. They never come onto the market. The Library of Congress has one, but it was given to us decades ago. I don't believe we could've afforded it otherwise."

"So how did Jonathan DeHaven get one?" Stone remarked.

With great reverence Caleb carefully eased the book back into the box and closed it. He placed the box in the safe and shut the door. "I don't know. The last *Psalm Book* came on the market over sixty years ago when it was purchased for what was then a record amount equaling millions of dollars in today's money. It's now at Yale." He shook his head. "For book collectors this is like finding a missing Rembrandt or Goya."

"Well, if there are only eleven in the world, it would be pretty simple to account for them," Milton suggested. "I could Google it."

Caleb looked at him with disdain. While Milton embraced every new advance of the computer, Caleb was a decided technophobe.

"You can't just *Google* a *Psalm Book*, Milton. And as far as I know, all of them are in institutions like Harvard, Yale and the Library of Congress."

"You're sure it's an original *Psalm Book*?" Stone asked.

"There were numerous subsequent editions, but I'm almost certain it's the 1640 version. It said so on the title page and has other points of the original that I'm familiar with," Caleb breathlessly replied.

"What exactly is it?" Reuben asked. "I could barely read any of the words."

"It's a hymnal that the Puritans commissioned a number of ministers to put together to give them religious enlightenment on a daily basis. The printing process was very primitive back then, which, coupled with the old-style spelling and script, makes it difficult to read."

"But if all the *Psalm Books are* in institutions?" Stone said.

Caleb glanced at him, a look of trepidation on his face. "I guess there's the possibility, however rare, that there are unaccounted-for *Psalm Books* out there. I mean, someone found half of the handwritten manuscript for *Huckleberry Finn* in her attic. And someone else turned up an original copy of the Declaration of Independence behind a picture in a frame, and then there was the discovery of some of Byron's writings in an old book. Over hundreds of years anything's possible."

Though the room was cool, Caleb wiped away a bead of perspiration from his forehead. "Do you know the enormous responsibility this entails? We're talking about a collection with a *Psalm Book* in it. A *Psalm Book*, for God's sake!"

Stone put a calming hand on his friend's shoulder. "I've never met anyone better qualified to do this than you, Caleb. And whatever we can do to help, we will."

"Yeah," Reuben said. "In fact, I've got a few bucks on me if you want to get a couple books out of the way before the real heavyweights start circling. What'll you take for that *Divine Comedy* thing? I could use a few laughs."

Milton piped in, "Reuben, none of us could even afford to buy the auction catalog they'll print the collection in."

"Well, that's just great," Reuben exclaimed in mock fury. "Now, I guess the next thing you'll tell me is I can't quit my crappy job at the loading dock."

"What the hell are you people doing here!" a voice cried out.

They all turned to look at the intruders who were standing just outside the vault door. There were two burly men in the uniforms of private security, their guns pointed at the Camel Club. The man in front of the two guards was short and thin with a shock of red hair, a trim beard of matching color and a pair of active blue eyes.

"I said what are you people doing here?" the redhead repeated.

Reuben growled, "Maybe we should be asking you the same thing, buddy."

Caleb stepped forward. "I'm Caleb Shaw with the Library of Congress, where I worked with Jonathan DeHaven. In his will he appointed me as his literary executor." He held up the house and vault keys. "I was given permission from Jonathan's lawyer to come here and look over the collection. My friends came along to help me." He reached in his pocket and presented his library ID to the man, whose demeanor quickly changed.

"Of course, of course, I'm sorry," the man said after gazing at Caleb's ID before handing it back to him. "I just saw people entering Jonathan's house, and the door was unlocked, and I suppose I jumped to conclusions." He nodded to his men to put away their guns.

"We never did catch your name," Reuben said, eyeing the man suspiciously.

Before he could answer, Stone said, "I believe we're in the company of Cornelius Behan, CEO of Paradigm Technologies, the country's third largest defense contractor."

Behan smiled. "Soon to be number one if I get my way, and I usually do."

"Well, Mr. Behan," Caleb began.

"Call me CB, everybody does." He took a step forward and glanced around the room. "So this is DeHaven's book collection."

"You knew Jonathan?" Caleb asked.

"I wouldn't call us friends, really. I had him over for one or two holiday parties. I knew he worked at the library and that he collected books. We'd occasionally pass each other on the street and chitchat. I was very stunned to hear of his death."

"As we all were," Caleb added somberly.

"So you're his literary executor, you said," Behan noted. "What does that mean?"

"It means I've been given the task of cataloging and appraising the collection and then selling it."

"Anything good in here?" Behan asked.

"Are you a collector?" Stone inquired.

"Oh, I've been known to collect a good many things," he answered vaguely.

"Well, it is a very good collection. It will be put up for auction," Caleb explained. "At least the most prominent parts of it will be."

"Right," Behan said absently. "Any new developments on Jonathan's death?"

Caleb shook his head. "So far it appears to be a heart attack."

"And he seemed so healthy. I guess that's a good reason to give it all we've got every day, because tomorrow . . . ?" He wheeled around and marched out, his men scurrying along in his wake.

As the sounds of the footsteps faded, Stone turned to Caleb. "Very considerate of him to come and check on the house of a man he occasionally *chitchatted* with."

"He was his neighbor, Oliver," Caleb pointed out. "He's naturally concerned."

"I didn't like him," Milton said. "He builds things that kill people."

"*Lots* of people," Reuben added. "In my book old CB's a shifty little peckerhead."

They spent hours going over the books and other articles until Caleb had a fairly complete list. Milton inputted these onto his laptop computer.

"Now what?" Milton asked as they closed the last book.

"Ordinarily, you'd bring in an appraiser from Sotheby's or Christie's," Caleb answered. "But I have someone else in mind. And in my opinion he's the best there is in the rare book field. And I want to find out if he knew that Jonathan had the *Psalm Book*."

"Is he in New York?" Stone asked.

"No, right here in D.C. Maybe twenty minutes by car."

"Who is it?" Reuben asked.

"Vincent Pearl."

Stone checked his watch. "We'll have to see him tomorrow, then. It's already eleven o'clock."

Caleb shook his head. "Oh, no, now is perfect. Vincent Pearl's rare book shop is only open at night."

14

As the Camel Club left De-Haven's home, two pairs of binoculars were trained on them. One was from an upper window of a house across from De-Haven's and another held by a man in the back of a van parked down the street that had stenciled on its side "D.C. Public Works."

When the motorcycle and Nova drove off, the van followed.

After the vehicles had disappeared, the pair of binoculars in the upper window of the house on Good Fellow Street continued to scan the area.

As Caleb predicted, it took twenty minutes to get to Vincent Pearl's rare book shop. There was no name on the storefront, only a sign that read "Hours 8 PM to Midnight, Monday to Saturday." Caleb marched up to the door and rang the bell.

Reuben looked around at the stout door and barred window. "I take it he's not into advertising."

"Anyone serious about book collecting knows exactly where to find Vincent Pearl," Caleb replied matter-of-factly.

"You know him well?" Stone asked.

"Oh, no. I hardly operate at the level of a Vincent Pearl. In fact, in the last ten years I've only met him personally twice, both times here at his shop. I've heard him lecture before, though. He's quite unforgettable."

The lighted dome of the Capitol was visible to the west. The neighborhood they were in was lined with ancient moss-covered brick and stone row houses and other dwellings that had once been a focal point of the burgeoning capital city.

"You sure he's here?" Milton asked just as a deep voice said in a demanding tone, "Who is it?"

Milton jumped, but Caleb spoke into a small loudspeaker barely visible under a strand of twisted ivy next to the door. "Mr. Pearl, it's Caleb Shaw. From the Library of Congress."

"Who?"

Caleb looked a little embarrassed and started speaking quickly. "Caleb Shaw. I work in the Rare Books reading room. We last met a few years ago when a collector of Lincoln memorabilia came to the library and I brought him around to you."

"You don't have an appointment for tonight." The tone was one of mild annoyance. Apparently, Pearl wasn't grateful for the referral Caleb had given him.

"No, but I come on some urgency. If you could just spare a few minutes."

A few seconds later the door clicked open. As the others entered, Stone noted a tiny reflection from above. The small surveillance camera was staring right at them, ingeniously disguised as a birdhouse. The reflection was from the streetlight hitting the lens. Most people would have missed such a device, but Oliver Stone was not most people, certainly when it came to things that spied on you.

As they passed into the store, Stone also noted two other things. The door, although it looked old and wooden, was actually made of reinforced steel, set in a steel frame, and the lock, to Stone's experienced eye, looked tamperproof. And the barred window was three-inch-thick polycarbonate glass.

The interior of the shop surprised Stone. He had expected to see a cluttered layout, with dusty books on bowed shelves and every crevice bursting with old parchments and tomes for sale. Instead, the place was clean, streamlined and well organized. The building itself was two stories in height. Tall ornate bookshelves lined every wall, and the books housed in them were behind locked sliding glass doors. A ladder on wheels ran on a long track tube attached to the tops of the nine-foot-high shelves. Three oval cherrywood reading tables with matching chairs sat in the middle of the long, narrow space. Overhead was a trio of bronze chandeliers that gave off surprisingly weak light. *They must be on dimmers,* Stone thought. A six-foot-wide spiral staircase led to the level above, which was partially open to the floor they were on. Up there Stone could see still more shelves, with a Chippendale-style banister running around the opening to the first floor.

A long wooden counter was at the end of the main room with still more shelves behind it. What Stone *wasn't* seeing surprised him. No computers, not even a cash register was visible from where he stood.

Reuben said, "Feels like a place you'd want to smoke a cigar in and have a tumbler or two of whiskey."

"Oh, no, Reuben," Caleb said in a shocked tone. "Smoke is deadly to old books. And one spilled drop can ruin a timeless treasure."

Reuben was about to say something when a heavily carved door behind the counter opened and an old man walked out. Everyone except Caleb did a double take because the gentleman's silvery beard was long and flowed down across his chest, and his long white hair cascaded down past his shoulders. His costume was even more eye-catching. Over his tall, potbellied frame he wore a full-length lavender robe with gold stripes across the sleeve. His rimless oval glasses were perched on his long wrinkled forehead, where wisps of grizzled hair lay in an untidy fashion. His eyes were, yes, they were black, Stone decided, unless the poor light was playing a trick on him.

"Is he a monk?" Reuben whispered to Caleb.

"Shh!" Caleb hissed as the man came forward.

"Well?" Pearl said, looking at Caleb expectantly. "Are you Shaw?"

"Yes."

"What is your matter of urgency?" Pearl suddenly glared at the others. "And who are these people?"

Caleb quickly introduced them, using only their first names.

Pearl's gaze lingered the longest on Stone. "I have seen you in Lafayette Park, have I not? In a tent, sir?" he said with exaggerated formality.

"You have," Stone replied.

Pearl continued, "Your sign says, if I recall correctly, 'I want the truth.' Have you found it?"

"I can't say that I have."

Pearl said, "Well, if I were inclined to seek the truth, I don't believe I would start my search across from the White House." Pearl turned back to Caleb. "Now, your business, sir?" he said briskly.

Caleb hastily explained about his being appointed DeHaven's literary executor and his request about the appraisal.

"Yes, it was certainly a tragedy about DeHaven," Pearl said solemnly. "And *you've* been named his literary executor, have you?" he added in a surprised tone.

"I helped Jonathan with his collection, and we worked together at the library," he answered defensively.

"I see," Pearl replied tersely. "But you still require an expert's eye, obviously."

Caleb turned slightly pink. "Uh, well, yes. We have an inventory of the collection on Milton's laptop."

"I would much prefer to deal in paper," Pearl replied firmly.

"If you have a printer here, I can take care of that," Milton said.

Pearl shook his head. "I have a printing press, but it's from the sixteenth century, and I doubt it's compatible with your contraption."

"No, it wouldn't be," mumbled a shocked Milton. A devoted lover of all things technological, he was obviously stunned at Pearl's lack thereof.

"Well, we can print one out and bring it to you tomorrow," Caleb suggested. He hesitated and then said, "Mr. Pearl, I might as well come right out and say it. Jonathan has a first-edition *Bay Psalm Book* in his collection. Did you know about it?"

Pearl lowered his glasses onto his eyes. "Excuse me, what did you say?"

"Jonathan has a 1640 *Bay Psalm Book.*"

"That is not possible."

"I held it."

"No, you did not."

"I did!" Caleb insisted.

Pearl waved a hand dismissively. "It's a later edition, then. Hardly earth-shattering."

"It has no music. That started with the ninth edition in 1698."

Pearl eyed Caleb severely. "Doubtless you won't be surprised to learn that I am aware of that. But, as you point out, there are *seven* other editions that have no music."

"It was the 1640 edition. The year was printed on the title page."

"Then, my dear sir, it's either a facsimile or a forgery. People are very clever. One ambitious fellow re-created the *Oath of a Freeman,* which antedates the *Psalm Book* by one year."

Stone interjected, "But I thought the 1640 *Bay Psalm Book* was the first printed book in America."

"It is," Pearl said impatiently. "The *Oath* wasn't a *book;* it was a one-page document called a broadsheet. As its name suggests, it was an oath, a pledge of allegiance if you will, that each Puritan male took in order to vote and enjoy other privileges in the Massachusetts Bay Colony."

"And it was forged?" Stone said.

"Ironically, the forger used a facsimile of the *Psalm Book.* He did so because it was struck on the same press as the *Oath* and by the same printer and thus utilized the same printing type." Pearl tapped Caleb on the chest. "The criminal was very ingenious, with the result that he very nearly duped *your* Library of Congress into buying it. Only when an expert in printing presses noted certain irregularities was the deceit uncovered."

Caleb said, "I've worked in the Rare Books Division for over a decade. I've examined the *Psalm Book* that we have. In my opinion Jonathan's is real."

Pearl eyed Caleb suspiciously. "What was your name again?"

Caleb's pink face now turned red. "Caleb Shaw!"

"Well, Shaw, did you run the standard authentication tests on the book?"

"No, but I looked at it, held it, smelled it."

"My God, man, you can't possibly be certain from such a rudimentary examination. DeHaven simply did not have that sort of a collection. A *Tamerlane,* a few incunabula, even the Dante, which I sold him, by the way, constituted the heart and soul of his rare books. No first-edition *Psalm Book* was ever a part thereof."

"So where did Jonathan get the book?" Caleb asked.

Pearl shook his head. "How could I possibly know that?" He looked at the others. "As your friend may have told you, there are only eleven existing *Bay Psalm Books* in the world out of the original print run. Just think about that, gentlemen. By comparison there are 228 Shakespeare First Folios, but only eleven *Psalm Books* on the entire earth. And of that number only *five* are in complete condition." He held up the fingers of his right hand. "Only five," he added with great solemnity.

As Stone stared at the luminous black eyes that seemed to pour out of the deep sockets like oil escaping the earth, it was clear to him that a spiritual diagnosis of Vincent Pearl would clearly reveal that he too suffered from bibliomania.

The bookseller turned back to Caleb. "And since all eleven are accounted for, I can hardly see how one made its way to the collection of Jonathan DeHaven."

"So why keep a forgery locked up in a vault?" Caleb countered.

"Perhaps he thought it was real."

"The head of the Rare Books Division fooled by a forged book?" Caleb said contemptuously. "I seriously doubt that."

Pearl was unperturbed. "As I said before, the library was nearly deceived into buying a fake *Oath*. People will believe what they want to believe, and book collectors are not immune to that impulse. In my experience self-delusion knows no boundaries."

"Maybe it would be better if you came by Jonathan's house so you can see for yourself that the *Psalm Book* is an original," Caleb said stubbornly.

Pearl stroked his unruly beard with the long, delicate fingers of his right hand while he kept his withering gaze on Caleb.

"And of course, I would welcome your expert opinion on the rest of the collection," Caleb added in a calmer tone.

"I believe I might have some time tomorrow evening," Pearl said in a clearly disinterested manner.

"That would be fine," Caleb said, handing him a card. "Here's my number at the library, just call to confirm. Do you have Jonathan's address?"

"Yes, in my files."

"I think it best not to mention the existence of the *Psalm Book* to anyone, Mr. Pearl, at least for now."

"I rarely *mention* anything to anyone," Pearl said. "Particularly things that are not true."

Caleb turned absolutely scarlet as Pearl ushered them quickly out.

"Okay," Reuben said outside as he pulled on his motorcycle helmet. "I think I just met Professor Dumbledore."

"Who?" Caleb exclaimed, obviously still furious from Pearl's parting shot.

"Dumbledore. From Harry Potter, you know."

"No, I *don't* know," Caleb snapped.

"What a bloody muggle," Reuben muttered as he slipped on his goggles.

Caleb said, "Well, Pearl obviously doesn't believe the *Psalm Book* is authentic." He paused, and then he said in a less confident tone, "And maybe he's right. I mean, I only looked at the thing for a few moments."

Reuben piped in, "Well, the way you told Pearl off in there *you* better be right."

Caleb flushed. "I can't believe I did that. I mean, he's famous in the book field. I'm just a government librarian."

"A first-rate librarian at one of the world's greatest institutions," Stone added.

"He may be terrific in his field, but he really needs to get a computer. And a printer that's not from the sixteenth century," Milton added.

The Nova pulled off. As Reuben kick-started the Indian, Stone, on the pretense of adjusting his tall body better in the sidecar, glanced behind him.

As they drove off, the van continued to follow.

When the Chevy Nova and the motorcycle split up, the van tailed the bike.

CHAPTER

15

Despite the lateness of the hour, Stone instructed Reuben to drop him near the White House instead of his caretaker's cottage at Mt. Zion Cemetery. He'd noticed the van following them and wanted to do something about it.

He quietly explained the situation to Reuben as he was getting out of the sidecar, describing the van to his friend.

Stone said, "Keep an eye out. If the van follows you, I'll call you on your cell phone."

"Shouldn't you call Alex Ford for some backup? After all, we did make him an honorary member of the Camel Club."

"Alex is no longer assigned to the White House. And I don't want to call him out on what might be nothing. But there are other Secret Service personnel here that can help me."

When Reuben pulled away, Stone slowly passed his tent, with the sign "I want the truth" next to it. No other protesters were here tonight, including his friend Adelphia. Then he made his way quickly toward a statue in the park of a Polish general who'd aided the Americans in the Revolutionary War. His reward for this good service had been a large memorial on which hundreds of birds crapped daily. Climbing up on the statue's pedestal, he saw that the van remained parked on 15th Street, outside the 1600 block of Pennsylvania Avenue closed to traffic.

Stone climbed back down and approached one of the uniformed guards who protected the White House perimeter.

"What's up tonight, Oliver?" the man said. He'd been guarding the White House for almost ten years and was well acquainted with Stone. For his part Stone was always polite and adhered strictly to the rules of the protest permit that he carried in his pocket.

"Hello, Joe, I wanted to give you the heads-up on something. It might not be anything, but I know the Service doesn't like to take chances." He quickly explained about the van, but without pointing toward it. "I thought you should know in case you wanted to check it out."

"Thanks, Oliver. I owe you."

As Stone had learned in all his years here, there was no detail too small for the Secret Service when it came to guarding the president. Thus, a couple minutes later he watched from nearby as Joe, joined by another armed guard, approached the D.C. Public Works van. Stone wished he had thought to bring his binoculars tonight, but they sat on his desk back at the cottage. He tensed when the driver's window of the van came down.

The next thing that happened was stunning. The two uniformed guards whirled around and walked quickly away from the van as the driver's window slid back up. The men did not come near Oliver Stone; they headed in the exact opposite direction as fast as they could go without running while the van remained where it was.

"Damn," Stone muttered under his breath.

Now he knew. The people in the van were members of a government agency with enough clout to send the Secret Service scurrying away like frightened children. Now was the time to run. But how? Should he call Reuben? Yet he didn't really want to involve his friend in this. A thought struck him.

Was his past finally catching up to him?

He quickly made up his mind and strode off across the park, reached H Street and turned left. The Farragut West Metro stop was only a couple blocks away. He checked his watch. *Damn!* The subway was closed. He changed direction, constantly looking over his shoulder for signs of the van. He decided to keep hoofing it down the street; he might catch a late-running bus.

When he reached the next intersection, the public works van screeched to a stop directly in front of him and the slide door started opening.

Then Stone heard the voice shouting at him.

"Oliver!"

He looked to his right. Reuben had driven his motorcycle up on the sidewalk and was speeding directly at him. He slowed just enough to allow Stone to dive into the sidecar. Reuben flew over the curb, back onto the street and gunned the motorcycle with Stone's long legs sticking straight up out of the sidecar.

Reuben, whose knowledge of the streets of D.C. nearly equaled Stone's, made a series of rights and lefts before he slowed the bike, eased into a dark alley and came to a stop behind a Dumpster. By this time Stone had righted himself in the sidecar. He looked up at his friend. "Your timing couldn't have been better, Reuben. Thanks."

"When you didn't call, I circled back around. The van started to move and I followed it."

"I'm surprised they didn't spot you. This motorcycle does tend to stick out."

"Who the hell are those guys?"

Stone told his friend about the run-in with the Secret Service.

Reuben said, "There aren't many agencies that can make the Service turn tail on its own turf."

"I can think of maybe two: CIA and NSA. Neither one gives me much comfort."

"What do you think they wanted?"

"I first spotted the van outside the rare book shop. It might have been following us before then, though."

"At DeHaven's?" Reuben snapped his fingers. "You think this has something to do with that Cornelius Behan prick? He's probably joined at the hip with the spy guys."

"It might, considering the timing." *Maybe this wasn't tied to his past, after all.*

Reuben looked nervous. "Oliver, if they were following us, do you think they might have had a tail on Caleb and Milton?"

Stone was already on his phone. He reached Caleb and told him some of what had happened and put his phone away. "He just dropped Milton off at home. They didn't see anyone, but they probably wouldn't have."

"But what did we do to get spooks after us? We told Behan what we were doing there. What interest could he have in DeHaven?"

"He might have an interest if he knew how DeHaven died. Or perhaps more accurately, how he was *murdered.*"

"You're saying Behan might have had his neighbor killed? Why?"

"You just said it, his *neighbor.* It's possible that DeHaven saw something he shouldn't have."

Reuben snorted. "On Good Fellow Street, with the rich and obnoxious?"

"It's all speculation, but the fact remains that if you hadn't shown up, I'm not sure what would've happened to me."

"So what do we do now?"

"Since it seems no one was concerned about us until we went

to Jonathan DeHaven's house, we start there. We find out whether the man was murdered or not."

"I was afraid that's what you were going to say."

Stone settled himself in the sidecar, this time with his legs where they ought to be. Reuben started the motorcycle and they set off.

Just like old times, Stone thought. And that clearly wasn't a good thing.

The men in the van reported in to a very upset Roger Seagraves.

"We could've taken the old guy even though his buddy showed up, but we figured it might be too dicey," one man said over the phone.

Seagraves stared at his secure phone for a moment, thinking what his next move should be. "They were at DeHaven's for how long?"

"Over five hours."

"And then to a rare book shop, and then you followed them to the White House."

"Yep. One of them has a tent in Lafayette Park. And according to the Secret Service, his name is Oliver Stone. What a joke!"

"He spotted your tail, so I don't know how much of a joke he is," Seagraves snapped. "And I don't like you flashing your creds around, especially to the Service."

"We just got in a jam and had to do it. But we *are* with the Agency," the other man countered.

"But not on official duty tonight," Seagraves shot back.

"So what do you want us to do?"

"Nothing. I want to check out Mr. Stone more thoroughly. I'll be in touch." Seagraves hung up.

A man calling himself Oliver Stone has a tent across from the White House, can spot expert surveillance and visited the house of a man I had killed. Seagraves could feel another thunderstorm coming on.

CHAPTER

16

IT WAS RAINING AND CHILLY IN Newark when the plane touched down. Annabelle now sported brown hair, cherry-red lipstick, sleek eyeglasses, funky clothes and blocky-heeled shoes. Her three companions were all dressed in two-piece suits with no ties. They didn't leave the airport together. They drove south and rendezvoused at a rental unit in Atlantic City.

Being back in the town after so many years, Annabelle could feel her tension level rising. The last time, she had come far too close to dying. But being tense could easily get her killed this time around. She would have to trust her nerves to weather what was coming. She had prepared nearly twenty years of her life for this moment. She did not intend to waste it.

Over the last week she'd wired the funds from the altered checks out of the corporate accounts. Those sums plus the stash from the ATM scam had been put into an overseas account that did not abide by a single U.S. banking regulation. With $3 million in seed money, the men were anxious to hear Annabelle's plan for the long con.

And yet she was clearly not ready to tell them. She spent much of the first day walking the town, scoping the casinos and in discussions with certain nameless people. The men spent the downtime playing cards and shooting the breeze. Leo and Freddy regaled young Tony with stories of old scams embellished and polished to the degree that only distant memories could inspire.

She finally called them all together.

"My plan is to turn our three million into a lot more, in a relatively short period of time," she informed them.

"I just love your style, Annabelle," Leo said.

"Specifically, I plan to turn our three million into at least *thirty-three* million. I walk away with thirteen point five, and you split the rest three ways. That's six and a half per. Anybody have a problem with that?"

The men sat there stunned for a full minute. Leo finally answered for them. "Yeah, boy, that just sucks."

She held up a warning hand. "If the scam doesn't work, we could lose some of the seed, but not all. Everybody all right with rolling that dice?" Each of them nodded. "The amount of money we're talking will necessitate taking certain risks on the back end."

Leo said, "Translation, whoever we're ripping off will never stop looking for us." He lit a cigarette. "And now I think it's time you told us who it is."

Annabelle sat back and slid her hands in her pockets. She never took her gaze off Leo's face, and he stared back in turn. Finally, he said nervously, "Is it really that bad?"

"We're hitting Jerry Bagger and the Pompeii Casino," she announced.

"Holy shit!" Leo yelled, his cigarette falling out of his mouth. It landed on his leg and burned a small hole in his pants. He angrily swiped at the burn mark and pointed a shaky finger at her. "I knew it! I knew you were gonna pull this crap."

Tony looked at each of them. "Who's Jerry Bagger?"

Leo said, "The meanest son of a bitch you hope you never cross paths with, sonny boy, that's who."

Annabelle joked, "Come on, Leo, it's my job to get him juiced about the scam. Keep that up, he'll want to take on Jerry all by himself."

"I'm not taking on Jerry effing Bagger for three million, thirty-three million or three hundred and thirty-three million because I won't live to enjoy it anyway."

"But you came here with us. And like you said, you knew I was going for him. You *knew* it, Leo." She stood, came around the table and draped a long arm around his shoulders. "And if the truth be known, you've been waiting for a shot to take that weasel down for the last twenty years. Admit it."

Leo suddenly looked embarrassed, lit another Winston and shakily blew smoke to the ceiling. "Anybody who's done business with that bastard wants to kill him. So what?"

"I don't want to kill him, Leo. I just want to steal so much money from Jerry that it'll hurt him where it matters the most. You could wipe out his whole family, and it wouldn't bother the guy nearly as much as knowing somebody got the money he's been piling up from the poor schmucks that trip through his casino every minute of every day."

"Sounds cool," Tony chimed, while Freddy still looked uncertain.

Leo stared in fury at the young man. "Cool? You think it's cool? Let me tell you something, you little know-nothing punk. You mess up in front of Jerry Bagger like you did at that bank, there won't be enough left of you to send in an envelope to your mama for burial." Leo turned and pointed a finger at Annabelle. "Let me make something real clear right now. I am not taking on

Jerry Bagger. But I am *really* not taking on Jerry Bagger with this screw-up along."

"Hey, I made *one* mistake. You never made a mistake?" Tony protested.

Leo didn't answer. He and Annabelle were engaged in a lengthy stare-down.

She said quietly, "Tony's role is limited to what he does best. He has no face time with Jerry." She glanced at Freddy. "And Freddy's backroom all the way. He just has to make some good-looking paper. The success of the scam depends on you. And me. So unless you think *we're* not good enough, I don't see a valid objection."

"They know us, Annabelle. We've been here before."

She walked around the table and opened a manila folder that sat on the table in front of her chair. She held up two glossies of a man and a woman.

"Who's that?" Freddy asked, puzzled.

Leo answered grudgingly as he gazed at the pictures. "Me and Annabelle, from a long time ago. In At-lan-tic Ci-ty," he spat out.

"Where'd you get the photos?" Tony asked.

Annabelle explained, "Every casino keeps a face bank, what they call the black book, of people who've tried to scam them, and they share that intelligence with the other casinos. You've never tried to rip a casino, Tony, and neither has Freddy, which is one reason I looked you two up. I still have a few contacts in this town; that's where I got the prints. They never actually caught us and photographed us. These were made from composites based on descriptions of us. If they had real photos, I'm not sure I'd be here."

"But you two don't look anything like that anymore," Tony said. "Some intelligence," he added with a sneer.

Annabelle pulled two more glossies out of the folder. These looked more like the real Leo and Annabelle. "Like the police do with missing children, the casinos hire experts to digitally alter the photos to take into account normal aging. They feed that into their black book and also into their electronic surveillance system that has face recognition software. That's why we'll look nothing like this when we make our run at Jerry."

"I'm *not* making a run at Jerry," Leo snarled.

"Come on, Leo, it'll be fun," Tony said.

"Don't piss me off, kid," Leo snapped. "Like I need an excuse to hate you!"

"Let's take a walk, Leo," Annabelle said. She held a hand up when Tony and Freddy stood to follow them. "Stay put. We'll be back," she said.

Outside, the sun was coming out from behind a patch of dark clouds. Annabelle pulled a hood over her head and slid on sunglasses. Leo pulled a ball cap low over his head and donned shades as well.

They walked along the Boardwalk, which ran between the casinos on the main strip and the wide beach, passing couples on benches staring at the ocean.

"They've fixed up the place since the last time we were here," Annabelle said. The casinos had stomped into town in the late seventies, plopping down billion-dollar gambling palaces in the middle of the seaside resort's stark decay. For years afterward a person would not want to venture far away from the casinos because the surrounding city was not the safest place. The powers-that-be had long promised a general cleanup of the area. And with the casinos throwing off lots of money and jobs, it looked like that promise was finally being fulfilled. They stopped and watched a large crane lifting steel beams up on top of a structure that a sign announced would soon be luxury condos. Everywhere they looked new construction and rehab of existing places was going on.

Leo veered toward the beach. He stopped to take off his shoes and socks while Annabelle slid off her flats and rolled up her pants. They walked along the sand, drawing close to the water. Finally, Leo stopped, bent down, grabbed a seashell and tossed it at an incoming wave.

"You ready to talk about it?" she asked, eyeing him closely.

"Why are you doing this?"

"Doing what? Running a con? That's what I've been doing all my life. You should know that better than anyone, Leo."

"No, I mean, why'd you come and get me, Freddy, the kid? You could've had your pick of just about anyone for this action."

"I didn't want just anyone. We go way back, Leo. And I thought you'd want to take another run at Jerry. Was I wrong?"

Leo threw another seashell into the water and watched it disappear. "Story of my life, Annabelle. I throw seashells at the waves, and they just keep coming."

"Don't get all philosophical on me."

He gave her a sideways glance. "Is this because of your old man?"

"And I don't need you playing my shrink either." She moved slightly away from him, crossed her arms over her chest and looked out to sea where at the edge of the horizon a ship slowly made its way somewhere.

"With thirteen million dollars I could buy a boat big enough to take across the ocean, couldn't I?" she asked.

He shrugged. "Don't know. I guess. I've never had a reason to price one." He looked down at his bare feet, crinkled the sand between his toes. "Annabelle, you were always smart about your money, a lot smarter than me. After all the cons you've pulled, I know you don't need the cash."

"Who ever has enough money?" she said, still watching the boat drift by.

He picked up another shell and hurled it. "You really want to do this, don't you?"

"Part of me doesn't. The part of me I listen to knows I have to."

"The kid says nothing?"

"The kid says nothing."

"If this goes bad, I don't even want to think about what'll happen to us."

"Then don't let it go bad."

"Do you have a single nerve in your body?"

"Not that I've noticed." She picked up a shell and chucked it into the face of a crashing wall of water, then let the ocean race across her feet and ankles. "Are we good?"

He slowly nodded. "Yeah, we're good."

"No more going ballistic on me?"

He cracked a smile. "That I can promise to no woman."

As they walked back to the hotel, he said, "I haven't heard anything about your mom in a long time. How's Tammy doing?"

"Not great."

"Is your old man even alive?"

"I wouldn't be the one to know that, would I?" Annabelle answered.

17

IT TOOK A FULL WEEK TO MAKE the preparations. As part of that work Annabelle gave a list of the documents and IDs she needed to Freddy. When he came to the end of the sheet, he did a double take.

"Four U.S. passports?"

Tony looked up from his computer. "Passports? What for?"

Leo stared at him contemptuously. "What? You think you cross nutcase Jerry Bagger and stay in the country? Give me a break. Yours truly is going to Mongolia and becoming a monk for a few years. I'd rather wear a robe and ride a yak around than let Bagger cut little pieces of my body off while he's screaming about wanting his dough back." He returned to working on his disguise.

Annabelle said, "We need the passports to get out of the country for a while until things cool down."

"Out of the country?" Tony exclaimed, half rising out of his chair.

"Jerry's not infallible, but there's no sense in being stupid. You can see the world, Tony. Learn Italian," she advised.

"What about my parents?" Tony said.

"Send 'em postcards," Leo growled over his shoulder as he

struggled to fit a toupee to his head. "Talk about your freaking amateur hour."

"U.S. passports are difficult to make, Annabelle," Freddy said. "They go for ten grand each on the street."

Annabelle gave him a hard stare. "Well, you're being paid six point five *million* to do these, Freddy."

The man swallowed nervously. "I see your point. You'll have them." Freddy went off with the list.

"I've never even been out of the country," Tony said.

"Best time to go is when you're young," Annabelle said, sitting down across from him at the table.

"Have you ever been out of the country?" he asked her.

Leo piped in. "Are you kidding? You think the States are the only place to run a con? Ha!"

"I've been around," Annabelle admitted.

Tony looked at her nervously. "Well, maybe we could travel together. You could show me around. You and Leo," he added quickly. "And I bet Freddy would want to come too."

Annabelle was already shaking her head. "We split up. Four apart is much harder to catch than four together."

"Right, okay, sure," Tony said.

"You'll have plenty of money to live on," she added.

Tony brightened. "A villa somewhere in Europe, with my own staff."

"*Don't* start throwing the cash around. That's a red flag. Start small and keep your head down. I'll get you out of the country, and then you take it from there." She sat forward. "And now here's exactly what I need from you." Annabelle explained Tony's task in great detail. "Can you do it?"

"No problem," he said immediately. She eyed him questioningly. "Look, I dropped out of MIT after two years because I was bored!"

"I know. That was the *other* reason I picked you."

Tony looked down at his laptop and started typing. "I've actually done it before and fooled the place with the best security in the world."

"Who's that, the Pentagon?" Leo asked.

"No. Wal-Mart."

Leo shot him a glance. "You're kidding me? Wal-Mart?"

"Hey, Wal-Mart doesn't mess around."

"How quickly can you do it?" Annabelle asked.

"Give me a couple days."

"No more than two. I want to test it."

"I've got no problem with that," he said confidently.

Leo rolled his eyes, said a silent prayer, made the sign of the cross and went back to his toupee.

While Freddy and Tony were working on their assignments, Leo and Annabelle donned disguises and headed to the Pompeii Casino. The largest casino on the Boardwalk and one of the newest, having risen from the ruins of an older gambling den, the Pompeii, true to its name, also sported a working volcano that "erupted" twice a day, at noon and six in the evening. What came out of the volcano wasn't lava, but certificates that one could use to get drinks and food. Since casinos practically gave food and alcohol away to keep people gambling, it was not much of a sacrifice on Bagger's part. However, people loved thinking they were getting something for nothing. Thus, the twice-daily eruptions were a surefire draw, the crowds lining up early and then proceeding to dump far more money in the casino than they would ever get back in food and liquor from the belches of the fake volcano.

"Leave it to Bagger to get morons to line up for that crap and then drop their paychecks in his casinos while they're getting fat and drunk," Leo snarled.

"Jerry collects chumps; that's the lifeblood of the casino business."

"I remember when the first casino opened here in '78," Leo said.

Annabelle nodded. "Resorts International, bigger than any Vegas casino at the time except the MGM. Paddy ran some crews here for a while at the beginning."

"Well, your old man never should have come back with you and me!" Leo lit a cigarette and pointed down the line of casinos. "I started out here. The casino crews back then were mostly locals. You had nurses, garbage truck drivers and gas jockeys all of a sudden dealing cards and running craps and roulette tables. They were so bad you could run any scam you wanted. Hell, you didn't even have to cheat. You could make money just off their mistakes. That lasted about four years. I sent both my kids through college on the money I made back then."

She looked at him. "You never talked to me about your family before."

"Yeah, like you're a real blabbermouth when it comes to that stuff."

"You knew my parents. What could I add to that?"

"I had kids early. They're grown and gone and so's my old lady."

"Did she know what you did for a living?"

"Hard to hide it after a while. She liked the money, just not the way I earned it. We never told the kids. I wasn't going to let them get near the business."

"Smart man."

"Yeah, they still ditched me."

"Don't look back, Leo, too many regrets start popping out."

He shrugged and then grinned. "We had a helluva roulette thing going here, didn't we? Any con can past-post craps and blackjack, but only real pros can do it long-term at roulette. It's as close as you can get to a long con at a casino table." He looked at her admiringly. "You were the best claimer I'd ever seen, Annabelle. You could bring the heat or the cool. The pit bosses melted every damn time. And you saw the steam coming before any of us," he added, referring to suspicious casino employees.

"And you were the best mechanic I ever worked with, Leo. Even when some rook cut into your move, you still nailed it before the dealer turned back around."

"Yeah, I was good, but the fact is you were just as good a mechanic as me. I think sometimes your old man kept me on because you said to."

"You give me way too much credit. Paddy Conroy only did what Paddy Conroy wanted to do. And what he ultimately did was screw us both."

"Yeah, and leave us for Bagger to feed on. And if you hadn't been cat-quick about it and made him miss by a couple inches?" He looked out toward the ocean. "Maybe we'd be out there somewhere."

She plucked the cigarette out of his mouth. "And now that we're done patting each other on the back down memory lane, let's get to work."

They started toward the casino entrance and then abruptly stopped. "Let the cattle drive get by," Leo warned.

Each casino had a bus drive where the charters would start lining up at eleven o'clock in the morning. They'd disgorge their usually elderly passengers who'd spend all day in the casino running through their Social Security money and eating junk food. Then they'd hop back on the bus and head home with little to live on for the rest of the month, but certain that they would be back when their next government check rolled in.

Leo and Annabelle watched the senior citizen brigades charge into the Pompeii in time for the first eruption of the day and then wandered in after them. They spent several hours walking the place and even played a few games of chance along the way. Leo had a nice ride at craps, while Annabelle stuck to blackjack, winning more than she lost.

They hooked up a little later and had a drink at one of the bars. As Leo watched a curvy thong-wearing waitress carry a load of drinks to a hot craps table three deep with bettors looking to ride some action to riches, Annabelle said in a low voice, "Well?"

He munched on some pecans and sipped his Jack and Coke. "Blackjack table number five. Looks like we got a little monkey business coming out of the shoe," he said, referring to the device that held the packs of cards.

"Dealer in on it?"

"Oh, yeah. How about you?"

Annabelle took a swallow of her wine before answering. "Roulette table next to the spinning car, we got a four-person past-posting team dragging and doing an okay job of it."

"I thought they taught the dealers to really case their bets now. And how about all the sophisticated eyes-in-the-sky and microcameras they got these days?"

"You know how crazy the roulette table is, that's why it's past-posting Mecca. And if you're good, anything's possible despite all the high-tech stuff."

He touched his drink against hers. "Don't we know that?"

"How's security look?"

"Nothing out of the ordinary. I'm assuming the vault's under a thousand tons of concrete surrounded by a million guys armed with machine guns."

"Good thing we're not going that route," she replied dryly.

"Yeah, you don't want to mess up your manicure." He put his drink down. "How old would Jerry be now?"

"Sixty-six," she answered promptly.

"I bet he hasn't mellowed with age," Leo said grumpily.

"He hasn't."

She sounded so sure, he looked at her suspiciously.

"You check out the mark, Leo, remember? Con Man 101."

"Damn, there's the asshole himself," Leo hissed, and immediately turned away.

As Annabelle watched, six men, all of them young, big and burly, walked by. They were surrounding another man, shorter but very fit, with broad shoulders and thick white hair. He was dressed in an expensive blue suit with a yellow tie. Jerry Bagger's face was heavily tanned. Down one cheek ran a scar, and it looked like the man's nose had been broken at least a couple times. Underneath his thick white eyebrows was a pair of canny eyes. His gaze darted across his casino, seemingly absorbing all sorts of interesting data from his empire of slots, cards and crushed hopes.

As soon as they passed by, Leo turned back around and struggled to regain his breath. A ticked-off Annabelle said, "Your hyperventilating when the guy is all the way across the casino didn't really figure into my plan, Leo."

He held up a hand. "Not to worry, I'm over it." He drew one last deep breath.

"We've never even met the guy face-to-face. It was his goons who tried to kill us back then. It's not like he's going to recognize you."

"I know, I know." He finished his drink. "What now?"

"When it's time to go, we go. Until then, we work our script and practice our cues and look for any edge we can get, because

Jerry's so damn unpredictable that even if we're perfect, it may not be enough."

"You know, I forgot what a cheerleader you are."

"Nothing wrong with stating the obvious. If he throws us a curve, we have to be ready to hit it out, or else."

"Yeah, we know all about *or else,* don't we?"

He and Annabelle both stared silently across the casino at Jerry Bagger and his army as they exited the casino, climbed into a mini-motorcade and headed off, perhaps to break somebody's kneecaps for cheating the casino king out of thirty bucks, much less 30 million.

CHAPTER

18

AT THE END OF A WEEK THEY were ready. Annabelle was dressed in a dark black skirt and high heels, and she wore minimal jewelry. Her hair was now blond and spiky. She looked nothing like her enhanced casino photo. Leo's appearance had been altered even more radically. His toupee was gray and thin, with a hard widow's peak. He sported a small goatee, slender glasses and a three-piece suit.

He said, "You know the only thing that bugs me about this is ratting out other cons."

"Like they wouldn't do it to *us* if they had the chance to walk away with millions? Besides, the ones we pegged aren't all that good. Sooner or later they'll get caught anyway. And it's not like the old days. No more bodies buried in the desert or chucked into the Atlantic. Past-posting's a conspiracy to commit theft by deception crime, something like a third-degree misdemeanor. They'll pay their fine or do their bit of time and go hit the casino boats in the Midwest or pester the Indians in New England until enough time passes and then they change their appearance, come back here to start all over again."

"Yeah, but it's still a raw deal."

She shrugged. "If it'll make you feel better, I'll get their names and send them twenty grand each for their troubles."

Leo brightened but then said, "Okay, just don't take it out of my share."

They had left Freddy and Tony and checked into one of the best hotels on the Boardwalk. They would have no further direct contact with either of the men from now on. Before leaving them she had admonished both, particularly Tony, to keep in mind that spies were everywhere in this town. "You don't flash cash, you don't joke, you don't say anything that might tip someone that a con is going down, because they'll go running to somebody to tell and collect some scratch. One slip and it could be over, for all of us."

She had looked directly at Tony when she added, "This is the real deal, Tony. No screwups."

"I'm covered. I swear," he'd declared.

Leo and Annabelle rode in a cab to the Pompeii and immediately took up their vigils. Annabelle watched a crew that she'd been observing running a past-posting scam at the roulette tables in casinos up and down the Boardwalk. There were various incarnations of past-posting, which had taken its name from a horse-racing scam where bets were laid down after the results of the race were known by the bettor. With roulette it involved surreptitiously sliding big dollar chips on winning numbers *after* the ball had dropped and then collecting. Some teams used a different technique. The bettor would hide the big chips under the cheaper ones *before* the ball dropped. Then the bettor would either "drag" or pull the big chips off the table if the number lost or do nothing except scream for joy if the number won, all right under the dealer's nose. The latter technique had the distinct advantage of taking the powerful eye-in-the-sky out of the equation because it would only be called into play if the bet won. Then the tape would show that the bettor had done *nothing* with the chips, since he would only pull the chip if the bet lost. Past-posting at the roulette table involved enormous amounts of practice, timing, teamwork, patience, natural skill and, most of all, nerve.

Annabelle and Leo had once been masters at this game. However, the surveillance technology in use today by the casinos drastically reduced the chances of anyone except the very best cheats being able to conduct the scam successfully over time. And the nature of the con meant that you could only work it a limited number of times at a casino before you were taken down, so the bet and the odds had better be large enough to justify the risk.

Leo kept his eye on a blackjack table and a gent who'd been playing and winning for a nice stretch. Not big enough to arouse suspicion, but cumulatively Leo figured the guy was making a lot more than the minimum wage for sitting on his butt and sipping free drinks. He used his cell phone to call Annabelle.

"You ready to do this?" he asked.

"Looks like my past-posters are just about ready to hit it, so let's go."

Annabelle walked over to a thickset man she'd easily sized up as a pit boss and whispered into his ear, inclining her head toward the roulette table where the scam was happening.

"There's a third-section-straight-up drag going down at table number six. The two women seated on the right side are the check-bettors. The mechanic's in the chair near the bottom of the table. The claimer's the skinny guy with glasses hanging back behind the dealer's left shoulder. Call up to the eye-in-the-sky and tell the layout camera to zoom in on the action and hold until the drag's executed."

Roulette tables were so large they were routinely covered by two ceiling cameras, one aimed on the wheel, the other on the table. The problem was the surveillance tech could only look at one camera at a time. The pit boss stared at her for a second, but Annabelle's authoritative description couldn't be ignored. He quickly spoke into his headset, relaying this order.

Meanwhile, Leo sidled up to the pit boss in his section and whispered, "At blackjack table number five you got a bad dealer doing the zero-shuffle. The player in seat number three has a card counter analyzer strapped to his right thigh. If you get close enough, you can see the impression through his pant leg. He's also got an intracranial in his right ear where he receives the call from the computer. The eye-in-the-sky won't pick up the deck cut because the dealer's movements obscure the slice, but if you get a handheld down here, you can record it easy enough from floor level."

As with Annabelle's warning, the pit boss only took a few seconds to call upstairs, and the handheld came down to take pictures.

Five minutes later the stunned cons were led away and the cops called.

Ten minutes after that, Annabelle and Leo found themselves in a part of the casino where no grandma with a Social Security check to blow would ever be invited.

Jerry Bagger rose from behind the huge desk in his lavish office, his hands in his pockets and several nice pieces of bling around his wrists and his muscular, tanned neck.

"Excuse me for not thanking you for saving me a few lousy grand," he said in a bark of a voice that revealed his Brooklyn background. "Fact is I'm not used to people doing me favors. It makes the hair on the back of my neck stand up. I don't like the hair on my neck standing up. The only thing I like erect on my body is what's behind my zipper."

The six other men in the room, all in high-dollar suits with big shoulders that were not the result of padding, stared at Leo and Annabelle, their hands clasped in front of them.

Annabelle stepped forward. "We didn't do it as a favor. We did it so we'd end up here to see you."

Bagger spread his hands. "So you're here. You've seen me. Now what?"

"A proposition."

Bagger rolled his eyes. "Oh, here we go." He sat down on a leather couch, picked out a walnut from a bowl on the table there and cracked it open using only his right hand. "Is this the part where you say you're going to make me a ton of money, even though I already got a ton of money?" He ate the bits of nut.

"Yes. And you can serve your country at the same time."

Bagger snarled, "My country? Is that the same country that keeps looking to lock my ass up for doing something that's perfectly legal?"

"We can help with that," Annabelle said.

"Oh, so now you're feds?" He looked at his men. "Hey, guys, we got feds in the casino. Call the fucking Orkin man."

The muscle all laughed on cue.

Annabelle sat down on the couch next to Bagger and handed him a card. He looked at it. "Pamela Young, International Management, Inc.," he read. "Means shit to me." He tossed it back to her. "My guys tell me you two really know your casino scams. They teaching that in fed school now? Not that I believe you're feds."

Leo said in a gruff tone, "You run what in a day, thirty, forty mil? You have to keep a certain level of reserves to comply with state gaming regs, but that leaves a lot of cash to float. So what do you do with the excess? Come on, tell us."

The casino owner looked at him in amazement. "I wallpaper my fucking house with it, asshole." He looked at his muscle. "Get this jerk-off outta my face."

His men moved forward, and two of them actually lifted Leo off the floor before Annabelle said, "What would you say to a ten percent return on that money?"

"I'd say that sucks." Bagger rose and went toward his desk.

"I meant ten percent every *two days*." He stopped, turned and looked at her. "What do you think of that?" she said.

"Too good to be true, so it is." He took a steel-gray $5,000 casino chip from a desk drawer and tossed it to her. "Go have some fun. No need to thank me. Consider it a gift from God. Don't let the door hit that nice ass on the way out." He signaled his men to let Leo go.

She said, "Just think about it, Mr. Bagger. We'll be back to-morrow to ask again. In accordance with my orders, we're required to ask twice. If you don't want in then, Uncle Sam will just go down the Boardwalk and give the deal to one of your competitors."

"Good luck on that."

She said confidently, "It worked in Vegas, it'll work here."

"Yeah, right. I wish I was smoking whatever it is you are."

"Gambling revenue topped out five years ago, Mr. Bagger. So how can the Vegas crowd keep putting up billion-dollar proper-ties? It's like they're printing money." She paused. "And they are. And helping their country at the same time."

He sat down behind his desk and stared at her with, for the first time, just a hint of interest. That was all Annabelle needed at this point.

"And did you ever wonder why none of the Vegas players

have been investigated by the feds in the last ten years? I'm not talking Mafia prosecutions, that's old news. But you and I know what goes on there. And yet like you said, the Justice Department is all over your butt." She paused. "And I know a man as smart as Jerry Bagger can't believe in that much luck." She laid her card down on his desk. "You can call anytime. People in my business don't keep regular office hours." She glanced at the big men who still hovered next to Leo. "And we can see ourselves out, fellows, thanks."

She and Leo left.

When the door closed behind the pair, Bagger snapped, "Tail 'em."

CHAPTER

19

ANNABELLE AND LEO WERE IN A cab; her gaze had never left the rear window.

"They back there?" Leo asked in a whisper.

"Of course. Where else would they be?"

"For a second there, I thought those damn goons were gonna toss me out the window. How come I always have to play bad cop to your good cop?"

"Because you play bad so incredibly good."

Leo gave a shiver. "The guy's the same nightmare I remember him being. You see him crack that nut with one hand?"

"Come on, he's a walking cliché from a bad mob movie."

The cab pulled in front of their hotel, and they got out. Annabelle walked down the street and then crossed it. She rapped on the window of the Hummer parked there. The glass slid down, revealing one of Bagger's burly men.

She said pleasantly, "You can tell Mr. Bagger that I'm staying in room 1412. Oh, here's another card for you in case he threw the other one away." She turned and rejoined Leo, and they walked into the hotel together. Her phone buzzed. It was Tony, calling to confirm he was in position. She'd bought him a very expensive pair of surveillance binoculars and had him check into a room of a hotel right across the street from the Pompeii, which had a fine view of the window line to Bagger's office suite.

The call to her room she'd been expecting came ten minutes later. She signaled Leo, who was standing by the window. He did a quick text message to Tony on his BlackBerry.

Annabelle poised her hand over the phone and motioned with the other one to Leo. "Come on, come on." The phone rang five times, six, seven.

On the ninth ring Leo got a confirming reply right back and nodded. Annabelle snatched up the phone. "Hello?"

"How'd you make my guys so fast?" Bagger bellowed.

"When it comes to surveillance, my . . . *employer* really can't be beat, Mr. Bagger," she informed him. "It's merely a question of thousands of assets on the ground and unlimited money." The truth was she knew he'd order them to be followed, and kept her gaze out the rear window of the cab. She'd seen on their earlier recon of the casino that Bagger's personal security all drove yellow Hummers. They weren't that hard to spot.

"Meaning I'm under surveillance?" he snapped.

"We're all being watched, Mr. Bagger. You shouldn't feel singled out."

"Cut the 'Mr. Bagger' shit. How do you know so much about casino scams that you were able to spot two going on in my place? Makes me think you're way too close to the con world."

"*I* didn't spot them. We had three teams in your casino today who were trolling for something I could use as bait to get to you. The members of those teams *are* experts in casino cons. They relayed the intel to us, and we told your pit bosses. Simple."

"Okay, we'll just let that go for now. What exactly do you want?"

"I thought I was clear in your office about my intentions—"

"Yeah, yeah! I know what you *said*. I want to know what you *meant* by it."

"This isn't something I'm prepared to discuss over the phone. NS—," she began, and then said quickly, "Hard-line phones aren't very secure."

"You were going to say NSA, weren't you?" he shot back. "The spooks, I know all about them."

"With all due respect, nobody knows all about NSA, not even POTUS," she said, dropping one more carefully scripted initialism.

There was a silence on the end of the line.

"Are you still there?" she asked.

He snapped, "I'm here!"

"Do you want to meet at your office?"

"That's no good. I'm, uh, I'm already headed out of town."

"No, you're not. You're sitting in your office right now." This information was what Tony had e-mailed Leo.

The line immediately went dead.

She put the phone down, looked at Leo and gave him a reassuring wink.

He let out a deep breath. "Deep waters we're treading in, Annie."

She looked amused. "You only called me Annie when you were really, really nervous, Leo."

He wiped a trickle of sweat from his forehead and lit up a Winston. "Yeah. Well, some things don't change, do they?"

The phone rang again. She picked it up.

"This is my town," Bagger said menacingly. "Nobody spies on me in *my* town."

She said calmly, "Mr. Bagger, since this whole thing seems to be upsetting you, I'll make it easy. I'll report back that you turned down our second and final offer. That way you won't have to worry about it anymore. And like I said, I'll just go elsewhere."

"There isn't a casino around here that would believe your half-ass story."

"It's not just a story. We wouldn't expect savvy casino operators to take this on faith. So we do trial runs. Let them make a lot of money very quickly, and then they decide. Either they're in or out. And they get to keep the profits regardless."

She could hear him breathing on the other end of the line.

"How much money?" he asked.

"How much do you want?"

"Why would the government offer me this kind of a deal?"

"There are many forms of 'the government.' Just because one part doesn't particularly care for you doesn't mean other elements don't see advantages. For us it's the very fact that Justice is after you that we're interested."

"How do you figure that as an advantage?"

"Because who'd ever believe that the U.S. government would be partnering with *you*?" she stated simply.

"Are you with NSA?"

"No."

"CIA?"

"I'm going to answer every question like that with an unqualified 'no.' And I don't carry my badge or creds in situations like this."

"I got politicians in my pocket in Washington. One call and I'll know."

"One call and you'll know nothing because the field I work in, the politicians know zip about. But call away. Call the CIA. They're in Langley, that's in McLean, Virginia, in case you didn't know. A lot of people think they're based in D.C. Believe it or not, they're actually listed in the phone book. You'll want the National Clandestine Service—it used to be called the Operations Directorate. But just to save you the call, they'll tell you they never heard of Pamela Young or International Management, Inc."

"How do I know this isn't some kind of sting operation the feds are running?"

"I'm not a lawyer, but I'd have to say it would be a pretty clear case of entrapment. And if you want to check us for a surveillance wire, feel free."

Bagger said, "What kind of trial run?"

"A few clicks on the computer."

"Explain that."

"Not over the phone. Face-to-face."

She could hear him sigh.

"You eaten dinner?" he asked.

"No."

"Pompeii, ten minutes. They'll meet you at the front door."

The line went dead.

She hung up and looked over at Leo. "We're in."

"And now comes the flash," he said.

"And now comes the flash," Annabelle agreed.

CHAPTER

20

AN HOUR LATER THEY WERE finishing an excellent dinner prepared by Bagger's personal chef. Bagger took his glass of bourbon and Annabelle and Leo their wine and settled down in comfortable leather chairs near a flickering gas fire.

Bagger had taken Annabelle up on her offer and had her and Leo checked for listening devices.

"Okay, bellies full, livers pickled, talk to me," Bagger ordered. He held up a finger. "First, what are you guys up to? And then tell me about the money."

Annabelle sat back cradling her drink, glanced at Leo and said, "You remember Iran-Contra?"

"Vaguely."

"There are occasions when the interests of America are best served by providing aid to countries and certain organizations that don't have popular support in the U.S."

"What, like giving guns to Osama to fight the Russians?" he sneered.

"It's a choice of the lesser of two evils. Goes on all the time."

"So what's that got to do with me?"

"We have money from very discreet sources, some of it private, but it needs to be 'finessed' before it can be deployed," she said, sipping her wine.

"You mean laundered," Bagger said.

She smiled coyly. "No, I mean finessed."

"I'm still not getting the connection."

"El Banco del Caribe. You know it?"

"Should I?"

Leo spoke up. "Isn't that where you park some of your casino cash? They specialize in disappearing money, for a price. No taxes."

Bagger had half risen from his seat.

Annabelle said, "It's part of our job to know things like that," she said. "Don't take it personally. You're not the only one we have a file on."

Bagger sat back down and eyed her spiky hair. "You don't look like a spy."

"Well, that's sort of the point, isn't it?" she said amiably, rising and pouring herself another glass of wine.

"Look, how do I know you're legit? I call anybody, they never heard of you. Where does that leave me?"

"Money talks and bullshit walks," she said, sitting back down.

"Meaning what exactly?"

"Meaning call your money guy in here."

Bagger looked at her suspiciously for a moment and then picked up the phone.

The man appeared a minute later. "Yes, sir?"

Annabelle took a slip of paper out of her pocket and handed it to him. "Pull this account up on your computer. It's at El Banco del Caribe. That's a onetime password along with the account number. And come back and tell Mr. Bagger the balance in that account."

The man looked at Bagger, who nodded. The man left and returned a few minutes later.

"Well?" Bagger said impatiently.

"Three million twelve thousand dollars and sixteen cents, sir."

Bagger stared at Annabelle, the new respect clear in his gaze. He waved his money guy gone. After the door had shut, he said, "Okay, you've got my attention."

"To further allay people's concerns, we usually do a trial run or runs, as the case may be."

"You mentioned that. How does it work?"

"You park money at El Banco for two days in an account of our designation; you collect the 'interest,' and then the money is put back into your account at your home bank."

"How much money are we talking?"

"A million is typical. The money you wire down gets 'mingled' with other funds. After two days you walk away with a hundred grand in profit. You can do it every two days if you want."

"Mingled? Don't you mean *finessed*?" Bagger said.

She raised her glass. "You learn fast."

Yet Bagger was scowling. "You want me to put a million bucks of my money in an account of *your* designation and wait two days for my money plus interest to come floating back to me? Do I look like I got cowshit for brains?"

Annabelle sat down next to him and gently touched his arm. "I tell you what, Jerry, I can call you Jerry, can't I?"

"I'll let it slide for now."

"For the two days your money is hanging out there, my associate and I will stay here at your hotel, with your boys watching us night and day. If your money doesn't come back into your account with interest just like I'm telling you, we're all yours. And I don't know about you, but public servant or not, I like my life way too much to give it up for a bunch of money that I'll never even see."

He looked her up and down, shook his head, rose and walked over to the window and looked out through the bulletproof glass. "This has got to be the craziest damn thing I've ever heard. And I'm a nutcase for even listening to it."

"It's not crazy when you look at the world today. Things have to be done to protect this country, action that is not always completely legal or popular. If the American people knew what really went on?" She shrugged. "But that's not my field task. My job is to make sure the money gets to where it needs to go. In exchange for your help, you get paid an extraordinary premium, it's that simple."

"But this money is all electronic. Why do you have to launder it?"

"Even digital dollars can be traced, Jerry. In fact, they can do it more easily than with real cash. The funds need to be commingled with other sources of money that are nongovernmental. It all gets washed out electronically, sort of like wiping fingerprints off a gun. Then the funds can go to where they're needed."

"And you say Vegas already does this? So if I call up and ask—"

She interrupted him. "They'll tell you nothing because that's what they've been instructed to do." She rose and stood beside him. "There's tremendous upside for you here, Jerry, but there's a downside too. And let me just lay that out for you. It's only fair that you know."

She led him back to the couch. "If it ever comes to certain people's attention that you've told anyone about this arrangement—"

Bagger laughed. "Don't threaten me, little girl. I invented the art of intimidation."

"This isn't intimidation, Jerry," she said quietly, her gaze directly on him. "If you tell anyone about this arrangement, men will come for you wherever you might be. These men will have no fear of anyone you could possibly hire to protect you. They are not bound by the laws of any country, and they will kill anyone remotely close to you, man, woman or child. Then they'll take you away." She paused to let this sink in. "I've been in the business a long time, and done some things that would probably surprise even you, but these are men I would never want to face, even with a squad of Navy SEALs surrounding me. They aren't the best of the best, Jerry. They are the worst of the absolute scum. And your last memory will be how could it have hurt so damn much."

Bagger exploded, "These whack jobs are on *our* government's payroll! No wonder we're so screwed up." When he took a sip of his bourbon, both Annabelle and Leo noted that his hand shook a bit. "So why the hell would I—" Bagger began.

Anticipating what he was going to say, she cut in. "But as I told my superiors, Jerry Bagger won't talk. He'll just collect his exorbitant profits and keep his mouth shut. I don't throw darts at names on a wall, Jerry. Guys like you are ideal for our purposes. You've got brains, guts, money, and you don't mind playing close to the edge." She studied Bagger closely and added, "I'd hate to give the action to one of the other casinos, Jerry, but my mission is clear."

After another minute he grinned and patted her leg. "I'm as patriotic as the next son of a bitch. So what the hell, let's do it."

CHAPTER

21

THE CAMEL CLUB HELD A
hastily called meeting at Stone's cottage at the cemetery the
morning following their visit to DeHaven's home. Stone explained to Milton and Caleb in greater detail what had happened
the night before.

"They could be watching us right now," a frightened Caleb
said as he glanced out the window.

"I would be astonished if they weren't," Stone replied calmly.

His cottage was small and sparsely furnished: an old bed, a
large, beaten-up desk covered with papers and journals, shelves
of books in various languages, all of which Stone spoke, a small
kitchen with a battered table, a tiny bathroom and a scattering of
mismatched chairs arranged around the large fireplace that was
the cottage's main source of heat.

"And that doesn't concern you?" Milton asked.

"It would have concerned me much more had they tried to
kill me, which they easily could have despite Reuben's heroics."

"So what now?" Reuben asked. He stood in front of the fireplace, trying to work the chill off. He checked his watch. "I need
to get to work."

Caleb added, "So do I."

Stone said, "Caleb, I need to get inside the vault at the library. Is that possible?"

Caleb looked uncertain. "Well, under normal conditions it would be. I mean, I have the authority to take people into the vaults, but I'll be questioned as to why. They don't really like people just bringing in friends and family without advance notice. And with Jonathan's death restrictions are even tighter."

"What if the visitor was a scholar from overseas?" Stone asked.

"Well, of course, that's different." He glanced at Stone. "What foreign scholar do you know?"

Reuben broke in. "I think he's talking about himself, Caleb."

Caleb looked sternly at his friend. "Oliver! I cannot possibly assist in perpetrating a fraud on the Library of Congress, for God's sake."

"Desperate times call for desperate measures. I believe we are now the targets of some very dangerous people because we're involved with Jonathan DeHaven. So we need to find out whether his death was natural or not. And looking at the place where he died may help me determine that."

"Well, we know how he died," Caleb countered. The others looked at him in surprise. "I just found out this morning," he said quickly. "A friend from the library called me at home. Jonathan died as the result of cardiopulmonary arrest, that's what the autopsy reported."

Milton said, "That's what *everybody* dies of. It just means your heart stopped."

Stone looked thoughtful. "Milton's right. And that also means the medical examiner doesn't know what actually killed De-Haven." He stood and looked down at Caleb. "I want to go into the vault this morning."

"Oliver, you can't just show up unannounced as some scholar."

"Why not?"

"It's just not done. There are protocols, procedures to follow."

"I'll say I was in town for a visit with family and wanted very much to see the world's greatest collection of books; a spur-of-the-moment thing."

"Well, that might work," Caleb grudgingly conceded. "But what if they ask you some question you don't know the answer to?"

"There's no one easier to impersonate than a scholar, Caleb," Stone assured him. Caleb looked very offended at this remark, but Stone disregarded his friend's annoyance and added, "I'll be at the library at eleven o'clock." He wrote something on a piece of paper and handed it to Caleb. "This is who I'll be."

Caleb glanced down at the paper and then looked up in surprise.

With that, the meeting of the Camel Club was adjourned, although Stone took Milton aside and started talking to him quietly.

A few hours later at the library Caleb was handing a book to Norman Janklow, an elderly man and reading room regular.

"Here it is, Norman." He handed him a copy of Ernest Hemingway's *A Farewell to Arms*. Janklow was a Hemingway fanatic. The novel he was holding was a first edition, inscribed by Hemingway.

"I would die to own this book, Caleb," Janklow said.

"I know, Norman, me too." A signed Hemingway first edition would fetch at least $35,000, Caleb knew, certainly beyond his financial means and probably Janklow's too. "But at least you can hold it."

"I'm getting started on my biography of Ernest."

"That's great." Actually, Janklow had been "getting started" on his Hemingway biography for the last two years. Still, the notion seemed to make him happy, and Caleb was more than willing to play along.

Janklow carefully fingered the volume. "They've repaired the cover," he said irritably.

"That's right. Many of our first-edition American masterpieces were housed in less-than-ideal conditions before the Rare Books Division really got up to speed. We've been going through the backlog for years now. That copy was long overdue for restoration, an administrative error, I guess. That happens when you have nearly a million volumes under one roof."

"I wish they'd keep them in their original condition."

"Well, our chief goal is preservation. That's why we have this book for you to enjoy, because it's been preserved."

"I met Hemingway once."

"I remember you telling me." *Over a hundred times.*

"He was a piece of work. We got drunk together at a café in Cuba."

"Right. I remember the story very well. I'll let you get to your research."

Janklow slipped on his reading glasses, took out his pieces of paper and a pencil and lost himself in the adventurous world of Ernest Hemingway's prodigious imagination and spare prose.

Promptly at eleven o'clock Oliver Stone arrived at the Rare Books reading room dressed in a rumpled three-piece tweed suit and holding a cane. His white hair was neatly combed, and he sported a very trim beard along with large black glasses that made his eyes buglike. That coupled with his walking with a stoop made him appear twenty years older than he was. Caleb rose from his desk at the back of the room, hardly recognizing his friend.

As one of the attendants at the front desk approached Stone, Caleb hurried forward. "I'll take care of him, Dorothy. I . . . I know the gentleman."

Stone made an elaborate show of producing a white business

card. "As promised, Herr Shaw, I am here to see the *books.*" His accent was thick and Germanic, and very well done.

As Dorothy, the woman behind the front desk, looked at him curiously, Caleb said, "This is Dr. Aust. We met years ago at a book conference in . . . Frankfurt, was it?"

"No, Mainz," Stone corrected. "I remember very clearly, because it was the season of *Spargel,* the white asparagus, and I always go to the Mainz conference and eat the white asparagus." He beamed at Dorothy, who smiled and went back to what she was doing.

Another man came into the reading room and stopped. "Caleb, I wanted to talk to you for a minute."

Caleb turned a shade paler. "Oh, hello, Kevin. Kevin, this is, uh, Dr. Aust from Germany. Dr. Aust, Kevin Philips. He's the acting director of the Rare Books Division. After Jonathan's—"

"Ah, yes, the very untimely death of Herr DeHaven," Stone said. "Very sad. Very sad."

"You knew Jonathan?" Philips said.

"Only by reputation. I think it clear that his paper on James Logan's metrical translation of Cato's *Moral Distichs* was the final word on the subject, don't you?"

Philips looked chagrined. "I must confess I haven't read it."

"An analysis of Logan's first translation from the classics to be produced in North America, it is well worth exploring," Stone advised kindly.

Philips said, "I'll be sure to add it to my list. Ironically, sometimes librarians don't have a lot of time to read."

"Then I will not burden you with copies of *my* books," Stone said with a smile. "They're in German anyway," he added with a chuckle.

"I invited Dr. Aust to take a tour of the vaults while he's in town," Caleb explained. "Sort of a spur-of-the-moment thing."

"Absolutely," Philips said. "We'd be honored." He lowered his voice. "Caleb, you heard the report about Jonathan?"

"Yes, I did."

"So that means he just had a heart attack, then?"

Caleb glanced at Stone, who, out of Philips' line of sight, gave a slight nod.

"Yes, I think that's exactly what it means."

Philips shook his head. "God, he was younger than me. It gives one pause, doesn't it?" He looked over at Stone. "Dr. Aust, would you like me to give you the fifty-cent tour?"

Stone smiled and leaned heavily on his cane. "No, Herr Philips, I would much prefer you to take that time and begin your friend's paper on *Moral Distichs.*"

Philips chuckled. "It's good to see that distinguished scholars can retain a healthy sense of humor."

"I try, sir, I try," Stone said with a slow bow.

After Philips had left them, Caleb and Stone headed into the vault.

"How did you find out about Jonathan's scholarly work?" Caleb asked once they were alone.

"I asked Milton to dig around. He located it on the Internet and brought me a copy. I scanned it in case someone like Philips showed up, to prove my scholarly pedigree." Caleb looked disgruntled. "What's the matter?" Stone asked.

"Well, it's a little deflating to one's ego to see how easily a scholar *can* be impersonated."

"I'm sure your validation of my pedigree made all the difference to your boss."

Caleb brightened. "Well, I'm sure it contributed somewhat to the success," he said modestly.

"All right, take me through your exact movements that day."

Caleb did so, ending on the top floor. He pointed at a spot.

"That's where his body was." Caleb shivered. "God, it really was terrible."

Stone looked around and then stopped and pointed at something on the wall.

"What's that?"

Caleb looked to where he was pointing. "Oh, that's a nozzle for the fire suppressant system."

"You use water in here with all these books?"

"Oh, no. It's a halon 1301 system."

"Halon 1301?" Stone asked.

"It's a gas, although it's really a liquid, but when it shoots out of the nozzle, it turns to gas. It smothers the fire without damaging the books."

Stone looked excited. "Smothers! My God!" His friend looked at him curiously. "Caleb, don't you see?"

What Stone was referring to suddenly dawned on Caleb. "Smothering? Oh, no, Oliver, no. It couldn't have been the cause of Jonathan's death."

"Why not?"

"Because a person would have several minutes to escape the area before he'd start feeling the effects. That's why they use halon in occupied places. And before the gas is discharged, a warning horn comes on. We're changing systems actually but not because it's dangerous."

"Why, then?"

"Halon significantly depletes the ozone layer. In fact, while it can still be used in this country and recycled for new applications, the manufacture of halon 1301 is banned in the U.S. and has been since the mid-nineties. Although the federal government is still the biggest user of it."

"You seem to know a lot about halon."

"Well, all employees were given an in-depth review of the system when it was first installed. And I did some extra reading on the subject."

"Why?"

He blurted out, "Because I come into this vault a lot, and I didn't want to die a horrible death! You know I lack any shred of personal courage."

Stone examined the nozzle. "Where's the gas stored?"

"Somewhere in the basement level of the building, and the gas is piped up here."

"You say it's stored as liquid and then comes out as a gas?"

"Yes. The speed with which it's blown out of the nozzle turns it into a gas."

"It must be very cold."

"If you're standing in front of the nozzle, you could get frost-bite, in fact."

"Anything else?"

"Well, if you stay in the room long enough, I suppose you *could* be asphyxiated. The rough rule of thumb is if there's not enough oxygen for a fire, there's not enough oxygen to sustain life."

"Could the gas cause a heart attack?"

"I don't know. But it doesn't matter. The system never came on. That horn can be heard throughout the building. The only way Jonathan wouldn't have heard it is if he was already dead."

"What if the horn was disconnected?"

"Who would have done that?" Caleb said skeptically.

"I don't know."

While he was talking, Stone was staring at a large register built onto one of the columns supporting a bookshelf. "Is that a vent for the HVAC system?" he asked. Caleb nodded. "Something must have fallen on it," Stone said, pointing to where two of the vent grilles had been bent.

"It happens with people bringing book carts in and out."

Stone said, "I'll have Milton research the halon system and see if anything else turns up. And Reuben has some friends at D.C. Homicide and the FBI from his days in military intelligence. I've asked Reuben to call them to see if he can find out something about the investigation."

"We have the meeting with Vincent Pearl tonight at Jonathan's house. In light of these developments, don't you think it best to call it off?"

Stone shook his head. "No. Those men can find us wherever we are, Caleb. If we're in danger, I'd rather try to find out the truth for myself than sit back and wait for the blow to fall."

As they were leaving the vault, Caleb muttered, "Why couldn't I have just joined a nice, boring *book* club?"

CHAPTER

22

THAT EVENING THEY ALL RODE to DeHaven's house in Caleb's Nova. In the meantime Milton had found out a lot about fire suppressant systems. He reported that "halon 1301 is odorless and colorless, and extinguishes fires by tweaking the combustion process, which includes the depletion of oxygen levels. It evaporates quickly, leaving no residue. Once the system is activated, it'll discharge in approximately ten seconds."

"Can it be lethal?" Stone asked.

"If you hang around long enough and depending on the concentration levels of the flooding agent, you can suffer asphyxiation. It can also cause a heart attack."

Stone looked triumphantly at Caleb.

"But the autopsy result said he suffered cardiopulmonary arrest," Milton reminded him. "If he'd suffered a heart attack, the cause of death would've been listed as a myocardial infarction. A heart attack or a stroke leaves very clear physiological signs. The medical examiner wouldn't have missed that."

Stone nodded. "All right. But asphyxiation can happen, you said."

"I don't really think so," Milton said. "Not after I spoke with Caleb earlier."

"I looked more into the library's halon system," Caleb explained. "It's rated as an NOAEL system. That stands for No Observed Adverse Effect Level, a standard protocol used in fire suppression. It relates to the cardio-sensitization levels present in a particular place in relation to the amount of flooding agent required to extinguish a fire. Bottom line, with a NOAEL level, you'd have plenty of time to escape the space before being affected. And even if the horn were disconnected for some reason, if the gas had come out of that nozzle, Jonathan would've heard it. There was no way halon could have incapacitated him so fast that he couldn't have escaped."

"Well, it looks like my theory on how Jonathan DeHaven died was incorrect," Stone admitted. He looked up ahead. They had just pulled onto Good Fellow Street.

"Is that Vincent Pearl?" he asked.

Caleb nodded and said irritably, "He's early, probably very eager to prove yours truly wrong about the *Psalm Book.*"

Reuben smirked. "I see he left the robes at home."

"Keep your eyes open," Stone warned as they got out of the car. "We are undoubtedly being watched."

True to Stone's words, the same pair of binoculars from the window across the street were trained on the group as they met Pearl and headed into the house. The person also had a camera and snapped a few shots of them.

Once inside, Stone suggested that the rare book dealer accompany Caleb to the vault alone. "It's not that large of a space, and you two are the experts in the area," he explained. "We'll just wait upstairs for you."

Caleb looked unhappily at Stone, doubtless for casting him

solo to Pearl. For his part Pearl gazed at Stone suspiciously for a moment and then shrugged. "I doubt it will take me long to show that it is *not* a first-edition *Psalm Book.*"

"Take your *time,*" Stone called to them as the two men stepped onto the elevator.

"Don't let the *book* bugs bite," Reuben added.

As the door closed, Stone said, "Okay, quick, let's search the place."

"Why don't we wait for Pearl to leave?" Milton asked. "Then we can take our time and Caleb can help us look."

"I'm not worried about Pearl. I don't want *Caleb* to know, since he would undoubtedly object."

They split up, and for the next thirty minutes they covered as much as they could.

Stone said in a disappointed tone, "Nothing. Not a diary, no letters."

"I did find this on a shelf in his bedroom closet," Reuben said, producing a photograph of a man and a woman in a small frame. "And that's DeHaven next to her. I recognize him from his picture in the paper."

Stone gazed at the photo and then turned it over. "No name or date. But judging from DeHaven's appearance, it was taken many years ago."

Milton said, "Caleb told us that the lawyer mentioned De-Haven was married once. I wonder if that was the bride?"

"Lucky guy if it is," Reuben commented. "And they look happy, which means it was early on in the marriage. That all changes with time, trust me."

Stone slipped the photo into his pocket. "We'll just hold on to it for now." He stopped and looked upward. "This home has a steeply pitched roof."

"So?" Reuben said.

"So homes with a pitched roof of this vintage usually have an attic."

Milton said, "I didn't see anything like that upstairs."

"You wouldn't if the access were hidden," Stone replied.

Reuben checked his watch. "What's taking the book geeks so long? You think they're fighting?"

"I don't really see those two chucking first editions at each other," Milton said.

"Whatever it is they're doing, let's just hope they keep it up for a little while longer," Stone said. "Milton, you stay down here and keep watch. If you hear the elevator, call up to us."

It took a few minutes, but Stone found the attic access behind a rack of clothes in DeHaven's closet. It was locked, but Stone had brought a pick and tension tool with him, and the lock quickly succumbed to his prodding.

"They must have added this closet later," Reuben said.

Stone nodded. "Walk-in closets weren't very popular in the nineteenth century."

They headed up the stairs. Along the way, Stone found and hit a light switch; this illuminated their path only weakly. They arrived at the top of the stairs and looked around the large space. It appeared unchanged since the day the home had been built. There were a few boxes and old suitcases, but a quick examination revealed them to be either empty or full of old junk.

Reuben spotted it first, positioned in front of a half-moon window of leaded glass. "Why a telescope here?" he asked.

"Well, you wouldn't have one in the *basement*, would you?"

Reuben looked through it. "Holy shit!"

"What?" Stone exclaimed.

"It's pointed at the house next door."

"Whose house is it?"

"How do I—" Reuben stopped and adjusted the eyepiece. "Damn!"

"What is it? Let me see."

"Now, wait a minute, Oliver," Reuben said. "Let me just execute a nice long recon."

Stone waited a few moments and then pushed his friend out of the way. Wiping the eyepiece clear, he gazed through a window of the house next to DeHaven's. The drapes were drawn, but this window also had a half-sphere of glass above, which the drapes didn't cover. It was only from this high vantage point that one could see into the room. And now Stone saw what had fully captured Reuben's attention. The room was a bedroom. And Cornelius Behan was sitting naked on a large four-poster while a tall and lovely brunet did a slow striptease for him. The dress had already hit the polished floor, as had a black slip. She was now undoing her bra. When this fell, she was left with nothing on save four-inch heels and a G-string.

"Come on, Oliver, it's my turn," Reuben called out, his big hand on Stone's shoulder. Stone didn't budge. "Hey, that's not fair, I saw the damn telescope first," Reuben protested.

As Stone continued to watch, the panties slid down the young woman's long legs. She stepped out of them and tossed them to Behan, who promptly put them over a certain part of his anatomy. She laughed, grasped one of the bedposts and proceeded to engage in a professional-looking pole dance. When she took off her shoes and slinked barefoot and naked toward the eagerly awaiting Behan, Stone gave up the telescope to his friend. "I've seen a picture of Mrs. Behan in the newspaper. That is not the woman."

Reuben adjusted the eyepiece. "Damn it, you got it all out of focus," he groused.

"Well, *you* fogged up the glass."

Reuben settled down to watch. "A little, homely man and that beautiful woman: How does that crap happen?"

"Oh, I could give you about a *billion* reasons." Stone added thoughtfully, "So DeHaven was a Peeping Tom."

"Hell, can you blame him?" Reuben exclaimed. "Ow, that looked like it hurt. Oh, it's okay. It looked worse than it was . . . Wow, the gal's limber too. Talk about heels over head."

Stone perked up. "What was that?"

Reuben was too busy giving the play-by-play to answer. "Okay, they're on the floor. Oh, get this, now she's lifted *him* up in the air."

"Reuben, that's Milton calling us. Caleb and Pearl must be coming."

Reuben didn't budge. "What the hell? I've never seen that move outside a monkey house. That chandelier must be *really* anchored to the damn ceiling."

"Reuben! Come on!"

"How is she doing that with *no* freaking hands?"

Stone grabbed his friend and pulled him toward the door. "Now!"

Stone managed to push him down the stairs with Reuben complaining the whole time. They arrived on the main level just as Caleb and Pearl emerged from the elevator.

As Milton shot Stone and Reuben murderous glances, no doubt for cutting it so close, the rare book dealer looked stunned while Caleb appeared triumphant.

"I know it must've been a shock," he said, patting Pearl on the shoulder. "But I *did* tell you it was an original."

"So it is a 1640 edition?" Stone asked.

Pearl nodded dumbly. "And I held it, in these two hands, I held it." He sat down in a chair. "I almost fainted down there. Shaw here had to fetch me some water."

"We all make mistakes," Caleb said in a sympathetic tone that was betrayed by his broad grin.

"This morning I called every institution that owns a *Psalm Book*," Pearl said. "Yale, the Library of Congress, Old South Church in Boston, everyone. They confirmed that all was fine." He wiped his face with a handkerchief.

Caleb took up the story. "We went over all the accepted points of authenticity regarding the book. That's what took us so long."

"I came convinced it was a forgery," Pearl admitted. "But even though we examined the entire book, I knew from the opening pages that it was real. I could tell largely from the uneven presswork. The printer thinned his ink sometimes, or else there were splotches of it across the printing elements. In first editions you will always see signs of dried ink caked in between the letters, which makes it very difficult to read. It was not the norm back then to wash one's typeset letters. The other points one would expect to see, indeed *have* to see in a first edition, are all there. All there," he repeated.

"Of course, the authenticity will have to be confirmed by a team of experts undertaking stylistic, historical and scientific analysis," Caleb noted.

"Precisely," Pearl agreed. "Still, I believe in my heart what their answer will be."

Stone said, "That there's a twelfth existing copy of the *Psalm Book*?"

"Indeed," Pearl confirmed quietly. "And Jonathan DeHaven had it." He shook his head. "I can't believe he never told me. To have one of the world's rarest books, one that some of the greatest collectors of all time never possessed. And to keep it a secret. Why?" He looked at Caleb helplessly. "Why, Shaw?"

"I don't know," Caleb acknowledged.

"What would something like that be worth?" Reuben asked.

"Worth?" Pearl exclaimed. "Worth? It's priceless!"

"Well, if you're going to sell it, somebody has to put a price on it."

Pearl stood and started pacing. "The price will be whatever the highest bid is. And it will run to many, many millions of dollars. There are some collectors and institutions flush with cash right now, and the interest will be extraordinary. There hasn't been a *Psalm Book* on the market for over six decades. This will be the positively last chance for some to get it for their collection." He stopped pacing and looked at Caleb. "And I would be honored to arrange the auction. I could do it in conjunction with Sotheby's or Christie's."

Caleb drew a deep breath. "This is a lot to take in, Mr. Pearl. Let me just think about everything for a day or two, and then I'll phone you."

Pearl looked disappointed but managed a smile. "I will eagerly await your call."

After Pearl had left, Stone said, "Caleb, while you were down in the vault, we searched the house."

"You did what!" Caleb exclaimed. "Oliver, that is outrageous. I'm only allowed in this house as Jonathan's literary executor. I have no right to go through his other possessions, and neither do you."

"Tell him about the telescope," Reuben prompted with a smug look.

Stone did so, and Caleb's anger was replaced with astonishment. He said, "Jonathan watching people having sex. That's repulsive."

"No, it's really not," Reuben replied earnestly. "It's actually very *uplifting* in a way. You wanna go check it out with me?"

"No, Reuben!" Stone said firmly. Then he showed Caleb the photo of the young woman and DeHaven.

"If she was Jonathan's wife, that was before I knew him," Caleb said.

"If he kept the photo, he might have been in touch with her," Milton suggested.

Stone said, "If so, she might be someone we need to find." He glanced at the book Caleb was holding. "What's that?"

"It's a book in Jonathan's collection that needs some work. It got some water damage somehow. I didn't notice it the last time we were here. I'm going to take it into the conservation department at the library. Our people are the best in the world. One of them does some freelance work on the side. I'm sure he can repair it."

Stone nodded and said in a warning tone, "Jonathan DeHaven inexplicably had one of the world's most rare books. He was spying on an adulterous defense contractor and maybe saw more than sex. And no one knows how he really died." He looked at his friends. "I think we have our work cut out for us."

"Why do we have to do anything?" Reuben asked.

Stone looked at him. "Jonathan DeHaven might have been murdered. Someone followed us. Caleb works at the library, and he's been commissioned to be DeHaven's literary executor. If Cornelius Behan was involved in DeHaven's death, he now might suspect that Caleb knows something. That might put Caleb at risk. So the sooner we find out the truth, the better."

"Wonderful," Caleb said sarcastically. "I just hope I manage to live through it."

CHAPTER

23

"YOU WILL RECEIVE AN E-MAIL from my people," Annabelle said. She was standing in the operations center at the Pompeii Casino with several of Bagger's people in attendance. "When you open the e-mail, it will provide you with detailed instructions."

One of the men spoke up. "We don't like opening e-mails if we don't know where they're from."

Annabelle nodded. "Hit it with all your antivirus stuff. I'm assuming you're state-of-the-art."

"We are," the same man said confidently.

"Then do like the lady told you and hit it hard," Bagger said impatiently.

Leo sat in one corner of the room, his gaze resolutely on the other men. His job was to note any degree of suspicion or concern while Annabelle went through her spiel. It didn't hurt matters that she was wearing a very clingy, short skirt, with no hose and a blouse with the top two buttons undone. Every guy in the room followed each glimpse of her upper thighs and cleavage. And if they were doing that, they weren't thinking as clearly as they should have been. Annabelle Conroy, Leo had long ago learned, used every asset in her arsenal.

"The only form of acceptable communication will be through the secure Web portal contained in the e-mail. Under no circumstances will you use your phone or fax, both of which can be monitored. Correction," she added, glancing at Bagger, "both of which *are* monitored."

Bagger raised his eyebrows on that comment but said, "You heard the woman. Nothing but the Net." Bagger was no doubt secure in his cooperation because he had an ace, or in this case, *two* aces in the hole. He would be holding Annabelle and Leo until his money came back.

"The e-mail will tell you where and how to send the funds. Two days later the funds will be automatically wired back to your account, plus the interest."

"And one million becomes one point one million in a couple of days, right?" Bagger said.

Annabelle nodded. "Just like we said, Jerry. Not a bad payday."

"It better be," he said ominously. "When can we start?"

Annabelle checked her watch. "The e-mail should be coming over your system right about now."

Bagger snapped his fingers, and one of his men checked the computer.

"Here it is," the man said. He hit a few buttons. "I'm just running it through some extra security scans to make sure it's clean."

Two minutes went by, and then the IT guy looked up. "Okay, it's good."

"Open it," Bagger ordered.

"You have your own money-wiring capabilities, right?" Annabelle asked, even though her careful background research had already provided the answer.

Bagger said, "Our system is piggybacked right onto the bank's. I don't like third parties controlling my money or necessarily knowing where my money's going. The funds come from the bank right to us, and we send the wire out ourselves. That's the way I like it."

I like it too, Annabelle said to herself.

Ten minutes later $1 million of Jerry Bagger's money was on its way to a very special account.

Leaving the office, Bagger said to Annabelle, "All right, you're my 'guest' for the next forty-eight hours. Give us a chance to get to know each other better." He smiled and let his gaze run up and down her long, lithe figure.

"Sounds good," Annabelle said.

"Yeah, sounds good," Leo added.

Bagger looked at Leo like he'd forgotten he was part of the deal. "Right," he muttered.

Over the next two days they ate breakfast, lunch and dinner with Bagger. At all other times Bagger's men stood outside their hotel rooms at the Pompeii and accompanied them wherever they went. Annabelle also sat up late into the night having drinks with the casino king, but expertly playing off his advances with just enough encouragement to allow the man to remain hopeful. She carefully let out facts of her "history," with just enough held back to guarantee intrigue and continued interest. He talked a lot about himself, with all the bravado and conceit one would have expected from such a man.

"I think you would've made a good spy, Jerry," she said admiringly as they relaxed on his couch over a couple of martinis. "You've got brains and nerve, that's a rare combination."

"Look who's talking." He slid closer to her, gave her thigh a pat. Then he tried to grab a quick kiss, but she turned away.

"Jerry, I could get into real trouble going down that road."

"Who's gonna tell? Look, we're all alone. I know I'm not a

spring chicken, but I work out every day, and I think I'll surprise you between the sheets, baby."

"Just give me some time. It's not like I'm not attracted to you, but I've got a lot going on right now. Okay?" She gave him a peck on the cheek, and he finally backed off.

At the end of the two-day period Bagger was $100,000 richer.

"Want to try for five million, Jerry? That'll get you half a million in interest in forty-eight hours." Annabelle was casually perched on Bagger's desk, her long legs crossed, while Leo sat on the couch.

"Only if you hang around until it comes back," Bagger said.

She winked. "That's part of the deal, Jerry. You get me all to yourself."

"So you keep telling me. Where'd my money go, by the way?"

"Like I told you, El Banco del Caribe."

"No, I mean, what overseas operation did it fund?"

Leo spoke up. "She could tell you, but then I'd have to kill you *both*." There were a few moments of awkward silence until Annabelle laughed. Then Leo and finally Bagger joined in, the latter a little reluctantly.

Two days later the $5-million wire had ballooned by $500,000.

"Damn," Bagger said, "this is better than printing money." He was again in his office with Annabelle and Leo. "I know Uncle Sam has got a ton of dough, but how can even the government afford this?"

Annabelle shrugged. "We can't. That's why we have trillion-dollar deficits. If we need more money, we just sell more T-bills to the Saudis and the Chinese. It won't work forever, but it does for now." She glanced at Bagger and put a hand on his arm. "But if you're feeling sorry for Uncle Sam, Jerry, you can let us use your money for free."

He laughed. "My motto hasn't changed in forty years: Every asshole for himself."

And a motto never fit anyone better than that one does you, Annabelle thought even as she smiled in mock admiration at the man.

Bagger leaned forward in his chair, glancing at Leo as he did so. In a low voice he said to her, "You ever lose the shadow?"

Annabelle said, "Depends."

"On what?"

"On how good of friends you and I become."

"I know how we can be really good friends."

"Tell me."

"We do a run for ten million, and I get an even mil for my troubles. Can Uncle Sam cover that action?"

"Just wire the money, Jerry."

"And you stay right here until I get it back?"

"We both do," Leo said.

Bagger grimaced and spoke in an even lower voice to her so Leo couldn't hear. "I suppose I'd get in deep shit for whacking him, wouldn't I?"

"You remember the scum of the scum I talked to you about? You harm him, they show up on your doorstep. I really wouldn't advise it."

"Well, damn," Bagger complained.

"It's not a total loss, Jerry. In two days you make a million bucks for doing nothing except eating and drinking with me."

"I wanna do more than that, you know that, don't you?"

"Jerry, I knew that the first time you tried to put your hand up my dress."

Bagger roared with laughter. "I like your style, lady. You're too good for the government. You should come and work for me. We'd take this town to a new level."

"I'm always open to future prospects. But for now why don't we work on the next million for you? I want you to be able to afford to keep me in the manner to which I've grown accustomed." She patted his hand, letting a fingernail dig lightly into his palm. She felt the shudder run through the man's entire body.

"You're killing me here, baby," he said in a pathetic whine.

Oh, no, that comes next.

CHAPTER

24

TWO DAYS LATER BAGGER WAS ahead by a total of $1.6 million since he'd run into Annabelle and Leo, never realizing, of course, that the money had come from the $3 million they'd accumulated from the two short cons. Tony had authorized transfer of these "interest" payments from their account into the one holding Bagger's money. It was similar in concept to a Ponzi scheme, which almost always self-destructed. Annabelle did not intend to allow that result to happen this time.

Bagger's happiness was palpable, particularly since he believed his dreaded antagonist, the government, was footing the bill. Sitting in her luxurious hotel room, upgraded to the presidential suite by Bagger himself after the latest payday, and awash in flowers sent by the casino king, Annabelle was scanning newspaper after newspaper for the kind of story she wanted, and finally found it. She and Leo could not speak frankly to each other anywhere in the casino. They had to assume that anything they said would be overheard either electronically or by one of Bagger's spies. Their only form of real communication was subtle hand and eye signals that the two had developed over the years and would not be recognizable to anyone else.

Passing each other in the hallway, Annabelle said good morning and then gave Leo a signal by adjusting a ring on her right index finger. He said hello back and then touched his tie knot and wiped his nose, thereby acknowledging both the receipt of her message and the action he would take.

Before she stepped onto the elevator that would take her to Bagger's office, Annabelle drew a deep breath. Contrary to what Leo had said, she did have nerves. This last step she was about to take was the whole ball game. If she didn't pull this off perfectly, everything they'd done over the last several weeks would be for naught. She'd not only lose the money she'd paid Bagger, she wouldn't live to enjoy her split of the remaining $1.4 million.

She arrived at his office and was quickly ushered in, the muscle having grown accustomed to seeing her around. Bagger greeted her with a hug that she allowed to drift down lower than it should have. His hand reached her bottom, gently squeezing before she removed it. Still, she'd let him go a little farther each time, which she knew was all he really required right now. Smiling, he stepped back and said, "What can I do for my magic money genie this morning?"

She frowned. "Bad news. I've been recalled to my field HQ, Jerry."

"What? What the hell does that mean?"

"It means I'm being reassigned."

"To where?" He looked at her face and said, "I know, you can't tell me."

She held up the section of the newspaper she'd brought with her. "This might give you a hint."

He took the paper and glanced at the article she was pointing to. It detailed the breaking story of a government corruption scandal involving a foreign contractor in Russia.

Bagger looked up at her, stunned. "You go from casinos to dirty contractors in Moscow?"

She took the paper back. "Not just any foreign contractor."

"You know them?"

"All I can say is it's in the best interests of the United States that this case never gets to court. That's where I come in."

"How long will you be gone?"

"Hard to say. And after Russia it'll be someplace else." She rubbed at her temple. "You got some Advil?"

He opened a drawer of his desk and handed her a bottle. She swallowed three with a glass of water he poured for her.

He sat down. "You don't look very good."

She perched on the edge of his desk and said wearily, "Jerry, I've been to so many places in the last year I've lost count. If I used a real passport, I'd have gone through about twenty of them. It just gets to you sometimes. Don't worry, I'll be fine."

"Why don't you get out, then?" he urged.

She laughed bitterly. "Get out? And what, screw my pension? I've put in too many years. Even civil servants have to eat."

"Come and work for me, then. I'll pay you more in one year than you'd make in twenty with those clowns."

"Yeah, right."

"I'm serious. I like you. You're good."

"You like the fact that I just made you over a million and a half bucks."

"Okay, I won't deny that. But I've got to know you. And I like what I see, Pam."

"My name's not even Pam. That's how well you really know me."

"That just adds to the fun. Think about it, willya?"

She hesitated and then said, "I *have* been thinking about my future lately. I'm not married; my life is my work and vice versa. And I'm not exactly a spring chicken anymore."

He stood and put an arm around her shoulders. "Are you kidding me? You're gorgeous. Any man would be lucky as hell to have you."

She patted his arm. "You haven't seen me in the morning before I've had my coffee and put on my face."

"Oh, baby, just say the word and we'll find out." His hand fell to her lower back and stayed, gently rubbing. He reached over and hit a button on his desk console, and the automatic window blinds lowered.

"What's that for?" she asked, her eyebrows hiked.

"I like my privacy." His hand moved lower.

Her phone buzzed, right on cue. She looked down at the number. "Oh, hell." She rose and moved away from him, staring at the screen.

"Who is it?" Bagger asked.

"My section chief. His number comes up all zeros." She composed herself and answered the phone. "Yes, sir?"

She said nothing else for several minutes and then clicked off. "Son of a bitch, that asshole!" she yelled.

"What is it, baby?"

She paced in a tight circle and then stopped, obviously still seething. "My esteemed section chief has seen fit to change my field orders. Instead of a trip to Russia, I'm being reassigned to—get this—Portland, Oregon."

"Oregon. They need spies in Oregon?"

"It's the graveyard, Jerry. It's where you get sent in my agency if people upstairs don't like you."

"How do you go from Russia to Oregon on the same morning?"

"The Russian gig came from my field supervisor. Oregon from my section chief, that's the next level up. His assignment takes priority."

"What's your section chief got against you?"

"I don't know. Maybe I'm doing my job too well." She started to say something else and then stopped.

Bagger quickly picked up on this. "Spill it. Come on, maybe I can help."

She sighed. "Well, believe it or not, the man wants to sleep with me. Only he's married, and I told him to back off."

Bagger nodded his head. "The bastard! It's always the same crap. The ladies don't put out, they get pushed out."

Annabelle was staring down at her hands. "This screws my career, Jerry. Portland! Damn it!" She hurled her phone against the wall, where it broke in half. Then she slumped in a chair. "Maybe I just should've slept with the guy."

Bagger started rubbing her shoulders. "No way. Guys like that, you do it once they keep expecting it. Then they get tired of you, or get a new honey. Then zip, it's Portland for your sweet ass anyway."

"I just want to nail that little son of a bitch so bad."

Bagger looked thoughtful. "Well, maybe that can be arranged."

She looked up at him warily. "Jerry, you can't put a hit on the guy, okay?"

"I'm not thinking about that, baby. You said he might be pissed because you're doing your job *too* well. How's that?"

"I bring in too much money, then all of a sudden people start looking at me to move up. I start moving up, then all of a sudden I'm a threat to his job. Believe it or not, Jerry, there aren't a lot of women doing what I do. There are some who would love to see another female in a section chief slot. If I keep bringing in people like you and flood our overseas operations with 'finessed' cash, it hurts him and helps me."

"Hell, only in the government sector do you get dinged for *overproducing*." He thought for a moment. "Okay, I see how we can turn the tables on this bozo."

"What are you talking about?"

"Our next run at El Banco."

"Jerry, I'm being reassigned. My associate and I are on a plane tonight."

"Okay, okay. But here's the deal. Until you leave you can do one last run, right?"

Annabelle seemed to consider this. "Well, yeah, I mean, I have the authorizations. But even a million bucks in *interest* isn't going to get me this guy's corner office."

"I'm not talking a measly million." He looked at her. "What's the largest single amount you've 'finessed'?"

She thought for a moment. "Most of the wires are one to five million. But I did fifteen million in Vegas. And twenty mil from New York, but that was two years ago."

"Chickenshit."

"Chickenshit? Right!"

"Tell me, what would really hurt this guy?"

"Jerry, I don't know. Thirty million."

"Let's make it forty million. And let's make it four days instead of two." He figured quickly in his head. "So that's twenty percent interest instead of ten. And that comes to eight million to yours truly. A nice piece of finessing."

"You've got forty million in cash?"

"Hey, who do you think you're talking to? And we had two championship fights here in the last week. I'm flush with green."

"But why are you doing this?"

"Eight mil in four days is nothing to sneeze at, even for a guy like me." He gave her neck a rub. "Plus, like I said, you're growing on me, lady."

"But I'm still going to Oregon. I can't disobey orders."

"Okay, you go to Oregon. But then you think about getting out and coming back here. I'll even give you ten percent of the eight and set you up nice."

"I'm not looking to be your kept woman, Jerry. I've got a brain."

"That you do, and I'll put it to good use. Along with the rest of you." He ran his hand down her back. "I'll call down to the boys."

"But like I said, I leave for Oregon tonight by private plane."

"I understand that."

"What I'm saying, Jerry, is there's no way you'll have your money back before I leave."

He laughed. "Oh, the hostage thing? I think we're past that, sweetie. You've made me one point six million and counting, so I think you've proved yourself."

"Only if you're sure. Forty mil is a lot of money."

"Hey, the gig was my idea, not yours. I'll handle it."

She stood. "I've run a lot of these ops, Jerry, and to me it's just a job." She paused. "Everybody else they just wanted to know how much, how much. Greedy bastards all of them." She paused again, seeming to search for the words, though she'd practiced them for a long time. "You're the first one to ever do something for me. And I appreciate it. More than you'll ever know." This was probably the first true statement she'd uttered in Bagger's presence.

They looked at each other, and then Annabelle slowly put her arms out and braced herself. He immediately crushed his body against hers. She almost gagged on his heavy cologne. His strong hands quickly found their way under her skirt, and she let them stay there, enduring his brutish groping in silence. She so wanted to slam a knee into his crotch. *Hold on, Annabelle, you can do this. You have to do this.*

"Oh, baby," Bagger moaned into her ear. "Come on, let's do it. One time before you hit the road. Right here on the couch. I'm dying here. Dying."

"Trust me, I can *feel* it against my leg, Jerry," she said as she managed finally to pry herself away from him. Annabelle adjusted her underwear and pulled her skirt back down. "Okay, stud, I can see I'm not going to be able to resist you much longer. Tell me, you ever been to Rome?"

He looked puzzled. "No. Why?"

"I rent a villa there every year when I go on my rare vacation time. I'll call you with all the details. And two weeks from today I'll meet you there."

"Why two weeks, why not now?"

"That'll give me time to report in to my new assignment, and maybe use the forty-mil run to leverage something better than Portland."

"But my offer to come back stands. And I can be pretty damn persuasive."

She ran a finger slowly over his mouth. "Show me how persuasive you are in Rome, *baby.*"

The $40-million wire left the Pompeii Casino two hours later. The e-mail that Tony had first sent to the Pompeii's operations center had a special component to it: ultrasophisticated spyware that had allowed Tony, from a remote location, to take control of the Pompeii's computer system. With that secret access he had written new code into their money-wiring program.

The three other wires had gone to El Banco, but when they'd sent the $40 million out, it had instead been automatically rerouted to another foreign bank and into an account controlled by Annabelle Conroy. While it would look to Bagger's people that the money had reached El Banco—a phony electronic receipt would be automatically sent to the Pompeii—not a dime of it would ever come back to him. Annabelle's scheme had been mainly for one purpose: to get the spyware on Bagger's computer system. With that done, she was golden. And then she had played her part and let Bagger's greed and lust bury the man, because the best way to con a mark was to let the mark suggest the con.

Four days from today to the minute, Bagger would grow a little nervous when his money didn't show up. An hour later he would be getting a sick feeling in his gut. An hour after that he would become homicidal. And Annabelle and her crew would be long gone with over 41 million tax-free dollars to keep them company.

Annabelle Conroy could buy her boat and sail the rest of her life away, leaving the endless cons behind. Yet it was still not enough punishment, she thought as she left Bagger's office to pack her suitcase. First, though, she was going to take a shower to get the man's grime off her.

As Annabelle was bathing, she thought again that the money loss was clearly not enough pain for the man who'd murdered her mother over ten thousand bucks that Paddy Conroy had duped Bagger out of. There was never enough pain for that. Yet even Annabelle had to admit, $40 million was a nice start.

CHAPTER

25

ROGER SEAGRAVES HAD DISCOV-
ered where Stone lived and had sent men to the cottage when it
was empty. They'd searched the cottage thoroughly, leaving no
sign that they had been there. And most important, they had left
with Stone's fingerprints, taken from a glass and a second off the
kitchen countertop.

Seagraves had run the fingerprints through the CIA's general
database, finding nothing. Using a password he'd stolen from a
fellow employee, he tried a highly restricted database. Access
was granted, and he placed the print in the hopper. A minute
later this led him to Subdirectory 666, one that he was certainly
well acquainted with, although his search request for Stone's
prints came back with "access denied." Seagraves was familiar
with Subdirectory 666 because it was where his own personnel
history was kept, or at least the sort of "personnel" he used to
be. He had often laughed at the "666" label, thinking it rather
cheeky, though accurate nonetheless.

Seagraves exited the computer system and pondered this development. Stone had worked for the CIA, judging from his age,
a long time ago. He had probably been an "eliminator" because
the Triple Six classification was never given to those who pushed

a pencil or pressed computer keys for the Agency. At present, Seagraves didn't quite know how to take this discovery. He'd since learned that Stone's librarian friend had been given the task of selling DeHaven's book collection. Unfortunately, his men's pursuit of Stone had raised the man's suspicions. And a Triple Six man was born with inherent paranoia; that was just one of the many qualifications for the job.

Should I kill him now? Or would that dig the hole even deeper? Seagraves eventually decided to forgo that lethal step. He would always have that option later. *Hell, I'll do it myself. One Triple Six to another. Young versus old, and young always won that battle. You get to live, Oliver Stone. For now.*

But he would have to do *something* about the man. And there was no time like the present.

Two days after their last visit to DeHaven's house Stone and Reuben rode on the latter's motorcycle to a rare book shop in Old Town Alexandria. The name of the shop was in Latin, and translated meant "Book of Four Sentences." Caleb had an ownership share in the place, which had once been named Doug's Books, until Caleb's brilliant idea to go completely upscale in the very affluent area. Stone was not here because he wanted to look at more old books. He kept some items at the shop that he needed to consult.

The owner of the shop, the aforementioned Doug, who now went by the more formal "Douglas," allowed Stone unfettered access to his hiding place. This was so because Douglas was terrified of Oliver Stone, a man who'd been described to him by Caleb (at Stone's prompting) as a homicidal maniac walking free solely on a legal technicality.

Stone's secret room was in the basement behind a false wall that was opened by pulling a wire hanging in an adjacent fireplace. A former priest's hole in the ancient building, it now contained many items from Stone's past life, plus a collection of his journals filled with cuttings from newspapers and magazines.

With Reuben's help he found and pulled several of these journals and took them with him. Reuben dropped him off at his cottage in the cemetery.

"Keep a close lookout, Oliver," Reuben warned. "If that little dipshit Behan is involved in this, he's got plenty of muscle and connections behind him."

Stone assured him that he would be careful, said good-bye and stepped inside the cottage. He brewed some strong coffee, settled at his desk and started going over the journals. The stories he'd selected dealt with the assassination of the Speaker of the House, Robert "Bob" Bradley. And also the nearly simultaneous destruction of his home, an event that only the most naive could've thought was a coincidence. Yet there seemed to be no connection between Bradley's obvious murder allegedly at the hands of a domestic terrorist group calling itself Americans Against 1984 and Jonathan DeHaven's seemingly innocent death. The FBI had received a note from the group which said that Bradley had been killed as a first step in the war against the federal government. The terrorists promised more attacks, and security in Washington had been heightened in response.

As he turned the pages of his journal, something nagged at Stone, but he couldn't quite pin it down. Bradley had been Speaker for a short period, after a political shake-up that had seen the incumbent Speaker and the majority leader both convicted of selling influence and laundering political campaign funds. Normally, the Speaker position would have followed party leadership lines, but with the top two men in jail, extraordinary measures were called for. And Bob Bradley, a powerful committee chairman with an impeccable reputation far removed

from the tainted leadership ladder of his party, had been the political Moses buttonholed to lead his people out of this nasty
thicket of impropriety.

He'd started by promising an ethical cleanup in the House of
Representatives and an end to partisan politics. Many had promised that, and few if any had delivered on that pledge, yet it was
thought that if anyone could do it, Bob Bradley could.

Stone turned to another journal and another story. This one
dealt with Cornelius Behan, recounting how he had come to this
country with no money in his pocket and built an international
conglomerate from nothing but his own sweat and nerve. Defense
contractors had the reputation, often well deserved, of playing
fast and loose with ethical rules. Paying off congressmen for political favors was one of the oldest games played in Washington,
and the tank and plane builders played it as well as anyone.

Stone finished reading the story on Behan, which detailed two
enormous and recent wins for his business. One was from the
Pentagon for a new generation conventional missile system and
the other to build a massive new bunker for the Congress outside of Washington for use in case of a cataclysmic attack. While
some cynics might argue that the best thing that could happen to
the country in case of such a catastrophe would be the elimina-
tion of that august body, Stone supposed the country needed
some continuity of government.

Each of these contracts was worth billions, and Behan had
won them both. As the article explained, he had outflanked his
opponents at every critical juncture. "It was as though he could
read their minds," the reporter had written. Stone didn't believe
in mind readers, but having been a spy as a young man, he did
believe in stealing secrets.

Stone leaned back in his chair and sipped his coffee. If Bradley's predecessor had been in Behan's pocket and Bradley had promised a crackdown on corruption, it might be worth it to take the new crusader out. There was no guarantee that Bradley's successor would be any more cooperative to folks like Behan, but there was also the factor of intimidation. Would a new Speaker be inclined to go full bore ahead with Bradley's pledge to bring ethics back when that same promise might have led to his colleague's violent death? The terrorist group could simply be a smoke screen, and an unverifiable one at that.

Stone had initially started thinking about Bradley's death because there was only one connection he could see between the man's murder and DeHaven's. And that connection was Cornelius Behan, a man who'd made billions by selling myriad things that killed lots of people, all in the name of peace.

Was it Behan's men in the D.C. Public Works van? Could they have somehow caused the Secret Service to retreat like that? Or was it another agency, working closely with Behan, that had taken on the role of running interference for him? People had debated for decades the existence of the military-industrial complex. Stone had never wondered about it. He had participated in that complex for years. If it was anything like it was thirty years ago, it was a potent force to be reckoned with. It was also a force that would not hesitate to eliminate people who got in the way. Stone also knew this from personal experience. After all, he used to be one of the "eliminators."

He would have Milton find out as much as possible about Bradley and Behan. Milton could get into databases that he had no business being on; yet those were always the most interesting ones. Stone would go to Bradley's demolished home to see if anything turned up there. And he needed to return to Jonathan DeHaven's house because he had to look through that telescope again, and not because he was anxious to be titillated by another episode of Behan's sex show. No, there was something very obvious that he had completely overlooked.

A sudden chill hit him, and he rose to start a fire. Then he stopped and rubbed his skin. He was cold, very cold. What the hell had the woman said? He struggled to recall her exact words. "Your temperature is coming back up." Yes, that's what the nurse taking care of Caleb had said. It had struck him as odd, because in a hospital one would normally hear that you were recovering if your temperature were coming *down*. But she had said he was almost *up* to normal, he was certain of it.

Stone grew very excited. Something was finally starting to make sense. He grabbed his cell phone to call the others but then stopped as he gazed out the window. From here he had a direct line of sight onto the street that bordered the cemetery. A white D.C. Public Works van was parked there. He could see it clearly under the streetlight.

Stone immediately drew away from the window. He called Reuben but it didn't go through. He looked at his cell phone. He had no power bars. Yet there was always a strong signal in this area. He glanced out the window. *Jammers.* He tried his hardline phone. It was dead.

He grabbed his coat and hurried to the back door. He would clamber over the rear fence and make his way through a labyrinth of Georgetown streets to an abandoned dwelling he occasionally used as a safe house. He cautiously opened the door and stepped outside. The fence was in sight.

The shot to his chest stopped him cold and dropped Stone to his knees. Already lapsing into unconsciousness, Stone looked over at the man standing there, wearing a black hood and holding the gun with both hands. It seemed to Stone that the man smiled even as his victim fell to the hard ground and lay still.

CHAPTER

26

IT WAS THE DARKNESS OF INTER-
rogation. Stone recognized this as soon as he awoke. It was so
black that not only could Stone not see any part of his body, but
it seemed as though he *had* no body. He was barefoot, painfully
thrust up on his tiptoes, and his hands were bound over his head.
The place he was in was very cold. These places were always cold
because cold wore you down faster than heat. He could sense
that not only was he shoeless, he was also naked.

The voice called out from the blackness. "Awake?"

Stone nodded.

"Say it," the voice commanded.

"Awake," Stone answered. He would only give them the minimum, nothing more. He had been through this before, albeit
three decades ago when a mission had gone awry and he had
found himself a prisoner in a land where no American would
ever want to be held captive.

"Name?"

This was exactly what he'd been dreading.

"Oliver Stone."

Something hard hit him on the back of the head, momentarily
stunning him.

"Name?"

"Oliver Stone," he said slowly, wondering if the blow had cracked his skull.

"Okay for now, *Oliver.* DeHaven?" the voice said.

"Who?"

Now Stone could feel something grasping his leg. He tried to kick out, but then realized his legs were pinned. The thing was crawling snakelike up his right leg. He took a deep breath and tried to fight the panic. It couldn't be a snake; they were just simulating it, he reasoned. Then whatever it was started to nudge Stone's flesh, not bite, but the pressure was growing heavier. *God, it felt like a damn snake. Maybe a boa?* In the total darkness even Stone's hardened nerves began to unravel.

"DeHaven?" the voice said again.

"What do you want to know?"

The pressure eased a bit, but it was still there as not-so-subtle intimidation.

"How did he die?"

"I don't know."

The pressure instantly intensified. It was now wrapping itself around Stone's belly. He was finding it hard to take a full breath. His arms and legs were aching, and his Achilles felt ready to pop from being forced to stand on tiptoe so long.

"I think he was murdered," Stone gasped.

The pressure released a few notches. He grabbed a quick breath, his lungs expanding painfully.

"How?"

Stone desperately tried to think of what to say. He had no idea who these people were and didn't want to give too much away. When he didn't say anything, the pressure fell away completely. Bewildered, he relaxed. He should have known better.

He fell to the floor as his bindings were released. He felt strong, gloved hands seize him. When he instinctively swung his arm out, it struck something hard; it was glass and metal, up near where his captor's face would be. *They have night-vision equipment.*

Stone was hoisted and carried somewhere. An instant later he was slammed down on a hard object, like a long board, and secured there. Then he was being tipped back and his face covered with cellophane. The water hit him hard, pushing the cellophane into his eyes, mouth and nose. He gagged. They were "waterboarding" him, a very effective torture technique. There were few things more terrifying than believing that you're drowning; especially upside down in total darkness while bound tightly to a board.

Suddenly, the gusher stopped and the cellophane was ripped off. As soon as he let out his breath, his head was plunged completely into cold water. He gagged again and strained to break free. Stone's heart was beating so fast he knew he would probably die of a heart attack before he did from drowning.

Then his head was pulled out from the water. He vomited, his retch covering his face.

"How?" the voice said calmly.

Yeah, the guy asking questions was always calm, Stone thought as he tried to shake the vomit out of his eyes. *He was probably sitting in a nice warm room with a cup of coffee while I'm getting the shit kicked out of me.*

"Suffocated," he spat out. "Just like you're doing to me, you *prick!*"

That got him another quick dunk. He'd done it on purpose, though, so the water would wash the puke off him. Stone had taken a quick breath before they plunged him in, and he came out in relatively decent shape.

"How?" the voice said.

"Not the halon 1301, something else."

"What?"

"I don't know yet."

Stone felt himself being tipped back for another plunge. He frantically shouted, "But I can find out."

The voice didn't immediately answer. Stone took that as a good sign. Interrogators hated to be at a loss for words.

The voice said, "We looked at your journals. You were reading up on Bradley. Why?"

"Seemed too coincidental. His death and then DeHaven's."

"They have nothing in common."

"You think so?"

Stone snatched a long breath, but they held him under so long this time he still almost drowned. He came out with his brain exploding from lack of oxygen, every limb quivering; his whole body was starting to shut down on him.

"What do you think they have in common?" the voice demanded.

"You're one dunk from killing me, so if that's your plan anyway, why don't you just get it over with?" he said feebly. He braced for the tip but it didn't come.

"What do you think they have in common?" the voice said again.

Stone took a shallow breath, which was all he could manage right now, and decided whether to answer or not. If it wasn't what they wanted to hear, he was dead. But he was nearly dead as it was.

He mustered his energy and said, "Cornelius Behan."

He braced for the last dunk. Instead, the voice said, "Why Behan?"

"Bradley was anticorruption. Behan won two major contracts under the old regime. Maybe Bradley found out something Behan didn't want known. So he killed him, burned his house down and blamed it on a fictitious terrorist group."

There was a long silence. All Stone could hear were the anguished smacks of his tortured heart. The sounds were terrifying, but at least he was still alive.

"DeHaven?"

"He's Behan's neighbor."

"Is that it?" the voice said, clearly disappointed.

Stone felt himself being tipped back. "No, that's not all! There was a telescope we found in DeHaven's attic pointed at Behan's house. DeHaven might have seen something he shouldn't have. So he has to be killed too, but not like Bradley."

"Why not?"

"People gunning for the Speaker wouldn't be that surprising. But DeHaven's a librarian and Behan's his neighbor. It had to be made to look like an accident away from DeHaven's and Behan's homes. Otherwise, fingers might start pointing at Behan."

Stone waited in silence, wondering if the answer had been the right one or not.

He lurched up as he felt the painful jab in his arm. A second later his eyes closed, and Oliver Stone let out a long breath and lay still.

From the corner of the room Roger Seagraves watched them carry Stone out. He was pretty tough for an old guy. Seagraves imagined that thirty years ago Stone might have been as good as he was. Now he at least knew that Stone suspected Cornelius Behan to be the man behind it all. And because of that, Oliver Stone would get to live another day.

CHAPTER

27

ANNABELLE'S HOTEL ROOM overlooked Central Park, and on impulse she decided to take a walk in it. Her hairstyle and color had changed once again. She was now a brunet with short hair, parted on the side, a look that matched the passport photo Freddy had made for her. Her clothes were typical New York, meaning black and stylish. She rambled through the park trails hiding behind a hat and sunglasses. Several people she passed stared at her, perhaps thinking she was someone famous. Ironically, Annabelle had never sought fame. Her whole life she had clung to the comforting shadows of obscurity where a talented con could find professional traction.

She bought a soft pretzel from a street vendor and carried it back to her room, where she sat on the bed and looked through her travel papers. Leo and she had parted company at the airport in Newark. Freddy was on his way out of the country already. She hadn't asked either man where they were going. She didn't want to know.

After arriving in New York she'd contacted Tony. As promised, Annabelle had made arrangements for him to fly to Paris.

After that, he was on his own, but with excellent if fake identification and travel documents and millions sitting in a readily accessible account. She'd given him one final warning: "Even though he never saw you, Bagger will know I needed some con really expert with computers, and you have that reputation. So lay low for a year or so out of the country. And do *not* flash the money around. Get a small place, dig in, learn the language, and lose yourself."

Tony promised her that he would do as she advised.

"I'll call and tell you where I end up."

"No, you won't," she'd told him.

She still had three days before Bagger's money was due back and he discovered he'd been conned. She would have given half the money back to be able to see his reaction. He would probably kill all of his IT and money guys first. Then he'd stalk through his casino with a pistol, popping off senior citizens playing the slots. Maybe a New Jersey SWAT team would swoop in and do the world a favor by putting the bastard out of his misery. Probably unrealistic, but she could always fantasize.

Her escape route would take her through eastern Europe and then Asia. That would last about a year. After that, it was on to the South Pacific, to a little island she'd discovered years ago and never been back to for fear of it not being as perfect the second time. Right now she'd be happy with almost perfect.

Her share of the take was currently parked in a series of offshore accounts. She'd live off the interest and investments the rest of her life, maybe occasionally dipping into the principal. She might even buy a boat, albeit a small one, and sail it herself. Not around the world; short excursions around a tropical cove would be just fine with her.

She had debated whether to send Bagger a note of triumph,

but in the end decided such bravado was both unworthy of her and the con she'd pulled. Let him spend the rest of his life guessing. Paddy Conroy's little girl wouldn't be high on his list of usual suspects because she was certain Bagger didn't even know Paddy had a daughter. Annabelle's relationship with her father had been truly unique, and he had never held her out to the con world as his child. Leo and a few others they'd worked with had eventually discovered the truth, but that was all.

Yet this time her picture *had* been captured on numerous Pompeii casino cameras. And she knew Bagger would take those photos and run around the con world paying people or even torturing them to get an ID on her. Every con she knew would cheer what she'd done to Bagger. Yet there might be someone who looked at the photo and let her name slip if Bagger threatened enough. *Well,* she thought, *let him come. He might find it a little harder to kill me than he thinks.* It wasn't the size of the dog in the fight, it was the size of the fight in the dog. Ironically, it wasn't her father that had told her that; it was her mother.

Tammy Conroy, despite her criminal ways, had been a good woman, and a long-suffering wife to Paddy. She'd been a cocktail waitress before tying her life to the charming Irishman, who had an endless supply of funny yarns and could sing any tune in a voice you'd want to keep listening to. Paddy Conroy dominated any room he was in. Perhaps that was why his potential as a con had never been fully realized. The best cons, you never even knew they were there. Paddy apparently didn't care, believing that his Irish luck, pluck and smile would save him every time. And it had, mostly. But it hadn't saved Tammy Conroy.

Jerry Bagger had personally put a bullet into her brain when she wouldn't rat out her husband. Paddy certainly hadn't returned his wife's loyalty. He'd fled when Bagger started to close in. Annabelle couldn't even attend her mother's funeral because

Bagger and his men were at the cemetery waiting for someone to show up. That was years ago, and Bagger was probably still looking for her father. Over ten lousy grand, when the man spent more on his suits than that. Yet Annabelle knew it ultimately wasn't about the money. It was about respect. And the only way you kept respect in Bagger's world was by doling out five licks for every one you took. And whether somebody stole ten grand or 10 million of his money, Bagger would hurt that person if he could get his hands on him. That's why when Annabelle ratted out the cons at the Pompeii, she had also called the police. With cops on the premises Bagger couldn't break any knees. If the cons were smart, they'd clear out fast after they'd done their time or paid their fines.

Bagger might have been a walking caricature of a casino chieftain in a bad mob film, but one thing that wasn't phony or funny about the guy was the easy manner in which he employed violence. If you conned other casinos, you went to jail. That was not how Bagger operated. He was a throwback to the days in Vegas when the way to deal with a pesky con was to first break the knees and then the head. His utter failure to bring his methods into modern times had led to his banishment from Sin City. While he hadn't completely cleaned up his act in Atlantic City, he had gotten far more discreet about it.

With all that, in Tammy Conroy's case, a ten-grand con wouldn't have ordinarily led to death. But it wasn't a simple case, because her father and Bagger had a long running war. Personally, Paddy kept out of Bagger's casinos, but he sent waves of teams in to do the con work for him, including, finally, his then teenage daughter and a much younger Leo. That almost led them to being fish food in the ocean the last time they visited Atlantic City. Yet over the years Bagger finally made the connection with Paddy and his casino's troubles. He eventually showed

up on Paddy's doorstep one night far away from Jersey. But
Paddy wasn't there. Some said he had a warning and cleared out.
If so, he forgot to let his wife in on it.

There was no evidence linking Bagger to the murder, of course,
and he'd had a million alibis, so no charges were ever filed in the
case. However, some veteran cons with inside knowledge that
Annabelle had talked to were absolutely certain as to what had
happened. Yet even if they'd seen the deed themselves, they
would never have testified against Bagger.

Having him so close to her over the last week, Annabelle
found herself thinking about putting a gun against his forehead
and firing. That would have evened one old score, but the forfeit
of her life would've been the price. No, this way was much better. Her father had never liked the long cons, arguing that it took
too much time and had too many potential pitfalls. Yet Tammy
Conroy would have truly appreciated the artistry and the execu-
tion of this one. And if somehow her mother had made it to
heaven, she hoped the woman would take a peek from up high
when Jerry Bagger discovered he'd been duped into a wild,
crafty ride with an admission price of 40 million bucks.

She picked up the TV remote and channel-surfed as she ate
her pretzel. The news was the same as always, all bad. More sol-
diers killed, more people starving to death, more people blowing
themselves and others up in the name of God. Done with TV,
she picked up the newspaper. Old habits died hard, and more
than once she found herself looking at stories and wondering
how to spin the details into a successful, creative con. That was
over now, she told herself. Nailing Bagger was the pinnacle of
her career; there was nowhere to go except down.

The last article she read caused her to sit up so fast she spilled
her pretzel and mustard on the bed. She stared wide-eyed at the
small, grainy photo that accompanied the back-page story. It

was a short tribute to a distinguished scholar and man of letters. There was no cause given for the death of Jonathan DeHaven, only that he had died suddenly while at work at the Library of Congress. Though he'd died some time ago, funeral arrangements were just now complete and burial was set for the next day in D.C. Annabelle had no way of knowing that the delay had been caused by the medical examiner's inability to find a cause of death. However, with no suspicious circumstances uncovered, the case had been set down to natural causes and the body released to the funeral home.

Annabelle grabbed her bag and started stuffing clothes in it. Her travel plans had just been changed. She was flying to Washington. To say good-bye to her ex-husband, Jonathan DeHaven, the only man who'd ever truly captured her heart.

CHAPTER

28

"OLIVER! OLIVER."

Stone slowly came to and sat up with difficulty. He was lying fully dressed on the floor of his cottage, his hair still damp.

"Oliver!" Someone was banging on his front door.

Stone rose, stumbled toward the door and opened it.

Reuben stared back at him with an amused expression. "What the hell's going on? You getting into the tequila again?" However, when he noted Stone's obvious distress, he quickly turned serious. "Oliver, are you okay?"

"I'm not dead. I take that as a positive."

He motioned for Reuben to come in, and Stone spent the next ten minutes filling him in on what had happened.

"Damn! You have no idea who they are?"

"Whoever it is, they're well up on their torture techniques," Stone said dryly, rubbing at the knot on his head. "I don't think I can even *drink* water again."

"So they know about the Behan connection?"

Stone nodded. "I'm not sure it was a total surprise to them, actually. But I think what I told them about Bradley and De-Haven was definitely new intelligence."

"Speaking of DeHaven, his funeral is today. That's what we were calling you about. Caleb is going, along with most of the Library of Congress. Milton's coming too, and I switched my shift at the dock so I could go. We thought it might be important."

Stone rose but immediately wobbled.

Reuben grabbed his arm. "Oliver, maybe you should just sit tight."

"One more torture session like that, you'll be attending *my* funeral. But the service today may be important. If only for those it happens to bring out into the open."

The service at St. John's Church next to Lafayette Park was very well attended by many library and government types. Also in attendance was Cornelius Behan with his wife, a tall, slender and very attractive woman in her early fifties with expertly colored blond hair. Her haughty air was intriguingly coupled with a wary, fragile bearing. Cornelius Behan was well known in Washington, and people continually went over to him, pressing the flesh and paying homage. He accepted it all with good graces, but Stone noted that he kept one hand on his wife's arm at all times, as though she might fall without such support.

At Stone's insistence the Camel Club members had scattered in the church so they could survey different sections of people. Though it was clear that whoever had kidnapped him knew of his involvement with the others, Stone didn't want to give those people, in case they were here, a reminder that he had three friends who would make nice targets.

Stone sat in the very back, and his gaze swept the area with a practiced motion, until it stopped on one woman who sat off to the side. As she turned and flicked her hair out of her face, Stone's gaze intensified. His previous training had made him highly skilled at remembering people's features, and he had seen that profile before, although the woman he was looking at now was older.

After the service was over, the Camel Club members left the church together, stepping in behind Behan and his wife. Behan whispered something to his wife before turning and speaking to Caleb.

"Sad day," he said.

"Yes, it is," Caleb said stiffly. He looked at Mrs. Behan.

"Oh," Behan said. "My wife, Marilyn. This is, uh . . ."

"Caleb Shaw. I worked at the library with Jonathan."

He introduced the other Camel Club members to her.

Behan glanced at the church where the pallbearers were bringing the casket out. "Who'd have thought? He looked so healthy."

"Many people do, right before they die," Stone said absently. His gaze was on the woman he had spotted earlier. She had put on a black hat and sunglasses and was dressed in a long black skirt and boots. Tall and lean, she cut quite a figure amid all the grief.

Behan looked searchingly at Stone and tried to follow his gaze, but Stone broke it off before the man could do so. "I suppose they're sure about his cause of death," Behan said. He added quickly, "I mean, they tend to get these things wrong sometimes."

Stone spoke up. "I suppose if they have, we'll know about it at some point. The media usually ferrets those things out."

"Yes, the journalists are rather good about that," Behan said with mild distaste.

"My husband knows a lot about instant death," Marilyn Behan blurted out. When they all stared at her, she hastily added, "I mean, because of what his company does."

Behan smiled at Caleb and the others and said, "Excuse us." He took his wife's arm firmly and led her away. Had Stone detected a hint of amusement in the lady's eyes?

Reuben's gaze trailed after them. "I can only visualize that guy now with a pair of panties flying at half-staff on his dinky. I had to cram my fist in my mouth to stop from ripping a laugh during the service."

"Nice of him to come today," Stone said. "I mean, for being such a *casual* acquaintance."

"The missus seems a complicated piece of work," Caleb commented.

"Well, she strikes me as sharp enough to know about her husband's indiscretions," Stone said. "I can't believe there's much love lost between them."

"And yet they stay together," Milton added.

"For love of money, power, social status," Caleb said in a disgusted tone.

"Hey, I wouldn't have minded some of that in my marriages," Reuben shot back. "I had the love, at least for a little while, but none of the other stuff."

Stone was now eyeing the lady in black. "That woman over there, does she look familiar to you?"

"How can one tell?" Caleb said. "She's wearing a hat and glasses."

Stone pulled out the photo. "I think she's this woman."

They all crowded around the picture, and then Caleb and Milton stared directly at the woman and took turns pointing.

Stone hissed, "Do you two think you could be a little more obvious?"

The funeral party headed to the cemetery. After the gravesite service was finished, people started heading back to their cars. The lady in black lingered by the raised coffin as two workmen in jeans and blue shirts waited nearby. Stone glanced around and noted that Behan and his wife had already returned to their limo. He scanned the surrounding area looking for folks to whom the administration of water torture might be a daily part of life. And you *could* spot such people, if you knew how to look for them, which Stone did. However, his surveillance turned up nothing.

He motioned for the others to follow as he walked over to the lady in black. She had placed a hand on the rosewood coffin and seemed to be mumbling something, perhaps a prayer.

They waited until she was done. When she turned toward them, Stone said, "Jonathan was in the prime of life. It's so sad."

From behind her glasses she said, "How did you know him?"

Caleb said, "I worked with him at the library. He was my boss. He'll be very missed."

The woman nodded. "Yes, he will."

"And how did you know him?" Stone asked casually.

"It was a long time ago," she said vaguely.

"Long friendships are becoming rarer these days."

"Yes, they are. Excuse me." She stepped past them and started to walk off.

"It's so curious, the medical examiner couldn't find a cause of death," Stone said loud enough for her to hear. The comment had the desired effect. She stopped and turned.

"The newspaper said he died of a heart attack," the woman said.

Caleb shook his head. "He died because his heart stopped, but he didn't have a heart attack. The papers just assumed, I guess."

She took a few steps toward them. "I didn't get your names."

"Caleb Shaw. I work in the Rare Books reading room at the Library of Congress. This is my friend—"

Stone put out his hand. "Sam Billings, nice to meet you." He motioned to the other two Camel Club members. "The big fellow is Reuben and that's Milton. And you are?"

She ignored Stone and focused on Caleb. "If you work at the library, you must love books as much as Jonathan did."

Caleb brightened as the subject changed to his specialty. "Oh, absolutely. In fact, in his will Jonathan named me his literary executor. I'm in the process right now of inventorying his collection, having it appraised and then sold, with the proceeds going to charity."

He stopped talking when he saw Stone motioning him to shut up.

She said, "That certainly sounds like Jonathan. I'm assuming his father and mother are dead?"

"Oh, yes, his father's been dead for years. His mother passed two years ago. Jonathan inherited their home."

It seemed to Stone that the woman was working hard not to smile at this last piece of information. *What had the lawyer told Caleb? That the marriage had been annulled? Perhaps not by the wife, but by the groom at the insistence of his parents?*

She said to Caleb, "It would be nice to see the house. And his collection. I'm sure it's very extensive by now."

"You knew about his collection?" Caleb asked.

"Jonathan and I shared a lot of things. I'm not going to be in town very long, so would tonight be okay?"

"As it happens, we were going over there this evening," Stone answered. "If you're staying at a hotel, we can pick you up."

The woman shook her head. "I'll meet you on Good Fellow Street." She quickly walked to a waiting cab.

"Do you think it wise to ask this woman to Jonathan's house?" Milton asked. "We really don't even know her."

Stone pulled the photo out of his pocket and held it up. "I think maybe we do. Or at least we will soon enough. On Good Fellow Street," he added thoughtfully.

CHAPTER

29

AFTER CLOSED-DOOR TESTI-mony was completed before the House Intelligence Committee, Seagraves and Trent had a cup of coffee in the cafeteria and later headed outside to stroll around the Capitol grounds. Since their official duties dictated that they spend a great deal of time together, this would raise no suspicions.

Seagraves paused to unwrap a stick of gum while Trent bent down to tie his shoe.

"So you really think this guy is ex-Agency?" Trent asked.

Seagraves nodded. "Triple Six, you know about that bunch, Albert?"

"Only vaguely. My clearance didn't go that high. The Agency recruited me for my analytical skills, not my ability in the field. And after ten years of their bullshit I'd had enough."

Seagraves smiled. "Jumping to the politico side really that much better?"

"It has been for us."

Seagraves watched as his colleague carefully combed his dozen strands back into place, somehow aligning each one perfectly against its neighbor without benefit of a mirror. "Why don't you just get a buzz cut?" Seagraves said. "A lot of ladies are into that macho look. And while you're at it get yourself in decent shape."

"After we finish our careers I'll have so much money that whatever foreign country I end up in the ladies there will take me any way I want."

"Suit yourself."

"This Triple Six guy might be a complication. We might be talking thunderstorm status."

Seagraves shook his head. "We do that, things will really heat up. For all I know he's still got connections. And if I did him, I'd have to do his friends. That's a lot of room to make a mistake and get the wrong people suspicious. For now he thinks Behan's the guy. If that changes, then the weather forecast might read differently."

"Are you really sure that's a good strategy?"

Seagraves' features turned a notch darker. "Let's do a reality check, Trent. While you sat safely behind your little wonk desk in nice, comfortable Washington, I was putting my ass on the line in places you're too scared to even watch on TV. You keep doing what you do, and let me worry about the strategic planning. Unless you think you can do it better than I can."

Trent tried to smile, but his fear didn't allow for it. "I wasn't questioning you."

"It sure as hell sounded like it." He suddenly grinned and clamped an arm around Trent's narrow shoulders. "No time to fight now, Albert. It's going way too well. Right?" He squeezed tightly and only released his grip when he felt the pain in the other man's body. It felt good, to feel another man's suffering up close like that. "I said, right?"

"Absolutely." Trent rubbed his shoulders and actually looked like he might start crying.

You must've had the crap kicked out of you on the playground every day.

Seagraves changed the subject. "Four State Department liaisons dead. That was some original spin." He'd actually known one of the murdered men; in fact, he'd served with him. A good agent, but millions of dollars easily trumped any friendship he'd ever had.

Trent said, "You expect the government to be creative? So what's next on the list?"

Seagraves tossed his cigarette down and glanced at his companion. "You'll see it when you see it, Albert." He was actually getting a little tired of his *junior* partner. That was partially what this little jam session was about, making it clear to Trent that he was and would always be a subordinate. And if things got dicey and it looked like the house of cards might tumble down, Trent would be the first person he'd kill for one simple reason: Mice always break under pressure.

He parted company with the staffer and walked to his car in a restricted area. He waved to the guard there who knew him by sight.

"Keeping my wheels safe?" Seagraves said with a grin.

"Yours and everybody else's," the guard said as he chewed on a toothpick. "You keeping the country safe?"

"Doing all I can." Actually, the next thing Seagraves would pass Trent would be key elements of the NSA's brand-new strategic surveillance plan for foreign terrorists. The media always assumed the NSA was doing things outside the law. They didn't know the half of it, and neither did the myopic folk up on Capitol Hill. But some well-heeled haters of America living seven thousand miles away and at least eight centuries in the past were willing to pay millions of dollars to know all about it. And money, man, money always carried the day; screw being a patriot. To Seagraves' mind, the only thing patriots got were a tri-folded flag for their troubles. And the major problem with that was you had to be dead to get one.

Seagraves drove back to his office, finished up a bit of work and headed home, which consisted of a thirty-year-old split-level rancher with three bedrooms and two baths, on a quarter acre of drainage-challenged dirt, that cost him nearly half his salary in mortgage and property taxes. He did a quick but intense workout and then opened the door of a small closet in the basement that he kept locked and protected by an alarm system.

Inside, arranged on the walls and on shelves, were mementos of his earlier career. Among other items was a brown glove trimmed with fur in a glass display box, a button from a coat in a small ring case, a pair of eyeglasses on a plastic holder, a shoe hanging from a peg on the wall, a wristwatch, two ladies' bracelets, a small, blank notebook with the monogram AFW, a turban on a shelf and a worn copy of the Qur'an under glass, a fur cap and a child's bib. The bib he felt a little remorse for. Yet when one killed the parents, often the child was sacrificed as well. A car bomb, after all, was indiscriminate in whom it destroyed. Each item was numbered from one to over fifty and held a history known only to him and a few others at the CIA.

Seagraves had gone to great pains and undertaken considerable risk to collect these objects, for that's what this was, his collection. Whether they realized it or not, everyone was a collector of some sort. A lot of people migrated to the ordinary end of the spectrum, collecting stamps, coins and books. Then there were those who accumulated broken hearts or sexual conquests. And then there were those who found gratification in the accumulation of lost souls. At the far end of the continuum, Roger Seagraves collected personal items from people he'd murdered, or assassinated rather, since he'd done it under the color of serving his country. Not that such a distinction made much difference to the victims; they were still dead, after all.

He had come here tonight to place two new objects in the room: a pen belonging to Robert Bradley and a leather book-mark of Jonathan DeHaven's. They were given places of honor on a shelf and in a shadow box respectively. He did so, placing a number on each one. He was approaching sixty in total. Years ago he had contemplated reaching a hundred, and he'd gotten off to a strong start, since at that time there were many in the world his country needed dead. Then his last few years on the job the pace had slowed considerably; a spineless administration and even weaker CIA bureaucracy had been the cause. He had long since given up his original goal total. He had instead gone for quality over quantity.

Any sane person being told the history of these items might judge Seagraves to be a psychopath maliciously collecting per-sonal items of murdered people. They would be wrong, he knew. It was actually a measure of respect accorded someone from whom you'd taken the most precious thing they had. If anyone ever succeeded in killing him, Seagraves trusted they'd be a worthy enough foe to afford him the same honor. He locked up his collection and went back upstairs to plan his next move. He had something to get, and with DeHaven dead and buried, now was the time to get it.

Annabelle Conroy sat in a rental car at the corner of Good Fel-low Street. It had been many years since she'd been here, and yet the place hadn't changed all that much. You could still smell the moldy stink of old money, though it was now mingled with the equally foul aroma of new currency. Annabelle, of course, had had neither, a fact that Jonathan DeHaven's mother, Elizabeth, had been quick to pounce on. No money and no breeding was what she had probably told her son over and over until the saying was ingrained on his very impressionable brain, finally allowing his mother to bully him into an annulment. Annabelle had not contested it, because what would the point have been?

Still, Annabelle held no ill feelings toward her ex. He was a man-child in many ways, erudite, kind, generous and affectionate. Yet he possessed not even a sliver of a backbone and ran from confrontation like the proverbial kid with glasses did from the bully. He had been no match for his omnipotent and acid-tongued mother; yet how many sons were? After the marriage had ended, he wrote Annabelle loving, moving letters, showered her with gifts, told her that he was thinking of her all the time. And she never doubted that he was. Deception was not part of his nature; *that* had been quite a new concept for her. Opposites apparently did indeed attract.

And yet he had never once asked her to come back. Still, compared to the men she'd known in her life, all of them like her on the wrong side of the good and bad equation, he was the light of pure innocence. He held her hand and was quick to open doors for his "lady." He talked to her about issues of importance in the world of normal people, a place as alien to her as a distant star. And yet Jonathan had made it less strange, less distant, in the brief time they'd spent together.

Annabelle had to admit she'd changed while with him. Jonathan DeHaven, though he would forever be firmly ensconced on the conservative side of life, had inched a little toward her, perhaps enjoying life in a way he never could've imagined before. He was a good man. And she was sorry he was dead.

She angrily swiped at a tear that fell far too easily down her cheek. The emotion was unusual and unwelcome. She did not cry anymore. She was not close enough to anyone to weep over death. Not even her mother's. It was true she'd avenged Tammy Conroy, but the daughter had also made herself rich in the process. Would she have done one without the other? Annabelle couldn't say for sure. Did it matter? Well, she had nearly 17 million reasons parked in a foreign bank account that said it didn't.

She watched as a gray Nova rattled up to the curb in front of DeHaven's house. Four men got out: the oddballs from the cemetery who'd said that Jonathan's death had no official cause. Well, she'd said her good-byes to Jonathan and would now walk through the house, for once without the wretched eye of Mama DeHaven following every swing of her daughter-in-law's irreverent hips. And then she would be on a plane out of here. Annabelle didn't want to be on the same continent when Jerry Bagger discovered he was $40 million poorer and erupted on a greater scale than his fake volcano ever had.

The burn of the lava could easily reach D.C.

She slid out of the car and walked toward the house and a life that could have very well been hers if things had worked out differently.

30

THEY WERE ALL IN THE BOOK vault after Annabelle had been given a brief tour of the main floor of the house. Caleb didn't open the small safe behind the painting. He had no intention of letting anyone else see the *Psalm Book*. After she'd seen the collection, they went back upstairs, where Annabelle walked though the elegant rooms with probably more interest than she cared to show.

"So you've been here before?" Stone said.

She looked at him blankly. "I don't remember saying whether I had or not."

"Well, you knew Jonathan lived on Good Fellow Street. I just assumed."

"People shouldn't assume so much, they'd be better off." She continued to look around. "The house hasn't changed much," she said, indirectly answering his question. "But at least he got rid of some of the uglier furniture. Probably after his mother died. I don't think that would've been allowed until *Elizabeth* drew her last breath."

"Where did you and Jonathan meet?" Caleb asked. She ignored this question. "He might've mentioned your name, but I don't know what it is," he persisted, drawing a warning look from Stone.

"Susan Farmer. We met out West."

"Did you *marry* out there as well?" Stone interjected.

He was very impressed because she didn't even flinch. But she didn't answer him either.

Stone decided to play his ace. He pulled the photo out of his pocket. "We were told that Jonathan's marriage had been annulled. Since you don't like people making assumptions, I'm *deducing* from your tone about Elizabeth DeHaven that she was the instigator of that action. He kept this photo. The woman bears a remarkable likeness to you. My experience is that men don't keep photos of women for just any reason. I think your case was special."

He handed the photo over to her. This time he got a reaction. As Annabelle took the picture, her hand, rock-steady all these years, shook a bit, and her eyes opened a smidgen wider and appeared a little moist. She said wistfully, "Jonathan was a very handsome man. Tall, thick brown hair and eyes that just made you feel good about yourself."

"And can I say you're as lovely now as you were then," Reuben added magnanimously, edging closer to her.

Annabelle didn't seem to have heard Reuben. She did something she hadn't done in a long time: She smiled, genuinely. "This was taken on the day of our wedding. It was my first, and only, marriage."

"Where were you married?" Caleb asked.

"Vegas—where else?" she said, her gaze holding fast on the photo. "Jonathan was in town for a book convention. We hooked up, hit it off and were married. All in a week's time. Pretty crazy, I know. At least that's how his mother saw it." She ran her finger along Jonathan's frozen smile. "But we were happy. For a time anyway. We even lived here for a while with his parents after we were married, until we found a place to live."

"Well, it *is* quite a large house," Caleb said.

"Funny, it seemed far too small back then," she remarked dryly.

"Were you out in Vegas for the book convention too?" Stone asked politely.

She handed the photo back, and Stone put it back in his jacket pocket. "Do you really need an answer to that question?"

"All right. Have you been in contact with Jonathan over the years?"

"And why would I need to tell you if I had?"

"And there's no reason for you to," Reuben piped in, scowling at Stone. "In fact, that's getting a little personal."

Stone was obviously put out by his smitten friend's traitorous comment but said, "We're doing our best to figure out what happened to Jonathan, and we need as much help as we can get."

"His heart stopped beating and he died. Is it that unusual?"

Milton explained, "The medical examiner apparently couldn't determine the cause of death. And Jonathan had just had a full cardio checkup at Johns Hopkins. He didn't have a heart attack or anything else, apparently."

"So you think someone killed him? Who could possibly have a problem with Jonathan? He was a *librarian*."

"It's not like librarians don't have enemies," Caleb said defensively. "Indeed, I've been around some colleagues who can get pretty mean-spirited after they've had a few glasses of merlot."

She looked at him incredulously. "Yeah, I bet. But no one's going to pop someone because they got fined for an overdue book."

"Let me show you something," Stone said. "It's up in the attic."

When they arrived there, Stone said, "That telescope is pointed toward the house next door."

Reuben added, "Yeah, it was looking into the owner's bed—"

Stone cut in. "I'll explain, Reuben, if you don't mind." He raised his eyebrows and glanced at Annabelle.

Reuben said, "Oh, right. Yeah, go ahead and explain, Oliv—I mean, it was Frank, right? Or Steve?"

"Thank you, *Reuben*!" Stone snapped. "As I said, the telescope is pointed at the house next door. It's owned by the head of Paradigm Technologies, one of the largest defense contractors in the country. The man's name is Cornelius Behan."

"He likes to be called CB," Caleb added.

"Okay," Annabelle said slowly.

Stone looked through the telescope, sweeping his gaze along the side of Behan's house, which stood across a sliver of grass from DeHaven's. "I thought so." He motioned for Annabelle to take his place. She focused the telescope's eyepiece on the spot where he'd been looking.

"It's an office or a study," she reported.

"That's right."

"You think Jonathan was spying on this guy?"

"Perhaps. Or he might have inadvertently seen something that led to his death."

"So this Cornelius Behan killed Jonathan?"

"We have no proof. But strange things have been happening."

"Like what?"

Stone hesitated. He had no intention of telling her about his being kidnapped. "Let's just say that there're enough questions here to make us look further. I think Jonathan DeHaven deserves that."

Annabelle studied him for a moment and then took another look through the telescope. "Tell me about this CB guy."

Stone briefly gave her a sketch of Behan and his company.

Next he mentioned the murder of the Speaker of the House, Bob Bradley.

Annabelle again looked skeptical. "You don't think that's connected to Jonathan? I thought terrorists had claimed responsibility."

Stone told her about the military contracts that Behan had won under the old regime. "Bradley's predecessor as Speaker had been convicted of unethical practices, so it's not a stretch to speculate that he might have been in Behan's pocket. And then Bradley comes along as Mr. Clean, and Behan might not have wanted certain things to be investigated. So Bradley had to die."

"And you're thinking that Jonathan stumbled on this conspiracy, and they had to kill him before he could tell anyone?" She still sounded unconvinced, but not as much.

"What we have are two unsolved deaths of government people with Cornelius Behan as a common denominator and a neighbor of one of the dead men."

Caleb added, "Behan was at the funeral today."

Annabelle said sharply, "Which one was he?"

"Little redheaded guy—"

Annabelle finished for him, "Who thinks way too much of himself and had the tall bottle-blond wife who despises him."

Stone looked impressed. "You sum people up quickly."

"I've always seen an advantage in it. Okay, what's our next move?"

Stone looked startled. "*Our* next move?"

"Yeah, once you give me a crash course on the info you're obviously holding back, maybe we can make some real headway."

"Miss Farmer," Stone began.

"Just call me Susan."

"I thought you said you weren't going to be in town long."

"Change of plan."

"Can I ask why?"

"You can ask. Can we meet tomorrow morning?"

"Absolutely," Reuben said. "And if you need a place to bunk—"

"I don't," she said.

"We can meet at my house," Stone suggested.

"Where's that?" she asked.

"At a cemetery," Milton said helpfully.

Annabelle didn't even raise an eyebrow.

Stone wrote down the address and directions. When she went to take it from him, she stumbled and fell against him, grabbing on to his jacket to keep from falling.

"Sorry," she said as her hand closed around the photo in his pocket. A second later she was pulling it out. And then something happened that had never happened before. Stone's hand closed around her wrist.

He said in a low voice so only she could hear, "All you had to do was ask for it." He released his grip, and she smoothly slid the photo into her pocket, her startled gaze on Stone's grim features. She regained her composure and faced the others. "I'll see you tomorrow."

Reuben took her hand, gently kissing it in the style of the centuries-ago French gentleman. "I want you to know what a true pleasure it's been making your acquaintance, *Susan.*"

She smirked. "Thanks, *Reuben.* Oh, there's a nice view of what I'm assuming is Behan's bedroom from up here. He's getting it on with some hot chick right now. You might want to check it out."

Reuben whipped around. "Oliver, you didn't tell me that."

Annabelle looked back at an exasperated Stone. "That's okay, *Oliver,* Susan's not *my* real name either. What a shock, huh?"

A minute later they heard the front door open and close. Reuben quickly took up post at the telescope, but just as quickly moaned, "Damn, they must have already finished." He turned to Stone and said reverently, "God, what a woman."

Yes, thought Stone, *what a woman indeed.*

Annabelle climbed into her car, started it and then pulled out the photo, rubbing her wrist where Stone had grabbed it. The guy named Oliver had actually caught her picking his pocket. Even as a kid assigned by her father to fleece tourists in L.A., she'd never been caught in the act. Tomorrow might prove to be very interesting.

Her attention turned to the photo. It was amazing how one picture could bring back so many memories. That year of her life was the only truly normal one she ever had. Some might have thought it boring, or at least uneventful. She had considered it wonderful. She'd stumbled across a man who'd fallen in love with her. No ulterior motive, no hidden agenda, no leveraging for a bigger con down the road. He'd fallen in love with just her. A bookman and a con girl. All odds were against them making it, and as she well knew, only a fool bet against the odds.

And yet a gentle man who collected books had somehow captured her heart, toughened and scarred as it was. Early on in their relationship Jonathan had asked her if she collected anything. Annabelle had told him no, yet maybe that wasn't true, she thought now. Perhaps she did collect something. Perhaps she collected lost chances.

She stared up at the big old house. In another life she and Jonathan might have lived there, with a passel of children, who knew? It was probably a good thing it hadn't turned out that way. She would've likely made a terrible mother.

Her thoughts turned to the obvious issue. Jerry Bagger would be erupting in two days. The smart move would be to leave the country now, despite what she'd told the men about meeting tomorrow. It didn't take her long to decide. She was staying and seeing it through. Maybe she owed it to Jonathan. Perhaps she owed it to herself. Because right now seemed a good time to end her collection of lost chances.

CHAPTER

31

ANNABELLE AND THE CAMEL Club gathered at Stone's cottage at seven o'clock the next morning.

"Nice digs," she said, gazing around the small interior. "And you have such quiet neighbors," she added, motioning out the window to the tombstones.

"There are some dead people whose company I would prefer over that of certain of my living acquaintances," Stone replied tersely.

"I can relate," Annabelle said cheerfully, sitting down in front of the empty fireplace. "Let's get to it, guys."

Reuben sat next to her looking for the world like a large puppy hoping for a little scratch around the ears. Caleb, Milton and Stone sat across from them.

"Here's my plan," Stone said. "Milton will find out as much as possible about Bob Bradley. There may be something about that we can use. I'll visit Bradley's house, or rather what's left of his house, and see what I can discover. Reuben used to be stationed at the Pentagon. He'll work his contacts there to find out what he can about Behan's military contracts that Bradley's dethroned predecessor might have helped push through."

Annabelle gazed at Reuben. "Pentagon, huh?"

He tried to appear modest. "Three tours of Nam too. Enough medals to decorate a damn Christmas tree. Hey, it's all about serving your country."

"I wouldn't know," Annabelle said, turning back to Stone. "But what about Jonathan's death? How do we find out if someone killed him?"

"I have a theory about that, but it'll require going to the Library of Congress and checking out the fire suppressant system there. The one problem with that is we don't know where it's located in the building. Caleb can't find out because it's classified for some reason. I guess so unauthorized persons couldn't sabotage it, although I think that's precisely what happened. The building is so massive that even if we could search room by room, it would take forever. We also need to see the configuration for the ventilation system for the room where Jonathan was found dead."

She asked, "What's this fire suppressant system got to do with anything?"

"I have a theory," is all Stone would say.

"Wouldn't the architect who did the building have the plans that would show both the fire system and the HVAC?" Annabelle pointed out.

"They would," Stone said. "Although the Jefferson Building was built in the late 1800s, it underwent extensive renovation about fifteen years ago. The Architect of the Capitol has the plans, but we have no access to them."

"Did they use a private architectural firm to help with the renovation?" she asked.

Caleb snapped his fingers. "You know, they did, one right here in D.C. I remember now, because the government was trying to stimulate the local economy and was getting more into public-private partnerships."

"There's your answer," Annabelle said.

"I'm not following you," Stone replied. "We still have no access to those plans."

She looked at Caleb. "Can you get me the name of the firm?"

"I believe so."

"The only issue will be whether they'll let us take pictures of the plans. I doubt they will, and copying them is probably out too." As she was thinking out loud, the Camel Club stared at her mystified. She finally noted this and said, "I'll get us into the architectural firm, but we need copies of the designs if we're going to locate the fire room and HVAC in the building."

Milton said, "I have a photographic memory. If I look at the plans once, I can memorize them."

She looked at him skeptically. "I've heard people make that claim before, and it never quite works out."

"I can assure you that it 'works out' with me," Milton said indignantly.

She grabbed a book off the shelf, opened it to a page in the middle and held it up in front of Milton. "Okay, read the page to yourself." He did so and nodded. Annabelle turned the book around and looked at the page. "All right, Mr. Photo, start regurgitating."

Milton read the page from memory, including punctuation marks, without one misstep.

For the first time in their company Annabelle looked impressed. "You ever been to Vegas?" she asked. He shook his head. "You might want to try it sometime."

"Isn't card counting illegal?" Stone asked, quickly deducing what she was alluding to.

She answered, "No, so long as you don't use a mechanical or computer device to do it."

"Wow," Milton exclaimed. "I could make a fortune."

Annabelle said, "But before you get your hopes up, even though it's not illegal if you're just using your brain, if they catch you, they'll beat the crap out of you."

"Oh!" Milton said, horrified. "Never mind."

She turned to Stone. "So how do you think Jonathan was killed? And no more doublespeak or I walk."

Stone studied her and then made up his mind. "Caleb found Jonathan's body. Right after that he fainted. At the hospital the nurse said that he was getting better and that his temperature was coming *up*, not down."

"And your point is?" Annabelle said.

"The fire suppressant system at the library uses a substance called halon 1301," Caleb said, taking up the explanation. "It starts as a liquid in the pipes but turns into a gas when it comes out of the nozzle. It puts out fires in part by eliminating oxygen in the atmosphere."

"Meaning Jonathan might have suffocated to death! Good God, you mean the police didn't stumble across that possibility and check to see whether the gas cylinder was empty?" Annabelle said angrily.

"There was no evidence that the system was even engaged," Stone said. "The warning horn didn't sound, and Caleb learned that it was operational, although it could have been disconnected and then reattached later. And the gas leaves no residue."

"And on top of that, halon 1301 could *not* have killed Jonathan, not at the levels that are used to suppress fires at the library," Caleb added. "I checked it. That's why it's used in spaces occupied by people."

"So where is this leading?" Annabelle asked. "You seem to be saying two different things. It was the gas but it wasn't the gas. Which is it?" she demanded.

Stone took up the discussion. "One element of the suppressant being engaged is the lowering of the temperature in the room. Caleb said he saw Jonathan's body, got an immediate chill and fainted. I believe the chill came from the gas, which led to the nurse's comment in the hospital about Caleb's temperature coming up. And I think Caleb fainted because the oxygen levels in the room *were* low, but not low enough to kill him, because he'd come into the room about a half hour after Jonathan."

Annabelle said, "So it obviously wasn't this halon 1301 stuff. So something else?"

"Exactly. We just have to find out what."

Annabelle stood. "Okay, I need to start doing some serious prep work."

Stone rose and faced her. "Susan, before you really become involved, you need to know that there are some very dangerous people tied up in this. I've already had evidence of that personally. It could be very risky for you."

"Oliver, let me put it this way. If it's any more dangerous than what I was involved in last week, I'd be floored."

Stone looked stunned by this comment and stepped back.

Annabelle hooked an arm through Milton's. "Okay, Milton, we need to spend some time together."

Reuben looked crushed. "Why Milton?"

"Because he's my little Xerox machine." She pinched Milton's cheek and he immediately turned red. "But first, we have to get him the right clothes, the right *style.*"

"What's wrong with my clothes?" Milton said, looking down at his red sweater and jeans, both of which were impeccably cleaned and pressed.

"Absolutely nothing," she said. "Except they're all wrong for what I need." She pointed at Caleb. "Call Milton with the name of the firm as soon as you get it." She snapped her fingers. "Let's go, Miltie."

She strode out the door. A shocked Milton looked helplessly at the others and hissed, "Miltie?"

"Milton!" Annabelle called from outside the cottage. "Now!"

Milton shot out of the door. Reuben immediately whirled on Stone. "Are you just going to let her take him?"

"What exactly would you suggest I do, Reuben?" Stone said bluntly. "That woman is a hurricane and earthquake all rolled into one."

"I don't know, you could . . . I mean . . ." He plopped down in a chair and growled, "Damn it, why couldn't *I* have a photographic memory!"

"Thank God you don't," Caleb exclaimed in a disgusted tone.

"What makes you say that?" Reuben demanded hotly.

"Because then she'd be calling you *Ruby*, and I'd have to be sick to my stomach."

CHAPTER

32

LATER THAT DAY AT THE LIBRARY
Caleb sent an e-mail to the administrative offices. An hour later
he found out the name of the private architectural firm that had
helped with the Jefferson Building's renovation. He telephoned
Milton with that information.

"How's it going with *that woman*?" he said in a low voice.

Milton whispered back, "She just bought me a black suit and a
really bright tie, and she wants to restyle my hair. You know,
jazz me up."

"Did she tell you why?"

"Not yet." He paused, then added, "Caleb, she sort of scares
me. She's so, she's so *confident*." Milton had no way of knowing,
but he had never uttered a truer statement.

"Well, you just hang in there, *Miltie*." Caleb hung up, chuckling.

He next phoned Vincent Pearl, knowing that he would get the
answering machine, since the rare book shop wasn't open until
later in the evening. The fact was he didn't want to talk to the
man because he hadn't made up his mind what to do about the
sale of Jonathan's collection yet, but most of all he didn't know
what to do about the *Psalm Book*. When its existence was revealed, there would be a positive uproar in the rare book world.

And he would be at the center of this maelstrom, a thought that terrified but also intrigued him. A little time in the spotlight wasn't such a bad thing, particularly for a person used to operating in the obscurity of a library.

The only thing that stopped him from going full bore ahead was a nagging thought. *What if Jonathan had gotten the* Psalm Book *somehow illegally?* That might account for his secrecy about the book. Caleb didn't want to do anything to besmirch his friend's memory.

Caleb put these unsettling thoughts aside and walked over to speak to Jewell English, who, like the Hemingway lover, Norman Janklow, had been a regular in the reading room over the last few years.

As he walked toward her, Jewell took off her glasses, tucked her pages of carefully written notes inside a small manila folder and motioned for him to sit down next to her. When he did, she clutched his arm and said excitedly, "Caleb, I got a line on a mint Beadle. *Maleska, the Indian Wife of the White Hunter.* It's a number one, Caleb."

"I think we have a copy of that volume," he said thoughtfully. "Make sure it's in true mint condition, Jewell. The Beadles were cheaply put together."

Jewell English clapped her hands together. "Oh, but, Caleb, isn't it exciting, though? A number one."

"Yes, it's very exciting. And if you want me to look at it first, I'd be glad to."

"Oh, you are a dear. I need to have you come over sometime for a drink. We have so much in common." She patted his arm and raised her carefully penciled-in eyebrows suggestively.

Caught off guard, Caleb said hurriedly, "Yes, well, that would be nice. Someday. Maybe. In the future. Sometime. Perhaps." He tried not to run back to his desk. Being hit on by a septuagenarian didn't really do much for his ego. He quickly recovered his good mood and surveyed the room. It was actually comforting to see bibliophiles like Jewell and Norman Janklow perched at the beautiful tables perusing old books. It made the world seem far saner than it actually was. Caleb loved giving in to such an illusion, at least for a few hours each day. *Oh, to be back in the world of foolscap and quill pen, if only for a little while.*

He was working at his desk about twenty minutes later when he heard the door to the reading room open. He glanced up and froze. Cornelius Behan was walking toward the reference desk when he spotted Caleb. He said something to the woman stationed at the desk, and she pointed to Caleb. He rose from his desk as Behan walked over, his hand out. He didn't have his bodyguards with him, Caleb noted. Perhaps security wouldn't let them through with their guns.

"Mr. Behan?" he said. Caleb had a sudden vision of Behan with a pair of panties flapping from his privates. He had to choke back a laugh. "Sorry," he said. "Air went down the wrong way."

"Please, just call me CB." They shook hands. Behan looked around the room. "I didn't even know this place existed. You should advertise better."

"We could do a better job of public awareness," Caleb conceded. "But with shrinking budgets it's hard to find the money."

"Trust me, I know all about government pecuniary shortfalls."

"Well, you've done very well dealing with Washington," Caleb commented, and then instantly regretted having said it as Behan looked at him with heightened scrutiny.

"It was a nice funeral," Behan said, abruptly changing the subject. "As far as funerals can be nice, of course."

"Yes, it was. It was good meeting your wife."

"Right. Anyway, I was downtown meeting with some folks on the Hill and thought I'd drop by. All this time I was

Jonathan's neighbor, and never once have I seen where he worked."

"Well, better late than never."

"I guess Jonathan really loved his work here?"

"He did. Always the first one in."

"Lots of friends here. I'm sure everyone liked him." He looked at Caleb questioningly.

"I think Jonathan got along well with everyone here."

"I understand you were at Jonathan's house last night with a woman?"

Caleb took this second abrupt change in subject in stride. "You should've come by if you saw us."

"I was busy."

I bet you were, Caleb thought.

"But some of my people saw you, they keep a tight lookout. So, this woman?"

"She's an expert in rare books. I had her come by to take a look at some of Jonathan's holdings as part of the appraisal process." Caleb was very proud of himself for coming up with that lie so quickly.

"So what'll happen to Jonathan's house?"

"I'm assuming it'll be sold. I'm not really involved in that part at all."

"I was thinking about buying the place and turning it into a guesthouse."

"Yours isn't big enough?" Caleb blurted out without really thinking.

Thankfully, Behan laughed. "Yeah, I know. You'd think it would be, but we have lots of guests. I thought you might have an inside track on what they're going to do with it. Maybe you've looked all through the place," he added in a casual tone.

"No. I've just confined myself to the vault."

Behan studied Caleb closely for a long moment. "I'll just call the lawyers then, let them earn their money." He hesitated and added, "So can you give me a tour of the place while I'm here? You keep really rare books here, I understand."

"Hence the name Rare Books reading room." Caleb had a sudden thought. It was against certain library protocols, but what the hell, it could be important in finding out who killed Jonathan. He said, "Would you like to go into the vaults?"

"Yes," Behan said almost too quickly.

Caleb gave him the standard tour, which he ended near the spot where Jonathan DeHaven had been killed. Was it Caleb's imagination, or did Behan's gaze linger just a beat too long on the fire suppressant gas nozzle sticking out of the wall. His suspicion was confirmed when Behan pointed at it.

"What's that?"

Caleb explained about the system. "We're actually going to replace the gas we use with another one that's more ozone-friendly."

Behan nodded. "Well, thanks for the tour."

After Behan had left, Caleb called Stone and told him about this encounter.

Stone remarked, "His roundabout way of asking if Jonathan had any enemies is very curious unless he's looking into the possibility of pinning the murder on someone else. And the fact that he wanted to know if you've looked *all* through Jonathan's house is very telling. I wonder if he knew about his neighbor's voyeuristic tendencies?"

After he had hung up with Stone, Caleb picked up the book he'd brought from DeHaven's vault and walked through a series of underground tunnels to the Madison Building where the Conservation and Preservation Division was located. The division was split into two large rooms, one for books and the other for everything else. Here almost one hundred conservators labored at restoring rare and not-so-rare items to better condition. Caleb went into the book room and headed to a table where a thin man wearing a green apron was carefully turning the pages of an incunabulum work from Germany. Around him was an assortment of tools, ranging from ultrasonic welders and Teflon spatulas to old-fashioned manual screw presses and X-acto knives.

"Hello, Monty," Caleb said.

Monty Chambers looked up from behind thick black glasses and rubbed his bald head with a gloved hand. He was clean-shaven and had a weak chin that seemed to melt into his face. He didn't speak but merely nodded at Caleb. Well into his sixties now, Monty had been the library's top book conservator for decades. He was given all the toughest assignments and had never failed to get the job done. It was said that he could coax even the most damaged and neglected books back to life. He was prized for the dexterity and sensitivity of his hands, his cleverness and creativity in restoring old works and his vast knowledge of book conservation and preservation techniques.

"Got a freelance job for you, Monty, if you have time." Caleb held up the book. "*The Sound and the Fury.* It has some water damage to the boards. It belonged to Jonathan DeHaven. I'm handling the sale of his collection."

Monty examined the novel and said in a high-pitched voice, "How soon?"

"Oh, you have plenty of time. We're in the early stages yet."

Conservators at Monty's level often worked on several major and smaller projects at a time. They worked late and also came in over some weekends when they wouldn't be interrupted as much. Caleb also knew that Monty had a fully equipped workshop at his home in D.C. where he did outside jobs on occasion.

Keller smiled. "Well, it sounds like this article will be good for business. In fact, we've been looking to branch out overseas."

"Then I think this is a match made in heaven," Annabelle replied.

"Any particular phase you'd like to look at?"

"All of it, really, but perhaps a focus on the basement and the second floor, which I heard were challenges too."

"It was all a challenge, Ms. Collins."

"Please, call me Regina. And the reconfig of the HVAC?"

"That *was* a bear."

"I can tell this is going to be a great article," Annabelle cooed.

Keller picked up the phone, and minutes later they were looking over the architectural plans. Milton positioned himself such that he took in every inch of the drawings, mentally filing every detail away in far reaches of his brain that most human beings could not access in theirs. Keller went over various points while Annabelle quickly sized up the plans and directed his attention and comments to the basement fire suppression room, the HVAC and the Rare Books reading room vaults.

"Now, the fire suppression equipment is centrally housed and piped through the slab?" she asked, drawing a finger along this part of the plan.

"Exactly. We were able to centrally locate it because of the delivery system we had. But they're in the process of changing the suppressant."

"Halon 1301," Milton volunteered, and Annabelle gave him a rewarding smile. "An ozone depletion monster. We have the same problem across the pond."

"Precisely," Keller agreed.

"And this HVAC duct runs right up to the vaults housed around the reading room," she pointed out.

"Yes, that was a little tricky because of the limited space, but we piggybacked some of the principal ductwork right onto the shelving columns."

"And still allow them to be load-bearing. That is very clever," Annabelle complimented.

They went over the drawings for another half hour until Annabelle pronounced herself satisfied. "Leslie," she said to Milton, "do you need to see anything else?"

He shook his head and, smiling, put his finger to his temple. "I've got it all up here."

Annabelle laughed and Keller quickly joined in.

She took a photo of Keller and his partner, Mahoney, for the story, and promised to send them a copy of the magazine when it came out. *Don't hold your breath, guys.*

As they were leaving, Keller said, "If you have any more questions, don't hesitate to give us a call."

"You've been more helpful than you could possibly imagine," Annabelle replied truthfully.

As they climbed into Annabelle's rented Ford, Milton said, "Thank God that's over. My palms are so sweaty I could barely open the car door."

"Milton, you did great. That halon comment was perfectly timed to put the mar—I mean, to put Keller at ease."

"It actually did feel good. Even though I felt like throwing up a couple of times."

"Forget about it; that comes with the territory. And you showed some style too with that 'got it all up here' comment."

Milton beamed. "You liked that one? It just came out."

"I can tell you're a natural at this."

He glanced at her. "You seem to do this stuff really well too."

She put the car in gear. "Just beginner's luck."

CHAPTER

34

WHILE ANNABELLE AND MIL-
ton were meeting with the architects, Stone had ventured into
the neighborhood where Bob Bradley had lived. He'd dressed in
a floppy hat, oversize coat and baggy pants, and he had on a
leash Goff, Caleb's mongrel dog, which had been named after
the first director of the Rare Books Division. This was a dodge
that he'd used before, and had actually originated in his old job
with the government. People just could not bring themselves to
be suspicious about someone walking a pet. Stone had no idea,
of course, that Roger Seagraves had used the same ploy in making his escape after killing Bradley.

As he strolled down the street, he could see that all that was
left of the town house was a blackened mass of toppled studs
and a scorched brick chimney. The two attached homes on
either side of Bradley's residence had also been extensively damaged. Stone looked around the area. It was not a particularly affluent part of town. Being a congressman was not the financial
windfall that some people thought it was. Members had to
maintain two residences, one in their home state and one in the
capital city, and the cost of housing in D.C. was extraordinarily
high. Some congressmen, particularly newer ones, often shared

homes in Washington or even slept in their offices for this reason. Yet the veteran Bradley had lived alone.

Milton managed to get Stone background information on the
man, and Stone had also consulted the journals kept at his hiding
place. Together they had presented an overall picture of Bradley.
Born in Kansas, he had had a typical politician's career, if there
was such a thing, serving twelve terms in the House and rising
through the ranks to head up the House Intelligence Committee
for over a decade before assuming the position of Speaker. With
his death at age fifty-nine, he left behind a wife and two grown
children, all back in Kansas. From what Stone could learn the
man had been honest and his career never threatened by scandal.
His stated purpose of cleaning up the Congress could very well
have made him many powerful enemies and led to his death.
Some might conclude that assassinating a man who was third in
line to succeed the president would be too audacious a move.
However, Stone knew that was a pipe dream: If one could kill
presidents, nobody was safe.

Officially, Bradley's murder was still an ongoing investigation, although the media, after a flurry of stories about it, had
been uncharacteristically mum. Perhaps the police were starting
to suspect that the terrorist group didn't really exist and Bradley's
death was due to something far more complex than the work of
bigoted and violent lunatics.

He stopped next to a tree so Goff could take a leak. Stone
could sense the presence of authority all around him. He'd been
in the spy business long enough to know that the truck parked
at the far end of the street was a recon vehicle, the two men inside assigned to ferret out any helpful details by watching the
dead man's home. One of the nearby townhomes had probably
been commandeered by the FBI with an investigative team working there 24/7. Binoculars and cameras were no doubt trained on

him right now. He pulled his hat down a bit lower, as though in response to the breeze.

As he was looking around, he caught sight of something, immediately turned around and walked the other way, dragging Goff along in his haste. A white D.C. Public Works van had turned the corner and was heading his way. He did not intend to find out if it was a real public works van or full of people who specialized in causing other humans enormous pain.

He turned right at the next corner and prayed that the van didn't follow. Although the area was crawling with feds, he could not assume that would protect him. The FBI might very well toss him in the van with the torturers and wave a hearty good-bye. He walked two more blocks before slowing down and letting Goff fuss at a bush while he slowly glanced behind him. No sign of the van. Yet it could've been a ruse, distracting him while they came at Stone from another direction. With this thought he called Reuben on his cell phone. The big man had just punched out at the loading dock.

"I'll be there in five minutes, Oliver," he said. "There's a police substation two blocks from where you are. Start heading that way. If the bastards make a move, you start screaming like bloody murder."

Stone walked in that direction. Reuben, for all his faults, was as loyal and as brave a friend as Stone could possibly want.

True to his word, Reuben came roaring down the road in his pickup truck, and Stone and Goff climbed in.

"Where's your motorcycle?" Stone asked.

"Jerk-offs have seen it. Figured I'd keep it on the q.t."

When they were far away from the area, Reuben slowed and then stopped.

"I've been checking the side mirror, Oliver," he reported. "I didn't see anything."

Stone didn't look convinced. "They must have seen me on the street."

"Your disguise fooled them."

Stone shook his head. "People like that aren't fooled so easily."

"Well, maybe they're keeping you on a short leash, hoping you'll lead them to the pot of gold."

"I'm afraid it'll be a long wait, then."

"Meant to tell you, buddy of mine from the Pentagon called me back. He didn't have a lot to say about Behan and that military contract, but he did tell me something interesting. I know some things have been reported in the press about secrets being stolen and leaks occurring. But it's a lot worse than the papers have reported. From what my friend said, there're some moles selling this country down the river to our enemies in the Middle East and Asia, among others."

Stone fiddled with Goff's leash and said, "Reuben, have your friends at D.C. Homicide or the FBI gotten back to you?"

"You know, that's really strange. Not one of them has called back. I don't get it."

Oh, I get it, Stone thought. *I get it loud and clear.*

CHAPTER

35

THEY MET AT STONE'S COTTAGE later that evening, and Annabelle and Milton reported on their session with the architects. Relying on his astonishing memory, Milton had drawn out a detailed plan of the locations of both the fire room and the HVAC line.

Caleb studied the drawings. "I know exactly where that is. I thought it was just a storage room."

"Is it locked?" Stone asked.

"I suppose it might be."

"I'm sure I have some keys that will probably fit it," Stone said.

Caleb looked startled. "Keys? What's that supposed to mean?"

"I think it means he's planning on breaking into the room," Annabelle said.

"Oliver, you can't be serious. Against my better judgment I let you impersonate a German scholar to get into the vault, but I absolutely draw the line on *burglarizing* the Library of Congress."

Annabelle looked at Stone with new respect. "You played a German scholar? That's impressive."

"Please do *not* encourage him," Caleb snapped. "Oliver, I am a federal employee."

"And have we ever held that against you?" Reuben quipped.

Stone said, "Caleb, if we don't get into that room, all the risk in getting the plan details will have been for nothing." He pointed at the drawing. "And you can see that the HVAC line running to the vault is also located in the fire suppression room. We can check both out at the same time."

Caleb shook his head. "That room is located off the main basement corridor. There are usually lots of people walking along there. We'll get caught."

"If we act like we're supposed to be there, no one will challenge us."

"He's right, Caleb," Annabelle said.

"I'm going too," Reuben added. "I'm tired of being left out of all the fun."

Milton piped in, "What about us?"

"I can't walk in with an army of people," Caleb wailed.

Annabelle said, "We can be backup, Milton. Every plan needs to allow for contingencies."

Stone looked at her strangely. "Fine, you can be our backup. We'll go tonight."

"Tonight!" Caleb exclaimed. "I'll need at least a week to work up the nerve. I'm a wimp. I started out as a librarian at an elementary school, but I couldn't take the pressure."

"You can do it, Caleb," Milton advised. "I felt the same way today, but it's not that hard to fool people. If I can do it to some architects, you can do it at the place where you work. What could they possibly ask you that you wouldn't have an answer for?"

"Oh, I don't know, how about where's my *brain* for agreeing to do this in the first place?" Caleb shot back. "And besides, the building will be closing by the time we get there."

"Can you still get us in with your library badge?"

"I don't know. Maybe, maybe not," he said evasively.

"Caleb," Stone said calmly. "We have to do this."

Caleb sighed. "I know. I know." He added sharply, "At least allow me the satisfaction of *pretending* I'm putting up a fight."

Annabelle put a hand on his shoulder and smiled. "Caleb, you remind me of somebody I know. His name's Leo. He likes to bitch and moan and act like a weenie, but in the end he always comes through."

"I guess I'll take that as a compliment," Caleb said stiffly.

Stone cleared his throat and opened one of the journals he'd brought with him. "I think I've discovered at least partly what it is we're up against."

They all turned their attention to him. Before he started speaking, he switched on his portable radio and classical music filtered into the room. "Just in case the cottage is being bugged," he explained. He cleared his throat again and told them about his trip to Bradley's destroyed house. "They killed the man and blew up his house. At first I thought it was to keep up the terrorist group subterfuge. Now I think there could be another reason: namely, that in spite of his reputation as an honest man, Bob Bradley was corrupt. And the evidence of that corruption disappeared in the explosion."

"That's not possible," Caleb said. "His predecessor was a crook, not Bradley. They elevated Bradley to the top spot to clean things up."

Stone shook his head. "In my experience in Washington one does not capture the Speaker's chair on an agenda of anticorruption. One gets there by building up powerful support and cultivating alliances over the years. Still, Bradley's ascension was out of the ordinary. If the majority leader hadn't been indicted along with the former Speaker, the job would've gone to him. And after him the party whip. But the leadership was so tainted that Bradley was brought in like the proverbial out-of-town sheriff to clean up the town. But I'm not talking about that sort of corruption.

"Bradley's role as Speaker obscures the other significant title he held: that of chairman of the House Intelligence Committee. In that role Bradley would have been briefed on virtually every covert operation going on in every American intelligence agency, including the CIA, NSA and the Pentagon. He and his staff would have been privy to secrets and classified documents worth a great deal to our enemies." Stone leafed through his journal. "Over the last several years there have been numerous accounts of espionage against American intelligence agencies, some of which have resulted in the deaths of undercover agents, four in the most recent instance that the press identified as State Department liaisons. And according to Reuben's sources, it's even worse than the media have reported."

"So you're saying Bradley was a spy?" Milton asked.

"I'm saying it's a possibility."

Caleb said, "But if Bradley was working with America's enemies, why would they kill him?"

"There are two possibilities," Stone replied. "First, he might have asked for more money in return for his acts of treason, and they decided to kill him instead. Or—"

Annabelle said, "Or *we* killed him."

Stone glanced at her and nodded slightly. The others looked stunned.

Caleb exclaimed, "We? As in our *government!*"

"Why kill him? Why not bring him to justice?" Milton added.

"Because doing that entails it all coming out," Stone said.

"And maybe the CIA and Pentagon don't want people to know they were beaten by the other side," Reuben added.

"And the CIA is not known for its compassion," Stone added

dryly. "Even the Speaker of the House may not be immune from their target sheet."

"But if it is our own government behind this, who were the people who kidnapped and tortured you, Oliver?" Milton asked.

Annabelle shot him a glance. "You were tortured?"

"I was interrogated thoroughly by some very experienced people," Stone replied.

"Thoroughly interrogated? They tried to drown you," Caleb snapped. "By . . . water-dunking you."

Reuben slapped his leg in fury. "Water-dunking! For God sakes, Caleb, that's what they do to clowns at the fair. What they did to Oliver was water-*boarding*, and it sure as hell ain't the same thing."

Stone said, "To address your question, Milton, I don't know how my abductors play into this yet. It doesn't make sense that if our government killed Bradley, they would also be interested in what we've found out. They'd already know."

"It would make sense if the agency that killed Bradley did the deed on its own, and another agency is trying to play catch-up," Annabelle offered. "We may have one agency pitted against another."

Stone looked at her with even more respect. "That's an interesting theory. How it plays out for us is hard to say right now."

"Are you still thinking this is tied to Jonathan's death?" Annabelle asked.

"The common denominator all along has been Cornelius Behan," Stone said. "His appearance at the library and his interest in the fire suppressant system only makes our suspicions seem more well founded. That's the tie to Jonathan. Cornelius Behan. And to get to the bottom of that, we have to find out how Jonathan died."

"So we have to burglarize the Library of Congress," Caleb groaned.

Stone put a hand on his friend's shoulder. "If it makes you feel any better, Caleb, it's not the first government building I've broken into."

CHAPTER

36

CALEB MANAGED TO GET STONE and Reuben through security on the strength of his credentials and the lie that they were important visitors looking at an exhibit after hours, although Caleb did so reluctantly and thus not very smoothly.

As they took the elevator down to the basement, Caleb complained, "Well, I don't feel all that different for having committed a *felony*!"

"Oh, the felony's coming up, Caleb," Stone said, showing his friend the ring of special keys. "What you did back there was probably no more than a misdemeanor." Caleb merely glared at him.

They located the room, which had large double doors. Stone quickly found the key on his ring that would fit the lock. A moment later they were inside the spacious room. The fire suppression equipment was against one wall.

"Now I see the reason for the large doors," Stone said.

The cylinders were huge, each probably weighing nearly a ton, and would not have fit through a regular-size door. Several of them were connected to pipes that ran to the ceiling and beyond.

The labels on the cylinders all read "Halon 1301." "Fire Control, Inc.," Stone said, reading the name of the company that had installed the equipment, which was also printed on the cylinders. He next studied the piping configuration. "There's a manual switch here to turn on the gas. And the pipes must run to a number of rooms in addition to the book vaults. But it's not clear which cylinder would be running to your space, Caleb."

Reuben looked over Stone's shoulders. "And you can't really tell if they've been discharged or not."

Stone moved to the HVAC ductwork and pulled out the drawing Milton had done. He glanced at a section of ductwork that rose straight to the ceiling.

"Why are you so interested in the HVAC, Oliver?" Reuben asked.

"If some sort of gas was used to kill Jonathan, then the killer would have to know that he'd be at an exact spot before knowing when to turn on the gas line from down here."

Caleb said, "That's right, I hadn't thought about that. Since there was no fire to trigger the gas, it had to have been turned on manually. But to do that, you'd have to be in this room. So how could the killer know that Jonathan would even be in that part of the vault?"

"I think he knew Jonathan's daily pattern. He was always the first one in the vault, and he regularly visited certain areas while he was inside, including the place where he died."

Reuben shook his head. "Okay, but from what Caleb told us he found DeHaven's body about twenty feet from one of the nozzles, meaning he was in the perfect place to be killed by the gas. But how would the person have known that all the way down here?"

Stone looked at Milton's drawing and then pointed to the HVAC. "This trunk line feeds directly into the book vault, running through all levels of it."

"So?"

Stone was looking around the HVAC and then stopped. On

the side not visible from the main area, Stone pointed at something. Reuben and Caleb looked at the spot.

"Why would you have an access panel cut into the ductwork?" Reuben wanted to know.

Stone opened the small panel and looked inside. "Caleb, remember the vent in the ductwork near where Jonathan's body was found. The grille was bent?"

"Yes, I remember you pointing that out. What about it?"

"If someone placed a camera attached to a long cable inside the ductwork in the book vault and bent the grille open, the camera would have a clean shot of the vault area where Jonathan was that morning. And if someone was down here with a receiver attached by that cable to the camera, I believe he could see everything going on up there, including Jonathan's movements."

"Damn," Reuben said. "And they used the ductwork—"

"Because that was the only way to run the cable. A wireless signal might not go through all the concrete and other obstructions," Stone said. "I think if we examine the ductwork inside the vault behind that bent grille, we'll note some evidence of how the camera was hung. The person waits down here, sees Jonathan on the camera and hits the manual switch, having disconnected the warning horn beforehand, and in ten seconds the gas is fully dispersed and Jonathan dies."

"But whoever did it would certainly have gone to retrieve the camera, so why didn't he bend the grille back then?" Reuben asked.

"He might have tried, but once you start bending those grilles, it's hard to get them back perfectly." He looked at Caleb. "Are you all right?"

Caleb was ashen-faced. "If what you're saying is true, then someone working at the library killed Jonathan. No one else could've entered the book vault unaccompanied."

"What the hell's that?" Reuben hissed.

Alarmed, Stone looked at the door. "Someone's coming. Quick, behind here."

They scrambled behind the HVAC system, Reuben having to half carry the terrified Caleb. They had barely gotten out of sight before the double doors opened. Four men came in, all wearing blue jumpsuits. Right behind them a forklift sailed into the room, driven by a fifth man. Another, obviously the boss, held a clipboard as the others gathered around him.

"Okay, we're taking this one, this one and that one," he said, pointing at three cylinders, including two attached to the piping. "And replacing them with the three on the forklift," he added.

The men went to work carefully unhooking the enormous pressurized cylinders from the pipes while Stone and the others watched from their hiding place.

Reuben glanced at Stone, who shook his head and put a finger to his lips. Caleb was shaking so badly that Stone grabbed one of his arms and Reuben the other to try and steady him.

A half hour later the three cylinders were lifted up by the forklift and strapped on. Next the three cylinders the men had brought in were attached to the piping system. Then the forklift moved out of the room, with the other men trailing. As soon as the doors closed behind the men, Stone went over to the newly installed cylinders and read the labels. "FM-200. Caleb, you said the library was scrapping the halon system. They must be replacing it with this type of fire suppressant."

"I suppose," Caleb replied.

"Okay, we've got to follow them," Stone said.

Caleb whimpered, "Please, Oliver, no."

"Caleb, we have to."

"I . . . don't . . . want to *die!*"

Stone shook him hard. "Get ahold of yourself, Caleb. Right now!"

Caleb looked at Stone in stunned amazement and then sputtered, "I don't appreciate you *assaulting* me."

Stone ignored this. "Which way is the loading dock?"

Caleb told him, and as they were heading out, Stone's cell phone buzzed. It was Milton. Stone told him what had happened. "We're going to follow the cylinders," he said. "We'll keep you posted."

Milton clicked off the phone and looked up at Annabelle. They were in her hotel room. He relayed what Stone had told him.

"That could be dangerous," she said. "They don't really know what they're getting into."

"But what can we do?"

"We're their backup, remember?"

She ran to the closet, pulled out a bag and slipped a small box out of it.

Milton immediately looked embarrassed because it was a tampon box.

She noted his discomfort. "Don't get all shy on me, Milton. Women always hide things they don't want found in their tampon box." She opened the box, took something out and slipped it in her pocket. "They said the name of the company was Fire Control. I'm assuming they're going to the company's storage facility. Can you find it?"

"Your hotel has WiFi, so I can look it up on the Net," Milton said, his fingers already flying over the keyboard.

"Good. Is there a novelty store around here somewhere?" she added.

He thought for a moment. "Yeah. It's got like magic stuff too. And it's open late."

"Perfect."

CHAPTER

37

THE NOVA FOLLOWED THE FIRE Control, Inc., truck at a discreet distance. Caleb was driving, Stone next to him and Reuben in the rear.

"Why don't we just call the police and let them handle it?" Caleb complained.

"And tell them what?" Stone said. "You said the library is having the old system scrapped. For all we know, that's all those men are doing. And it might alert the wrong people that we're on to something. We need stealth here, not the cops."

Caleb snapped, "Terrific! So I have to go in harm's way instead of the police? What the hell I pay taxes for I'm sure I don't know."

The truck turned left and then hung a right. They had passed through the Capitol Hill area and entered a run-down part of town.

"Slow down," Stone said. "The truck's stopping."

Caleb eased the car to the curb. The truck had halted at a chain-link gate that another man inside the complex was now opening.

"It's the storage facility," Stone said.

The truck pulled through, and the gate was locked behind it.

"Well, that's all we can do here," Caleb said in a relieved tone. "My God, do I need a decaf cappuccino after this nightmare of an evening."

Stone said, "We need to get inside the fence."

"Right," Reuben agreed.

"Are you both insane!" Caleb cried out.

"You can wait in the car, Caleb," Stone said. "But I have to check out what's going on in there."

"But if you get caught?"

"Then we get caught. I think it's worth it," Stone replied.

"And I can stay in the car?" Caleb said slowly. "But that doesn't seem fair if you two are risking—"

Stone cut him off. "If we need to get away quickly, it's better to have you in the car, ready to roll."

"Absolutely, Caleb," Reuben agreed.

"Well, if you say so." Caleb tightened his grip on the wheel and got a determined look. "I have been known to lay down rubber on occasion."

Stone and Reuben slipped out of the car and made their way toward the fence. Hiding behind a stack of old boards outside the storage complex, they watched as the truck parked in a corner of the lot. The men climbed off the truck and walked into the main building. A few minutes later the men, wearing their street clothes, drove off in their own cars. A security guard locked the gate behind them and went back into the main building.

"Our best bet is probably to scale the fence on the other side where the truck's parked," Reuben said. "That way the truck is between us and the building in case the guard comes back out."

"Good plan," Stone said.

They hustled around to the other side of the fence. Before they started climbing, Stone tossed a stick at the fence. "Wanted to make sure it wasn't electrified."

"Right."

They slowly scaled the fence and quietly dropped down on the other side, squatted low and started making their way toward the truck. Halfway there, Stone stopped and motioned for Reuben to drop to his belly. They scanned the area but saw no one. They waited another minute and started moving again. Stone suddenly veered away from the truck toward a small concrete-block building near the rear of the fence. Reuben hurried after him.

The door had a lock, but one of Stone's keys fit it.

Inside, the place was filled with large cylinders. Stone took out a small flashlight he'd brought with him and shone it around. There was a workbench littered with tools, and a small paint machine in one corner next to some cans of paints and solvent. Hanging on one wall was a portable oxygen tank and mask. Stone flicked his light on some of the cylinders and read off, "FM-200. INERGEN. Halon 1301, CO_2, FE-25." He stopped and came back to the CO_2 cylinder, studying the markings closely.

Reuben nudged him. "Look," he said, pointing at a sign on the wall.

"Fire Control, Inc. We know that," Stone said impatiently.

"Read the name below that."

Stone sucked in a breath. "Fire Control is a subsidiary of Paradigm, Technologies, Inc."

"Cornelius Behan's company," Reuben muttered.

Caleb sat fidgeting in the Nova, his gaze on the fenced area. "Come on," he said. "What's taking so long?"

He suddenly plopped down sideways in his seat. A car passed by him on its way to the storage facility. After it had gone past, he sat back up and his heart nearly skipped a beat. It was a private security cruiser; in the backseat was a large German shepherd.

Caleb pulled out his cell phone to call Stone, but the battery was dead. He was forever forgetting to charge the damn thing because he didn't like talking on it in the first place.

"Dear God!" Caleb groaned. He took a deep breath. "You can do this, Caleb Shaw. You can *do* this." He let out a deep breath, focused and then quoted dramatically from one of his favorite poems to pluck up his courage. "Half a league, half a league, / Half a league onward, / All in the valley of Death / Rode the six hundred. / 'Forward, the Light Brigade! / Charge for the guns!' he said: / Into the valley of Death / Rode the six hundred." He paused and looked up ahead where the real-life drama was unfolding with attack dogs and armed men, and his backbone began to bend ominously. The rest of his courage faded as he reflected on the fact that the damn Light Brigade had been wiped out.

He snapped, "Tennyson didn't know shit about real danger!"

Caleb climbed out of the car and made his way hesitantly toward the fence.

Back outside, Stone and Reuben headed toward the truck.

Stone said, "Keep a lookout while I check." He scampered up in the bed of the truck; it had an open back, with wooden slats all around to keep the cargo in. He used his light to see the painted labels on the cylinders. All but one read "Halon 1301." The other's label read "FM-200." Stone pulled from his jacket pocket a small can of turpentine and a rag that he'd taken from the storage building, and started applying turpentine over the cylinder with the label FM-200.

"Come on, come on," Reuben said, his gaze darting in all directions.

As the coat of paint started to dissolve, Stone stopped rubbing and shone his light on the label that had been painted over. He rubbed some more until it was finally revealed. "CO_2," he read. "Five thousand ppm."

"Oh, hell!" Reuben hissed. "Run for it, Oliver."

Stone looked over the side of the truck. The canine was just stepping out of the security cruiser near the front gate.

Stone jumped down, and keeping the truck between them and the cruiser, they hustled toward the fence. However, the truck could not hide their *scent* from the dog. Stone and Reuben heard it howl, and then they could hear the four legs headed their way, followed by the two guards.

Stone and Reuben sprang onto the fence and started climbing. The dog reached them and sank its teeth into Reuben's pant leg.

Outside the gate, Caleb watched helplessly from a hiding place, uncertain of what to do but trying to screw up his courage to attempt some action.

"Hold it right there," a voice called out. Reuben was trying to kick his leg free, but the dog was holding on tight. Stone looked down and saw the two guards, their guns pointed at them.

"Come down from there, or the dog'll take your leg off," a guard snapped. "Now!"

Stone and Reuben slowly climbed down. The same guard called off the dog. It retreated a bit, its teeth still bared.

"I think this is all a simple misunderstanding," Stone began.

"Right, tell it to the cops," the other guard snarled.

"We'll take over from here, boys," a woman's voice called out.

They all looked over. Standing outside the gate beside her black sedan was Annabelle. Milton stood next to her, wearing a blue windbreaker and a ball cap with "FBI" stenciled on it.

"Who the hell are you?" one of the guards said.

"FBI Agents McCallister and Dupree." She held up her creds and opened her jacket so they could see her badge and also the gun on her belt holster. "Open the gate and keep the damn doggie off us," she snapped.

"What the hell is the FBI doing around here?" the same guard said nervously as he ran over to the gate and unlocked it.

Annabelle and Milton stepped through. She said to Milton, "Read 'em their rights and cuff 'em." Milton took out two pairs of handcuffs and headed over to Stone and Reuben.

"Wait a minute," the other guard said. "We catch anybody trespassing, our orders are to call the police."

Annabelle got in the plump young man's face, looking him up and down. "How long have you been in, uh, security, kid?"

"Thirteen months. I'm weapons-certified," he said defiantly.

"Sure you are. But put your damn gun away before you accidentally shoot somebody, like *me*." He reluctantly holstered his weapon as Annabelle held up her creds again. "This trumps the local cops every time, okay?" The realistic-looking credentials, which were part of a packet she'd had Freddy make for her just in case, were what Annabelle kept in her tampon box.

The guard swallowed nervously. "But we got procedures." He pointed at Stone and Reuben, whom Milton was handcuffing. On the back of Milton's windbreaker was also stenciled "FBI." They'd gotten that at the novelty shop along with their fake guns, badges and handcuffs. "And they were trespassing."

Annabelle laughed. "Trespassing!" She put her hands on her hips. "Do you even know who you've got here? Do you?"

The guards glanced at each other. "Two old bums?" one of them answered.

"Hey, you little son of a bitch," a handcuffed Reuben roared in mock fury, and jumped forward. Milton instantly drew his pistol and placed it against the side of Reuben's head, shouting, "Shut the hell up, lard-ass, before I blow your damn head off."

Reuben immediately froze.

Annabelle said, "The big 'pleasant' guy over there is Randall Weathers, wanted on four counts of drug dealing, money laundering, two charges of murder in the first and the bombing of a federal judge's home in Georgia. The other guy is Paul Mason, aka Peter Dawson, among sixteen other phony names. This asshole's got a direct line to a Middle East terrorist cell operating in the shadow of the Capitol. We've been running a wiretap on his cell phone and e-mail. We picked up his trail tonight and followed it right here. Looks like they were doing a recon to steal some explosive gas. We think they were targeting the Supreme Court this time. Park a truck of that stuff in front with a timer and watch all nine justices get blown right to hell." She looked over at Stone and Reuben in disgust. "You guys are going down all the way this time. *All* the way," she added ominously.

"Damn, Earl," one of the guards said excitedly to his partner. "Terrorists!"

Annabelle took out a notebook. "Let me get your names. The Bureau will want to know who to give commendations to for helping with the bust." She smiled. "And I think I see big raises in both your futures."

The two guards looked at each other, grinning. "Hot damn," the one named Earl exclaimed. They gave her their names and then she turned to Milton. "Get 'em in the cruiser, Dupree. The sooner these slimeballs are at WFO, the better." She turned back to the guards. "We'll bring the locals in, but only after we've done a little 'interrogation' of these boys, FBI-style." She winked at the guards. "But you didn't hear that from me."

They both grinned knowingly at her. "Kick the crap out of 'em both," Earl said.

She said, "Roger that. We'll be in touch."

They put Stone and Reuben in the backseat of the sedan and drove off.

Caleb waited until the guards were out of sight, then raced back to the Nova and followed Annabelle's car.

Inside the sedan, Milton took the handcuffs off Stone and Reuben.

"Milton, you were talking some serious trash back there," Reuben said proudly.

Milton beamed. He took his ball cap off, and his long hair streamed down.

Stone said to Annabelle, "When you do backup, you *really* do backup. Thanks."

"In for a dime, in for a dollar," she said. "Where to now?"

"My place," Stone answered. "We have a lot to talk about."

CHAPTER

38

ROGER SEAGRAVES DROVE HIS rental car slowly through the quiet streets of the affluent D.C. neighborhood, turning left onto Good Fellow Street. At this hour most of the large homes were dark. As he passed the late Jonathan DeHaven's house, he seemed not to even glance over. *Another thunderstorm had come his way. He was getting a little tired of the weather pattern. But it really was the perfect setup; he couldn't let it pass.* He kept driving slowly, as though he were just on a leisurely tour admiring the old mansions. Next he drove around the block and made his way down the parallel street, carefully noting the lay of the land.

Observing it and coming up with a plan, however, were two very different things. He needed time to think. One observation had caught his eye: the house across the street from Behan's. A person with a pair of binoculars was in there watching. Watching what? Regardless, he would have to take that into account when preparing his attack. And when eyes were watching, there was only one way to kill and then get away.

After he had finished his reconnoiter, Seagraves parked his rental car at a hotel. Gripping a briefcase, he walked into the bar, had a drink and then took the elevator up as though going to his room. He waited an hour and then took the stairs down. Exiting the building through another door, Seagraves slid into another car he had waiting in an adjacent parking lot. He had something else to do tonight besides contemplating another murder.

He drove to a motel, drawing a key out of his pocket as he exited his car. With ten quick strides he was at the door of a room on the second level overlooking the parking lot. He opened the door but did not turn on the light. He walked quickly to the door connecting to the next room, unlocked it and went through. As he stepped into the second room, Seagraves could sense the other person's presence but said nothing. He took off his clothes and climbed into bed with her. She was soft, curvy, warm and, most important of all for his purposes, a shift supervisor at NSA.

An hour later, each of them satisfied, he dressed and smoked a cigarette while she showered. He knew that she had taken the same steps he had to avoid being followed, and the NSA had so many employees it simply couldn't keep track of them all. And she'd never given anyone any reason to show interest in her, which was why he'd recruited her for his operation. And they were both single, so even if the rendezvous were discovered, it would be put down to simple sex between two consenting adults who happened to be federal employees, which, as yet, was not illegal in America.

The water in the shower stopped. He knocked on the bathroom door and opened it. He helped her out of the shower, gave her naked ass a squeeze and dropped another kiss on her.

"I love you," she said, nuzzling his ear.

"You mean you love the money," he answered back.

"That too," she cooed, dropping her hand to his crotch and pressing against him.

"One a night," he said. "I'm not eighteen anymore."

She gripped his muscular shoulders. "Could've fooled me, baby."

"Next time," he said, slapping her butt hard and leaving a red mark.

"Be rough again," she said, breathing in his ear. "Make me hurt."

"I don't know any other way."

She pushed him against the wall, her damp breasts wetting his shirt, and ripped at his hair as she tried to stick her tongue all the way down his throat. "God, you are so damn sexy," she moaned.

"That's what they tell me."

He tried to pull away but she wouldn't let go. "The money wire goes out on schedule?" she asked in between jabs of her tongue.

"As soon as I get my cash, you get yours, sweetie." And she cooed again, and this time let him free after he'd given her butt another hard slap, leaving a mark on the other cheek.

Yes, stupid, it really was all about the money.

While she finished in the bathroom, he walked back into the other room, flicked on a light, grabbed her purse off the night-stand and slid the digital camera out of one of the inner pockets. He thumbed the twenty-gig hard drive out of the slot and used his fingernail to scrape off a small black veneer from the back of the inch-long drive. He stared at the miniature object for a few seconds. Tiny in size, it represented at least $10 million, maybe more, to an eager buyer in the Middle East who did not like America knowing his plans of death and destruction for those who opposed him.

The information on this black gem would balance out the fight, at least for a little while, until NSA figured out that their new surveillance program had been compromised. Then they'd change it, Seagraves would get another call and he, in turn, would make a call. Then a few days later he'd go to another motel, screw the lady again, peel off another veneer and make another eight figures. Repeat business was his staple. They'd continue to do it until NSA started to realize that the mole was somewhere close. Then Seagraves would shut the operation down at NSA, for a while anyway, since bureaucrats tended to have short memories. In the meantime he'd just go after another target. And there were so many.

He used a bit of gum to stick the piece of veneer containing digital details of NSA's surveillance program behind one of his front teeth. Then he went to the first motel room he'd entered, where another change of clothes hung in the closet. He showered, changed and left, walking along the street for a few blocks, then grabbed a bus, rode it to a rental car shop, slid into another leased ride and drove home.

He spent an hour digging the information out of the tiny device and another hour putting it in proper form for passing on. As a spy Seagraves had long been an enthusiastic student of secret codes and the history of cryptology in general. Nowadays computers encrypted and decrypted messages automatically. The most secure systems used keys consisting of hundreds or even thousands of digits—far longer than the actual messages being encrypted. At the very least, breaking the strongest of these keys required enormous computing power and thousands if not millions of years. This was so because modern-day cryptologists assumed that the coded messages would be intercepted and thus had engineered their encryption systems for that eventuality. Their mantra could be: You can intercept it, but you almost certainly can't read it.

Seagraves had opted for a more vintage method of encryption, one that, because of the way the messages were communicated, might be even more unbreakable than the modern-day, computer-generated juggernauts for one simple reason: If you couldn't intercept the message, you had zero chance of reading it. There was something to be said, he mused, for the old ways. Even the NSA, with all its technological might, could learn a lesson from that.

After he had finished that task, he fell into bed.

Instead of sleeping, though, all he could think about was his next kill. That would enhance his precious "collection" by one.

Back at his cottage, Stone quickly brought the others up to date on what they'd found. When he'd mentioned the hidden lettering on the cylinder reading "CO_2, 5,000 ppm," Milton had immediately gotten on his laptop where he'd stored pertinent downloaded files from the Internet. After Stone had finished speaking, Milton said, "CO_2 is almost never used in occupied spaces because it can suffocate people as it instantly takes oxygen content out of the air to extinguish fires. At five thousand parts per million it would be rapidly fatal for someone standing nearby; he'd be overcome before he could escape. And it's not a pleasant way to die."

Annabelle made a coughing noise, stood and went over to look out the window.

"And I presume it has a cooling effect," Stone said hastily, eyeing her with concern.

Milton nodded as he scanned his screen. "With high-pressure systems there's a discharge of dry ice particles. They call it a snow effect because it rapidly absorbs heat, reduces ambient temp and helps prevent flash and reignition of the fire. The snow turns to vapor under normal temperatures and leaves no residue."

Stone added, "By the time Caleb and DeHaven were found in

the vault, the O_2 levels had probably returned to almost normal, and any lingering chill would be put down to the extraordinary levels of cooling in the vaults."

"But if DeHaven were killed by CO_2 suffocation, wouldn't that have turned up in the autopsy?" Reuben asked.

While they'd been talking, Milton's hands had been flying over his keyboard. "Not necessarily. This is information I downloaded earlier from a site sponsored by a national medical examiners' organization. While carbon *monoxide* poisoning can be detected postmortem by the cherry-red appearance of the skin, carbon *dioxide* exposure doesn't leave such clear-cut signs." Reading from the screen, Milton said, "The only way to detect low levels of oxygen in a person is through a blood gas test which measures the ratio of oxygen to carbon dioxide in a person's blood. But that test is only done on the *living* to see if oxygen levels need to be increased. It's never done postmortem for the simple fact that the person's dead."

Caleb added, "From what I was told afterward Jonathan was pronounced dead in the vault. He wasn't even taken to the emergency room."

Stone said, "The cylinder they removed with the label FM-200 was the one I focused on, for obvious reasons."

"I'm not getting what you mean," Reuben replied.

"The library's scrapping the halon system. If I'm right and they brought in a cylinder full of deadly CO_2 with the wrong label to disguise it, they wouldn't have been bringing halon *back* to the library; that would have raised suspicion."

"Right, they'd have to bring in the gas they were replacing the halon with. FM-200," Caleb added. "And they took it out tonight with a bunch of halon cylinders. If we hadn't been there, no one would've noticed."

Stone nodded. "And I'm certain that the cylinder connected

to the piping tonight was full of halon. The empty cylinder that had contained the CO_2 was probably disconnected from the piping right after it was discharged. Then if the police happened to check, they'd find nothing out of the ordinary. They wouldn't check every cylinder in the place, certainly. And even if they did check, they'd have to send it to Fire Control, Inc., for that purpose. I doubt they'd get an accurate answer back because whoever orchestrated this is obviously employed by the company."

"The perfect murder," Annabelle said grimly as she sat back down. "The question is why. Why would anyone want to kill Jonathan that badly?"

"That takes us back to Cornelius Behan," Stone said. "Now we know that the lethal CO_2 cylinder that killed DeHaven was switched for the halon. We also know that Fire Control is owned by Behan. The man obviously had DeHaven killed. Behan showed up at the reading room to see Caleb on the very same day the cylinders were removed from the library. I'm sure he was trying to determine if there was any interest in the nozzle And there must be some connection between Behan and Bob Bradley."

Reuben ventured, "Maybe Bradley and Behan were part of the spy ring we think is operating here. Bradley comes to visit Behan at his home, and Jonathan saw or heard something he wasn't supposed to. Or he might have seen something that tied Behan to Bradley's murder. Behan found out about it and had him killed before DeHaven could tell anybody and lead the investigation to him."

Stone said, "It's possible. We have a lot of ground to cover, so we need to split up. Caleb, you go into the vault first thing tomorrow and check behind that air-conditioning grille for evidence of a camera having been placed there. Next examine the video surveillance tapes for people going in the vault."

"What?" Caleb exclaimed. "Why?"

"You yourself said that whoever killed Jonathan would have to have access to both the library and the vault. I want to know who went in that vault a few days before DeHaven's death and then after he was murdered."

"I can't just walk into security and demand to see the tapes. What possible reason would I give?"

"I'll help you think of one, Caleb," Annabelle said.

"Oh, great," Reuben said under his breath. "First Milton gets to play with the lady and now Caleb. But *moi*? Nooo."

Stone continued, "Reuben, I want you to make an anonymous call to the D.C. police and tip them off about the CO_2 cylinder. Use a pay phone so they can't trace the call. I don't know if they'll take it seriously or not. And by the time they get there, it'll probably be too late, but we have to try."

Caleb said, "But won't that let certain people know that we're on to them?"

"Maybe it will," Stone said. "But right now that's the only evidence we have that DeHaven was murdered. After you do that, Reuben, I want you to take up surveillance on Good Fellow Street starting tonight."

"It's not the greatest place to spy on people, Oliver. Where do I post myself?"

"Caleb can give you the key and pass code to get into DeHaven's house. You can slip in through the back without anyone seeing you."

Milton asked, "What do you want me to do?"

"Your task is to find out as much as possible about any connection between the late Bob Bradley and Cornelius Behan. Nothing is too small to overlook."

Annabelle said, "And what are you going to do, Oliver?"

"I'm going to think."

As the others were leaving, Annabelle drew Caleb aside. "How much do you trust your buddy, Oliver?"

Caleb blanched. "I'd trust him with my life. In fact, I *have* trusted him with my life."

"I'll admit he seems to know what he's doing."

"He most assuredly does," Caleb said loyally. "Now, you said you were going to help me get that video material. How?"

"You'll be the first to know when I think of it."

CHAPTER

39

AT TEN-FIFTEEN IN THE MORN-
ing EST the state of New Jersey suffered its first earthquake in
recent memory. The epicenter was Atlantic City, right where the
Pompeii Casino rose from the Boardwalk. Jerry Bagger had
erupted slowly at first. Warning gases and rising rock temperature started off when his $48 million didn't appear at ten o'clock
sharp. At ten past the hour, when he was told there was some
confusion about the whereabouts of the money, even his muscle-
men started to retreat a bit from his presence. Five minutes later
the casino king was told by his money guy, after contacting El
Banco, that not only was the $8 million in interest not coming
his way, but neither was his original $40 mil, since the bank had
never received it.

The first thing Bagger did was to try and kill the messenger.
His rage uncontrollable, he most certainly would've beaten the
moneyman to death if his security people hadn't pulled him off,
pleading that the murder would be hard to cover up. Bagger
next got on the phone and threatened to jump on a plane and fly
down to El Banco and rip their hearts out one by one. The bank
president challenged him to come, secure in the fact, he told

Bagger, that he had an entire army guarding the premises complete with tanks and artillery.

They *did* send him an accounting that showed the first three money transfers *had* been received. And that funds from another account had been ordered transferred into Bagger's deposit equaling a 10 percent return over two days. Then the amounts had been returned to Bagger each of the three times. The fourth wire had never reached them. When the electronic receipt Bagger's wire department had gotten back was more closely examined, it turned out not to have the bank's complete authorization coding, although it would have taken very close scrutiny to find the subtle discrepancy.

On hearing that, Bagger attacked the unfortunate head of his wiring department with one of the man's own office chairs. It was revealed two hours later, after an intense evaluation, that very sophisticated spyware had been placed on the Pompeii's computer system enabling the casino's money wires to be controlled by a third party. With that revelation Bagger demanded a sterilized pistol and ordered the head of his IT department to report to his office. However, the doomed man was smart enough to make a run for it instead. Bagger's men caught up with him in Trenton. After an interrogation that would have made the CIA proud, it was clear the man was not part of the scam, but had been duped. The only thing this earned him from Bagger was a bullet to the brain delivered by the casino king himself. Later that night the body went into a landfill. And still, with all that murderous energy released, the quake continued to rumble unabated.

"I will kill that bitch, do you hear me!" Bagger was at the windows of his office screaming this over and over to the people far below on the Boardwalk. He hustled back to his desk and took out her card. Pamela Young, International Management, Inc. He ripped the card to shreds and looked wild-eyed at his head of security. "I wanna kill somebody. I need to kill somebody right now, damn it."

"Boss, please, we gotta keep a handle on this. The money guy's in the hospital along with the wire punk. And you whacked the IT geek yourself. That's a lot for one day. The lawyers say it's gonna be hard keeping the police out of it as it is."

"I'm going to find her," Bagger said, looking back out the window. "I'm going to find her. And I'm gonna kill her slow."

"From your lips to God's ear, boss," the muscle said encouragingly.

"Forty million dollars of my money. Forty million!" Bagger said this in such a deranged tone that the burly security chief backed toward the door.

"We'll get her, I swear, boss."

Bagger finally seemed to calm a bit. "I want everything you can dig up on the bitch and the jerk-off with her. Pull all the tapes off the cameras and take it around and get an ID. She's not some walk-off-the-street con. And get some of the cops we have on the payroll to go over her room with the fingerprint crap. Call in every marker I have."

"You got it." The man started to hustle out.

"Wait!" Bagger said. The man turned hesitantly back. "Nobody knows that I got scammed, you got that? Jerry Bagger is nobody's mark. You *got* that?"

"Loud and clear, boss. Loud and clear."

"Well, get on it!"

The man fled the room.

Bagger sat down at his desk and looked at the tiny shreds of Annabelle's business card lying on the carpet. *She's going to look just like that,* he thought. *After I finish with her.*

CHAPTER

40

"You're looking unusually happy this morning, Albert," Seagraves said as they sat sipping coffee from Styrofoam cups in Trent's office on the Hill.

"Stock market had a big rally yesterday; my 401(k)'s looking good."

Seagraves slid a sheaf of papers across the table. "Good for you. Here's the latest from Central Intelligence. We have two senior levels that'll give the formal briefings. Your guys can take a week to digest the report, and then we'll schedule the face-to-face."

Trent took the pages and nodded. "I'll check the members' schedule and get back to you with some dates. Any surprises in here?" he added, tapping the pages.

"Read 'em for yourself."

"Not to worry, I always do."

Trent would take the pages home and shortly thereafter would have everything he needed to pass the stolen NSA secrets on to the next stage.

Outside, Seagraves jogged down the steps of the Capitol. And to think, spies used to just drop stuff in the park and pick up their money in cash either at the drop spot or from a P.O. box.

And either place was usually where the arrest took place. Sea-graves shook his head. *No way was he ever ending up on the wall at CIA with the likes of Aldrich Ames and other busted stooges playing at being spies.* As a government killer he'd ago-nized over even the smallest detail. As a spy he saw no reason to change his M.O.

Seagraves was obsessing over a detail right now. His mole at Fire Control, Inc., had called with some unwelcome informa-tion. Two guys had been caught sneaking into the storage facil-ity last night, but the rental cops had had to turn them over to the FBI. Seagraves had checked with some of his contacts at the Bureau. According to them, no such arrest had ever happened. His mole had also told him that the rental cops had spotted an-other guy running away from Fire Control's storage yard. He'd gotten into an old piece of junk, a Nova, his guy had told him. The description of both the car and the man fit someone well known to Seagraves, though he'd never met him. Now, he de-cided, would be a good time to remedy that situation. And in Seagraves' world of sweating the details, you just never knew when a face-to-face might come in really handy later on.

Caleb arrived at work early to find Kevin Philips, the acting di-rector, opening the doors to the reading room. They chitchatted a bit about Jonathan and ongoing projects at the library. Caleb asked Philips if he'd known about the new fire suppressant sys-tem going in, but Philips said he hadn't. "I'm not sure they even kept Jonathan apprised of that information," Philips told him. "I doubt he knew what gas was being used."

"You can say that again," Caleb whispered under his breath.

After Philips had left and before anyone else arrived, Caleb rummaged in his desk and withdrew a small screwdriver and a penlight. With his back to the surveillance camera he slipped these into his pocket and went inside the vault. Quickly making his way to the top floor, he stopped next to the air vent, his gaze averted from the spot where his friend had died. He used the screwdriver to open the vent, noting with satisfaction that the screws came out very easily, as though someone had removed the covering recently. He set the vent down next to the shelf column and shone his light inside the opening. At first he didn't see anything unusual, but when he swung his light around a third time, he saw it: a small screw hole in the rear wall of the duct. That could have been used to suspend a camera. He held the vent cover back up and eyeballed it. Judging from the position of the screw and the bent grille, the camera would've had a clear field of vision of the room.

Caleb screwed the vent cover back on and left the vault. He called Stone and reported what he'd found. He was just settling down to work when someone came in.

"Hello, Monty. What've you got there?"

Monty Chambers, the library's top book conservator, was standing by the front desk, carrying several items. He still had on his green work apron, and his shirtsleeves were rolled up.

"The *Doctrina* and the *Constable's Pocket-Book,*" he said succinctly.

"You've been busy. I didn't even know the *Doctrina* was out for preservation work." The *Doctrina breve* had been written by Juan de Zumárraga, the first bishop of Mexico. It dated from 1544 and had the distinction of being the oldest complete book in the Western Hemisphere that has survived the centuries. The *Constable* dated from 1710.

"Kevin Philips ordered it," Chambers replied. "Three months back. The *Constable* too. Minor stuff, I just had a backlog. You in the vault? Or me?"

"What? Oh, I'll take them. Thanks." Caleb carefully accepted the wrapped books from his colleague and set them on his desk. He tried not to think about the fact that between the *Doctrina* and the *Constable* he was in possession of a small fortune's worth of history.

"I'll get to your Faulkner soon," Chambers muttered. "Might take some time. Water damage, tricky."

"Right, that's perfectly fine. Thank you." As Chambers turned to leave, Caleb said, "Uh, Monty."

Chambers turned back around, looking a little impatient. "Yeah?"

"Have you checked our copy of the *Psalm Book* recently?" Caleb had had a horrible thought while in the vault, and taking the rare books from Chambers had forced this nightmarish theory to take the form of an awkward question.

Chambers looked suspicious. "The *Psalm Book*? What for? Anything wrong?"

"Oh, no, no. I just mean, well, I haven't seen it in some time. Years, in fact."

"Well, neither have I. You don't just walk in and check out the *Psalm Book*. It's in the national treasures section, for God's sake."

Caleb nodded. He had authority to look at virtually any book in the vaults, but the *Psalm Book* and some others were designated as "national treasures," the library's most important category of possessions. These works were numbered and housed in a special section of the vaults. In the event of war or natural catastrophe they would be whisked away to designated secure locations. Hopefully, there would be people left to enjoy them.

Chambers continued, with uncharacteristic loquaciousness, "I told them a long time ago we should repair the cover and redo the support stitches and reinforce the spine—all reversible, of course—but they never acted on it. Don't know why not. But if they don't do something, the *Psalm Book* won't hold up much longer. Why don't you tell them that?"

"I will. Thanks, Monty." After Chambers had left, Caleb wondered what to do. If the library's copy of the *Psalm Book* was missing? My God, it couldn't be. He hadn't seen the book in, what was it, three years at least. It certainly resembled the one he had found in Jonathan's collection. Six of the eleven existing *Psalm Books* were incomplete and in various stages of disrepair. Jonathan's edition had been complete, though in a run-down condition, similar to the library's. The only way to tell for sure was to take a look at the *Psalm Book* the library had. Kevin Philips would probably allow him to do that. He'd make up some excuse, maybe relaying what Monty had just told him. Yes, that would do it.

He put the books Chambers had brought him back in the vaults after signing them back in on the system. Then he called Philips. Though sounding a bit puzzled, Philips authorized Caleb to check the *Psalm Book*. For security purposes, and to preclude anyone from later accusing him of damaging the book, Caleb brought another library staffer with him. After examining the book he could confirm that what Chambers had said was true, the book did need preservation work. However, he could not tell if it was the book he'd remembered seeing three years ago. It looked like it. But then it also looked like the one in Jonathan's collection. If Jonathan had somehow taken the library's *Psalm Book* and substituted a forgery, the book Caleb had looked at three years ago wouldn't have been the real one anyway.

Wait a minute. How stupid. The library used a secret coding in its rare books on the exact same page to verify their owner-ship. He turned to that certain page and scanned down it. The symbol was there! He breathed a sigh of relief that was short-lived. It could've been forged too; particularly by someone like Jonathan. And did the *Psalm Book* in Jonathan's collection have such a symbol as well? He would have to check. If it did, it would prove that Jonathan had stolen it from the library. Then what did Caleb do? He cursed the day he'd been appointed the man's literary executor. *I thought you liked me, Jonathan.*

He spent the rest of the afternoon working on several scholars' requests, a major collector's inquiry, handling a pair of international phone calls from universities in England and Switzerland and helping patrons of the reading room.

Jewell English and Norman Janklow were both there today. Though of the same age and both avid book collectors, they never spoke to each other; indeed, they avoided one another entirely. Caleb knew how the feud had started; it was one of the most painful moments of his professional life. English had expressed her enthusiasm about Beadle's *Dime Novels* to Janklow one day. The old man's response had been a little unexpected, to say the least. Caleb clearly recalled Janklow's words. "Beadles are idiotic rubbish, candy wrappers for the bottom-feeding mindless masses, and poor candy wrappers at that."

Understandably, Jewell English had not taken this crushing rebuke to her life's passion very well. And the old woman was not about to take it lying down. Well aware of Janklow's favorite author, she'd told the old boy that Hemingway was *at best* a second-rate bum of a writer who used simplistic language because that's all he knew. And the fact that he'd won a Nobel Prize for churning out that *crap* invalidated forever more the award in her mind. To add insult to injury, she also said that Hemingway wasn't worthy to lick F. Scott Fitzgerald's patent-leather shoes, and—Caleb cringed when he recalled it—she'd intimated that manly hunter and fisherman Ernest Hemingway preferred men over the ladies, the younger the better.

Janklow's face had turned so red that Caleb had been certain the old man was going to keel over from a coronary. That was the first and only time that Caleb could ever remember having to separate two patrons of the Rare Books reading room, both of them well into their seventies. It really very nearly had come to blows, and Caleb had snatched up the rare books each had at their tables to prevent them from being used as weapons. He'd admonished them both about proper library etiquette and even threatened to suspend their reading room privileges if they didn't back the hell off. Janklow looked like he wanted to take a swing at Caleb, but he'd held firm. He could've taken the old shriveled man, easy.

Caleb kept looking up from his work to ensure that nothing like that altercation happened again. But Janklow was happily going through his book, his big pencil strolling lazily over the notepaper, only stopping on occasion while he cleaned his thick glasses with a wipe. For her part Jewell English's face was glued to her book. She looked up, saw him eyeing her, closed her book and motioned him over.

As he sat down next to her, she whispered, "That Beadle I was telling you about?"

"Yes, the number one?"

"I got it. I got it." She clapped her hands silently.

"Congratulations, that's wonderful. So it was in good condition?"

"Oh, yes, otherwise I would've called you in. I mean, you *are* an expert."

"Well," Caleb said modestly. She took hold of his hand in her gnarled one. The strength of her grip was surprising.

"Would you like to come and see it sometime?"

He tried to delicately extricate himself from her clawlike hand, but she wouldn't budge. "Oh, um, I'll have to check my calendar. I tell you what, next time you're in, give me some dates and I'll see what I have available."

She said coquettishly, "Oh, Caleb, I'm *always* available." She actually batted her false lashes at him.

"Isn't that nice?" He again tried to wrench his hand free, but the elderly woman held firm.

"So let's pick a date right now," she said sweetly.

In desperation Caleb glanced over at Janklow, who was eyeing them suspiciously. He and Jewell typically fought over Caleb's time like two wolves over a side of beef. He would have to spend a few minutes with Janklow before he left, to balance things out, or the man would complain about it for weeks. And yet as Caleb stared at the old gentleman, he had a sudden thought.

"Jewell, I bet if you asked him to, Norman would love to see your new Beadle. I'm sure he regrets his previous outburst terribly."

She immediately released his hand. "I don't talk shop with Neanderthals," she said testily. She opened her bag for him to inspect and then stalked out of the room.

A smiling Caleb rubbed his hand and spent some time with Janklow, silently thanking the man for giving him the ability to ditch English. Then he returned to his work.

Yet his mind continued to jump from the mysterious *Psalm Book* to the dead Jonathan DeHaven to the equally dead Speaker of the House, Bob Bradley, and finally to Cornelius Behan, a rich, adulterous defense contractor who'd apparently murdered his neighbor.

And to think he became a librarian partly because he hated pressure. Maybe he should apply for a job at the CIA, just to catch a little downtime.

CHAPTER

41

ANNABELLE HAD A ROOM service dinner, showered, wrapped herself in a towel and started combing out her hair. As she sat in front of the vanity mirror, she started mulling things over. The fourth day had arrived, and Jerry Bagger was now aware that he was $40 million poorer. She should've been at least six thousand miles away from the man, but in fact was barely a short plane hop south. She had never failed to follow the exit plan before, but then again, she'd never had an ex-husband murdered before either.

She was intrigued by Oliver and Milton, though Caleb was a little "special" and Reuben was more than a little amusing with his puppy-dog crush. And Annabelle had to admit she kind of liked hanging around with the odd bunch. Despite having a loner personality, Annabelle had always been part of a team, and a side of her still needed that. It had started with her parents and had continued into adulthood when she began running her own crews. Oliver and the others were filling this need in her life, albeit in a different way. But she still shouldn't be here.

She stopped combing her hair, slipped off the towel and pulled a long T-shirt on. She crossed to the window and looked out at the busy street below. In the swirl of traffic and fast-walking pedestrians, she mentally retraced what she'd done so far: Impersonated a magazine editor, knowingly aided Oliver in breaking into the Library of Congress, committed a felony by impersonating an FBI agent, and she was now supposed to come up with a way for Caleb to look at the security tapes to try and figure out what had happened to Jonathan. And if Oliver was right, some people who might be even more dangerous than Jerry Bagger could be aligned against them.

She turned back from the window, sat on the bed and started putting lotion on her legs. "This is crazy, Annabelle," she told herself. "Bagger will move the ends of the earth to kill you, and here you are, not even out of the damn country." And yet she had promised the others to help them. Actually, she reminded herself, she'd insisted on being part of it. "Should I stick it out and take a chance that Jerry's radar doesn't hit D.C.?" she said out loud. Someone had killed Jonathan. And she wanted revenge if for no other reason than she was furious that someone had made the decision to end his life long before it should have been over.

She had a sudden thought and checked her watch. She had no idea what time zone he was in, but she needed to know. She ran to the desk against one corner and snatched up her cell phone. She punched in the numbers and waited impatiently while it rang. She'd given him this number and an international phone so they could keep in contact for a while after the con. If one heard anything about Jerry, he or she was supposed to call the other.

Leo finally answered. "Hey."

"Hey yourself. I didn't think you were going to pick up."

"I was in the pool."

"In the pool, nice. Where in the pool?"

"The deep end."

"No, I meant where in the world?"

"No can answer. What if Bagger's standing right there?"

"I see your point. Heard from anybody else?"

"Not a peep."

"How about Bagger?"

"No, I took old Jerry off my Rolodex," he said dryly.

"I meant, have you heard any of the fallout?"

"Just some scuttlebutt. Didn't want to get too close, you know. You can bet the dude's homicidal."

"You know he'll never stop looking for us as long as he's breathing."

"Then let's pray for a massive heart attack. I don't want the guy to suffer." Leo paused and said, "Something I should've told you before, Annabelle. Now, don't get pissed."

She sat up straighter. "What did you do?"

"I sort of let it slip to Freddy a little about your history."

She stood. "How much of my history?"

"Your last name, your stuff with Paddy."

She screamed into the phone, "Are you out of your damn mind?"

"I know, I know, it was stupid. It just came up. I just wanted him to know that you weren't like your old man. But I didn't tell Tony. I'm not that dumb."

"Thanks, Leo, thanks a hell of a lot."

She clicked off and stood in the middle of the room. Freddy knew her last name and also that her father was Paddy Conroy, Jerry Bagger's mortal enemy. If Jerry got to him, he'd make Freddy talk. And then the man would come for her, and she could predict her fate with reasonable accuracy. Jerry would feed her into a wood chipper body part by body part.

Annabelle started packing her bag. *Sorry, Jonathan.*

When Caleb returned to his condo later that night, he found someone waiting for him out in the parking lot.

"Mr. Pearl, what are you doing here?"

Vincent Pearl didn't look like Professor Dumbledore this evening, principally because he wasn't wearing a long lavender robe. He had on a two-piece suit, open-collared shirt, shiny shoes, and his long thick hair and beard were carefully combed. He looked thinner in the suit than he had in the robe. The chubby Caleb made a mental note never to start dressing in robes. Pearl's spectacles were halfway down his nose as he silently studied Caleb with such a condescending look that the librarian started getting a little perturbed.

"Well?" Caleb finally asked.

In a deep, offended voice Pearl said, "You haven't returned my calls. I thought a personal appearance would help remind you of my interest in the *Psalm Book*."

"Right, I see."

Pearl looked around. "A parking lot seems hardly appropriate to engage in conversation about one of the world's most important books."

Caleb sighed. "Very well, come on up."

They rode the elevator to Caleb's floor. The two men sat across from each other in the small living room.

"I was afraid that you'd decided to go straight to Sotheby's or Christie's with the *Psalm Book*."

"No, it's nothing like that. I haven't even been back to the house after you were there. I didn't call you because I'm still thinking."

Pearl looked very relieved by this statement. "At the very least it would behoove us to obtain definitive tests on the *Psalm Book*. I know several firms with impeccable reputations that can do this. And I see no need to wait."

"Well," Caleb said hesitantly.

"The longer you procrastinate, the less control you have over the public learning about the existence of a twelfth *Psalm Book*."

"What do you mean by that?" Caleb said sharply as he sat forward.

"I'm not sure you adequately realize the significance of this discovery, Shaw."

"On the contrary, I realize very clearly the enormity of it."

"I mean that there might be leaks."

"How? I've certainly told no one."

"Your friends?"

"They're completely trustworthy."

"I see. Well, pardon me if I don't share your confidence. But if there is a leak, people might start making accusations. Jonathan's reputation may suffer considerably."

"What sort of accusations?"

"Oh, for heaven sakes, man, let me just spell it out for you: accusations that the book was stolen."

Caleb's thoughts leaped to his own theory about the library's *Psalm Book* being a forgery. Yet he said as earnestly as he could, "Stolen? Who would believe such a thing?"

Pearl took a deep breath. "No other owner of one of those treasures in the long and celebrated history of book collecting has ever kept it a secret. Until now."

"And you think it's because Jonathan stole it? Preposterous. He's as much a thief as I am." *Please, please, let that be true.*

"But he might have purchased it from someone who *had* stolen it, perhaps unwittingly, perhaps not. At least he might have had a suspicion, which would explain the secrecy he kept about owning the book."

"And where exactly would the book have been stolen from? You said you checked with the other places that own one."

"What the hell would you expect them to say?" Pearl snapped. "Do you think they would admit it to me if their *Psalm Book* had been stolen? And maybe they don't even know. What if a very clever forgery was left in its place? It's not like these places check their literary treasures daily to assure their authenticity." He added, "Did you find any paperwork relating to the book? A bill of sale? Anything to show where it came from?"

"No," Caleb admitted, his heart sinking. "But I haven't looked through Jonathan's personal papers. My work was limited to the book collection."

"No, your work *extends* to all evidence of ownership of his books. Do you really think that Christie's or Sotheby's will put a *Psalm Book* up for auction without being absolutely certain of both its authenticity and the legal authority under which Jonathan DeHaven's estate will be selling the book?"

"Of course, I was aware that they would need to know that."

"Well, Shaw, if I were you, I would set about immediately to find that evidence. But if you can't, the clear impression will be that Jonathan came by it through means that are not verifiable. And in the rare book field that is tantamount to saying that he stole it himself or knowingly purchased it from someone who did."

"I suppose I could ask his attorneys if I could search through his papers. Or perhaps they could do it if I told them what to look for."

"If you go that route, they will want to know why. And when you tell them, you will have most certainly lost control of the situation."

"Do you expect me to look all by myself?"

"Yes! You're his literary executor, start acting like it."

"I don't care to be talked to in that manner," Caleb said angrily.

"Are you paid a percentage of the sale price of auction?"

"I don't have to answer that," Caleb retorted.

"I'll take that as a yes. Well, if you try to auction this *Psalm Book* off without finding ironclad proof that DeHaven came by it honestly and it's later found that he didn't, it won't only be *his* reputation down the toilet, will it? When a great deal of money is involved, people always assume the worst."

Caleb didn't say anything as this slowly sank in. As repugnant as he found Pearl's remarks, the man had a point. It was devastating to think that his deceased friend's reputation would suffer a shipwreck, but Caleb certainly didn't want to sink to the bottom along with it.

"I suppose I could go through Jonathan's things at his house." He knew that Oliver and the others had already searched the house, but they hadn't been looking for ownership documents for the book collection.

"Will you go tonight?"

"It's late already." *And he'd given the key to Reuben.*

"Well, tomorrow, then?"

"Yes, tomorrow."

"Very well. Please let me know what you find. Or *don't* find."

After Pearl had left, Caleb poured himself a glass of sherry and drank it while eating a bowl of greasy potato chips, one of his favorite snacks. He was under too much pressure to adhere to any sort of diet now. As he sat drinking, he ran his gaze over his own small collection of books he kept on a set of shelves in his den.

Who would've thought book collecting could get so damn complicated?

CHAPTER

42

VERY EARLY THE NEXT MORNING Reuben reported to Stone that nothing had happened the previous night at DeHaven's; this was a repeat of the report he'd given the night before.

"Nothing?" Stone said skeptically.

"No action in the bedroom, if that's what you're implying. I saw Behan and his wife come home around midnight. But apparently, they don't use that bedroom, because the light never came on. Maybe that venue's reserved for the strippers."

"Did you see anything else? The white van, for instance?"

"No, and I think I got in and out of the place without anyone seeing me the last two nights. A ten-foot hedge runs all the way around the rear area. There's an alarm pad right inside the back door, so that was easy enough."

"Are you sure you didn't notice anything that could help us?"

Reuben looked uncertain. "Well, it might be nothing, but around one in the morning I thought I saw a glint of something in a window of the house across the street."

"Maybe the owners were up and about."

"That's the thing. It doesn't look like anybody's living there.

No car and no trash cans out front. And today's trash day because all the other houses had them out on the curb last night."

Stone stared at him curiously. "That *is* interesting. Could the glint have been an optics signature?"

"Not from a gun, I don't think. But maybe a pair of binoculars."

"Keep an eye on that place as well. What about the call to the police?"

"I did it from a pay phone like you said. I took it as a bad sign when the woman told me to stop making crank calls to the police."

"Okay, call me with your next report tomorrow morning."

"Great, but when exactly am I supposed to sleep, Oliver? I'm leaving for the loading dock right now, and I've been up all night."

"When do you get off work?"

"Two."

"Sleep then. You won't have to be at DeHaven's until ten or so."

"Thanks a lot. Can I at least eat the man's food?"

"Yes, so long as you replace it."

Reuben snorted. "Man, living in a mansion ain't what it's cracked up to be."

"See, you haven't missed anything."

"And while I'm out here busting my ass, what's Your Highness doing?"

"Your Highness is still thinking."

"Have you heard from Susan?" Reuben added hopefully.

"Not a word."

A half hour later Stone was out working in the graveyard when a taxi pulled up by the gates and Milton climbed out. Stone rose, dusted off his hands, and the two went in the cottage together. While Stone poured out some lemonade, Milton opened his laptop and a paper file he'd brought with him.

"I've found out a lot about Cornelius Behan and Robert Bradley," he said. "I just don't know how helpful it'll be."

Stone sat down at his desk and pulled the file toward him. Twenty minutes later he looked up from the pages. "It does not appear that Behan and Bradley were friends at all."

"*Enemies,* more accurately. Although Behan's company won those two big government contracts, Bradley thwarted him on three others, in part by floating allegations that Behan was into buying influence. I got that last bit from a couple of Hill staffers I know. They wouldn't come out and say it, of course, but it was pretty clear that Bradley went out of his way to spearhead the attack on Behan. And it's also clear he thought Behan was corrupt. It doesn't sound like they're part of a spy ring."

"No, it doesn't, unless it's a cover. But I agree with the late Speaker. I believe Behan is corrupt too. Is he corrupt enough to kill? In DeHaven's case I would say yes."

"So maybe Behan had Bradley killed too. He'd have a clear motive if the man was interfering with his business."

Stone said, "We've established that DeHaven was killed by CO_2 poisoning and that the lethal cylinder came from one of Behan's companies. Caleb called me yesterday. He went into the vault and checked behind the bent air vent. There was a small screw hole in the wall of the duct that could have been used to secure the camera. And he also reported that the grille screws came out very easily, as though they had been taken out recently. But it's not enough to prove a camera was ever there."

"So if Bradley and Behan weren't in cahoots together, Jonathan couldn't have seen them at Behan's house. So why kill Jonathan?"

Stone shook his head. "I simply don't know, Milton."

After Milton had left, Stone went back to work in the cemetery. He hauled a lawn mower out of a small storage shed, cranked it up and ran it over a patch of grass in a field to the left of the cottage. When he finished and cut the motor, he turned to find her watching him. She had on a big floppy hat, sunglasses and a three-quarter-length brown leather coat over her short skirt. Behind her he saw the rental car parked just outside the gates.

He wiped his face with a rag and pushed the lawn mower over to the cottage's front porch, where Annabelle was standing. She slipped off her glasses.

"How's it going, Oliver?"

He didn't say anything for a few moments. "You look dressed to go somewhere."

"Actually, that's why I came by. To let you know of a change in plan. I have to leave town. My flight heads out in a couple hours. I won't be back."

"Is that right?"

"That's right," she said, her tone more firm.

"Well, I can't blame you; things *are* getting a little dangerous."

Her gaze went to his face. "If you believe that's why I'm bugging out, you're not nearly as smart as I thought you were."

He studied her for another moment. "Whoever's after you must be pretty dangerous."

"You strike me as a man who has his enemies too."

"I don't go looking to make mine. They just seem to find me."

"I wish I could relate. I tend to make *my* enemies."

"Are you going to tell the others?"

She shook her head. "I thought you could do it for me."

"They'll be disappointed. Especially Reuben. And I haven't seen Milton this happy in years. And of course, Caleb won't admit that he likes having you around, but he will pout for the longest time."

"And how about you?" she said, her gaze downcast.

He used his boot to scrape the grass off the lawn mower's wheels. "You certainly have some remarkable skills."

"Speaking of, you caught me picking your pocket. That hadn't happened since I was eight years old." She looked at him questioningly.

"I'm sure you were a very precocious child," he said.

She gave him a tiny smirk. "Anyway, it's been fun. And you guys look out for yourselves. Like you said, enemies tend to find you."

She turned to leave.

"Uh, Susan, if we do figure this all out, do you want us to contact you, let you know about Jonathan?"

She faced him. "I think I should let the past stay right where it is. In the past."

"I just thought you'd like to know. Losing a spouse that way, you don't really get over it."

"You sound like you speak from experience?"

"My wife. It was a long time ago."

"Had you two divorced?"

"No."

"It wasn't the same with me and Jonathan. He decided to end our marriage. I'm not sure why I even came here."

"I see. Well, could I have the picture back, then?"

"What?" she said, appearing startled.

"The picture of Jonathan. I wanted to return it to his home."

"Oh, I . . . I don't have it with me."

"Well, when you get to wherever you're going, you can send it along."

"You're far too trusting, Oliver. There's nothing to make me send it back to you."

"That's right. Nothing at all."

She gazed at him curiously. "You're one of the most unusual people I've ever met, and let me tell you that's saying something."

"You should get going, don't want to miss your flight."

She glanced around at the tombstones. "You're surrounded by death here. Way too depressing. You really might want to think about getting another job."

"You see death and sadness in these sunken patches of dirt, I see lives lived fully and the good deeds of past generations influencing the future ones."

"That's way too altruistic for me."

"I thought that once too."

"Good luck." She turned to leave.

"If you ever need a friend, you know where to find me."

Her shoulders tensed for an instant as he said this. Then she was gone.

Stone put the lawn mower away and sat on the porch gazing solemnly at his tombstones as a chilly wind started to sweep across.

CHAPTER

43

CALEB ROSE AND GREETED THE man as he came into the reading room.

"Can I help you?"

Roger Seagraves showed Caleb his library card, which anyone could obtain in the Madison Building across the street by showing a driver's license or passport, fake or not. The name on the library card was William Foxworth, and the photo on the card matched the man. The same information had been loaded into the library's computer system.

Seagraves glanced around at the tables where a few people sat. "I'm looking for a particular book." Seagraves named the one he wanted.

"Fine. Do you have a particular interest in that era?"

"I have lots of interests," Seagraves said. "That's just one of them." He studied Caleb for a moment as though thinking of what he wanted to say. Actually, the script had been carefully planned, and he had done his homework on Caleb Shaw. "I'm also a collector but a novice one, I'm afraid. I have a few recent purchases in English literature that I'd like someone to evaluate for me. I guess I should have had that done before I bought them, but as I said, I'm just starting out collecting. I came into some money a while back, and my mother worked at a library for years. I've always had an interest in books, but serious collecting is a whole other ball game, I've found."

"It absolutely is. And it can be quite ruthless," Caleb said, and then hastily added, "In a dignified way, of course. As it happens, one of my areas of expertise is eighteenth-century English literature."

"Wow, that's terrific," Seagraves said. "My lucky day."

"What are the books, Mr. Foxworth?"

"Please, call me Bill. A first-edition Defoe."

"*Robinson Crusoe? Moll Flanders?*"

Seagraves said, "*Moll Flanders.*"

"Excellent. What else?"

"Goldsmith's *The Life of Richard Nash.* And a Horace Walpole."

"The *Castle of Otranto,* 1765?"

"That's the one. It's in pretty good shape, actually."

"You don't see many of those. I'd be glad to take a look at them for you. As you can imagine, there are many variations in editions. And some people buy books thinking they're true first editions, but they turn out to be something else altogether. It even happens with some of the better dealers." He added quickly, "Inadvertently, I'm sure."

"I could bring them in the next time I'm here."

"Well, I'm not sure that's a good idea, Bill, because you'd have a hard time getting them past security unless prior arrangements have been made. They might think you stole the books from us, you see. You don't want to be arrested."

Seagraves paled. "Oh, right, I hadn't thought of that. My God, the police. I've never even had a parking ticket."

"Calm down, it's okay." Caleb added a little pompously, "The world of the rare book can be very, how shall I say, sophisti-

place. *How long had he been unconscious?* The next thing he saw drove all other thoughts from his mind.

There were twin bullet holes in the bedroom window and matching ones in the window he was looking out of. "Oh, shit!" Reuben exclaimed as he ran for the door, stumbled again and fell. He reached out to catch himself, and his hand closed around it. When he stood back up, he was holding the rifle that he was certain had been used to kill two people. He immediately dropped it and took the steps two at a time. As he raced through the kitchen and saw the food that he'd left out, he realized his prints would be all over the damn place, yet he had no time to worry about that. He stepped through the back door.

The light hit him flush in the face, and he put a hand up to block the glare.

"Freeze!" the voice bellowed out. "Police!"

CHAPTER

44

"I WAS ABLE TO GET HIM A lawyer," Caleb said. "Although he was so young and so *cheap*, I don't know how effective he'll be. But I told a little white lie and said that Reuben was staying there at my request to watch over the book collection, which is why he had the house keys and the alarm code. And I also gave that statement to the police. I told them Jonathan's lawyer's name so he could confirm my role as literary executor."

Milton and Caleb were at Stone's cottage. The stunning news of Reuben's arrest for the murders of Cornelius Behan and his lady friend was evident in the group's somber looks.

"Will he get out on bail?" Milton asked.

Stone shook his head. "It's doubtful considering Reuben's personal situation and the circumstances of the case. But perhaps with the information Caleb gave them they'll reconsider the charges."

Caleb said, "I saw Reuben briefly this morning. He said he was watching Behan's house when he noticed the fire and then someone hit him on the head and knocked him out. When he came to, he saw that Behan and his girlfriend were dead. When he tried to leave, the police nabbed him."

"The papers have had a field day with Behan being found dead with his naked mistress. Apparently, Mrs. Behan was in New York last night," Milton added.

Stone said, "What we have to do is find the real killer."

Milton said, "How exactly do we accomplish that?"

"By following through on our investigation." He glanced sharply at Caleb. "We have to get a look at those security videos from the library."

"Susan said she was going to help me do that. I haven't heard from her."

"I suggest you come up with your own way, then."

Caleb looked surprised but didn't question Stone's instruction.

Stone said, "I think we can safely assume that Behan and Bradley were not friends. I initially thought that Behan had Bradley killed, and that may still be true, but then who killed Behan and why?"

Milton suggested, "Revenge for his killing Bradley?"

"If so, we have to look at possible suspects from that angle." Stone glanced at Milton. "I'll need to see members of Bradley's staff, known associates, perhaps friends in the military or intelligence communities who had the skill and other means to kill Behan."

Milton nodded. "There's something called the Unelected Directory that could be helpful. It might take longer to get anything on the military and intelligence end, though."

"Whoever killed Behan knew that Reuben was in the house and framed him for it. That means they were watching the place as well."

"The people in the house across the street that Reuben mentioned?" Caleb hazarded.

Stone shook his head. "No. The fire was probably set by an

accomplice of the killer. They must've known that there was sur-veillance going on inside that house. The fire was a distraction, giving them an opportunity to get in the house, kill Behan and escape."

"Pretty clever," Caleb commented.

Stone said, "I'm going downtown to see Reuben."

"Won't they ask for ID or something, Oliver?" Milton pointed out.

"They can ask, but the last time I checked, not having any wasn't a crime."

"I bet Susan can get you an ID," Milton suggested. "She had FBI credentials that looked like the real thing."

Caleb said, "Where is our intrepid colleague?"

"She had other plans," Stone answered.

Jerry Bagger sat in his office with a look of defeat rare in the man. Photos of Annabelle and Leo had been discreetly circu-lated to every corner of the con world, and no one had come for-ward to offer an ID. It wasn't surprising considering there was not one single clear shot of her or her grunt. It was like they knew exactly where the surveillance cameras were posted. And though his people had done their best to forestall it, news of the con against Bagger had leaked out in bits and pieces, which was probably worse than the truth all being revealed, since it allowed ample room for speculation. In sum, the casino king was a laughingstock. That only fueled his desire to find the pair and run them through a buzz saw while he videotaped their last hor-rendous moments on earth.

Their rooms had been gone over, and not a single print had been found. Any drinking glasses that the woman and her side-kick touched had long since been cleaned. The cell phone she'd thrown against the wall had gone in the Dumpster and was now resting in the landfill of whatever state Jersey shipped its garbage to. The four-day window had dried up their trail. Bagger put his head in his hands. And he'd been the one to suggest the extended time frame. He had, in effect, conned himself.

And that was the bitch's plan all along. She gave me just enough rope to hang myself.

He rose and went over to the wall of windows. He'd prided himself on being able to sniff out scams long before they had a chance to do him any harm. However, the fact was this was the first con perpetrated on him directly; all others had been focused on his casino. Those were short cons, aimed at relieving money from his craps, blackjack and roulette tables. This had been a long con orchestrated by a woman who knew exactly what she was doing, and used every asset she had, including that old reliable, sex.

Yet she had been so damn convincing. He went through her spiel over and over in his mind. She had turned the tap on and off at just the right interval. She had him convinced that she was a spy working for the government. And these days, with all the crap the feds were involved in, it was hard not to believe even the most outrageous stories.

He gazed out the window, and his mind went back to that telephone call, the one where she wanted to meet after ferreting out his security detail following her. He'd lied that he was already gone from the office, heading out of town. She'd told him point-blank that he was still in his office. That one comment had made him believe that she was legit, that the spooks were really watching him. *Watching him!*

He stared across the street at the hotel. It reached twenty-three stories off the Boardwalk, identical to his building. The line of windows there looked right into his office. *Son of a bitch! That was it!* He screamed for his security chief.

After a bit of hassle and tough questioning and finally a call to Reuben's lawyer, Oliver Stone was allowed in to see his friend in his cell. When the door clanged shut behind him, Stone jumped slightly. He had been imprisoned before, though not in an American facility. No, that wasn't right, he corrected himself. His recent torture had certainly been by fellow Americans on U.S. soil.

Assuming that the room was being monitored, Stone and Reuben talked in low voices using few words. And Stone started tapping his feet on the concrete floor.

Reuben caught on to what he was doing. "Think the sound will mess up their electronic eavesdropping?" he whispered, his look skeptical.

"Not really, but it'll make me feel better."

Reuben smiled and started tap-dancing too. "The fire?" he muttered.

"Yes, I know," Stone said. "You okay?"

"Just a knock in the head. My lawyer's going to use that as a defense."

"Prints on the gun?"

"Accidental touch."

"Caleb explained things to the police. You were there guarding the books." Reuben nodded. "Anything else?"

The other man shook his head. "Other than the peep show. Never saw it coming."

"Following through, just so you know."

"Connected?"

Stone gave a barely perceptible nod. "Need anything?"

"Yeah, Johnnie Cochran. Too bad he's in the big courtroom in the sky." He paused. "Susan?"

Stone hesitated. "Busy."

As Stone left the building later, he noted that two men—obviously police—were following at a discreet distance.

"I'll let you hang with me but just for a little while," he muttered to himself. He was already thinking about the next person he needed to talk to.

CHAPTER

45

ROGER SEAGRAVES READ THE news story off his computer screen at work. The murder suspect had been identified as Reuben Rhodes. Former military and DIA with a drinking problem who'd burned just about every bridge he had over the years. He worked at a loading dock in D.C. and lived in basically a shack in the outer reaches of northern Virginia. The guy was a walking time bomb, the story had clearly implied. And this hater of war had killed a man who'd made a fortune from providing the deadly toys all armies needed to fight. It really was too good to be true.

When Seagraves first saw the big man entering the house through the back door, he didn't know what to make of it. A burglar, he thought at first, yet the house alarm hadn't gone off, and the man came out early the next morning with nothing in his hands. When he returned the following night, Seagraves knew he had a golden opportunity to put a very nice buffer between him and the police.

He pulled his hours for the government and then punched off the federal clock. Now the time was his alone. Seagraves had another little pickup to do. It wouldn't be as pleasant as his sack time with the lady from NSA, but business couldn't always be

like that. It was important to keep his sources happy and func-
tioning and, at the same time, ensure that no suspicion was
falling on them. It was fortunate that with his position at CIA he
had informal access to some of the investigations going on regarding domestic spy rings. While it was true that the FBI also
played a large role in such matters, and he had few contacts
there, it was still an asset to know which persons his agency had
deemed "of interest."

It was a testament to his skill that the arrow had never pointed
his way. It seemed the CIA couldn't believe that one of its former assassins would ever go into business on his own. Did they
really think that was how the world worked? If so, he sincerely
feared for his country's safety if its premier intelligence agency
could be so easily hoodwinked. Yet then there was Aldrich
Ames, after all. But Seagraves was far different than that spy.

Seagraves had killed people under orders from his government.
Thus, normal rules of engagement—to wit, law and order—did
not apply to him. He was like a professional athlete, able to get
away with much because of what he could bring on the field. Yet
the traits that made them so formidable on the court or gridiron
also made them dangerously aggressive off it. If Seagraves could
get away with killing all those years, he felt there was nothing he
couldn't do. And even when he pulled a trigger for a living, he
never really felt like he was working for someone else. It was his
ass out there, whether in the Middle or Far East or any other
place he was directed to go and snuff out a life. He was a loner,
his psychological profile had confirmed that, and was one reason he'd been recruited as an assassin in the first place.

He drove to a fitness facility in McLean, Virginia, a short
drive down Chain Bridge Road from CIA headquarters. He was
playing tennis with his section chief, a man who prided himself
on his patriotism, job efficiency and his top spin backhand.

They split the first two sets, and Seagraves debated whether to let his boss win the third set. Finally, his competitive spirit won out, though he made it look close. He had fifteen years on the guy, after all.

"Kicked my butt, Roger," his boss said.

"I was just on my game tonight. But you didn't make it easy on me. If we were the same age, I don't think I could hang with you on the court."

This man had been a career seat warmer at Langley. The closest he got to real danger were the thriller novels he liked to read. His boss knew very little of Seagraves' past work for the Agency. The Triple Six Club was a closely guarded secret, for obvious reasons. However, the man did know that Seagraves had worked in the field for many years, in places that the Agency had consistently rated as top "hot spots." For this reason Seagraves was accorded far more deference and respect than the average wonk down the hall.

Back in the locker room while his boss finished his shower, Seagraves opened his locker and took a towel out. He wiped his face and then went to dry his hair. He and his boss drove to the Reston Town Center and had dinner at Clyde's Restaurant, settling in near the gas fireplace in the center of the elegant dining area. After eating they parted company. While his boss drove off, Seagraves strolled along the town center's Main Street, pausing in front of the movie theater.

It was in places like this and in local area parks that spies in the past had made their drops or picked up their money. Seagraves envisioned the subtle handing off of a bucket of popcorn with something more than extra butter lying within; a subtle but ultimately clumsy practice of the art of espionage. He had already made his pickup spending the evening with his section chief, and there was no chance anyone had observed how it had been done.

The CIA almost never undertook surveillance of *two* employees out together, particularly for tennis and dinner. Their notion of traditional spies mandated that it was a solitary occupation, which was why he'd invited his clueless boss to come along.

He drove home, took the towel he'd kept from the locker room and walked into a small room in his basement that was concrete with specialized lining, his little "safe" room of sorts that kept prying eyes away. He set the towel down on a table along with a handheld steamer. The fitness center's logo was woven into the towel's surface. Well, it would have been if this had actually been the fitness center's towel. It was a very acceptable facsimile, but the logo was merely sitting on top of the fabric, like iron-on patches kids put on their clothes. The steamer quickly removed the logo. On the other side of it was the thing Seagraves had sweated through three sets of tennis for: four two-inch-long slivers of tape.

Using a sophisticated magnifying device that, for some reason, his employer allowed its personnel at certain levels to possess, he read and decrypted the information contained on the slivers. He then reencrypted it and put it in proper form to transport to Albert Trent. This took him until midnight but he didn't mind. As a killer he had often worked at night, and old habits *died* hard.

Finished with that, he had one more task to perform before he would call it a night. He went down to his special closet, unlocked and disarmed it and stepped inside. He came here at least once a day to look at his collection. And tonight he had one addition to make, although he was irked it was only one, since it should have been a pair. He withdrew the object from his coat pocket. It was a cuff link of Cornelius Behan's that an associate of Seagraves', who worked for Fire Control, Inc., had given him. Behan had apparently dropped it while visiting the storage facility, a visit that had ultimately cost him his life. Behan had apparently figured out the cause of Jonathan DeHaven's death, and he couldn't be allowed to share that with anyone.

Seagraves placed the cuff link on a small shelf on the wall next to the baby's bib. He had nothing as yet of the young woman he'd shot. He'd eventually track her identity down and obtain something of hers. He'd shot Behan first. The man had slumped over, leaving him with a clean angle to take out the girl. She was about to perform a lewd act on Behan. On her knees she stared out the window, where the first shot had come from. Seagraves had no idea if she could see him, but it didn't really matter. He didn't even give her a chance to scream. The bullet really did a number on her pretty face. It would no doubt be a closed casket, the same for Behan. The exit wound was always bigger than the entrance.

As he stared at the empty space next to the cuff link, Seagraves made a promise that he would find an item of hers and his collection would be 100 percent up-to-date. Just the way he liked it.

CHAPTER

46

IT TOOK STONE SOME EFFORT, but he managed to lose the men tailing him. He immediately went to an abandoned home near the graveyard that he used as a safe house. He changed clothes and headed to Good Fellow Street. He passed DeHaven's house and then Behan's. There were reporters camped outside Behan's manse obviously waiting for an appearance by the unfortunate and humiliated widow. The damaged home across the street appeared to be empty.

As he watched the Behan house from the corner while pretending to consult a map, a large furniture van pulled up in front of the home and two burly men got out. A maid opened the front door as the reporters tensed. The men went inside and a few minutes later came out carrying a large wooden chest. Even though the men were obviously very strong, they struggled with the weight. Stone could sense the thoughts of the reporters: Mrs. Behan was hidden in the chest to escape the media. What a scoop that would be!

The cell phones came out, and a number of the journalists leaped into their cars and followed the van as it pulled down the road. Two cars covering the rear of the house zoomed in from the block behind the Behans'. However, a few reporters remained behind, obviously sensing a trick. They pretended to move off down the street but took up positions just out of sight of the Behans'. A minute later the front door opened again and a woman in a maid's uniform appeared, wearing a big floppy hat. She climbed into a car parked in the front courtyard of the house and drove out.

Again Stone could sense the reporters' collective thoughts. The furniture van was a decoy, and the missus was disguised as the maid. The remaining journalists ran for their vehicles and followed the maid's car. Two more journalists came from the next street over, no doubt alerted to this development by their colleagues.

Stone promptly walked around the corner and down to the next block that abutted the rear of the Behans' property. There was an alleyway here, and he waited behind a nearby hedge. His wait was a short one. Marilyn Behan appeared a few minutes later, wearing slacks, a long black coat and a wide-brimmed hat pulled low. When she got to the end of the alley, she cautiously peered around.

Stone stepped out from the cover of the hedge. "Mrs. Behan?"

She jumped and looked around at him.

"Who are you? A damn reporter?" she snapped.

"No, I'm a friend of Caleb Shaw's. He works at the Library of Congress. We met at Jonathan DeHaven's funeral."

She seemed to be searching her memory. From her demeanor she seemed a little stoned, he thought. There was no smell of liquor on her breath, though. So was it drugs?

"Oh, yes, I remember now. I made my little quip about CB understanding instant death." She suddenly coughed and reached in her handbag for a tissue.

"I wanted to offer my condolences," Stone said, hoping that the woman wouldn't remember that Reuben, her husband's alleged killer, had also been in their group.

"Thank you." She glanced back down the alley. "I guess this seems a little odd and all."

"I saw the reporters, Mrs. Behan. It must be a nightmarish situation for you. But you did fool them. That's not easy to do."

"When you're married to a very wealthy man who stirs up controversy, you learn how to duck the media."

"Could I talk to you for a few minutes? Maybe over a cup of coffee."

She seemed flustered. "I don't know. This is a very difficult time for me." Her face screwed up. "I just lost my husband, damn it!"

Stone remained unperturbed. "This concerns your husband's death. I wanted to ask you about something he said at the funeral."

She froze and then asked suspiciously, "What do you know about his death?"

"Not nearly as much as I'd like to. But I think it might have some connection to Jonathan DeHaven's death. It seems very mysterious, after all, that two next-door neighbors should die under such . . . unusual circumstances."

She suddenly looked very calculating. "You don't think De-Haven died of a heart attack *either,* do you?"

Either? "Mrs. DeHaven, can you spare a few minutes? Please, it's important."

They had coffee at a nearby deli. Sitting at a back table, Stone said bluntly, "Your husband mentioned something to you about DeHaven's death, didn't he?"

She sipped her coffee, pulled her hat down lower and said quietly, "CB didn't believe he'd had a heart attack, I can tell you that."

"Why not? What did he know?"

"I'm not sure. He never really said anything directly to me about it."

"Then how do you know he had doubts?"

Marilyn Behan hesitated. "I'm not sure why I should tell you anything."

"Let me be honest with you in the hopes that you'll return the favor." He told her about Reuben and why he was in the house, though he tactfully didn't mention the telescope. "He didn't kill your husband, Mrs. Behan. He was only there because I told him to watch the house. There are a lot of strange things going on, on Good Fellow Street."

"Like what?"

"Like the person in the house across the street."

She said nervously, "I didn't know anything about that. And CB never mentioned it. I know that he felt that people were spying on him though. Like the FBI, trying to dig up some dirt on him. Maybe they were, maybe they weren't, but he's made a lot of enemies."

"You said he didn't say anything directly to you about Jonathan's death, but at the funeral he seemed to want assurance that it was indeed a heart attack that killed him. He mentioned that autopsies are sometimes wrong."

She put down her coffee and rubbed nervously at the red lipstick on the rim of the cup. "I overheard CB on the phone one day. I wasn't eavesdropping or anything," she added quickly. "I was looking for a book, and he was in the library on a call. The door was partially open."

"I'm sure it was unintentional on your part," Stone said.

"Well, he was telling someone that he'd found out DeHaven had just had a heart workup at Johns Hopkins and that he was in fine shape. And then he said he'd pulled some strings with the

D.C. police and learned that DeHaven's autopsy results were not making people happy at all. They just didn't add up. He sounded worried and said he wanted to check more into it.' "

"And did he?"

"Well, I don't usually ask him where he's going, and he accorded me the same courtesy. I mean, the circumstances of his death evidently showed that he strayed at times. I was flying to New York and was in a bit of a hurry, but for some reason, I don't know, maybe it was his concerned look, I asked him where he was going, if anything was wrong. I didn't even know he owned the damn company, to tell the truth."

"Company? What company?"

"Fire Control, Inc., I think it was. Something like that anyway."

"He went to Fire Control?"

"Yes."

"Did he tell you why?"

"Just that he wanted to check something out. Oh, he did mention the library, or at least the place where Jonathan worked. Something about his company having the contract to protect it against fire and such. And that he'd learned that some cylinders had been recently removed from there. He also said there seemed to be an inventory screwup."

"Do you know if he found anything?"

"No. As I said, I went to New York. He didn't call me. But when I called him, he didn't mention it, and I had forgotten about it by then."

"Did he sound disturbed when you talked to him?"

"No more than usual." She paused. "Oh, he did say he was going to check the pipes in our house. I thought he was joking."

"The pipes? What was he referring to?"

"I don't know. I assumed our gas line pipes. I guess they can leak, and there could be an explosion."

Stone initially thought, *Like what happened to Speaker of the House Bob Bradley.* But then something else occurred to him.

"Mrs. Behan, do you have a sprinkler system in your house?"

"Oh, no. We have a large collection of artwork, so water was out of the question. But CB *was* concerned about fire. I mean, look what happened across the street. He had another system put in, one that put out fire without using water. I'm not sure how it works."

"That's all right, I think I know."

"So you believe whoever killed Jonathan also murdered CB?"

Stone nodded. "I do. And if I were you, I'd go and stay at another of your homes, as far away from here as possible."

Her eyes widened. "You think I'm in danger?"

"I think you might be."

"I'll go back to New York, then. I'll leave this afternoon."

"I think that would be wise."

"I suppose the police will let me. I had to give them my passport, though. I suppose I'm a suspect. I am the wife, after all. My alibi is ironclad, but I suppose I could have hired someone to kill him while I was away."

"It has been done before," Stone conceded.

They sat in silence for a minute or so. "You know, CB really did love me."

"I'm sure he did," Stone said politely.

"No, I know what you're thinking. But he *did* love me. The other women, they were just playthings. They came and they went. I was the only one who got him to walk down the aisle. And he left everything to me." She took another sip of her coffee. "You know it's ironic, he made a fortune building tools of war, but CB actually hated guns, never even owned one. His background was in engineering. He was a brilliant man, and he worked harder than anyone else." She paused. "He loved me. A woman can tell, you know. And I loved him. With all his faults. I still can't believe he's gone. A part of me died with him." She wiped away a tear from her right eye.

"Mrs. Behan, why lie to me?"

"What?"

"Why lie to me? You don't even know me. So why bother?"

"What the hell are you talking about? I'm not lying. I did love him."

"If you really loved him, you wouldn't have hired a private detective to watch your house from across the street. Was he taking pictures of the comings and goings of the women your husband enjoyed?"

"How dare you! I had nothing to do with that. They were probably the FBI spying on CB."

"No, the FBI would've been smart enough to have a team of agents there, at least one man and a woman to make it seem like a normal household. They would've also taken the trash out and performed other ordinary tasks, and they wouldn't have let themselves be seen during the surveillance. And why would the FBI be watching your home? Would they think it even remotely likely that your husband would meet with some incriminating person *there*? Not even the FBI has an unlimited budget to cover every base, however implausible." He shook his head. "I hope you didn't pay the firm a lot of money, since they were hardly worth it."

She half rose from her chair. "You bastard!"

"You could've just divorced him. Gotten half and walked away a free woman."

"After he humiliated me like that? Paraded those whores through *my* house? I wanted to make him suffer. You're right: I hired a private detective and set him up in that house. So what? And the pictures he'd already taken of my husband and his paid bitches? Well, with those I was going to make old CB bleed and force him to turn over everything to me. Otherwise, it all comes out, and let me tell you, the federal government doesn't like its contractors putting themselves in compromising positions. CB had top-secret clearances. Maybe he wouldn't have if the government knew he was doing something he could be blackmailed for. And after he signed everything over to me, then I was going to dump *him*. He wasn't the only one playing around. I've had my share of lovers, and I've picked the one I'm spending the rest of my life with. But now I get everything without even blackmailing him. It's the perfect revenge."

"You might want to keep your voice down. As you said, the police no doubt still consider you a suspect. And it's not smart to give them unnecessary ammo."

Marilyn Behan looked around at the people in the café staring at her. She paled and sat back down.

Now Stone stood. "Thanks for your time. Your information was very useful." He added with a completely straight face, "And I'm sorry for your loss."

She hissed, "Go to hell."

"Well, if I do, I surely won't be alone, will I?"

CHAPTER

47

ANNABELLE WAS WAITING FOR her connecting flight out of Atlanta. As she looked over her new itinerary, she inwardly seethed at Leo's stupid move. How could he have done that? If she had wanted Freddy to know who she was, she would have told him herself.

Her flight was called, but she waited as the passengers lined up. Even though she was in first class and could have boarded early, out of old habit she liked to see who was getting on the plane. As the line thinned, she picked up her carry-on bag. She had dumped most of her clothes back in D.C. She never checked a bag when flying; it was an invitation for someone to snoop on her. She would buy more clothes when she got to her destination.

As she was walking up to the line to get on the plane, she glanced over at an airport TV tuned to CNN and stopped moving. Reuben's face peered back at her. She hurried over closer to the TV and read the subtitles. Vietnam vet Reuben Rhodes arrested. Defense contractor magnate Cornelius Behan and a woman murdered by shots fired from the home next door. Rhodes being held. . .

"My God," Annabelle said to herself.

Over the PA came, "Last call for flight 3457 nonstop to Honolulu. Last call for passengers on flight 3457 nonstop to
Honolulu."

Annabelle looked at the departure gate for her plane. They
were about to close the door. She turned to look back at the
screen. Shots from the house next door? Behan dead. Reuben arrested. What the hell was going on? She had to find out.

Then her thoughts just as suddenly swung the other way. *This
is not your concern, Annabelle. You need to go. Jerry Bagger is
coming for you. Let the old guys handle it. There was no way
Reuben could have murdered Behan, but they'll figure it out.
And if they don't, it's not your problem. It's not.*

Still, she stood there frozen. Never before had she been so in-
decisive.

"Last call, door's closing for flight 3457."

She whispered desperately, "Go, Annabelle, damn it, just go.
You don't need this. It's not your fight. You don't owe these
people anything. You don't owe Jonathan anything."

She watched as the door to her flight from Jerry Bagger
slammed shut and the ticket-taker marched off to another gate.
She watched ten minutes later as the Boeing 777 pulled away
from the gate. As it soared into the sky right on schedule, Annabelle was booking another flight north taking her squarely within
the vicinity of Jerry Bagger and his wood chipper. And she didn't
even know why. Yet somewhere in her soul maybe she did.

Albert Trent was finishing up some things at his office at home.
He'd gotten a late start after a long night of work and decided to
catch up on some things before he drove in. The tasks were all
related to his position as the senior staff member on the House
Intelligence Committee. It was one he'd held for years now, and
he was well grounded in nearly all aspects of the intelligence

business, at least the part the agencies shared with their congressional overseers. He smoothed his few strands of hair down, finished his coffee and cheese Danish, packed his briefcase and a few minutes later pulled down the street in his Honda two-door. Five years from now he would be driving something much nicer in, say, Argentina, or he'd heard the South Pacific was truly paradise.

His secret account now contained millions. He should be able to double that in the next half-decade. The secrets Roger Seagraves was selling were at the very top end of the payment scale. It wasn't like the Cold War where you dropped a package off and picked up twenty thousand bucks in return. The people Seagraves was dealing with operated only in the seven-figure range, but they expected a lot for their money. Trent had never questioned Seagraves either about his sources or the people he was selling to. The man would never have revealed anything, and, in fact, Trent didn't want to know. His sole but critical piece of the equation was getting the information Seagraves passed to him to the next leg of the journey. His method for doing so was unique and probably foolproof. Indeed, it was the main reason the American intelligence community was currently in shambles.

There were many energetic and skilled counterintelligence agents out in the field trying to ferret out how the secrets were being stolen and then communicated to the enemy. In his official capacity Trent had been privy to some of these investigative efforts. The agents talking to him had no reason to suspect that a mere staffer with a bad hairdo who drove an eight-year-old Honda and lived in a crummy house and labored under the same bills and limited income every other civil servant had was part of a sophisticated espionage crew that was decimating American intelligence efforts.

The authorities had to know by now that the source was

deeply buried inside, but with fifteen major intelligence agencies eating up 50 billion in budget dollars a year spread over 120,000 employees, the haystacks were enormous and the needles beyond microscopic. And Roger Seagraves, Trent had found, was chillingly efficient and never missed any of the details, however small and seemingly trivial.

Trent had tried to find out some background on him when they first started talking, yet could discover exactly zero on the man. To an experienced intelligence staffer like Trent, he knew this meant Seagraves had had an entirely covert past professional life. That made him a man you would never want to cross. And Trent never intended to. He would much rather die old and rich far away from this place.

As he puttered along in his dented Honda, he imagined how that new life would look. It would be very different, that was for certain. However, he never dwelled on how many lives had been lost because of his greed. Traitors seldom had such pangs of conscience.

Stone had just returned from his visit with Marilyn Behan when someone knocked on his cottage door.

"Hello, Oliver," Annabelle said as he peered out.

He exhibited no surprise at her reappearance, but simply motioned her inside. They sat in front of the fireplace in two rickety chairs.

"How was your trip?" he asked pleasantly.

"Come off it, I didn't go."

"Really?"

"Have you told the others I left?"

"No."

"Why not?"

"Because I knew you'd be back."

She said angrily, "Okay, that really pisses me off. You don't *know* me."

"Obviously, I do, because here you are."

She stared at him, shaking her head. "You have got to be the most unusual cemetery worker I've ever met."

"You've met many, have you?"

"I heard what happened to Reuben."

"The police are wrong, of course, but they just don't know it yet."

"We have to get him out of jail."

"We're working on that and Reuben's doing fine. I don't think many people will give him trouble in there. I've seen him take out five men in a bar fight. In addition to his great physical strength, he is one of the most ruthless and dirtiest fighters I've ever seen. I greatly admire that in a person."

"But somebody got the drop on him at Jonathan's?"

"Yes, someone did."

"Why do it? Why kill Behan?"

"Because he found out how Jonathan died. That was enough reason." Stone explained his conversation with Marilyn Behan.

"So they take out Behan and blame it on Reuben because he was ever so conveniently there?"

"They probably saw him coming and going from the house, figured the attic would be a good shot line, and they executed upon that plan. They may have ascertained that Behan brought women by and that they always spent time in that room."

"Pretty tough competition we're up against. So what do we do now?"

"For starters we need to see the tapes of the reading room vault."

"On the way back I actually thought of how to do that."

"I had no doubt you would." He paused. "I don't think we could have finished this without you. In fact, I'm sure of it."

"Don't flatter me too much. We're still not there yet."

The pair sat in silence for a few moments.

Annabelle gazed out the window. "You know it *is* peaceful here."

"With dead people? I'm starting to find it very depressing."

She smiled and rose. "I'll call Caleb about my idea."

Stone stood too, stretching out his lean, six-foot-two frame. "I'm afraid I've reached the age where simply cutting the grass does awful things to my joints."

"Take some Advil. I'll give you a call later, once I'm settled back in."

As she passed Stone on the way out, he said quietly, "I'm glad you're back."

If she heard him, Annabelle didn't react. He watched the lady climb into her car and drive off.

CHAPTER

48

AFTER HIS REVELATION JERRY Bagger had summoned the manager of the hotel across the street to his office and demanded details of every guest who'd taken a room on the twenty-third floor on the side facing his building on a certain day. And in Atlantic City, when Jerry Bagger said to come, you went. As usual, some of Bagger's men hovered in the background.

The hotel manager, a young, good-looking man who was obviously ambitious and intent on performing his duties to the best of his abilities, was not inclined to let the casino chief see anything.

"Just so you understand the situation, if you don't give me what I want, you will die," Bagger said.

The manager had flinched. "Are you threatening me?"

"No. A threat is when there's a chance it won't happen. This is what in the trade we call a sure thing."

The manager paled but bravely said, "The information you're requesting is confidential. I can't possibly hand it over to you. Our guests expect their affairs to be kept private, and we have the highest standards at the—"

Bagger cut him off. "Yeah, yeah. Look, I'll go the easy route first. How much you want for it?"

"You're trying to bribe me?"

"Now we're getting somewhere."

"You can't possibly be serious—"

"Hundred thou."

"A hundred thousand dollars!"

Bagger looked at his men. "Boy, this guy's quick, ain't he? Maybe I should hire him to run my place. Yeah, a hundred thousand dollars slipped right into your personal account if you let me look at the records." The man seemed to be considering the offer, but Bagger was quickly growing impatient. "And if you don't, I tell you what, I'm not gonna kill you. Instead, I'll break every bone in your body, mess with your brain so you can't tell anybody what happened to you, and you can spend the rest of your life in a nursing home pissing all over yourself while some freak-offs drill you every night. Now to me there's no real choice there, but I'm a reasonable man, so I'll let you make the decision. You got five seconds."

An hour later Bagger had all the information he'd requested and quickly culled down his list of potential suspects. Next he questioned hotel personnel about some of the guests in question. It didn't take him long to hit the jackpot because of some extra services one of the guests had taken advantage of during his stay.

"Yeah, I gave him a massage," the young woman named Cindy said. She was petite and dark-haired with a cute face, alluring curves and a streetwise manner. She popped gum and played with her hair while talking to Bagger in a private room in the hotel's sumptuous spa area.

He eyed her closely. "You know who I am?"

Cindy nodded. "You're Jerry Bagger. My mom, Dolores, works a craps table for you at the Pompeii."

"Right, good old Dolores. You like this spa shit?"

"Pay sucks, but tips are great. The old guys like to feel a young lady's hands on 'em. A few get a hard-on while I'm doing it. Pretty disgusting on an eighty-year-old, but like I said, they tip good."

"This guy you worked on." Bagger glanced at the name he'd written down. "This Robby Thomas, tell me about him, starting with what he looks like."

Cindy gave him a physical description. "Good-looking guy but way too cocky. He really thought a lot of himself. I don't like that in a man. And he was too thin and pretty, if you know what I mean. I could've probably taken him in arm wrestling. I like my guys big and rugged."

"I bet. So this pretty boy, you only give him a massage? Or something extra?"

Cindy crossed her arms and stopped popping her gum. "I'm a licensed professional, Mr. Bagger."

In response he pulled ten hundred-dollar bills from his wallet. "This enough to buy your license?"

Cindy eyed the money. "I guess what I do on my own time is my business."

"Can't argue with that." He held out the money. "So tell me about it."

But she hesitated in taking the cash. "I could maybe lose my job if—"

"Cindy, I don't give a shit if you're screwing dead people at this two-bit joint, okay?" He pushed the money down the inside of her shirt. "Now talk to me. And don't lie. Lying to me is a very bad thing."

She started speaking fast. "Okay, like he was all over me from the get-go. I was massaging him, and all of a sudden I felt his hand against my leg. And then his hand moved way past where it should've been."

"Yeah, a real animal. What happened next?"

"He started coming on to me really hard. At first I blew him off. Then he started talking high-and-mighty. Said he was making a big score and I should be nice to him."

"A big score, huh? Keep going."

"He flashed some money, said there was a lot more where that came from. After I finished work, he was waiting for me. We had a couple drinks; I started getting a little looped. I'm not real good with holding my liquor."

"Yeah, yeah, let's keep it moving here, Cin," Bagger said impatiently. "I got serious ADD."

She went on hurriedly. "So anyway, we ended up in his room. I gave him a mouth job to get things going, but the asshole popped early. Let me tell you I was pissed. I mean, I didn't even know the jerk. He was really upset, crying like a baby. Guy gave me a hundred bucks. A lousy hundred bucks! Then he was in the bathroom puking for about ten minutes. When he came out, he said he hadn't had any in a long time and that was the reason he came so freaking fast. Like I gave a crap."

"What a jerk. What happened next?"

"Well, that was pretty much it. I mean, there wasn't any reason for me to stay after that, was there? It's not like we were on a date or nothing."

"He didn't say anything else? Where he was from? Where he was going? What the big score was?" She shook her head. He studied her closely and said, "Okay, you look like an enterprising gal. Did you maybe rip off some cash from his wallet while he was puking in the john?"

She said angrily, "I'm not some kind of trash! Who do you think you are accusing me of that?"

"Let's do a little reality check here, Cin." He touched his chest. "I'm Jerry Bagger. You're a lowlife who lets strangers shoot off in her mouth for chump change. So I'm going to ask you one more time: Did you rip off some cash to bump the C-note he gave you?"

"I don't know, I might have," she said. "But I don't feel like talking no more."

Bagger clamped a hand around her chin and jerked her head around so they were looking eye-to-eye. "Did your old lady ever tell you anything about me?"

A scared Cindy swallowed nervously. "She said you were real good to work for."

"Anything else?"

"She said anybody ever tries to cross you is one dumb son of a bitch."

"That's right. Your mama's smart." He squeezed tighter on her chin, and Cindy gave a little yelp. "So if you wanna see mama again, take a real deep breath and tell me what you saw in pretty boy's wallet."

"Okay, okay. It was weird because he had a couple of IDs."

"And?"

"And one was the name he gave me at the spa, Robby Thomas from Michigan. The other one was a driver's license from California."

"The name?" Bagger said calmly.

"Tony. Tony Wallace."

Bagger let go of the woman's face. "See, that wasn't so hard. Now, why don't you go back to rubbing the old farts' cocks?"

She rose on trembling legs. As she turned to leave, Bagger said, "Hey, Cindy, aren't you forgetting something?"

She slowly turned back around. "What's that, Mr. Bagger?" she said nervously.

"I paid you a thousand bucks. Pretty boy gave you a tenth of that, and he got a blow job. You never even asked me if I wanted one. That's not nice, Cindy. That's something a guy like me re-members for a long time." He waited, staring at her.

Her voice quavering, she said, "Do you want me to give you a blow job, Mr. Bagger?" She hastily added, "It'd be an honor."

"No, I don't."

CHAPTER

49

Annabelle and Caleb were walking down a hallway in the Jefferson Building. Annabelle had on a red knee-length skirt, black jacket and a beige blouse. She appeared professional, confident and inspired. Caleb looked ready to slash his wrists.

"All you have to do," she said, "is act sad and depressed."

"Well, that should be easy, since I *am* sad, and I *am* depressed," he snapped.

Before they entered the security office for the library, Annabelle stopped and put on a pair of glasses attached to a chain around her neck.

"Are you sure this will work?" Caleb hissed. He was starting to wheeze a bit.

"You can never be sure a scam will work until it does."

"Oh, that's just great!"

A few minutes later they were sitting with the head of security in his office. Caleb sat with his head bowed and his gaze on his shoes while Annabelle talked away.

"So as I explained, Caleb has retained me as his psychologist to help him through the process."

The chief looked puzzled. "You say he's having trouble going into the vault?"

"Yes. As you know, he found the body of a dear friend and colleague in there. The vaults are a place that Caleb normally loves. It's been a part of his life for many years." She glanced over at Caleb, who, on cue, let out a deep sigh and dabbed at his eyes with a tissue.

"Now the venue that has represented so many positive memories for him has become a place of deep sadness, even horror."

The chief looked over at Caleb. "I'm sure it was rough on you, Mr. Shaw."

Caleb's hands were shaking so badly that finally Annabelle grabbed hold of one of them.

"Please call him Caleb, we're all friends here," Annabelle said encouragingly, signaling the chief without Caleb seeing her even as she gave Caleb's hand a crushing squeeze.

"Oh, right, yes, we are friends, sure," the chief said awkwardly. "But what does this have to do with my department?"

"My plan is to let Caleb watch the tapes of the reading room, people coming and going from the vault, everything normal, everything as it should be, as a way to empower him to navigate this difficult period and turn the reading room and the vault back into purely a positive experience for him."

"Well, I don't know about letting you see the tapes," the chief said. "It's a highly unusual request."

Caleb started to get up in defeat, but a scathing look from Annabelle caused him to freeze in midrise. She said, "Well, it's an *unusual* situation. I'm sure that you would do anything within your power to see a fellow employee successfully get on with his life."

"Well, sure, but—"

"So would now be a good time to see the tapes?" She shot a

furious glance at Caleb, who was still halfway out of his chair. "I mean, you can see that he's desperate."

Caleb slumped in his chair, his head hanging between his knees.

Annabelle looked back at the chief and eyed his name tag. "Dale, I can call you Dale, can't I?"

"Well, sure. Okay."

"Dale, do you see the clothes I have on?"

Dale looked at her attractive figure and said sheepishly, "Yeah, I noticed."

"You see that my skirt color is red. That's an empowering, positive color, Dale. But my jacket is black, a negative vibe, and my blouse is beige, a neutral color. This represents that I'm halfway through my goal of helping this man back to a normal, healthy life. But I need your help, Dale, to finish the job. I want to be able to wear all red for Caleb. And I'm sure you want me to as well. I say let's finish the job, Dale. Let's just do it." She ran an appraising eye over him. "I can tell, you're with me, aren't you?"

Dale looked at the miserable Caleb and said, "Well, okay, I'll get the tapes for you."

After he had left the room, Caleb said, "You handled yourself very professionally."

"Thank you," she said tersely.

When she said nothing further, Caleb added, "And I think I did reasonably well."

She stared at him in disbelief. "Do you really?"

Hours later Annabelle and Caleb sat back after watching the comings and goings in the reading room before and after De-Haven's murder.

"It's just the typical flow of traffic," Caleb said. "There's nothing there."

Annabelle ran a tape over again. "Who's that?"

"Kevin Philips. He's the acting director after Jonathan died. He came down to ask me about Jonathan's death. And there's Oliver dressed as a German scholar."

"Nice," Annabelle said admiringly. "He carries it off very well."

They looked through some more footage. Caleb pointed at one scene. "That's when I got the notice about becoming Jonathan's literary executor." He stared at the screen more closely. "Am I really that chubby?" He pressed a hand to his stomach.

"Who gave you the notice?"

"Kevin Philips."

Annabelle watched on the tape as Caleb stumbled and broke his glasses.

He said, "I'm not usually that clumsy. I wouldn't have been able to read the damn thing if Jewell English hadn't lent me her glasses."

"Yeah, but why did she do a switch on you?"

"What?"

"She switched out the glasses she was wearing with another pair in her bag." Annabelle rewound the tape. "See? It's a pretty first-rate move, actually. She'd make a good mechanic . . . I mean, she's very nimble-fingered."

Caleb watched in surprise as Jewell English palmed the glasses she was wearing and drew out another pair from her bag. It was this pair she gave to Caleb.

"I don't know, maybe that was a special pair. The ones she gave me worked well enough. I could read the message."

"Who is this Jewell English?"

"Just an elderly lady who's a book fanatic and reading room regular."

"And she has hand moves like a Vegas blackjack dealer," Annabelle pointed out. "I wonder why that is," she added thoughtfully.

CHAPTER

50

STONE WAS SITTING IN HIS COT-
tage thinking about his conversation with Marilyn Behan. If she
was telling the truth, and he had no reason to think that the bit-
ter woman wasn't, then Stone had been wrong. Cornelius Behan
hadn't killed Jonathan DeHaven or Bob Bradley. However, he'd
apparently stumbled on the method used to kill the unfortunate
librarian and, in doing so, had prompted others to murder him.
So who else benefited from DeHaven's death? Or Bradley's,
for that matter? He desperately needed something to connect
the dots.

"Oliver?"

He glanced up. Milton was standing in the doorway.

Milton said, "I knocked but no one came."

"I'm sorry, I guess I was preoccupied."

Milton carried his laptop as usual and a small briefcase. He
put them both down on the desk and drew out a folder. "Here's
what I could find on Bradley's staff."

Stone took the papers and read through them carefully. There
were numerous documents highlighting Bradley's political career, including the House Intelligence Committee that he'd
chaired for years.

"Bradley was a very capable politician, and he instituted many good reforms in the intelligence fields," Milton said.

"Which maybe got him killed," Stone commented. "Nice reward."

Stone started going through the backgrounds and photos of both Bradley's congressional office staff and his underlings on the intelligence committee. As soon as he finished, Annabelle and Caleb arrived. Stone told them and Milton about his encounter with Marilyn Behan.

"Well, that certainly kills the theory about Behan's involvement in Jonathan's death," Caleb said.

"Appears so," Stone said. "What did you two find out today with the tapes?"

"Well, our initial hunch that we might see someone coming in or out of the vault that might be helpful didn't play out. But we did find something else that might be very important." Annabelle explained about the sleight of hand pulled by Jewell English.

"You're sure about this?" Stone asked, looking puzzled.

"Trust me, I've seen that move a million times."

And done it yourself at least as often, Stone thought. He turned to Caleb. "What do you know about this woman?"

"Just that she's an elderly widow, a regular patron, a lover of old books, very nice and enthusiastic and . . ." He turned red.

"And what?" Stone asked.

"And she's always hitting on me," he said in a low, embarrassed voice.

Annabelle had to hold back a laugh.

Stone said, "But presumably, you know all these things about her because she told them to you. They're not verified."

"That's true," Caleb conceded.

"So why the glasses switch?"

"Oliver, it could simply be that she didn't want to give me

those because they're special to her for some reason. She lent me another pair so I wouldn't read too much into it."

"I wouldn't read too much into it either, Caleb, except one wouldn't expect elderly widows who frequent rare book reading rooms to have such exceptional sleight-of-hand skills. If she didn't want you to wear those glasses, why not just say so and hand you the spare pair?"

Caleb started to say something and then stopped. "I don't have an answer to that."

"I don't either, but I'm starting to believe that we need to find an answer if we're going to discover what happened to Jonathan DeHaven."

"You can't possibly believe that sweet old Jewell English had anything to do with Jonathan's death," Caleb protested.

"We can't rule that out right now. And Behan was killed because he guessed how DeHaven died. I think he discovered that the gas cylinders at the library had been deliberately mislabeled. That may be why he came to the reading room asking questions and wanting to look at the vault, Caleb. He was fishing for information as to why DeHaven might have been killed. Remember, he wanted to know if DeHaven was friendly with everyone at the library. He wasn't looking to pin the murder on someone else, he genuinely wanted to know if DeHaven had any enemies."

"In other words, the key isn't Behan, but DeHaven, and maybe something at the *library*?" Annabelle said.

"Possibly," Stone replied. "Or something in his private life."

Caleb flinched at this remark but remained silent.

"But where does the murdered Bob Bradley figure into all this?" she asked. "You said you thought that was connected."

"We know that Bradley was killed by a bullet from a rifle fired through a window in another building. Behan died in the exact same way. That can't be a coincidence. Indeed, it could very well be the exact same killer. Professional assassins like to use the same method of killing because they become so proficient at it. It reduces the chances of an error in the assignment."

"You sound like you know a lot about that sort of thing," Annabelle said.

He smiled innocently. "As Caleb can tell you, I'm a voracious reader of thriller novels. I find them not only entertaining but informative." He looked at Caleb. "Is there any way we can get a look at the woman's glasses without her knowing?"

Caleb said sarcastically, "Sure, we can burglarize her home in the middle of the night and steal them."

Stone said, "Good idea. Can you find out where she lives?"

Caleb sputtered, "Oliver, you can't be serious."

"I might have a better way," Annabelle said. They all looked at her. "Does she come into the reading room on a regular basis?"

"Fairly regularly."

"If she sticks to that schedule, when is she due next?"

Caleb thought quickly. "Actually, tomorrow."

"Fine. I'll go to the library with you tomorrow. You point her out to me and then let me handle it."

"What are you going to do?" Caleb demanded.

Annabelle rose. "Give her a taste of her own medicine."

After Annabelle had left, Caleb said, "I couldn't talk in front of her obviously, but, Oliver, what if all this has something to do with the *Bay Psalm Book*? It's incredibly valuable, and we can't find out where Jonathan got it. Maybe it's stolen and maybe someone else wants it. They could have killed Jonathan to get it."

"But they didn't get it, Caleb," Stone countered. "The person who knocked out Reuben was in the house. They could have broken into the vault and taken it then. And why kill Cornelius Behan? Or Bradley? They could have no connection with the

Psalm Book. Behan didn't even know DeHaven had a book collection. And there's no evidence that Bradley even knew your colleague at all."

After a depressed and confused Caleb had left, Milton and Stone sat talking while Stone flipped through the file on Bradley's staffers. He said, "Michael Avery went to Yale, clerked for a Supreme Court justice, did a stint at NIC before going on the intelligence committee staff. He moved with Bradley when he became Speaker." He looked at some of the other pictures and bios. "Dennis Warren, another Yalie, was at DOJ early in his career. He was Bradley's chief of staff and kept that position when Bradley became Speaker. Albert Trent was on Bradley's intelligence committee staff for years; a Harvard-educated lawyer and CIA employee for a time. They're all Ivy Leaguers, all highly experienced. It looks like Bradley had a first-rate team."

"A congressman is only as good as his staff, isn't that the old saying?"

Stone looked thoughtful. "You know, one thing we've never really looked at were the circumstances of Bradley's murder."

"How do we remedy that?" Milton asked.

"Our lady friend is very good at impersonation."

"The best."

"How would you like to do a similar run with me?"

"I'm your man."

CHAPTER

51

ALBERT TRENT AND ROGER
Seagraves were meeting in Trent's office on Capitol Hill. Seagraves had just handed Trent a file with some briefing material.
Trent would make a copy of the file and put it in the committee's
intake system. Embedded within the original file were critical
secrets from the Pentagon detailing U.S. military strategies in
Afghanistan, Iraq and Iran. Trent would use a pre-agreed decryption method to ease these secrets from the pages. With this
business finished, Seagraves said, "Got a minute?"

They strolled around the Capitol grounds. "Boy, Roger, you
got lucky with Behan, and the other guy getting blamed for it,"
Trent said.

"Understand one thing, Albert: Nothing I do is tied to luck. I
saw an opportunity and took it."

"Okay, okay, no offense meant. You think the charges will
stick?"

"Doubtful. I'm not sure why he was there, but he *was* watching Behan's house. And he's buddies with Caleb Shaw at the
reading room. And on top of that, the guy I nabbed and 'talked'
to, this Oliver Stone, is with the same group."

"Shaw is DeHaven's literary executor. That's why he's been going to the house."

Seagraves looked disdainfully at his colleague. "I *know* that, Albert. I did a face-to-face with Shaw to set up a future move if it becomes necessary. It's not just books they have on their minds. The guy I interrogated used to be at CIA in a very special capacity."

Trent exclaimed, "You didn't tell me that."

"You didn't need to know, Albert. Now you do."

"Why do I need to know now?"

"Because I said so." Seagraves gazed at the Jefferson Building, where the Rare Books reading room was located. "These guys have also been snooping around Fire Control, Inc. My man there said the paint on one of the cylinders they pulled from the library had been rubbed off. So they probably know about the CO_2."

Trent turned pale. "This is really not looking good, Roger."

"Don't start sweating yet, Albert. I've got a plan. I've always got a plan. We got the last payment in. How fast can you move the new stuff?"

He checked his watch. "Tomorrow at the earliest, but it'll be tight."

"Make it happen."

"Roger, maybe we should just shut it down."

"We've got a lot of customers to service. That wouldn't be good business."

"It also wouldn't be good business to go to prison for treason."

"Oh, I'm not going to prison, Albert."

"You can't know that for certain."

"Yes, I can. Because they don't put dead men in jail."

"Okay, but we don't have to go that route. Maybe we should think about at least slowing down a bit. Let things cool off."

"Things rarely cool down after they heat up. We'll just keep doing what we're doing, and like I said, I have a plan."

"Care to share it?"

Seagraves ignored the question. "I'm doing another pickup tonight. And this one might top ten mil if it's as good as I think it is. But keep your eyes and ears open. Anything looks strange, you know where to find me."

"You think you might have to, you know, kill again?"

"Part of me sure hopes so." Seagraves walked off.

Later that night Seagraves drove to the Kennedy Center to attend a performance of the National Symphony Orchestra, NSO. Perched on the edge of the Potomac, the plain, boxy Kennedy Center had often been declared one of the country's blandest memorials built in honor of a deceased president. Seagraves didn't care about the aesthetics of the structure. He didn't care about the NSO either. His handsome features and tall, muscular physique drew stares from many of the women he passed as he walked down the hall toward the auditorium where the NSO would be performing. He took no notice of this. Tonight was strictly a working night.

Later, during the brief intermission, Seagraves joined other patrons in going outside the auditorium to get a drink and gaze over the memorabilia for sale. He also made a pit stop in one of the men's rooms. After that, the lights dimmed, signaling the start of the last part of the program. In a crush of people he made his way back to the theater.

An hour later he had a drink at a late night bar across from the Kennedy Center. He pulled his program out of his side jacket pocket and studied it. This was not *his* program, of course. It had been slipped into his pocket during the crush of the crowd getting back into the theater. There was no possibility that anyone could have seen this. Spies who skirted crowds were always caught. For that reason, Seagraves embraced the masses for the protective cover they provided.

Back home in his workshop, Seagraves finessed the secrets from the pages of the "program" and put them in the proper format to send along to Albert Trent the next time he saw the man. He smiled. What he was staring at was no less than the final pieces he needed for the decryption keys for high-level diplomatic communications emanating from the State Department to its overseas branches. Now he was thinking $10 million was too cheap. Maybe $20 million. Then Seagraves decided he would start at $25 million to leave himself some wiggle room. He conducted all his negotiations over various prearranged Internet chat sites. And the secrets were only delivered once the money had been wired into his numbered account. He had taken the very reasonable position of not trusting anyone he did business with. Yet he was kept honest on his end by the efficiencies of the free market. The first time he collected money without delivering the merchandise, he would be out of business. And probably dead.

The only possible thing that could upset that plan was some old guys who had a habit of snooping. If it had only been the librarian, he wouldn't have been too worried. But thrown into the mix was the Triple Six, a man not to be taken lightly. Seagraves could sense another storm brewing. For that reason, when he'd earlier kidnapped Stone and tortured him, he'd taken one of his shirts from the man's cottage; to add to his collection, if the need arose.

CHAPTER

52

STONE AND MILTON ARRIVED at the Federalist Club around ten the next morning.

They gave their request and were escorted into the manager's office. He looked at their crisp, official-looking identification cards that Milton had run off his laser printer the night before.

"You've been hired by Bradley's family back in Kansas to investigate his death? But the police here are handling it. And the FBI. They've *all* been here, numerous times," the manager added in an annoyed tone.

"The family wanted its own representation, as I'm sure you can understand," Stone said. He and Milton were dressed in suit jackets, ties and dark slacks. Milton's longish hair was hidden under a fedora that he'd declined to remove. "They don't feel as if adequate progress is being made."

"Well, since the police haven't caught anyone, I can't argue with that opinion."

Stone said, "You can call them if you want to verify our representation of their interests. Mrs. Bradley is out of the country, but you can talk to the family's local lawyer in Maryland." On the card was Milton's phone number. He'd recorded a message posing as the attorney in the off chance the manager took them up on the offer.

"No, that's all right. What would you like to know?"

"Why was Bradley at the club that night?"

"It was a private celebration, for his election as Speaker of the House."

"I see. Who arranged it?"

"His staff, I believe."

"Anyone in particular?"

"Not that I can remember. We received instructions by fax. I assumed it was a surprise of some sort."

"And he was killed in the front drawing room?"

"We call it the James Madison Room. You know the Federalist Papers thing. I can show you if you like."

He led them to the large room fronting the street. Stone looked out the broad bay window at the upper story of the building across the street. To his skilled eye it was a perfect shot trajectory, which clearly demonstrated not only advance intelligence but someone on the inside.

Following through on this thought, Stone asked, "And he came in here why?"

The manager was wiping a speck of dust off the marble fireplace mantel. "Oh, it was for the toast, in his honor." He shivered. "It was ghastly. Senator Pierce had just finished speaking when Bradley was shot. It was absolutely horrifying, blood everywhere. A very expensive Persian rug was a total loss, and blood even seeped into the wood. That cost a small fortune to have bleached out and then restained. The police just let us do it recently. We couldn't even cover it because they said it might taint the evidence. People had to walk by looking at it. Cut down on membership traffic here, I can tell you that."

"Who owns the building across the street?" Milton asked.

"I don't know. I assume the authorities have found out by now. It used to be a private home and then an art gallery. It's been just sitting there for about five years now, a real eyesore, but what can you do? I had heard, though, that it was being renovated. Into condos, I think. They just hadn't started the work yet."

"So who summoned Bradley into the room for the toast?" Stone asked.

The manager thought for a moment. "There were so many people here, I'm not sure. I really wasn't involved in that part of the celebration. I *was* standing by the window when the shot came. I think I actually felt it whiz by my ear. I was limp for days after."

"I'm sure. Anyone else that might be able to tell us anything?"

"Well, one of the waiters, and the bartender who worked the event. They're both in now if you want to talk to them."

The bartender knew nothing. However, the waiter, Tom, said, "It was one of his staff, I think, who got everybody together for the toast. At least that's what I recall. I helped pull people in from the other rooms, and then they went and got Congressman Bradley."

"Do you remember who it was? The staff person?"

"No, not really. There were a lot of people. And I don't think he ever said his name."

"So it was a man?" Tom nodded. Stone held up a copy of pictures of Bradley's staff. "Recognize anyone? How about him?" He pointed to Dennis Warren. "He was Bradley's chief of staff. It would make sense for him to organize the toast."

"No, it wasn't him."

"Him," Stone said, pointing to Albert Trent. "He was also high up on Bradley's staff."

"Nope." The waiter ran his gaze down the photos, finally stopping at one. "That's him. Now I remember. Really efficient."

Stone stared at the photo of Michael Avery, who'd served on Bradley's staff at the intelligence committee.

As they were leaving the Federalist Club, Milton asked, "What now?"

"Now we talk to some people who worked for Bradley."

"Not Avery? That would tip him off."

"No, but Trent or Warren."

"But we can't tell them we're investigating on behalf of Bradley's family; they'd probably know we were lying."

"No, we're going to tell them the truth."

"What?"

"We're going to tell them we're investigating the death of Jonathan DeHaven."

Dennis Warren was at home when Stone called, after looking him up in the directory, and he agreed to meet with them. Over the phone he'd said that while he'd heard about DeHaven's death, he didn't know the man. He'd commented ruefully that "I don't even have a library card, I'm ashamed to admit."

Milton and Stone rode the Metro to Warren's Falls Church, Virginia, home. It was a modest place in an older neighborhood. It was clear that Warren was not the outdoor or handyman type. His lawn was full of weeds, and the house was desperately in need of painting.

However, inside, the place was cozy and comfortable, and, despite Warren's comment on not having a library card, the shelves were full of books. Stacks of worn tennis shoes, varsity jackets and teen-related junk showed that he was also a father.

Warren was a tall, portly man with thinning brown hair and a wide pockmarked face. His filmy, translucent skin bespoke of decades laboring for his country under fluorescent light. He led them through the hall to the living room.

"Don't mind the mess," Warren said. "Three sons ages fourteen to eighteen means your life and home are not your own. I can stand up in a meeting and present a cogent argument on complex geopolitical intelligence strategies to the Joint Chiefs or the secretary of defense, but I can't seem to get any of my sons to bathe on a consistent basis or eat anything other than cheeseburgers."

"We know you were on the intelligence committee staff," Stone began.

"Right. I moved with Bradley when he became Speaker. Currently, I'm unemployed."

"Because of his death?" Milton said.

Warren nodded. "I served at his pleasure, and it was a pleasure serving him. He was a great man. A man we needed in this day and age; rock-solid and honest."

"You couldn't stay with the intelligence committee?" Stone asked.

"Not really an option. Bradley wanted me to come with him, so I did. And I wanted to go. There's only one Speaker of the House and only one chief of staff to a Speaker. Lot of action and everybody returns your phone calls. Plus, the new chairman of the intel committee had his own people he wanted to move up. That's how it is on the Hill. You're attached to your member's coattails. And when those coattails move or go away, well, that's why I'm home in the middle of the day. Good thing my wife's a lawyer, or we'd be up a creek financially. To tell the truth, I'm still getting over the shock of what happened and haven't really started looking for another job." He paused and eyed them closely. "But you said you were investigating this DeHaven guy's death? What's that got to do with Bradley?"

"Maybe nothing or maybe a lot," Stone said vaguely. "You've heard about Cornelius Behan's murder?"

"Who hasn't? Pretty embarrassing for the wife, I'd say."

"Yes, well, DeHaven lived next door to Behan, and the killer used DeHaven's house to shoot from."

"Damn, I hadn't heard that. But I still don't get the connection to Congressman Bradley."

Stone admitted, "I'm trying to connect the dots myself, frankly. Were you at the Federalist Club that night?"

Warren nodded slowly. "It was supposed to be a tribute to the old man and ended up being a nightmare."

"You actually saw it happen?" Milton asked.

"I had that great misfortune. I was next to Mike, Mike Avery. Senator Pierce had just finished a nice toast and *bam*, shot came out of nowhere. It all happened so fast. I had my glass of champagne next to my lips. Spilled it all over me. It was awful. I was sick to my stomach, a lot of people were."

"You know Avery well?"

"I should, we worked together, day *and* night, for ten years."

"Where is he now?"

"Moved with me when Bradley became Speaker. He's out of a job now too."

"We understand that he was the one who put together the event at the club and arranged for the toast."

"No, he didn't. Mike and I drove over there together. We were just part of the guest list."

"We were told he was getting people in the room for the toast."

"So was I. We were just helping out."

"Who were you helping?"

"Albert. Albert Trent. He was the one who suggested the toast. Albert was always thinking of stuff like that. I'm just a poor wonk with limited social skills."

"Albert Trent? Did he put the whole event together?"

"Don't know. But he was certainly working the room that night."

"Is he out of a job now too?"

"Oh, no. Albert stayed behind at the intel committee."

"But I thought you said you followed your congressman?" Stone said, puzzled.

"Normally, you do. But Albert didn't want to leave. Bradley wasn't happy about it, I can tell you that. Albert had cut some deal with the new intel chairman coming up to be his top aide. Albert has a way of making himself indispensable. But there's a lot to do at the Speaker's office, and not having Albert left us shorthanded. I'm not telling tales out of school. That was public knowledge."

"But Bradley let him have his way?"

Warren smiled. "You obviously didn't know Bob Bradley. Like I said, the guy was incredibly decent, honest, hardworking, but you don't get to his position in life without being tough as hell and persistent. And the man didn't like having a subordinate buck him. Dollars to doughnuts, Albert was going to end up in the Speaker's office sooner rather than later."

"But with Bradley dead, that became a moot point?"

"Of course. Me and Mike tried to do the right thing, and we're unemployed. Albert bucks the old man and he's sitting pretty. And Mike's got four kids and his wife stays home. Trent's single and no kids. Tell me how that's fair."

After they had left, Milton said, "I know, everything I can find on Albert Trent."

Stone nodded. "Everything."

"That seems a pretty clear motive for murder, though. I'm surprised the police haven't jumped on it. Warren didn't even seem to catch it."

"What motive?" Stone asked.

"Oliver, it's obvious. If Bradley lives, Trent has to leave the intelligence committee. If he dies, Trent gets to stay where he is."

"So you think the man murders the Speaker of the House to avoid changing jobs? And he didn't pull the trigger because he was at the club. So he'd have to hire a hit man to do it for him. That seems a little extreme to keep a midlevel government position. And like Warren said, the Speaker's office is far more prestigious."

"Then there has to be something more."

"Agreed. But right now we don't know what that is."

Inside the house, Dennis Warren picked up the phone and spoke with his friend and former colleague Mike Avery. Then he punched in a second number.

"Albert? Hey, it's Dennis. Look, sorry to bother you at work, but some guys were here asking some weird questions. I called Mike Avery too, to give him a heads-up. It's probably nothing, but I thought I'd call you anyway."

Trent said, "I appreciate that. What exactly did they want to know?"

Warren recounted the conversation and then added, "I told them you'd organized the toast for Bob and that you'd stayed behind at the committee."

"What did they look like?"

Warren described Stone and Milton. "Do you know them?"

"No, not at all. That *is* weird."

"Well, again, I just thought I'd give you a heads-up. Hope I didn't say anything I shouldn't have."

"I have no secrets," Trent replied.

"Hey, Albert, if anything opens on the committee staff, let me know, willya? I'm tired of twiddling my thumbs."

"Will do and thanks for the info."

Albert immediately left his office and made a call from a pay phone and arranged to meet with Seagraves outside the Capitol later.

When Seagraves arrived, Trent said, "We've got a problem."

Seagraves listened and said, "Well, their next move is obvious."

"You'll take care of it?"

"I always take care of it."

CHAPTER

53

WHILE MILTON AND STONE were making their investigative rounds, Caleb glanced up from his desk in the reading room as Annabelle walked in, wearing a black pleated skirt and matching jacket, white blouse and low pumps. She had a tote bag slung over her shoulder and was holding her newly minted library card with her picture on it. Caleb approached her.

"Can I help you, Miss . . . ?"

"Charlotte Abruzzio. Yes, I was looking for a certain book."

"Well, you came to the right place. After all, this *is* a library." Caleb laughed.

Annabelle didn't even crack a smile. She'd told him to keep the conversation to a minimum and not to attempt any lame jokes, but he'd gone and done it anyway, the little dork. She gave him the name of the book she wanted. It was one he'd suggested the night before when they'd gone over the plan.

Caleb retrieved the volume from the vault, and Annabelle sat down at a table with it. She was seated facing the door and also where she could easily see Caleb.

An hour later Caleb jumped up. "Ah, *Jewell,* how are you?

Jewell, it's so good to see you," he said, advancing quickly on the older lady after giving Annabelle a "that's her" look.

At her seat Annabelle gritted her teeth. *What a piece of work.* The man could not have been more obvious if he'd pulled out a pair of handcuffs and tackled the old woman. Luckily, Jewell English seemed not to have noticed because she was fumbling in her bag.

A few minutes later Caleb gave Jewell a book from the vault, and she settled down with it. Caleb kept going back over to her often and then glancing at Annabelle as though she might have somehow missed the identity of the target. In exasperation Annabelle finally gave him such a fierce glare that he fled back to his desk.

When Jewell was done an hour later, she packed her bag, said good-bye to Caleb and left. Annabelle followed her a minute later and caught up with her out on the street where the elderly woman was looking for a cab. Annabelle had wrapped a scarf around her head and put on a long jacket she'd carried in her bag. As a cab pulled up to the curb, Annabelle made her move. She bumped into Jewell, jostling the woman's bag. Her hand slipped in and out of it so fast, a person standing right next to them would've been unable to follow the move.

"Oh, my Gawd," Annabelle said in a deep southern voice. "Honey, I am sooo sorry. My mama didn't raise me to run into nice ladies like you."

"That's all right, dear," Jewell said, a little out of breath from the collision.

"Y'all have a nice day," Annabelle said.

"You too," Jewell said pleasantly as she climbed into the cab.

Annabelle fingered the flowered glass case in her pocket as she walked slowly away. A few minutes later she was back in the reading room. There was a different person working the front desk. Caleb hurried over to Annabelle. "Dawn," he said to the woman at the front desk, "I'm going to give Ms. Abruzzio a quick tour of the vault. She's in from out of town. I, uh, already cleared it with the higher-ups," he lied. This sort of flouting of the rules would have been unthinkable a short time ago, but with all that had happened, Caleb considered finding Jonathan's killer more important than following library rules.

"All right, Caleb," Dawn said.

The pair went inside the vault, and Caleb led Annabelle to the Jefferson Room, where they could talk in private. She held up the glasses. "Want to try them on? I did and couldn't see much."

Caleb did so and then immediately pulled them off. "My God, that's weird; it's like looking through three or four layers of different glass, with little sunspots. I don't understand. I could see through her other pair perfectly."

"Which is why she gave you those glasses and not these. Otherwise, you would've been suspicious. Do you have the book she was looking at?"

He held up the Beadle. "I just pretended to reshelve it."

Annabelle took the book. "Looks pretty cheap."

"That's the whole point. They're *dime* novels from the nineteenth century."

"The thing is she looked like she was reading this book okay with these glasses. I mean, she was taking notes."

"Yes, she was, wasn't she?" Caleb slowly put the glasses on and, squinting, opened the book.

"Can you read anything?" Annabelle asked.

"It's a bit blurry." As he turned the pages, he suddenly stopped. "Wait a minute, what's that?"

"What's what?" she said.

He pointed to a word on the page. "This letter is highlighted. Don't you see, it's glowing yellow, bright as day."

Annabelle looked at where he was pointing. "I don't see any-thing like that."

"Right there!" he exclaimed, putting his finger on a letter *e* in a word on the first line.

"It's not glowing to me, and—" She broke off. "Caleb, give me the glasses." Annabelle slipped them on and looked at the page. The letter was now a vibrant yellow, literally jumping off the page. She slowly took the specs off. "These are *really* special glasses."

Caleb was staring at the page with his naked eye. No glow. He put the glasses back on, and the letter *e* glowed. "And there's a highlighted *w* and an *h* and an *f*." He flipped to the next page. "And there's another *w* and an *s* and a *p*. And a lot more letters. All highlighted." He took off the glasses. "*E, w, h, f, w, s, p.* That's gibberish."

"No, it's a code, Caleb," Annabelle said. "These letters form a secret code, and you need these special glasses to see them."

He looked astonished. "A secret code?"

"Do you know what other books she's looked at recently?"

"They're all Beadles, but I can check the call slips."

A few minutes later he'd rounded up six books. He went through them page by page wearing the glasses, but there were no glowing letters. "I don't understand. Was it just the one book?"

"It can't be," Annabelle replied in frustration. She held up the book with the glowing letters. "Can I check it out?"

"No, this is not a lending library."

"Not even you?"

"Well, yes, I can. But I'd have to fill out a four-part call slip."

"So someone at the library could know you've checked it out?"

"Well, yes, they could."

"That's no good. We could inadvertently tip someone off."

"What do you mean by that?"

"Caleb, someone here had to highlight those letters. If you take home one of the books involved, it could alert people who are behind whatever the scheme is."

"Are you saying that someone at the Library of Congress is involved in putting secret codes in rare books?"

"Yes!" she said in exasperation. "Give me the book. I'll get it out of the building. It's small and thin, it won't be a problem. Wait a minute, do the books have electronic antitheft devices built into them?"

He looked appalled by the suggestion. "My God, woman, these are rare books; that would be tantamount to desecrating them."

"Yeah? Well, it seems that someone already did that by making the letters glow. So I'll just borrow the book for a while."

"Borrow it! That book is the property of the Library of Congress!"

"Caleb, don't make me hit you. I'm taking the book." He started to protest again but she cut him off. "This might have something to do with Jonathan's death," she said. "And if it does, I don't care what the rules are here, I want the truth about how he died. You were his friend. Don't you want to know too?"

Caleb quickly calmed and said, "Yes, I do. But getting the book out of here won't be easy. Technically, we have to check every bag before anyone leaves the room. I can *pretend* to search yours, of course, but the guards also look into every bag before it leaves the building, and they're very thorough."

"Like I said, it *won't* be a problem. I'm taking this to Oliver's place tonight. Meet me there after you get off work. He strikes me as someone who could be able to understand all this."

"What do you mean? Granted, it seems that he has certain skills and knowledge that are somewhat out of the ordinary, but secret codes? That's spy stuff."

"You know, for a man who spends all his time around books, you are the most *clueless* person I've ever met!" she said.

"That is a highly offensive and *rude* remark," he said, bristling.

"Good, it was supposed to be!" she snapped. "Now get me some tape."

"Tape, what for?"

"Just go get it."

He reluctantly retrieved the tape from a storage cabinet inside the main vault area.

"Now turn around," she said.

"What?"

She spun him around. While his back was turned, Annabelle hiked her skirt up to her waist, positioned the paperback book around the inside of her left thigh and secured it there with the tape. "That'll hold it, although it's not going to be fun getting it off."

"Please tell me you are not doing anything to damage that book," he said sternly. "It is a vital piece of history."

"Turn around and see for yourself."

He whipped around, saw the book, and also her exposed pale thighs and a thin line of her panties, and gasped.

She said in a breathy voice, "I think the book will be *very* happy there, Caleb, don't you?"

"Never in all my years as a librarian at this *venerable* institution," he began, his voice quavering with shock; however, Caleb didn't once take his eyes off her legs even as his heart thundered in his chest.

She slowly pulled her skirt back down, smiling impishly. "And you loved every second of it." She bumped him with her hip as she passed by. "I'll see you at Oliver's, *stud*!"

had found out at the Federalist Club and from their talk with Dennis Warren.

"So this Albert Trent stuck at the intelligence committee," Annabelle said. "What does that mean?"

Reuben spoke up. "It means he'd have access to secrets worth selling, I can tell you that. When I worked at DIA, we had briefings all the time with the Hill. The intelligence committee members and their staff all had to have top-secret clearances."

"But spies are notorious for not telling Congress everything," Milton said, looking up from the book. "Would Trent really know enough of value that he could sell?"

"Remember," Stone said, "Trent was not always a staffer there. He'd once been at the CIA."

"So he could have contacts there. Hell, maybe there, NSA, NIC, the whole alphabet," Reuben commented. "He might have assembled a minimart for espionage."

"But how do you get from a mole like Trent to secret codes in rare books?" Annabelle asked as she shifted her weight on the old chair she was sitting on and rubbed her tender thigh where she'd had to tear the tape off to get the book free.

"I don't know," Stone admitted. "We have to find out more about this Jewell English. If we could get her to crack, we could trace it back to the source. She must know the glasses are missing by now."

"Get her to crack?" Reuben exclaimed. "Oliver, we can't splay her out on a rack and smack her around until she talks."

"But we can go to the FBI, show them the book and glasses, tell them our theories and let them take it from there," Stone suggested.

"Now you're talking," Reuben said. "The more distance we put between us and them, whoever they are, the better."

Stone looked over at Caleb, who hadn't spoken one word and was sitting disconsolate in a corner.

"Caleb, what's wrong?"

The pudgy librarian took a quick breath but didn't make eye contact with any of them.

Annabelle, now concerned, said, "Caleb, I'm sorry if I was tough on you today. You actually did a good job." She bit her lip as she finished the lie.

He shook his head. "It's not that. You're right, I'm totally inept when it comes to the stuff you do."

"So what is it?" Stone asked again impatiently.

He took one long breath and looked up. "The police came to the library today. They gave me the keys to Jonathan's house. The first thing I did was check on the collection." He paused, glanced at Annabelle and leaned over and whispered into Stone's ear. "The *Psalm Book*'s been stolen."

Stone froze for an instant while Milton and Reuben stared at Caleb. "Not *the* book," Milton asked, and Caleb nodded miserably.

Annabelle said, "Hey, if five's a crowd, I can always leave. I'm not really that into books."

"How could it have been taken?" Stone asked, putting up a hand to stop her from departing.

"I don't know. You need pass codes to get into the vault and safe. And neither of them was forced."

"Who else has the codes?" Reuben asked.

"I'm not sure."

"Well, certainly, the lawyer for one," Stone said. "He had the keys and code to the main vault. He could've written the code down before he gave it to you and made a duplicate of the key."

"That's right, I hadn't thought of that. But what about the small safe? He didn't have the code to that."

Stone said, "You thought of it, he could have too. I mean, it wasn't that hard. If the lawyer knew Jonathan well and had visited him at the reading room, it could have easily occurred to him. Or perhaps Jonathan gave him that code, but he didn't give it to you for some reason."

Caleb said, "But if he was going to steal it, why not do it before he met with me? That way I'd never even have known the book was there."

Stone looked puzzled. "That's true. Although I still don't believe it's connected to the murders."

Caleb groaned. "Great, but Vincent Pearl will kill *me* when he finds out. This was going to be the crown jewel in his career. I bet he even accuses me of stealing it."

"Well, maybe *he* stole it," Milton said, glancing up from the book.

"How? He couldn't get in the house, and he didn't have the keys or the codes to the vault," Caleb said. "And he well knows that that book is impossible to sell without the proper papers. He couldn't make any money off it. He'd be arrested if he tried."

They all sat silently until Reuben said, "It's bad news about the book, but let's not forget the main agenda. We go to the FBI tomorrow. At least that's something."

"What about Jewell English?" Milton asked.

Caleb sat up straighter, probably happy to get his mind off the stolen *Psalm Book.* "If she comes back to the library, I can tell her that I'll check for her glasses in lost and found."

Reuben said, "Hell, if she is a spy, she's probably already out of the country."

"It's possible she doesn't know the glasses are missing yet," Stone said. "She'd only use them when looking for the coded letters. That means she might not pull them out until she comes to the reading room."

Caleb said, "So if we get them back to her before she realizes they're gone, she might not get suspicious."

"We'll need them for the FBI, but if we explain our plan, they might let us get them back to her and they can set up surveillance," Reuben said. "Then she gets more code, passes it on to somebody, and the FBI is there to nab 'em."

"A good plan," Stone said.

"Actually, it's not," Milton said suddenly. "We can't take the book to the FBI."

They all looked over at him. While they'd been talking, he'd gone back and reread through the slim volume, his hands flipping through the pages faster and faster. He took the glasses off and held up the book, his hand trembling.

"Why not?" Caleb asked irritably.

In answer, Milton handed the glasses and book to Caleb. "See for yourself."

Caleb put on the glasses and opened the book. He turned one page and then another and another. Frantic, his fingers whipped through the last part of the book. He slammed it shut, his face a mix of anger and incredulity.

Stone, his eyes squinty with concern, said, "What is it?"

Caleb said slowly, "The highlighted marks are all gone."

CHAPTER

55

STONE PUT ON THE GLASSES AND flipped through the book. He ran his finger across one of the letters he knew had been highlighted earlier. It was as dull and lifeless as the others now. He closed the book, took off the glasses and sighed. "The highlighting chemical wash they used had a time limit built in. Then it evaporates."

"Like vanishing ink?" Milton said.

"Somewhat more sophisticated than that," Stone said. He added in anger, "I should have thought of that."

"Do you know about this sort of chemical, Oliver?" Caleb asked.

"Not this process, no. But it would make sense. If you're a spy and it's possible that the glasses might fall into the wrong hands, the book will reveal nothing if enough time passes." He looked at Caleb. "Whoever put the chemical wash on had to know that Jewell English would have access to the book before the effect wore off. How could that be accomplished?"

Caleb thought for a moment. "Someone would have to go into the vault and doctor the book there. Then contact her somehow and tell her which one to ask for. She comes to the library right away and asks to see it."

Stone studied the cover of the book. "It seems that it would be quite a tedious process to mark each appropriate letter. If nothing else, it would take some time."

"Well, people are in and out of the vaults fairly frequently. But some of the interior vaults don't see a lot of use. However, if one of the library staff were in there for hours on end, it would be noticed, certainly."

Reuben said, "Maybe whoever did it is really good, can do it quickly, maybe using some sort of template."

"What about after hours?" Stone asked.

Caleb looked uncertain. "In the vault? That would be limited to a very few. The director and the Librarian of Congress are the only two I can think of. The computer is programmed to deny access to other people after hours unless special arrangements have been made. It certainly wouldn't be an everyday thing."

"So DeHaven would've had access to the vault after hours?" Stone said.

Caleb nodded slowly. "Yes, he would. Do you think he was part of the spy ring? And that's why he was killed?"

Annabelle started to protest, then seemed to think better of it.

"I don't know, Caleb." Stone rose. "What we need to do now is act. Caleb, call Jewell English and tell her you've found her glasses where she dropped them in the reading room. Tell her you'll bring them by to her."

"Tonight? It's already nine o'clock," Caleb said.

"You have to try! It's clear to me that we're operating on a very tight time frame now. And if she's made a run for it, we need to know."

Annabelle said, "Oliver, that might be dangerous. What if she's still around and suspects something's up?"

"Caleb will wear a listening device. I know that Milton has some of those gadgets at his home." Milton nodded. Stone continued, "Milton will go with him to English's but remain hidden outside. If something happens, he can call the police."

"What if the something that happens is bodily harm to *me*?" Caleb whined.

"You described her as an elderly lady, Caleb," Stone reminded him. "I think you should be able to handle the situation. However, I believe the more likely scenario is that you'll find she's gone. If so, try to get into her house and discover what you can."

Caleb was squeezing his hands nervously. "But what if she hasn't left? And what if she has some big thug around who attacks me when I go to see her?"

Stone shrugged. "Well, of course, that would be unfortunate."

The librarian turned crimson. "*Unfortunate?* That's easy for you to say. Pray tell what will *you* be doing while I'm risking *my* life?"

"Breaking into Albert Trent's home." He glanced at Annabelle. "Are you game?"

"Oh, absolutely," Annabelle said, smiling broadly.

"What about me, Oliver?" Reuben said pitifully. "I thought *I* was your Tonto."

Stone shook his head. "You've been arrested once and you're still a suspect, Reuben. We can't risk it. You'll have to sit this one out, I'm afraid."

"Well, that's just great," Reuben grumbled, slapping his thigh in frustration. "Some people get all the fun."

Caleb looked ready to strangle the big man.

CHAPTER

56

CALEB PULLED HIS NOVA WITH the rattling tailpipe to the end of the quiet cul-de-sac and shut off the motor, glancing at Milton nervously. His friend was dressed all in black with his long hair bunched under a knit ski cap; he'd also darkened his face.

"My God, Milton, you look like a poster boy for Criminals Are Us."

"It's just standard-issue surveillance dress. How's the wire?"

Caleb rubbed his arm under his jacket where Milton had attached the listening device. He also had a power pack stuck in the back of his waistband. "It's itching the crap out of me, and the power pack's making my pants so tight, I can barely breathe."

"It's actually probably just nerves," Milton commented.

Caleb glared at him. "You *think*?" He slid out of the car. "Just make sure 911 is on your speed dial, *burglar boy.*"

"Roger that," Milton replied as he took out a pair of night binoculars and scanned the area. He'd also brought a high-speed camera and a Taser gun.

Jewell English had answered Caleb's phone call and seemed delighted that he'd found her glasses. Tonight would be fine regardless of the late hour, she'd said. "I don't sleep much," she confided to Caleb on the phone. "But I might be in my night-gown," she added in a girlish voice.

"That's nice," he'd answered dully.

As he walked toward her home, he took note of the other houses. They were all aged tiny brick ranches with cookie-cutter yards and darkened interiors. A cat snuck across one lawn, startling him. He took several deep breaths and muttered, "She's just an old lady who lost her glasses. Just an old lady who lost her glasses. Just an old lady who could be a spy with henchmen waiting to slit my throat." He glanced back at the car. He couldn't see Milton but assumed his sidekick was busily snapping photos of a suspicious-looking robin lurking on a tree branch.

The lights were on in Jewell's home. He could see lace curtains in the windows and through the big living room glass, knickknacks and bric-a-brac positioned on the painted fireplace mantel. There was no car in the rusty carport. He assumed she'd either quit driving or her ride was in the repair shop. Her lawn was neatly cut, and two columns of rosebushes guarded the front of her house. He rang the bell and waited. No one came. He rang it again. No footsteps reached his ears. He glanced around. The street was empty, quiet. *Maybe too quiet, as they say in the movies; right before you're shot, stabbed or eaten.*

He'd called her a little over an hour ago. What could have happened in the interim? He'd heard the bell buzz, but maybe she couldn't hear it. He knocked on the door, hard. "Jewell?" He said her name again, louder. From somewhere a dog started barking, and he jumped. It wasn't from inside the house, though, probably a neighbor's mutt. He knocked again, harder, and the door swung open.

He turned, poised to run. You never ever went into a house when the door just opened like that. The next sound nearly pushed his heart into defib.

"Caleb?"

He shrieked and grabbed the handrail on the front stoop to avoid pitching over into the bushes in his fright.

"Caleb!" the voice said again urgently.

"What? Who? Dear God!" He spun frantically around trying to see who was calling his name, his feet slipping and sliding on the damp concrete. He became so dizzy, he was almost sick to his stomach.

"It's me, Milton."

Caleb froze in a half-squat, his hands clamped to his thighs as he desperately tried to keep from heaving his dinner into the fragrant roses. "Milton?"

"Yes!"

"Where are you?" he hissed.

"I'm still in the car. I'm speaking to you through the wire. It has communication capability as well as being a surveillance device."

"Why the hell didn't you tell me that?"

"I did. I guess you forgot. I know you're under pressure."

"You can hear me clearly?" Caleb said between gritted teeth.

"Oh, yes, very clear."

The language that erupted from the staid librarian would have caused the filthiest rap singer in the world to concede his lewd speech title to Mr. Caleb Shaw.

There was a long pause after this explosion. Finally, a stunned Milton said, "I can tell you're a little upset."

"Yep!" Caleb took a deep breath and willed his food to remain in his belly. He slowly stood erect and stretched out his back even as his poor heart continued to race. If he keeled over with a coronary right now, Caleb swore he'd come back and haunt the little techno-geek every second of every day.

"Okay, she's not answering. I just knocked on the door, and it swung open. What would you suggest I do?"

"I'd leave right now," Milton answered automatically.

"I was hoping you'd say that." Caleb started to back down the steps, afraid to turn around lest something leap out at him from the house. Then he stopped. What if she was lying on the bathroom floor with a broken hip or had suffered a heart attack? The thing was, despite the evidence, part of Caleb could not believe that the same sweet lady who was such an enthusiastic lover of books could be wrapped up in the spy business. Or if she was, maybe she was simply an innocent dupe.

"Caleb? Have you left yet?"

"No," he snapped. "I'm thinking."

"Thinking about what?"

"About whether I should go in and check on her."

"Do you want me to come with you?"

He hesitated. Milton *did* have a Taser gun. If Jewell *were* a spy and came at them with a meat cleaver, they could take the old crone down, *hard.*

"No, Milton, just stay put. I'm sure it's nothing." Caleb pushed open the door and went in. The living room was empty, as was the small kitchen. There was a frying pan on the stove with bits of onion and what looked like ground beef; this matched the aroma in the air. There was one plate, a cup and a fork in the sink, all dirty. On the way back through the living room he picked up a heavy brass candleholder as a weapon and moved slowly down the hallway. He reached the bathroom first and looked in. The toilet seat was down, the shower curtain open, and no bloody body was lying in the tub. He didn't check the medicine cabinet primarily because he didn't want to see how absolutely terrified he looked in the mirror.

The first bedroom was empty, the small closet full of towels and bedsheets.

There was only one room left. He hoisted the candleholder above his head and nudged the door open with his foot. It was dark inside, and it took a moment for his eyes to adjust. His breath left him in a rush. There was a lump under the bedcover.

He whispered, "There's someone in the bed. The covers are over her face."

"Is she dead?" Milton asked.

"I don't know, but why would she be asleep with the covers over her face?"

"Should I call the police?"

"Just hang on a sec."

There was a small closet in the room, its door partially open. Caleb stood to one side, his candleholder at the ready. He again used his foot to push the door open and then jumped back. A short rack of clothes hung there without a murderer in sight.

He turned back to the bed, his heart beating so fast, he wondered if he should have Milton call an ambulance for *him.* He looked down at his shaky hands. "Okay, okay, a dead body can't hurt you." Still, he didn't want to see her, not like that. He suddenly realized something. If they *had* killed her, he was partly responsible, for taking her glasses and exposing the old woman. This somber thought depressed but also calmed him somewhat.

"I'm sorry, Jewell, even if you were a spy," he mumbled solemnly.

He gripped the top of the bedcover and jerked it down.

A dead *man* stared up at him. It was Norman Janklow, the Hemingway lover and Jewell English's nemesis in the Rare Books reading room.

CHAPTER

57

ALBERT TRENT LIVED IN AN OLD house with a broad front porch set far back from a rural road in western Fairfax County.

"Must be a hike for him to get into D.C. every day from here," Stone noted as he eyeballed the place with a pair of binoculars from behind a copse of towering river birch. Annabelle, dressed in black jeans, dark tennis shoes and a black hooded jacket, crouched next to him. Stone carried a small knapsack.

"Does it look occupied?" she asked.

He shook his head. "No lights that I can see from here, but the garage is closed, so we can't tell if there's a car in there."

"A guy in the intelligence field probably has an alarm system."

Stone nodded. "I would be stunned if he didn't. We'll disable that first, before we go inside."

"You know how to do that?"

"As I once told Reuben when he asked me that, the library is open to everyone."

There wasn't another house within their line of sight, but they still approached the rear of the house to avoid being seen. This required crawling on their bellies, then their knees, and finally crab-walking down a gentle slope twenty yards from the house.

They halted here and Stone took another reconnoiter. The home had a walk-out basement with a pressure-treated deck on one end. The back was as dark as the front. With no streetlights and just a dash of ambient light, Stone's night binoculars were working optimally. Through the green haze of the coated optics he could see everything he needed to.

"I'm not spotting any movement, but make the call anyway," he told Annabelle.

Milton had gotten Trent's home phone number off the Internet, a far more dangerous threat to America's privacy than the poor National Security Agency ever thought of being. Annabelle used her cell phone to call. After four rings the voice mail kicked in, and they listened to a man's voice instructing them to leave a message.

"Our spy seems to be out in the cold tonight," she said. "Are you armed?"

"I don't own a gun. You?"

She shook her head. "I'm not into that. I go for brains over bullets."

"Good, guns aren't great things to be into."

"You sound like you speak from experience."

"Now is not the time to swap life stories."

"I know, I'm just foreshadowing for when will be a good time."

"I didn't think you'd be sticking around after this."

"I didn't think I'd be sticking around *for* this. So you never know."

"Okay, the phone box is hanging on a foundation wall underneath the deck. Let's move, keep it nice and slow."

As they crawled forward, a horse whinnied somewhere in the distance. There were small family farms scattered around here, though they were being rapidly ground under by northern Virginia's colossal residential housing machine that randomly spit out condos, town houses, modest single-family homes and mansions with numbing speed. They'd passed several such farms on the way to Trent's place, all of which had stalls, hay bales, paddocks and large critters nibbling grass. Fat piles of horse manure left on the streets had served as an exclamation point for the equines' presence. Stone had almost stepped in some getting out of Annabelle's rental car.

They reached the phone box, and Stone spent five minutes evaluating the security system hardwired into it, and took another five minutes to disable it. After he'd rerouted the last wire, he said, "Let's try the window right here. The doors probably have dead bolts. I brought a tool to force them, but let's take the point of least resistance first."

That point was not the window, which was nailed shut.

They moved down the rear of the house and finally found one window that was secured with window pins. Stone cut a circle of glass out, reached in, pulled out the pins and popped the lock. A minute later they were roaming down the hallway toward what looked to be the kitchen, with Stone in the lead holding a flashlight.

"Nice place, but he appears to be a minimalist," Annabelle noted. Trent's taste in interior decoration did tend toward the spartan: a chair here, a table there. The kitchen was barren.

Stone said, "He's a bachelor. He probably eats out a lot."

"Where do you want to start?"

"Let's see if he has an office of some kind here. Most D.C. bureaucrats tend to bring their work home."

They found the office, but it was nearly as bare as the rest of the house, no papers or files. There were some photos on the credenza behind the desk. Stone pointed to one. A big, bearish man with a bluff, honest face, white hair and thick gray eyebrows was standing next to a smaller, flabby man with a bad comb-over but who possessed a pair of cagey brown eyes and a furtive expression.

Stone said, "The big man is Bob Bradley. Trent's next to him."

"Trent *looks* like a little weasel." She stiffened. "What's that vibrating sound?"

"Damn, that's my phone." Stone unclipped his cell and looked at the screen. "It's Caleb. I wonder what they found."

He never got a chance to hear.

The heavy blow from behind knocked Stone unconscious.

Annabelle let out a scream an instant before a wet cloth held by a very strong hand covered her mouth and nose. As she breathed in the chemical fumes and started to collapse, her gaze fell on a mirror hanging on a wall across the room. In the reflection she could see two men wearing black masks. One had her, and the other was standing over Stone. And behind them she saw a third man. It was the man in the picture, Albert Trent. He smiled, not realizing she had seen his reflection. Within a few moments her eyelids started fluttering, then closed, and she became limp.

In accordance with Roger Seagraves' instructions, one of the men removed the watch from Annabelle's wrist. Seagraves already had a shirt of Stone's. Although he was not killing them himself, Seagraves *was* orchestrating their deaths, which satisfied his collection criteria. He would especially covet the addition of a Triple Six, a first for his collection. Seagraves intended on giving it a particularly special place of honor.

CHAPTER

58

ANNABELLE REGAINED CON-
sciousness first. As her eyes came into focus, she saw the two
men working away. One stood on a ladder while the other one
was handing him things. She was lying bound hand and foot on
a cold concrete floor. Directly across and facing her was Stone,
his eyes closed. As she watched, his eyelids fluttered several
times and then remained open. When he saw her, her gaze directed him to the two men. Their mouths weren't bound, but
neither wanted to alert their captors that they were awake.

As Stone took in the room, his belly tensed. They were being
held in the storage room at Fire Control, Inc. He squinted to see
the label on the cylinder the men were preparing overhead. It
was suspended from the ceiling by chains, which was why they
were using a ladder to reach it.

"Carbon dioxide, five thousand ppm," he mouthed as Annabelle tried to understand him.

*The men were going to kill them the same way Jonathan De-
Haven had died.*

Stone looked frantically around for something, anything, he
could use to cut through his bindings. They probably wouldn't
have much time after the men had left the room before the gas

would shoot out of the cylinder and devour the oxygen in the air, leaving them to suffocate. He spotted it about the time the men finished their work.

"That should do it," one of them said, climbing down.

As the man stepped into the wash of the overhead light, Stone recognized him. It was the foreman from the team that had removed the cylinders from the library.

When the men glanced over, Stone instantly closed his eyes. Acting on his cue, Annabelle did likewise.

"Okay," the foreman said, "let's not waste time. The gas release triggers in three minutes. We'll let it clear out and then get them out of here."

"Where are we dumping them?" the other man said.

"A real out-of-the-way place. But it won't matter if they're found. The cops won't be able to tell how they died. That's what's so sweet about this setup."

They grabbed the ladder and left. The instant the two men shut and locked the door behind them, Stone sat up and slid on his butt over to the worktable. He levered himself up, snatched a box cutter off the table, sat back down and propelled back over to Annabelle.

He whispered, "Quick, take this knife and cut through my ropes. Hurry! We've got less than three minutes."

As they lay back-to-back, Annabelle moved the blade up and down as quickly as she could from such an awkward position. Once, she hit flesh and heard Stone grunt in pain, but he said, "Keep going, don't worry about that. Hurry! Hurry!" His eyes were on the suspended cylinder. Facing the way he was, he could see what Annabelle couldn't. There was a timer on the cylinder, and it was counting down fast.

Annabelle cut as quickly as she could until she felt her arms would drop from her shoulders. Sweat was leaching into her eyes from the effort.

Finally, Stone felt the rope start to give way. They had one minute left. He pulled his hands apart, giving her more room to work. She cut more and the ropes fell completely away. Stone sat up, undid the bindings on his feet and jumped up. He made no attempt to reach the cylinder. It was too high up, and even if he could get to it and figure out how to stop the countdown, the men would know something was wrong when they didn't hear the gas release. He grabbed the oxygen tank and face mask that he'd seen on his previous visit and raced to Annabelle's side. They had thirty seconds.

He grabbed her bound hands and slid Annabelle to a far corner behind a pile of equipment. He threw a tarp over them, placed his head next to Annabelle's, strapped the large oxygen shield over both their faces and turned on the feed line. A low hiss and the feeling of a light breeze in their faces showed that the line was working.

A moment later they heard a sound like a small explosion followed by the roar of a waterfall up close. For ten long seconds it continued, the CO_2 coming out so fast and furiously that it covered the entire room almost instantly. As the "snow effect" took place, the temperature dropped dramatically, and Stone and Annabelle began to shake uncontrollably. They sucked deeply on the life-giving oxygen. Yet on the fringes of the air pocket provided by the O_2 Stone could feel the draining clutches of an atmosphere that was far closer to the moon's than Earth's. It tore at them, trying to rip the molecules of oxygen away, but Stone kept the mask crushed to their faces even as Annabelle gripped him with the strength of extreme panic.

Despite the supply of oxygen, Stone's thoughts still became

muddled. He felt as though he were in a fighter jet soaring ever higher, the g-forces pulling his face back and up, threatening to rip his head off. Stone could only imagine the horror that Jonathan DeHaven, who'd had no oxygen to draw on, had endured in his final moments of life.

Finally, the roar stopped just as instantly as it had started. Annabelle moved to push the mask away, but Stone stopped her. Whispering, he said, "The oxygen levels are still depleted. We have to wait."

Then he heard what sounded like a ventilator fan come on. Time passed, and with each tick Stone kept his eye on the door. Finally, he moved the mask from his face but kept it on Annabelle's. He drew a careful breath and then another. He tossed off the blanket, lifted her up and over his shoulder and carried Annabelle to the exact spot where she'd been. Moving as quietly as possible, Stone grabbed up the nearly empty oxygen tank and stood behind the door to the room.

He didn't have long to wait. A minute later the door opened and the first man came through. Stone waited. When the second man appeared, Stone swung the cylinder and caught him dead on the skull, crushing it. He dropped as though poleaxed.

The other man turned in alarm, ripping at the gun on his belt. The tank hit him flush in the face, driving him back against the worktable and into the hard metal of the vise attached there. He screamed in pain and clutched wildly at his injured back as the blood slicked his face. Stone slung the tank once more, catching the guy square on the temple. As the man fell to the floor, Stone dropped the tank, raced to Annabelle and untied her. She rose on shaky legs and looked down at the two battered men.

"Remind me never to piss you off," she said, her face very pale.

"Let's go before somebody else shows up."

They raced out the door, scaled the fence and ran down the street. Three minutes later they had to pull up, breathing hard, sweat running down the dirty creases of their skin. They sucked in delicious air and then jogged another quarter mile until their legs were dead. They slumped down against the brick wall of what looked to be a warehouse.

"They took my phone," Stone said, gasping for extra oxygen. "And by the way, I'm way too old for this shit. I seriously mean it."

"Mine too . . . and me too," she answered in halting breaths. "Oliver, I saw Trent in the house. His reflection in the mirror."

"You're sure?"

She nodded. "It was definitely him."

Stone glanced around. "We have to get in touch with Caleb or Milton."

"After what happened to us, do you think they're okay?"

"I don't know," he said shakily. He lurched to his feet, held out a hand and pulled her up.

As they started walking fast down the street, she slowed and said quietly, "Is that how Jonathan died?"

He stopped and turned to her. "Yes. I'm sorry."

She shrugged noncommittally but wiped a tear from her eye. "My God." Her voice shook.

"Yes, my God," Stone agreed. "Look, Susan, I never should have let you get involved in this."

"First of all, my name's not Susan."

"Okay."

"Second of all . . . tell me your real name and I'll tell you mine."

Stone hesitated just for a second. "Franklin, but my friends call me Frank. You?"

"Eleanor, my friends call me Ellie."

"Franklin and Eleanor?" he said, looking bemused.

"You started it." She smiled even as her eyes filled with tears and her body began to shake. "Oh, Jonathan."

Stone reached out and gripped her shoulder, steadying the woman.

"I can't believe this," she said. "I haven't even seen the man in forever."

"It's okay if you still care about him."

"I wasn't sure I did until right now."

"There's no law against it."

"I'll be okay. Believe me, I've been through far worse." As soon as Annabelle said that, she started to sob uncontrollably. Stone pulled her close as her legs failed. They both sank to the cement, and Stone kept holding her as her fingers dug into him, her tears dampening his shirt and his skin.

Five minutes later she stopped except for a couple of last heaves. Pushing away from him, Annabelle rubbed her swollen eyes and her runny nose with her sleeve.

She said, "I'm sorry. I never, and I mean never, lose control like that."

"Crying because you lost someone you love isn't exactly unusual."

"It's just not . . . I mean . . . You never—"

Stone put his hand against her mouth and said quietly, "My real name is John. John Carr."

Annabelle tensed for an instant and then relaxed. "I'm Annabelle Conroy. It's nice to meet you, John." She exhaled a deep breath. "Whoa, that's not something I do very often."

"Use your real name? I can sympathize. The last person I told tried to kill me."

He stood and helped her up. As he turned, she kept ahold of his hand.

"Thank you, *John*, for . . . everything."

He was clearly embarrassed by her gratitude, but she came to the rescue. "Let's go and see if Milton and Caleb need saving. Okay?" Annabelle said.

A moment later they were jogging down the road.

CHAPTER

59

ANNABELLE AND STONE MADE A phone call from a service station, reaching Caleb. He had not yet fully recovered from finding Norman Janklow's body but was able to relay some of what had happened. Stone called Reuben, and all arranged to meet back at Stone's safe house. An hour later they were reassembled, and Stone and Annabelle reported their experience first.

"Damn," Reuben said. "Good thing you thought of the oxygen, Oliver."

Caleb and Milton told their story next.

Caleb added, "We called the police from a pay phone. Only took about an hour to find one in our cell-happy world. Thank goodness I remembered to take the candleholder; it has my fingerprints on it."

"Did you touch anything else?" Stone asked.

Caleb looked worried. "I grabbed the handrail on the outside stoop." He glared at Milton. "Because gadget boy here decided to scare the crap out of me. And I might have touched something else inside the house, I don't remember. I've actually tried to block it out of my memory."

"Your prints are in the federal database?" Stone said.

"Of course." Caleb gave a resigned sigh. "Well, it won't be the first time the coppers have come for me, and I doubt it'll be the last."

"What connection could this Norman Janklow have to all this?" Reuben asked.

Stone answered, "Janklow could've been a spy, like English. That means the books he looked at could've been secretly coded too."

"They must've only pretended to dislike each other," Caleb said. "To help maintain their cover."

"Okay, but why kill Janklow?" Reuben persisted.

"If he was a spy, once we exposed English, maybe the whole thing started to unravel, and they had to start tying up loose ends," Annabelle ventured. "They might have gotten English out of the way and left Janklow there dead to confuse things."

"I'd say they accomplished their goal, then," Caleb pointed out.

"We should go to the police now," Milton said anxiously.

"And tell them what?" Stone argued. "The marks in the book have disappeared. And if we explain that we were almost killed tonight, we'd have to admit to having broken into Albert Trent's home. I'm sure he's already called the police to report the burglary."

He glanced at Annabelle. "And even though you saw him, it's your word against his. And I didn't call the police about what happened at Fire Control, Inc., because I felt sure by the time they got there, the two men I attacked would've disappeared." He looked at Caleb. "And since Caleb was at Jewell English's home and his prints might be found there, if we go to the police, he'll instantly become a suspect. Couple that with the fact that the authorities already have Caleb and Reuben on their radar, it's all far too complicated for the police to believe."

"Well, hell," was Reuben's sole comment to that analysis.

Annabelle said, "So what do we do? Wait for them to come after us again?"

Stone shook his head. "No. Caleb will go to work tomorrow as if nothing's happened. The library will be in an uproar having lost a director and a patron in such a short time. Caleb, find out what you can. The news will give us some hint as to what the police think. And if they've killed English too, the body might turn up."

Milton said, "I'll keep my eye peeled on the Net for any of that. That's where it'll break first."

Stone continued, "Bob Bradley, Jonathan DeHaven, Cornelius Behan and now Norman Janklow have been murdered. I believe Bradley died because he was forcing Albert Trent to leave the intelligence committee staff. Trent couldn't do that, because if I'm right, Trent was using that position to pass secrets. DeHaven was killed either because he was involved in the reading room being used to convey these stolen secrets or he stumbled on the scheme and had to be silenced. That might be the same for Norman Janklow, or else he was also a spy like English. Behan was killed because he figured out that one of his companies' equipment was used to murder DeHaven and would no doubt have investigated further. Trent had a mole at Fire Control who probably tipped him off about Behan's suspicions, and he had to be eliminated."

Caleb said, "But how could Jonathan, Jewell English or Norman Janklow become involved in a spy ring? Who would think to use the Rare Books reading room to communicate stolen secrets through coded letters in the first place?"

Stone said, "Well, because one wouldn't logically think of it makes it a good plan. And remember, most spies are captured because they're placed under surveillance for some reason, and then they're observed making the drop of information, usually in a public place. Instead, we have coded letters in rare books. There's no surveillance possible. Old people read old books and go home. No one would even consider them remotely suspicious."

Caleb said, "But you still have to get the secrets Trent was presumably stealing to the library somehow. It wasn't Albert Trent highlighting those letters in the books. And Jonathan couldn't have done it in the Beadle we took from the library. He was dead by then."

"Agreed. And that's the part we still have to figure out. In fact, that's the most important part, because it's our main hope of solving this case. If Janklow, English or DeHaven were spies, there has to be some evidence of that."

Milton said, "We've already searched DeHaven's house and found nothing."

"And I looked through Jewell's," Caleb said, "and only found a dead body."

Stone nodded. "Perhaps Norman Janklow's home may yield some results."

Reuben interjected, "The only problem with that is the police will be crawling all over it now. Same with English's place."

Stone said, "Things *are* getting very dangerous now, and we all have to be extremely careful. I suggest that we double up from now on. Milton and Caleb, you two can stay at Milton's house; it has a very good security system. Reuben, you and I can stay at your place, since certain people already know where I live." He looked at Annabelle. "You can stay with us too."

Reuben looked hopeful. "My shack's not much to look at, but I've got plenty of beer, chips and a wide-screen plasma. And I do a mean chili. On the protection side, I've got one nasty pit bull named Delta Dawn, who'll take a bite out of anyone I tell her to."

"I think I'll stick to my hotel. But I'll watch out for myself, don't worry."

"Are you sure?" Stone said.

"I'm sure. But thanks for the offer. I'm really more of a loner, actually. That's how I prefer it," she added, averting her gaze from Stone.

As the meeting broke up, Stone stopped Annabelle on the way out.

"Are you okay?" he asked.

"I'm fine, why shouldn't I be? Just another day in the life."

"Almost being killed isn't such a normal thing."

"Maybe it is and maybe it isn't."

"Okay, are you game for another run at Albert Trent?" She hesitated. "I don't mean breaking into his house again. I mean tailing him."

"You think he's still around?" she said.

Stone nodded. "They have no idea really what we know or don't know. My guess is they'll maintain the status quo until conditions dictate otherwise. If he skips town now, it's all over. If this is a spy ring, they might want to see if things can be salvaged. These people have obviously worked hard to put it together."

"*These* people don't play around, do they?"

"Neither do I," Stone replied.

Roger Seagraves was a very unhappy man. While Janklow had been sacrificed to muddy the waters and silence a potential witness, English was in a secure place far away from D.C. Yet because she'd allowed her glasses to be taken and their operation blown, Seagraves didn't see her remaining alive for long. That was the good news. The bad news was Oliver Stone and the woman had escaped, costing him two men in the process. The

Triple Six had somehow managed to beat the death chamber and smash their skulls in. That was impressive, especially for a guy who must be sixty by now. Seagraves chastised himself for not killing the man when he had the chance. He had cleaned up the bodies at Fire Control, but the police were all over Jewell English's place. Fortunately, she had kept nothing incriminating at her home, and the same for Janklow. However, Seagraves' perfect scheme was ruined.

Now he only had one goal. To go right to the source and end it once and for all.

From the small table next to him, he picked up Stone's old shirt and the watch taken from Annabelle. Seagraves promised himself that these items would still become part of his collection.

CHAPTER

60

He woke, stretched, turned over and gazed out the window. The weather today was just like it had been yesterday. Sunny and beautiful with an ocean breeze apparently designed solely to inspire contentment in all it touched. He got up, wrapped a sheet around his waist and strolled to the window. Situated on several acres of land that included a sandy beach pounded by the ocean, the villa was his, at least for a year, the length of the lease, but he was thinking about buying it outright. The isolated estate boasted a saltwater infinity swimming pool, a wine cellar, a tennis court and a cabana with a daybed that was useful for more than drying out after a dip, for he seldom swam alone or with a bathing suit on. In the two-car garage sat a Maserati coupé and a Ducati for his driving pleasure. A cook, maid and gardener came with the place for less money than he'd paid in condo fees back in L.A. He drew a deep breath and knew he could spend the rest of his life here.

He hadn't exactly followed Annabelle's instructions about not flashing the cash, but this place had been immediately available for someone with the money. He'd actually seen the listing on the Internet before they'd done the scam but after Annabelle had told them they stood to make millions. It was never too early to plan for such a large purchase. And once he had leased the house, he had to have the toys that went with it. He wasn't worried about Bagger finding him. The guy had never even seen him. And there were lots of rich, young people around this part of the world. He was cool. In fact, he was great.

Tony heard her coming up the stone stairs and retreated back to his bed, letting the sheet fall away. When she opened the door, he saw that she carried a tray with his breakfast only. It was funny; she'd slept with him after the second night but wouldn't eat breakfast with him. It probably had to do with her being the maid.

"*Dos huevos, jugo de naranja, tostada y café con leche,*" she said. Her Spanish accent was pleasantly lyrical.

"And you." He smiled, pulling her to him after she had set the tray down on the table next to the bed. She kissed him on the lips and let him slip off her strapless nightie, which was all she happened to be wearing. He traced the finely developed muscles in her long brown neck, stroked her large breasts, moved his hand down her flat belly and then went lower still.

"*Tu no tienes hambre?*" she cooed, rubbing her bare leg against his and nuzzling his neck with her lips.

"*Hambre* for you," he said, nibbling her ear.

He scooted around and let her fall back on the bed. He took one of her shapely legs in each of his arms and stood poised between her thighs. She licked her fingers and then squeezed her breasts.

"Damn, you drive me loco, Carmela!" he said.

She lunged forward, grabbed him by the shoulders and pulled him down on her.

The door smashing back against the wall made the couple forget about screwing before breakfast.

Four big men came in, trailed by a smaller broad-shouldered

fellow wearing a two-piece suit and open-collared shirt and sporting a devilish look of triumph.

Jerry Bagger said, "Hey, Tony, nice place you got here. I really like it. It's amazing what you can buy with someone else's money, ain't it?"

He sat down on the bed as the terrified Carmela tried to cover herself with the sheet.

"Hey, honey, you don't have to do that," Bagger said. "You're really pretty, how do you say, *bonita*! That's right. *Muy bonita, bitch.*" He motioned to one of his men. This gent picked up Carmela, carried her over to the open window and tossed the lady out.

They all listened to one long scream and then a thud.

Bagger picked up the glass of orange juice on the tray and drank it down in one long gulp. He wiped his mouth with a napkin and said, "I drink orange juice every day. You know why? It's got a ton of calcium. I'm sixty-six, but do I look it? Hell no! Feel this muscle, Tony, go ahead and feel it." Bagger flexed his right biceps. Tony, however, seemed paralyzed.

Bagger feigned surprise. "Why so upset? Oh, because of the bitch going out the window? Don't worry about that." He looked at the man who'd done the tossing. "Hey, Mike, you aimed for the swimming pool, right, like in that James Bond movie? Which one was that again?"

"*Diamonds Are Forever,* Mr. Bagger," Mike said promptly.

Bagger smiled. "That's right, *Diamonds Are Forever.* Damn, I love that James Bond shit. That's the one with what's-her-name in the teeny bikini where you can see her butt crack. Stephanie Powers?"

"Jill St. John, Mr. Bagger," Mike corrected politely.

"Right, right, I always get those two broads mixed up. Bitches look just alike when they ain't got nothing on. Go figure."

"I didn't quite make the pool with the lady, Mr. Bagger," Mike admitted.

"But you tried, Mike, you tried, that's the important thing." He turned back to Tony. "That's the most important thing, right, Tony?"

Tony was obviously too horrified to speak.

"Besides, it's better this way, because the two old folks downstairs? You're not gonna believe this, they just keeled over and died when we walked in. And there's no way a pretty little thing like that bonita bitch could've kept up a big place like this all by herself. I look at it as a favor what we did, don't you, Tony?"

Tony nodded with great difficulty.

"Now feel my muscle. I want you to feel the *strength* I got in this body."

Not waiting for Tony to take the initiative, Bagger grabbed his hand and pulled it over to his flexed biceps. "You feel how hard that is, Tony? Do you understand how strong I am now? You got a real good sense of that?"

Tony wailed, "Please don't kill me, Mr. Bagger. Please. I'm sorry. I'm sorry."

Bagger gave Tony's fingers a crushing grip and let them go. "Come on, don't do that, apologies make a man look weak. Besides, it was a great scam, really first-rate. Everybody in the whole gambling world knows that you guys put one over on my ass to the tune of forty mil." Bagger looked away and drew a deep, calming breath, apparently trying hard to keep from dismembering the young man with his bare hands, at least for a few more minutes.

"But first, let's get one important thing squared away. I want you to ask me *how* I found you. I want you to know how smart I am and how fucking dumb you are. So ask me, Tony, how did I track you down, with all the places you could've gone in the whole freaking world after ripping me off?" Bagger grabbed ahold of Tony's slender neck and jerked him close. "*Ask* me, you little prick." A vein throbbed in Bagger's temple.

Tony said haltingly, "How did you find me, Mr. Bagger?"

Bagger slammed a forearm into Tony's shallow chest, knocking him back against the bed. Then the casino chief stood and paced. "I'm glad you asked me that. See, the bitch who ran the scam, she had you watching me that first night to make it look like I was under surveillance. Now, the only way to look into my office is to get a room on the twenty-third floor of the hotel across from my casino. So I go over there and make some inquiries about who occupied any rooms on that floor on that day that looked out onto my place. And I checked out every single person on that list."

He stopped pacing and grinned at Tony. "Until I found you. You were smart not to use your own name at the hotel, but you made a slip that the bitch and her sidekick didn't. That's why I couldn't track them down, 'cause they left nothing behind." Bagger wagged a finger at him. "But you, you went and got a massage, because I checked on that. And you hit on the chick that gave you the rubdown, looking for a little action on the side. But you didn't last too long with the lady and then ran into the bathroom to puke your guts out. While you were in there the bitch rolled your wallet and took some cash to add to the lousy C-note you gave her for popping early. And that's where she saw the driver's license with your real name. It was pretty dumb to keep it in there, Tony.

"So while you thought the BJ only cost you a hundred bucks, you can see the price tag really turned out to be a whole lot more. And the lowlife told me everything I needed to know for a lousy grand. Don't ever trust the bitches, Tony, they'll screw you every time, and don't I know it."

He sat back down next to Tony, who was now quietly sobbing. "You got a rep, young man. Gadget boy, do anything with a computer. Like putting spy shit on my bank wiring system and stealing forty million of my money. I mean, that's talent. So anyway, I greased a lot of palms, checked your friends, your family, traced some calls you made back home, killed a few uncooperative people, and now I find myself sitting here with you on the sunny coast of Spain or fucking Portugal or wherever the hell we are." He slapped Tony's bare leg.

"Okay, good, now I got that off my chest, we can move on." He motioned to one of his men, who pulled a compact pistol out of his jacket holster, spun a suppressor on the muzzle, chambered a round and handed it to Bagger.

"No, please, no," Tony whimpered before Bagger silenced him by jamming the pistol in the young man's mouth, breaking his two front teeth in the process.

Bagger wedged a forearm against Tony's windpipe, holding him down on the bed and sliding his finger near the trigger.

"Okay, Tony boy, here's the drill. You get one chance at this. One chance," he repeated slowly. "And it's only because I feel generous. Why, I don't know. Maybe I'm mellowing in my old age." He paused, licked his lips and said, "The bitch. I want her name and everything else you know about her. You tell me that, you get to live." He looked around the cavernous bedroom. "Not here, not on *my* dime. But you get to live. You don't tell me, well?" Bagger abruptly slid the pistol out of Tony's mouth, its muzzle covered in his blood and bits of teeth. "Oh, you thought I was just going to shoot you?" Bagger laughed. "No, no, that's not how this works. That's way too fast." He gave the gun to another man and held out his hand. Mike slapped a serrated knife into his palm.

"We do this stuff slow, and we have lots of practice." Bagger held out his other hand, and another of his men slipped a plastic glove on it.

Bagger continued, "You didn't used to have to do this glove stuff except because of fingerprints. But now what with all the diseases and crap everywhere, you can't take chances. I mean like the bonita bitch, how do you know she wasn't bonking every muchacho in town before you started banging her ripe ass? I hope you were at least wearing a rubber."

Bagger reached his gloved hand down, grabbed Tony's crotch and pulled hard.

Tony screamed in agony, but the other men held him down. Bagger studied Tony's private parts and said, "Frankly, I don't understand what bonita saw in you." He raised the knife up. "Okay, the bitch's name, where my money is and everything else. Then you get to live. Otherwise, I start with your balls, and then it gets really painful after that. What's it gonna be, Tony? You got five seconds. And once I start cutting, I don't stop for nothing."

Tony made a sound.

"What was that? I didn't quite get it."

"A-Ann—"

"Speak the hell up, you little asshole, my hearing's not that great."

"Annabelle!" he screamed.

"Annabelle? Annabelle who?" Bagger yelled so hard, spit flew out of his mouth.

"Annabelle . . . Conroy. Paddy Conroy's daughter."

Bagger slowly lowered the knife and let go of Tony's privates. He handed the blade to one of his men and stripped off the glove. Jerry Bagger stood and walked over to the window and looked out. His gaze didn't even linger for a second on the dead

Carmela, who'd landed flush on an ornate stone lion positioned next to the back door. Instead, he stared out at the ocean.

Annabelle *Conroy*? He'd never even known Paddy had a kid. Yet now it started to make sense. Paddy Conroy's little girl had been in his casino, in his office, played him like a fool and screwed him out of far more than her old man ever had.

Okay, Annabelle, I did your mama, now it's your turn.

He cracked his knuckles, turned back around and looked at bloody-mouthed Tony lying there on the bed weeping, a hand over his privates.

"What else?" he said. "Everything. And you get to keep breathing."

And Tony told him, finishing up with Annabelle's instructions on keeping a low profile and not spending his money all in one place.

Bagger said, "Well, you should've listened to the woman." He snapped his fingers. "Okay, guys, get to it. We don't have all day."

One of the men opened a black case he'd brought with him. Inside were four baseball bats. He handed three to the other men and kept one for himself.

As they raised the bats overhead, Tony shrieked. "But you said if I told you, you'd let me live. You said so."

Bagger shrugged. "That's right. And after the boys finish with you, you'll still be alive. Barely. Jerry Bagger is a man of his word."

As he walked out, he heard the first blow land, breaking Tony's right knee. Bagger started whistling, closed the door to muffle the screams and went downstairs for a cup of coffee.

CHAPTER

61

THE NEXT MORNING THE LI-
brary *was* in an uproar. Norman Janklow's murder, so soon after
DeHaven's death, had sent shock waves the length and breadth
of the Jefferson Building. When Caleb arrived for work, the
police and FBI were already interrogating everyone. Caleb did
his best to answer the questions with short answers. It didn't
help that the same two homicide detectives who'd given him
back the keys to DeHaven's house were also there. He sensed
that they were keeping a very close eye on him. Had someone
spotted him at Jewell's house? Had they found his prints there?
And Reuben had been released in time to commit the murder.
Did they suspect him as well? There was no way to tell.

Next his thoughts turned to the Beadle that Annabelle had
taken. He had brought it with him today. It had been relatively
easy, though Caleb was still a nervous wreck. The guards didn't
check bags going in, only coming out, and only visitors had their
bags run through the X-ray machine. Still, the presence of the
police only added to his tension. He breathed a sigh of relief
after he'd safely run the gauntlet of authority and put the book
away in his desk.

When a conservator showed up with some repaired books to be returned to the vault, Caleb volunteered to do it. This would give him the perfect opportunity to reshelve the Beadle. He put the dime novel in the stack with the others and went into the vault. He put away the repaired tomes and then headed to the section where the Beadles were kept. However, when he started to slide the book onto the shelf, he noticed that the tape Annabelle had used to secure it to her thigh had torn a corner of the cover when she pulled it off.

"Great, you'd have thought she could have been a little more careful, considering she *stole* the damn book in the first place," he muttered to himself. He'd have to take the Beadle to conservation. He left the vault, filled out the necessary paperwork and had the conservation request inputted on the computer system. Then he walked through the tunnels to the Madison Building, barely glancing at the room where the gas cylinder that had killed Jonathan DeHaven once lurked. Reaching the conservation department, he presented the book to Rachel Jeffries, a woman who did very thorough work and performed it promptly.

After chatting briefly with her about the latest awful news, Caleb returned to the reading room and sat at his desk. He looked around the space, so beautiful, so perfect for contemplation, so very empty right now after the deaths of two men associated with it.

He jerked when the door opened and Kevin Philips came in, looking gaunt and stricken. The two men spoke for a few minutes. Philips told Caleb he was thinking of resigning. "It's too much for my nerves," he explained. "I've lost ten pounds since Jonathan died. And with his neighbor being murdered and now with Janklow's death, the police don't think Jonathan's death was innocent."

"Well, they could be right."

"What do you think is going on, Caleb? I mean, this is a library. This stuff isn't supposed to happen to us."

"I wish I could tell you, Kevin."

Later Caleb spoke with Milton, who'd been keeping his eyes and ears glued to the media outlets. He reported that there was much speculation about Janklow's death, but no official cause had been reported. Jewell English's home had been rented by her two years earlier. The only connection between the woman and the dead man was their regular visits to the reading room. English was now missing. Inquiries into her background had come to a dead end. She apparently wasn't who she appeared to be. Perhaps Janklow wasn't either.

Big surprise there, Caleb thought as he hung up with Milton. Every time the door to the reading room opened, Caleb would tense. The place, so long a haven of peace and genteelness, was now like a recurrent nightmare. He just wanted to get out of its suffocating depths. *Suffocating! God, that was an unfortunate choice of words.* Yet he stayed because it was his job, and while he was often weak and impulsive in other aspects of his life, he was serious about his work. There were, not surprisingly, no patrons in the reading room today. At least this would give Caleb time to catch up on some tasks. However, that was not to be. Suddenly realizing that he was famished, Caleb decided to run out and get a sandwich.

"Mr. Foxworth?" Caleb said as the tall, good-looking man approached him out on the street in front of the Jefferson Building.

Seagraves nodded and smiled. "Please—Bill, remember? I was coming by to see you today." Actually, Seagraves had been waiting for Caleb to come outside.

"I'm just going to get a sandwich. I'm sure someone else can help you find a book in the reading room."

"Well, I was actually wondering if *you'd* like to see *my* books."

"What?"

"My collection. It's in my office. It's only a few blocks from here. I'm a lobbyist, specializing in the oil industry. It pays to be close to Capitol Hill in my business."

"I'm sure it does."

"Do you think you could spare a few minutes? I know it's a lot to ask."

"All right. Mind if I get a sandwich on the way? I haven't had lunch."

"Not at all. I also wanted to tell you that I have on a five-day inspection period works by Ann Radcliffe and Henry Fielding."

"Excellent. Which books?"

"Radcliffe's *The Romance of the Forest* and Fielding's *The History of the Adventures of Joseph Andrews.*"

"Very good choices, Bill. Radcliffe was a genius at Gothic mystery. People think horror writers today are on the edge? They should try reading Radcliffe. Her stuff will still scare the pants off you. *Joseph Andrews* is a fine parody of Richardson's *Pamela.* Fielding's ironic in that he was a true poet at heart whose greatest fame was as a novelist and playwright. It's said that his most popular play, *Tom Thumb,* made Jonathan Swift laugh for only the second time in his life." Caleb chuckled. "I'm not sure what the first was, though I have a few theories."

"Fascinating," Seagraves said as they walked down the street. "The thing is the dealer in Philly where I got the books says that they're first editions, and his letter makes the usual claims about typical points and other indicia, but I really need an expert opinion. These books aren't cheap."

"I would imagine not. Well, I'll take a look at them, and if I can't tell, which, without blowing my own horn too loudly, is doubtful, I can certainly put you in touch with someone who can."

"Mr. Shaw, I can't tell you how much I appreciate this."

"Please, call me Caleb."

Caleb grabbed a sandwich at a deli on Independence Avenue a block down from the Madison Building and then followed Seagraves to his office building.

It was located in a brownstone, Seagraves said, but they'd have to enter from the alley. "They're doing repairs on the lobby, and it's a mess. But there's an elevator we can ride from the basement right to my office."

As they walked down the alley, Seagraves kept a running conversation going about old books and his hopes of building an adequate collection.

"It takes time," Caleb said. "I have a part ownership interest in a rare book shop in Old Town Alexandria. You should drop by sometime."

"I'll certainly do that."

Seagraves stopped at a door in the alley, unlocked it and ushered Caleb inside.

He closed the door behind them. "The elevator's just around the corner."

"Fine. I think—"

Caleb didn't finish what he was thinking as he slumped to the floor unconscious. Seagraves stood over him, holding the blackjack he'd earlier hidden in a crevice of the interior wall. He hadn't lied. The brownstone's lobby *was* being renovated—the entire building was, in fact—and had been recently shut down so construction work could begin in a week.

Seagraves tied and gagged Caleb and then placed him in a box that sat open against one wall after taking off a ring from Caleb's right middle finger. He nailed the lid of the box shut and made a call. Five minutes later a van pulled into the alley. With the driver's help Seagraves lifted the box into the van. The men climbed in and the van pulled off.

CHAPTER

62

ANNABELLE HAD PICKED STONE
up before the crack of dawn, and they'd driven out to Trent's
home and settled themselves down where they could see his
driveway. They'd left Annabelle's rental car for Reuben to use
and taken his battered pickup truck for the surveillance. It fit in
a lot better in horse country than her Chrysler Le Baron had the
night before. Because she and Stone had been kidnapped, that
car was still parked on a dirt road about five hundred yards from
where they were. Annabelle had rented another car the previous
night at Dulles Airport.

Stone was looking through a pair of binoculars. It was dark,
chilly and damp, and with the truck's engine off, the interior
quickly became very cold. Annabelle snuggled down in her coat.
Stone seemed oblivious to the elements. They had only seen one
other car pass by, its headlights cutting through the fog that hovered a few feet above the ground. Stone and Annabelle had
ducked down in the truck's cab until it had gone by. The sleepy
driver was on his cell phone, gulping coffee and reading snatches
of a newspaper draped across the steering wheel.

An hour later, just as dawn was breaking, Stone tensed. "Okay,
something's coming."

A car had pulled out from Trent's driveway. As it slowed to make the turn onto the road, Stone focused his binoculars on the driver's side.

"It's Trent."

Annabelle looked around at the deserted area. "It might be a little obvious if we start tailing him."

"We're going to have to chance it."

Luckily, another car pulled past them, a station wagon with a mom driving and three small kids in the backseat. Trent pulled ahead of the station wagon.

Stone said, "Okay, that car's our buffer. If he checks the mirror, he'll see a family, nothing more. Hit it."

Annabelle put the truck in gear and pulled into line behind the second car.

They made it to Route 7 twenty minutes later through a series of back roads. As they did so, a few other cars joined the procession, but Annabelle managed to keep behind the station wagon, which, in turn, was right behind Trent. When they reached Route 7, a main artery into Tyson's Corner, Virginia, and Washington, D.C., the traffic picked up considerably. D.C. was an early-to-work sort of place, and major roads were routinely jammed as early as five-thirty.

"Don't lose him," Stone said urgently.

"I've got it covered." She expertly maneuvered the truck through traffic, keeping Trent's sedan within sight. It helped that it was getting light now.

Stone glanced at her. "You seem to have tailed people before."

"Just like I told Milton when he asked me a similar question, beginner's luck. So where do you think Trent's headed?"

"I hope to work."

Forty minutes later Stone was proved correct as Trent led

them to Capitol Hill. As he turned into a restricted area, they had to break off surveillance, but they watched as an automatic security barrier lowered into the ground and a guard waved him in.

Annabelle said, "If only that guard knew the guy's a spy and a murderer."

"Well, we have to prove that he is; otherwise, he's not. That's the way it works in a democracy."

"Almost makes you wish we were fascists in this country, doesn't it?"

"No, it doesn't," Stone said firmly.

"So what now?"

"Now we wait and watch."

Even before 9/11 undertaking surveillance near the Capitol was not easy going. Now it was nearly impossible unless one was nimble and tenacious. Annabelle continually had to move the truck, until they'd found a place close enough to see the exit Trent would have to come out of, and far enough away that the cops would not hassle them. Twice Stone had dashed across the street and bought them coffee and food. They listened to the radio and swapped a little bit more of their personal histories, along with large doses of conjecture on what their next move should be.

Milton had phoned Stone on a cell phone he'd loaned his friend. He had little to report. The police were being very tight-lipped about things, and consequently, the media kept running the same information over and over. Stone put the phone away and settled back in his seat, took a sip of coffee and glanced at his partner. "I'm surprised you're not complaining about the monotony. Stakeouts aren't easy."

"The gold always comes to patient people."

Stone looked around. "I'm assuming Trent will be working a full day, but we can't chance that."

"Isn't the Library of Congress around here somewhere?"

Stone pointed up ahead. "A block that way is the Jefferson Building, where Caleb works. I wonder how he's getting on. I'm sure the police were there today."

"Why don't you call him?" she suggested.

Stone phoned his friend's cell but Caleb didn't answer. He called the reading room next. A woman picked up and Stone asked for Caleb.

"He left a while ago to get some lunch."

"Did he say how long he'd be gone?"

The woman said, "Can I ask what this is in reference to?"

Stone clicked off and sat back.

"Anything wrong?" Annabelle asked.

"I don't think so. Caleb just went off to get some lunch."

Stone's phone rang. He recognized the number on the screen. "It's Caleb." He put the phone up to his ear. "Caleb, where are you?"

Stone stiffened. A minute later he put the phone down.

"What's up?" Annabelle asked. "What did Caleb say?"

"It wasn't Caleb. It was the people who are holding Caleb."

"What!"

"He's been kidnapped."

"My God, what do they want? And why are they calling you?"

"They got the number from Milton. They want to meet to discuss things. Any sign of the police, they kill him."

"What do they mean they want to meet?"

"They want you, me, Milton and Reuben to come."

"So they can kill us?"

"Yes, so they can kill us. But if we don't go, they'll kill Caleb."

"How do we know he's not already dead?"

"At ten o'clock tonight they said they'd call and let him talk to us. That's when they'll tell us where and when the meeting is."

Annabelle drummed her fingers on the worn steering wheel. "So what do we do?"

Stone studied the Capitol dome in the distance. "You play poker?"

"I don't like to gamble," she answered with a straight face.

"Well, Caleb's their full house. So we need at least that or better to be able to play this hand. And I know where to get the cards we need." However, Stone knew that his plan would test the limits of friendship to the max. Yet he had no choice. He punched in the number, which he knew by heart.

"Alex, this is Oliver. I need your help. Badly."

Alex Ford sat forward in his chair at the Secret Service's Washington Field Office.

"What's going on, Oliver?"

"It's a long story, but you need to hear it all."

When Stone finished, Ford sat back and let out a long breath. "Damn."

"Can you help us?"

"I'll do my best."

"I've got a plan."

"I hope you do. It sounds like we don't have much time to pull this together."

Albert Trent left Capitol Hill that evening and drove home. Leaving Route 7, he followed the meandering back roads to his isolated neighborhood. He slowed as he approached the last turn before his driveway. A pickup truck had run off the road and hit something. An ambulance and a utility truck were there along with a police car. A uniformed cop was standing in the middle of the road. Trent drove cautiously ahead until the policeman stepped forward with his hand up. Trent rolled down his window and the cop leaned in.

"I'm going to have to ask you to turn around, sir. That truck skidded off the road and hit an aboveground natural gas pressure regulator and caused a major surge in the pipes. Damn lucky he didn't blow himself and the neighborhood sky-high."

"But I live right around the bend. And I don't have gas in my house."

"Okay, I'll need to see some ID with your address on it."

Trent dug into his jacket pocket and handed the officer his driver's license. The cop hit it with his flashlight and then handed it back.

"All right, Mr. Trent."

"How soon will they fix it?"

"That's a question for the gas company. Oh, one more thing."

He reached his other hand in the window and sprayed something from a small canister directly into Trent's face. The man coughed once and slumped over in his seat.

On cue, out of the ambulance stepped Stone, Milton and Reuben. With the cop's help Reuben lifted Trent out of the car and into another car that pulled forward, Annabelle at the wheel. Alex Ford emerged from the ambulance and handed Stone a leather canvas knapsack. "You need me to show you how to use it again?"

Stone shook his head. "I've got it. Alex, I know this is a stretch for you, and I really appreciate it. I didn't know where else to turn."

"Oliver, we'll get Caleb back. And if this is the spy ring that people have been whispering about and we can bust it, you guys all deserve medals. When you get the call, let us know the details. I've got multiagency support on this. Just so you know, I didn't have to beg for volunteers on this one because a lot of guys are itching to nail these bastards."

Stone climbed into the car with the others.

"And now we play the hand," Annabelle said.

"Now we play the hand," Stone affirmed.

CHAPTER

63

THE CALL CAME AT PRECISELY
ten o'clock. Stone and the rest of the group were in a downtown
hotel suite. The man on the other end started to dictate the time
and place to meet, but Stone cut him off.

"We're not going to do that. We have Albert Trent. You want
him back, then we'll do an exchange on *our* terms."

"That is not acceptable," the voice said.

"Fine, then we turn your buddy over to the CIA and they can
'coax' the truth out of him, including naming names, and believe
me, what I've seen of Trent, it won't take long. You won't even
have time to pack a bag before the FBI knocks down your door."

"Do you want your friend to die?" the man snapped.

"I'm telling you how they both can *live,* and you can avoid
going to prison for the rest of your life."

"How do we know this isn't a trick?"

"How do I know you're not planning to put a bullet into me
when I show up? Simple, we have to trust each other."

There was a long pause. "Where?"

Stone told him where and when.

"Do you realize what tomorrow will be like down there?"

"That's why I picked it. We'll see you at noon. And one more thing: If you harm Caleb, I will kill you personally." Stone clicked off and turned to the others.

Milton looked fearful but determined. Reuben was examining the contents of the leather pack Alex Ford had given them. Annabelle's gaze was directly on Stone.

Stone went over to Reuben. "How's it look?"

He held up two syringes and two bottles of liquid. "Amazing stuff, Oliver. What will they think of next?"

Stone walked into the adjoining room, where an unconscious Albert Trent was strapped to the bed. Stone stood there, fighting a strong impulse to attack the sleeping man who'd caused them all such pain.

A minute later he rejoined the others. "Tomorrow will be a long day, so we need to get some sleep. We'll run two-hour shifts watching Trent. I'll take the first one."

Milton immediately curled up on the couch while Reuben lay down on one of the double beds. Both men were asleep within a few minutes. Stone went back into the other room, sat down in a chair next to Trent and stared at the floor. He jerked when Annabelle pulled up a chair beside his and handed him a cup of coffee she'd made. She was still dressed in jeans and a sweater, but her feet were bare. She curled one long leg under her as she sat down.

He thanked her for the coffee and added, "You should get some sleep."

"I'm more of a night person, actually." She glanced at Trent. "So what are the odds of everything going perfectly tomorrow?"

"Zero," Stone answered. "It's always zero. Then you do all you can to beat that number, but sometimes it's out of your hands."

"You speak from experience, don't you?"

"What else do you speak from?"

"Bullshit, like most people, but not you."

He sipped his coffee and stared off. "Alex Ford is a good man. I'd go into battle with him anytime. I have, in fact. We actually have a decent shot at doing this clean."

"I want to kill that little creep," she said, watching the unconscious Trent.

Stone nodded and ran his gaze over the man. "He looks like a mouse, a desk jockey, which is exactly what he is, to most people. Wouldn't hurt a fly. He just gets other people to do it for him, and this cruelty has no limit because he doesn't have to see it or dirty his hands. Because of people like him, our country has been put at great risk."

"All for money?"

"I've known some to claim it was about a cause, about following their beliefs, even about the excitement, but it's always really about the money."

She eyed him curiously. "You've known other traitors?"

He glanced sideways at her. "Why do you find any of this interesting?"

"I find *you* interesting." When he remained silent, she said, "We were talking about other traitors?"

He shrugged. "I've known more of them than I cared to. But I didn't know them for long." He rose and went over to the window. "In fact, most of them I only saw for a few seconds before they died," he added barely in a whisper.

"Is that what you were? The assassin of American traitors?" Stone's shoulders tensed and she added hurriedly, "I'm sorry, John, I shouldn't have said that."

He turned to face her. "I guess I failed to mention that John Carr is dead. So why don't you make it 'Oliver' from now on?" He sat back down without looking at her. "I *really* think you need to get some sleep."

As she rose to leave, she glanced back. Stone sat rigid in the chair seemingly staring at Albert Trent, but Annabelle didn't believe the man was looking at the handcuffed spy. His thoughts were probably far in the past, perhaps recollecting how to give a bad man a quick death.

Not that far away Roger Seagraves was marshaling his own team, trying to anticipate every move the other side would make. He hadn't been back to his house because he'd suspected something had happened to Trent. He and his partner had implemented a system whereby each would call the other by a certain time in the evening if everything was okay. He obviously hadn't gotten that call. Their capturing Trent complicated matters but didn't make things insurmountable. He had to assume that Oliver Stone and the others had gone to the authorities by now, so there were several levels of opposition he would have to bust through to get Trent clear, if the man hadn't already ratted him out. However, rather than fearing tomorrow, Seagraves was looking forward to it. It was such times that the man lived for. And it was only the best man that would survive. And Seagraves was certain he would be that man tomorrow. Just as certain as he was that Oliver Stone and his friends would be dead.

CHAPTER

64

THE NEXT DAY BROKE CLEAR AND warm. Stone and the others left the hotel, transporting Trent in a large trunk that they loaded into a van. Inside the van, Stone squatted over Albert Trent and gave him an injection in the arm using one of the syringes. He waited ten minutes and then injected Trent with the other syringe. A minute later the man's eyes fluttered open. As he came to, Trent looked wildly around and tried to sit up.

Stone pressed a hand against his chest and then took a knife out of a sheath on his belt. Holding the blade in front of Trent's quivering face, he slid it between the man's skin and the gag, severing the cloth.

Trent said in a shaky voice, "What are you doing? I'm a federal employee. You could go to jail for this."

"Save it, Trent. We know everything. And if you don't do anything stupid, we're going to give you up for Caleb Shaw in a nice, easy exchange. But if you don't cooperate, I'll kill you myself, or would you rather spend the rest of your life in prison for treason?"

"I have no idea—"

Stone held the blade up. "That's not what I meant by being cooperative. We have the book and the code and the evidence that you set up Bradley to be killed. And we know about Jonathan DeHaven and Cornelius Behan. And you almost added me and her to your bag, but we decided it wasn't our time to go." He inclined his head in Annabelle's direction.

She said, smiling, "If you're going to have thugs jump people at your house and then try and murder them, you shouldn't stand in a spot where the mirror captures your reflection, Al. And if it were up to me, I'd slit your throat and toss your body in a landfill. That's where you're supposed to deposit garbage, right?"

Stone unlocked the handcuffs around the man's hands and feet. "We're doing a one-to-one exchange. We get Caleb, you go free."

"How can I be sure of that?"

"The same way Caleb can be, you just have to trust. Now get up!"

Trent rose on shaky legs and looked at the others arrayed around him in the back of the van. "Are you the only ones who know? If you've called in the police—"

"Just shut up," Stone snapped. "And I hope you have your fake passport and plane tickets ready."

Reuben opened the van doors and they all stepped out, with Trent in the middle.

"My God," Trent said, "what the hell is going on here?" He was looking at a sea of people.

Stone said, "Don't you read the papers? It's the National Book Festival on the Mall."

"And a march against poverty," Milton added.

"Two hundred thousand people total," Reuben chimed in.

"What a great day in the capital city. Reading books and fighting for the poor." He gave Trent a poke in the side. "Let's get going, ass-wipe, we don't want to be late."

The National Mall stretched for nearly two miles, bracketed on the west by the Lincoln Memorial and on the east by the Capitol and encircled by vast museums and imposing government buildings.

The National Book Festival, an annual event, had grown to over 100,000 attendees. Circus-size tents had been erected on the Mall emblazoned with banners reading Fiction, History, Children's Literature, Thrillers and Poetry, among others. In these tents writers, illustrators, storytellers and others held large crowds enraptured with their readings and anecdotes.

On Constitution Avenue the March Against Poverty was ramping up, with its destination the Capitol. After that, many of the marchers would join in the book festival, which was free and open to the public.

Stone had carefully planned the exchange point with input from Alex Ford. It was near the Smithsonian Castle on Jefferson Street. With thousands of people around, it would be nearly impossible for a shooter to get off a clean shot even at a distance. In his knapsack Stone carried the one device that would allow him to complete this mission the right way, for once he had Caleb back safely, Stone had no intention of allowing Albert Trent and his fellow spies to escape.

Reuben said, "Up ahead, two o'clock, by the bike rack."

Stone nodded, and his gaze caught Caleb standing on a small grass plot partially encircled by a waist-high hedge, with a large and elaborate fountain beyond that. It offered some privacy and a buffer from the throngs of people. Behind Caleb were two men with hoods pulled up and wearing dark sunglasses. Stone was sure they were armed, but he also knew that federal snipers were stationed on the roof of the castle, their beads no doubt already drawn on the men. Yet they would only fire if necessary. He also knew that Alex Ford was around helping to coordinate the operation.

Stone eyed Caleb, trying to get his attention, but there were so many people around, it was difficult. Caleb looked panicked, which was normal, but Stone detected something else in his friend's eyes that he didn't like: hopelessness.

And that's when Stone saw the thing around Caleb's neck.

"My God!" he muttered. "Reuben, do you see it?"

The big man looked stricken. "Those bastards!"

Stone turned to Milton and Annabelle, who were following behind. "Stay back!"

"What?" Annabelle said.

"But, Oliver," Milton protested.

"Just do it!" Stone snapped.

The two stopped. Annabelle looked particularly stung by Stone's order, and Milton seemed paralyzed. Reuben, Stone and Trent moved on until they came face-to-face with Caleb and his captors.

Caleb moaned over the sound of the fountain in the background and pointed to what looked like a dog collar around his neck. "Oliver?"

"I know, Caleb, I know." He pointed to the device and said to the hooded men, "Take that off him. Now!"

Both men shook their heads. One held up a small black box with two buttons sprouting from it. "Only when we're safely away."

"You think I'm letting you walk away leaving a bomb locked on my friend's neck?"

"As soon as we're away, we'll deactivate it," the man said.

"And I'm just supposed to trust you?"

"That's right."

"Then you're not leaving, and if you detonate the bomb, we all die."

"It's not a bomb," the same man said. He held up the black box. "I push the red button, enough toxin to kill an elephant goes right into him. He'll be dead before I let go of the button. I push the black button, the system is disengaged and you can take the collar off without releasing the poison. Don't try to take the control from me forcibly. And if a sniper shoots, my reflex will involuntarily push the button." He let his finger hover over the red button as he smiled at Stone's obvious dilemma.

"You enjoying this, asshole?" Reuben spat out.

The man kept his gaze on Stone. "We're assuming you've got cops everywhere just waiting to take us once your friend here is safe. So excuse us for taking obvious precautions."

Stone said, "And what's to prevent you from triggering it once you're gone? And don't give me the trust answer again. It'll make me upset."

"My orders were not to kill him unless our escape was blocked. If you let us go, he lives."

"What exact point do you need to get to before you deactivate the poison?"

"Not very far away at all. In three minutes we'll be gone. But if we wait too long, I push the red button."

Stone gazed at Caleb, then at the furious Reuben and back at Caleb. "Caleb, listen to me. We have to trust them."

"Oh, God, Oliver. Please help me." Caleb didn't appear willing to trust anyone.

"I will, Caleb, I will." In desperation Stone said, "How many loaded darts do you have in that damn thing?"

"What?" The man looked startled.

"How many!"

"Two. One on the left and one on the right."

Stone turned and gave his knapsack to Reuben and whispered. "If we die, don't let us die in vain."

Reuben took the knapsack and nodded, his face pale, but his manner rock-steady.

Stone turned back around and held up his left hand. "Let me slide my hand under the collar so the left dart will hit me instead of my friend."

The man now looked totally flustered. "But then you'll both die."

"That's right. We'll both die *together*!"

Caleb stopped shaking and stared directly at Stone. "Oliver, you can't do that."

"Caleb, shut up." Stone looked at the man. "Tell me where to put my hand."

"I don't know if this—"

"Tell me!" Stone shouted.

The man pointed to a spot, and Stone squeezed his hand in the narrow space, his skin now resting against Caleb's.

"Okay," Stone said. "When will I know it's been disarmed?"

"When the red light on the side there turns green," the man said, pointing to a small crimson glass bubble on the collar. "Then you can undo the clasp and it comes right off. But if you try to force it off before, it automatically engages."

"Understood." He glanced at Trent. "Now, take that scum and get the hell out of here."

Albert Trent pulled away from Reuben's grasp and marched over to the hooded men. As they started walking away, Trent turned back and grinned. "Adios!"

Stone kept his eyes tight on Caleb's face. He was also talking to his friend in a low voice, even as onlookers slowed and pointed at what must have seemed a very unusual scene, one man's hand jammed under a collar on another man's neck.

"Deep breaths, Caleb. They're not going to kill us. They're not going to kill us. Deep breaths." He checked his watch. Sixty seconds had passed since the men had left with Trent and disappeared into the crowd. "Two more minutes and we're home free. We're good, we're in great shape." He looked at his watch. "Ninety seconds. We're almost there. Hang with me. Hang with me, Caleb."

Caleb was holding Stone's arm in a death grip, his face flushed, his breath coming in mangled gasps, but he was standing firm and finally said, "I'm okay, Oliver."

Once, a suspicious Park Police officer started heading their way, but two men in white jumpsuits who'd been cleaning out trash cans intercepted the cop and sent him on his way. They'd already relayed the situation to the snipers, who'd stood down.

Meantime, Milton and Annabelle had crept forward, and Reuben whispered to them what was going on. Tears fell down Milton's horrified face while Annabelle put a trembling hand to her mouth and watched as the two men clung to each other.

"Thirty seconds, Caleb, we're almost there." Stone's gaze was now directly on the red light on the collar as he counted off the ticks. "Okay, ten seconds and we're free."

Stone and Caleb together mouthed the final countdown. But the light didn't turn to green. Caleb couldn't see this and said, "Oliver, can you take it off now?"

Even Stone's nerves began to fail now, yet he never once thought of pulling his hand free. He closed his eyes for a second, awaiting the sting of the needle and the poison right behind it.

"Oliver!" This was Annabelle calling out to him. "Look."

Stone opened his eyes and stared at the beautiful little drop of green in the bubble.

"Reuben! Help me," he called out.

Reuben shot forward, and together they unlocked the collar and slipped it off Caleb's neck. The librarian fell to his knees as the others crowded around him. When he finally looked up, he grabbed Stone's hand.

He gushed, "That was the bravest thing anyone's ever done, Oliver. Thank you."

Stone looked around at the others, and then the truth hit home. It took him barely an instant to react. He shouted, "Get down!" He grabbed the collar and threw it over the hedge, and it landed in the large fountain.

Two ticks later the collar exploded, sending geysers of water and chunks of concrete shooting into the air. The crowds on the Mall panicked and started running. When Stone and the others slowly got to their feet, Caleb said, "My God, Oliver, how did you know?"

"It's an old tactic, Caleb, to draw us all in and let down our guard. And he told me where the poisoned needles were in the collar because he knew the bomb would kill us, not the poison, if there ever was any poison in it." Stone took the knapsack from Reuben and pulled from it a small flat object with a small screen on it. On the screen a blob of red was moving fast.

"Now we finish this," he said.

CHAPTER

65

"THEY'VE GONE INTO THE Smithsonian Metro entrance," Reuben said, eyeing the small screen Stone was holding as the group raced across the Mall and pushed their way through the panicked crowds and small blocks of police.

"That's why we picked that exchange spot," Stone answered.

"But the Metro will be jammed," Milton said. "How will we find them in there?"

"We took a page from Trent and company. You know the chemical wash they put on the letters in the book to make them glow?"

"Sure, so?" Milton said.

Stone said, "I injected Trent with a chemical provided by Alex Ford that transmits a signal to this receiver. It's like the man's glowing for us. Using this, we can pick him out of a crowd of thousands. Alex and his men also have a receiver. We're going to pin them down."

"I hope it works," Caleb said as they forced their way through the swells of people. He rubbed his neck. "I want to see them rot in jail. And no *books* to read. Ever! That'll serve them right."

Suddenly, screams poured out of the station below.

"Come on!" Stone shouted, and they dashed down the escalator.

While Trent and the two men were waiting for the next train, a pair of agents disguised as maintenance workers had approached from their rear. Before they had a chance to draw their weapons, both men fell forward with gaping bullet wounds in their backs. Behind them Roger Seagraves, wearing a cloak, replaced the silenced pistols in his twin belt holsters. The noise of the crowds had covered the suppressed shots, but when the men fell, and the people saw the blood, the screams started, and panicked citizens began running in all directions. An instant before one of the agents died, he rallied, pulled his gun and shot one of the hooded men in the head. As this man dropped, the detonator device he still carried in his hand clattered to the stone tile floor.

A westbound train roared into the station and disgorged still more passengers, who ran headlong into the growing chaos.

Trent and his remaining guard used this panic to jump onto one of this train's cars. Seagraves did likewise, but with the riptide of the crowd he could only manage to scramble onto the next car down.

Right before the doors closed, Stone and the others fought their way through the mass of people and clambered aboard. The train car was packed, but Stone checked his tracking device and saw that Trent was very close by. He scanned the interior and finally spotted him at the other end. Stone quickly noted that only one hooded man remained with him. The problem was that at any moment Trent or his bodyguard could spot them.

A few moments later Alex Ford and several other agents ran

through the crowd, but the train was already pulling out. He yelled at his men, and they ran back out of the station.

Inside the moving train, Stone said, "Reuben, sit down, quick!" Reuben towered over everyone and thus was the one most likely to be spotted. Reuben pushed some teenage boys out of the way and sat on the floor. Stone ducked down and kept his gaze on Trent. He was talking to his bodyguard and holding his hands up to his ears for some reason. Facing the way he was, Stone couldn't see Roger Seagraves in the car behind him, watching him through the glass. Seagraves had been stunned to see that Caleb and the others were still alive. He was lining up for a shot to Stone's head when the train sped into the next station and lurched to a stop. People pushed and pulled to get on and off, and Seagraves was levered away from his kill position.

The train took off again and gained speed rapidly. Stone was now making his way through the crowd toward Trent. He palmed his knife, keeping the blade tucked against his forearm under his sleeve. He visualized plunging the knife up to the hilt into Trent's chest. Yet that wasn't his plan. He would kill the guard, but Stone had no intention of cheating Trent out of spending the rest of his life in prison.

Stone was closing in on his target when his plans were foiled. The train rocketed into Metro Center, came to a stop, and the doors burst open. Metro Center was the busiest station in the entire subway system. Trent and his guard jumped through the open door. In the next car down Seagraves did likewise. Stone and the others pushed their way out and into a crush of passengers rushing to and from trains arriving and departing on two different levels and from several different directions.

Stone kept his gaze on Trent and the hooded figure next to

him. From the corner of his eye he saw two men in white jump-suits heading toward Trent. What he didn't see was Roger Sea-graves slide a small metal object out of his pocket, pull a pin with his teeth and let it fly, even as he turned his back and made sure his ears were plugged.

Stone saw the oblong cylinder sail past him through the air and knew instantly what it was. He whirled around and screamed to Reuben and the others, "Get down and cover your ears!" A couple seconds later the "flash-bang" went off, and dozens of people around it collapsed to the floor holding their ears, cover-ing their eyes and screaming in pain.

Trent and his bodyguard had been unaffected by the explo-sion. They'd put ear protectors on and had averted their gaze from the "flash" part of the flash-bang.

Stone, woozy despite having put his face to the floor and jammed his coat sleeves into his ears, looked up and saw shoes and feet flying in front of him. As he tried to get up, a large man fleeing the panic barreled into him, knocking him down. Stone felt the tracker fly out of his hands, and he watched with a sick-ening feeling as it slid across the floor, over the edge and onto the tracks under the train as it pulled out of the station. When the end car cleared the station, he lunged to the edge and looked down. The box had been crushed.

He turned back around and saw that Reuben had attacked the hooded man. Stone sprang to his friend's aid, not that the big man needed it. Reuben put the smaller man in a half nelson, lifted him off the floor and slammed him headfirst into a metal pole. Then Reuben flung the man away, and he slid across the slick floor as people scrambled to get out of the way. As Reuben stormed toward him, Stone hit him from behind, knocking his friend down.

"What the hell—" Reuben grunted as the shot fired by the man sailed by overhead. Stone had seen the gun and knocked Reuben out of the way just in time.

The hooded man rose on one knee and prepared for a point-blank shot but was dropped by the impact of three rounds in his chest fired by two federal agents who came running up followed by uniformed police.

Stone helped Reuben up and looked around for the others.

Annabelle waved from a far corner, Milton and Caleb beside her.

"Where's Trent?" Stone called out.

Annabelle shook her head and held her hands up in a helpless gesture.

Stone stared hopelessly around the crowded platform. They'd lost him.

Suddenly, Caleb screamed, "There, going up the escalator. That's the man who kidnapped me. Foxworth!"

"And Trent!" Milton added.

They all looked upward. At the sound of his alias Seagraves glanced over his shoulder, and his hood fell away, giving them all a good look at him and Albert Trent, who was beside him.

"Damn," Seagraves muttered. He maneuvered Trent through the crowd, and they raced out of the train station.

Up on the street Seagraves pushed Albert Trent into a cab and gave an address to the driver. He whispered to Trent, "I'll meet you there later. I've got a private plane ready to take us out of the country. Here're your travel papers and new ID pack. We'll get your appearance altered." He shoved a thick wad of documents and a passport into Trent's hands.

Seagraves started to slam the cab door shut and then abruptly stopped. "Albert, give me your watch."

"What?"

Seagraves didn't ask again. He ripped the watch off Trent's wrist and closed the cab door. It drove off, a panicked Trent looking back at him through the window. Seagraves planned to kill Trent later, and he had to have something belonging to him. He was very angry about having to leave his collection behind, because he couldn't risk returning to his house. And Seagraves was also upset because he hadn't been able to get any items from the two agents he'd killed in the Metro.

Well, I can always start a new collection.

He ran across the street to an alleyway, climbed into a van he'd parked there and changed his clothes. Then he waited for his pursuers to appear. And this time he wouldn't miss.

CHAPTER

66

STONE AND THE OTHERS RODE
the escalator out of the Metro along with hundreds of other panicked people. While sirens filled the air and a small army of police converged on the area to investigate the rampage, they walked down the street aimlessly.

"Thank goodness Caleb's okay," Milton said.

"Absolutely," Reuben bellowed. He grabbed Caleb around the shoulders. "What the hell would we do without you to tease?"

"Caleb, how did you come to be abducted?" Stone asked curiously.

Caleb quickly explained about the man calling himself William Foxworth. "He said he had books for me to look at, and then the next thing I know, I'm unconscious."

"Foxworth, that was the name he used?" Stone asked.

"Yes, it was on his library card, so he would've had to show some ID to get it."

"Undoubtedly not his real name. At least we got a look at him."

"What do we do now?" Annabelle asked.

"What I still don't understand is how the chemical wash was put in the books," Milton said. "Albert Trent works on the intelligence committee staff. He gets the secrets somehow and then passes them on to whom? And how do they end up in books at the reading room where Jewell English and presumably Norman Janklow see and write them down using their special glasses?"

While they were all mulling those questions, Stone used his cell phone to check in with Alex Ford. They were still looking for Trent, but Ford advised Stone and the others to pull back from the chase. "No sense in putting yourselves in more danger," he said. "You've done enough."

After Stone had told them that, Caleb said, "So where do we go? Home?"

Stone shook his head. "The Library of Congress is near here. I want to go there."

Caleb wanted to know why.

"Because that's where this all started, and a library is always a good place to get answers."

Caleb was able to get them into the library but not the reading room because it was closed on Saturday. Wandering the halls, Stone said to the others, "What confuses me most of all is the timing of events." He paused, marshaling his thoughts. "Jewell English came to the reading room two days ago, and the highlights were in the Beadle book. Later that night, when we had the book, the highlights vanished. That is a very tight time frame."

Caleb said, "It is amazing, really, because most books in the vault sit unread for years, even decades. The highlighting would have to go on the letters, and Jewell would have to be contacted to come in with the name of the book to ask for. Then, like you said, that very same day the highlights disappear."

Stone stopped walking and leaned against a marble banister. "Yet how could they be so sure the timing would work? You wouldn't want the wash to remain on the pages very long in case the police got their hands on them. Indeed, if we'd acted a little sooner, we might have gotten the book to the FBI before the chemical evaporated. So logically, the highlighting had to have taken place close to the time English came in."

Caleb said, "I'd been in and out of the vaults before Jewell came in that day. I didn't see anyone in there other than some of the staff, and none stayed longer than ten or fifteen minutes. That wouldn't have been nearly long enough to highlight all those letters. And they couldn't have done it anywhere else, because that would require them taking the book home." He jerked. "Wait a minute. If any of the staff *had* taken it home, I can check that. They'd have to fill out the four-part call slip. Come on! The reading room's closed, but I can check from another place."

He led them to the library's main reference desk, talked to the woman there for a few moments and then stepped behind the counter, logged on the computer and started typing. A minute later he looked disappointed. "No Beadles have been checked out. In fact, no books at all have been checked out by library personnel in over four months."

While they all were standing there, Rachel Jeffries walked by. She was the conservator Caleb had brought the Beadle dime novel containing the highlights to for repair.

She said, "Oh, hello, Caleb, I didn't think you came in on weekends anymore."

"Hi, Rachel, just doing some research."

"I'm trying to catch up on some backlog at conservation. I popped over here to meet with someone on a project I'm doing. Oh, while I have you, I wanted to let you know that the Beadle you gave me to work on had just recently been returned to the vault after repairs."

"What?" Caleb said, stunned.

"It had some back cover damage and a few loose pages. When

I looked up its conservation history, I was really surprised because, like I said, it had just been brought back to the vault. Any idea how it was damaged again?"

"When *exactly* had it been brought back to the vault?" Caleb asked, ignoring her question.

"Why, the day before you gave it to me."

"Rachel, hang on a minute." Caleb started tapping on the computer keyboard again. He was looking for how many Beadles had been sent to conservation in the recent past. His answer came back quickly as the software churned through the data.

"Thirty-six Beadles repaired over the last two years," he said to the others. Next he checked the records for books Jewell English and Norman Janklow had requested, together with *all* books that had gone to the conservation department over the last six months. He found that Jewell English had requested 70 percent of the Beadles that had been repaired in the last six months. And she'd requested them on the exact day they had come back from conservation. He found a similar pattern for Norman Janklow.

He told the others the results of his search. "The Beadles require a lot of preservation work because they were so cheaply made."

Stone, whose mind had raced ahead of the others, looked at Rachel Jeffries. "Can you tell us which conservator repaired that particular Beadle?"

"Oh, sure, it was Monty Chambers."

Stone and the others started running down the long corridor. Caleb called back over his shoulder, "Rachel, I love you."

She immediately blushed but managed to say, "Caleb, you know I'm *married*. But maybe we can have a drink sometime."

"Do you know where Chambers lives?" Stone asked Caleb as they ran out onto the street.

Caleb nodded. "It's actually not too far from here." They hailed two cabs and sped off. Fifteen minutes later the cabs slowed as they turned onto a quiet residential street lined with old row houses that were in good repair. Each had a small square of front yard enclosed by two-foot-high wrought-iron railings.

"This area looks familiar for some reason," Stone said.

"There are a lot of neighborhoods just like this one around here," Caleb explained.

They climbed out of the cabs, and Caleb led them up to one of the homes. The brick was painted blue and the shutters were coal black. Flowers sat in pots on the windowsill.

"You've been here before, obviously," Stone said, and Caleb nodded.

"Monty has a workshop at home where he repairs books freelance. I've referred several people to him. He's even repaired a couple of my books. I can't believe he'd be mixed up in something like this. He's the best conservator LOC has, been there for decades."

"Everyone has their price, and a conservator would be the perfect person to doctor the books," Stone remarked, looking cautiously at the front of the house. "I doubt that he's hanging around here, but you never know. Reuben and I will knock on the door while you all stay back."

The knock prompted no response. Stone glanced around. There was no one on the street. "Give me some cover, Reuben," he said.

Reuben turned around and placed his wide body between Stone and the street. A minute later the lock clicked open. Stone went in first, followed by Reuben. The main floor revealed nothing of interest. The furniture was old, but hardly antique, the pictures on the walls were prints, the refrigerator had some old takeout in it, the dishwasher was empty. The two bedrooms upstairs yielded little of interest. Some slacks, shirts and jackets hung in one closet, underwear and socks in the small bureau. The bathroom held the usual items, though Stone picked up a couple objects with a puzzled look. The medicine cabinet held the typical assortment of prescriptions and toiletries. They found nothing that might indicate where Chambers had gone.

When they got back downstairs, the others were standing in the foyer.

"Anything?" Caleb asked anxiously.

Stone answered, "You mentioned a workshop?"

"Lower level."

They trooped down and searched through Chambers' work space. It had all the things one would expect to see in a book conservator's arsenal and nothing else.

"Dead end," Reuben proclaimed.

The lower level was a walk-out, and Stone glanced out the window. "Opens into an alleyway with a row of buildings on the other side."

"So?" Reuben said irritably. "I doubt a fleeing traitor would be lurking in an alley waiting for the feds to show up."

Stone opened the door, stepped out and looked up and down the alley. "Wait here!" He ran down the alley, turned the corner and disappeared from view. When he returned a few minutes later, his eyes were gleaming.

Reuben was watching his friend closely. "You remembered why this place looks familiar. You've been here before?"

"We've *all* been here before, Reuben."

STONE LED THEM AROUND THE
corner and down the street along the front of the row houses that
backed to the alley opposite Chambers' home. Stone stopped in
the middle of the block and motioned the others to stay put as he
stared upward at something on the building they were in front of.

"Good Lord," Caleb said, looking around and realizing
where he was. "I didn't recognize it in the daytime."

"Caleb, ring the bell," Stone instructed.

Caleb did so and a deep voice said, "Yes, who is it?"

Stone motioned to Caleb. "Oh, it's me, Mr. Pearl, Caleb Shaw.
I, uh, I wanted to talk to you about the *Psalm Book.*"

"I am not open. My hours are clearly posted on the sign."

"It's very urgent," Caleb said. "Please? It won't take long."

A long moment passed and then they heard a click. Caleb
pulled the door open and they all went inside. When Vincent
Pearl appeared a moment later, he was not dressed in long robes,
but in black pants, white shirt and a green work apron. His long
hair was disheveled and his beard untidy. He appeared startled
to see the others with Caleb and said angrily, "I'm very busy
right now, Shaw. I cannot drop everything simply because you
show up unannounced."

Stone stepped forward. "Where's Albert Trent? In the back room?"

Pearl gaped at him. "Excuse me? Who?"

Stone pushed past him, kicked open the door to the back room and went in. He came out a minute later. "Upstairs, then?"

"What the hell are you doing?" Pearl screamed. "I'll call the police."

Stone darted past him for the spiral stairs and motioned for Reuben to follow him upstairs. "Watch out, Foxworth might be with him." The pair disappeared upstairs, and a minute later the others heard screams and a struggle. Then the noise abruptly stopped, and Stone and Reuben marched downstairs holding firmly to Albert Trent.

They threw the man in a chair, and Reuben stood next to him. The intelligence committee staffer looked thoroughly beaten, but Reuben still growled, "Just give me an excuse to snap your scrawny neck."

Stone turned to face Pearl, who, unlike Trent, had lost none of his composure.

"I have no idea what you think you're doing," Pearl said as he lifted the apron over his shoulders. "This man is a friend of mine, and he's here at my invitation."

"Where's Chambers?" Caleb blurted out. "Is he here at your invitation too?"

"Who?" Pearl said.

Caleb looked exasperated. "Monty Chambers."

"He's right here, Caleb," Stone said. He reached over and tugged hard on Pearl's beard. It started to come off. With his other hand Stone moved to grab a chunk of the bushy hair, but Pearl stopped him.

"Please allow me." He pulled first the beard and then the wig off, revealing a smooth, bald head.

Stone said, "To really hide your identity, don't leave a hairbrush and shampoo in the bathroom. Bald men rarely need those items."

Pearl sat down heavily in a chair and ran his hand along the fake hair. "I'd wash this and my beard in the sink and then brush them out. It was a pain, but there you are. Much of life is a pain."

Caleb was still staring at Vincent Pearl, who was now Monty Chambers.

"I can't believe I never saw that you two were one and the same man."

"The disguise was very effective, Caleb," Stone said. "Hair and a beard, different type of glasses, the added weight, unusual clothes. It all adds up to a very unique look. And by your own admission you'd seen Pearl privately here at the shop only twice before. And only at night, and the lighting is not that good."

Caleb nodded. "And you spoke very little at the library. And when you did, your voice was high and squeaky. So which came first," he demanded, "Vincent Pearl or Monty Chambers?"

Pearl smiled weakly. "Monty Chambers is my real name. Vincent Pearl was simply my alter ego."

"Why have one at all?" Stone asked.

At first Chambers appeared reluctant to answer. But finally, he shrugged and said, "I suppose it doesn't matter now. I used to be an actor, in my youth. I loved dressing up, playing the role. But my talent outstripped my opportunities, I guess you could say. My other passion was books. As a young man I apprenticed with an excellent conservator and learned the trade. I was hired by the library and had the beginnings of a good career. But I also wanted to collect books. And the salary at the library didn't allow for that. So I became a rare book dealer. I certainly had the knowledge and experience. But who would engage a humble conservator at the library for that? Not the rich, which was the clientele I was aiming for. So I invented someone they would pursue with vigor: Vincent Pearl, theatrical, mysterious, infallible."

"And whose shop was only open at night to accommodate his day job," Stone added.

"I bought this shop because it was across the alley from my home. I could put on my disguise and walk out the door and into my shop a new man. It worked very well. Over the years my reputation as a dealer flourished."

"How do you go from book dealer to spy?" Caleb asked, his voice trembling. "How do you go from book conservator to someone who kills people?"

Trent spoke up. "Don't say anything! They have nothing on us."

"We have the codes," Milton said.

"No, you don't," Trent sneered. "If you'd had them, you'd have gone to the police."

"*E, w, h, f, w, s, p, j, e, m, r, t, i, z.* Shall I go on?" Milton asked politely.

They all looked at him, dumbfounded.

Caleb said, "Milton, why didn't you tell us before?"

"I didn't think it mattered, because we didn't have the proof in the book. But I read the highlighted letters before they vanished. And once I see something, I never forget it," he said helpfully to the stunned Trent. "Anyway, it just occurred to me that since I remembered all the letters, the authorities could try and decrypt it once I told them."

Chambers looked at Trent and shrugged. "Albert's father and I were friends, meaning friends with me as Monty Chambers. When he passed away, I became a father figure to Albert, I guess, or at least a mentor. This was years ago. Albert came back to Washington after he finished school, and joined the CIA. He and I had talks over the years about the spy world. Then he

moved to the Hill. And we had more discussions. By this time
I'd let him in on my secret. He didn't like books all that much. A
character flaw that I, unfortunately, never held against him."

"The spying?" Stone prompted.

Trent screamed at Chambers, "You old fool, shut up!"

"Okay, that's it, bedtime, junior." Reuben slugged Trent flush
in the jaw, knocking him out. He straightened up and said encouragingly to the book dealer, "Go right ahead."

Chambers eyed the unconscious Trent. "Yes, I wonder that I
am an old *fool*. Little by little, Albert told me how there was
money to be made in selling what he called *minor* secrets. He explained that it wasn't so much spying as just the normal course
of business. He said in his position on the committee staff he'd
met a man who had contacts in all the intelligence agencies and
who was very interested in doing business with him. It turned
out later that this man was very dangerous. But Albert said lots
of people sold secrets, on both sides. It was almost expected."

"And you believed that?" Stone said.

"A part of me didn't. A part of me wanted to because book
collecting is an expensive passion and the money could come in
handy. I see clearly now that it was wrong, but back then it
didn't seem that bad. Albert said the problem was that all spies
eventually got caught when they did a drop. He said he'd figured a way around that that depended on me."

"Your skill as a conservator with rare books; you had expertise and access to the library," Caleb said.

"Yes. And Albert and I were old friends, so there was nothing
suspicious about him bringing me a book; that was my specialty,
after all. Inside the books, certain letters were marked with a
tiny dot. I'd take the coded letters he'd given me and put them in
the library books using the chemical stain. With incunabula
works I always loved the beautifully highlighted letters that the

craftsmen created during the cradle of printing and beyond. To me they were really paintings in miniature, hundreds of years old, and with proper care they can look as vibrant today as the day they were first done. In my own way I'd been experimenting with materials like that for years, just as a hobby. There's no market for that sort of thing anymore. It actually wasn't too difficult to come up with a chemical to make the letters react under the right type of lenses, which I also constructed. Along with old books, chemistry and the power and manipulability of light have always fascinated me. I do so enjoy my work at the library." He paused. "Well, at least I did enjoy it, as my career is now, of course, over." He sighed heavily. "On the other end, Albert and his people arranged for people to come to the reading room with these special glasses. I understand they came in on a regular basis, not always simply to get the coded messages, so as not to raise suspicion."

"Little old ladies and men coming in and reading rare books would never incite suspicion anyway," Stone added. "They could take the secrets, put them in an old-fashioned letter to a 'relative' living out of the country, and not even the mighty NSA, with all its supercomputers and satellites, would ever know. It really was a perfect plan."

"I would tell Albert which book was ready to go, and he would place little phrases on certain Internet sites that would tell them when to come in and what book to ask for. I'd deliver that book on the morning of their visit. I had an endless supply of volumes in for repair that were freely circulated in the reading room, so that was no problem. They came in, copied down the highlighted letters and went on their way. Some hours after that, the chemical wash evaporated and the evidence with it."

"And you get paid very well, with the money sent to a foreign account," Annabelle said.

"Something like that," he admitted.

"But like you said, Vincent Pearl was a big success. Why not go with that identity full-time?" Stone asked.

"As I said, I loved the work I did at the library. And it was fun fooling everyone. I guess I wanted the best of both worlds."

Caleb spoke up. "Spying is bad enough, but murder! Bob Bradley, Cornelius Behan, Norman Janklow, probably Jewell English? And Jonathan? You had Jonathan killed!"

"I didn't have any of them killed!" Chambers protested fiercely. He pointed at Trent. "He did that; he and whoever he's working with."

"Mr. Foxworth," Stone said slowly.

"But why Jonathan?" Caleb asked bitterly. "Why him?"

Chambers nervously rubbed his hands together. "He came into the conservation room unexpectedly after hours one night and saw me doctoring a book. I was just applying the chemicals to the pages. I tried to explain it away, but I'm not sure he believed me. I immediately told Albert what had happened, and the next thing I know, Jonathan was dead. Albert told me later that because the reading room was our base of exchange, they had to make the death seem natural. If we lost the reading room, we'd be out of business."

"But you knew what had happened, and yet you still didn't come forward?" Caleb said accusingly.

Chambers exclaimed, "How could I? I'd rot in jail."

"Which you will now," Stone said firmly. "And him," he added, looking at the slumped-over Trent.

A voice said, "Or maybe not."

They all whirled around and watched as Roger Seagraves stepped toward them, a pistol in each hand.

"Mr. Foxworth?" Caleb said.

"Shut up!" Seagraves said impatiently. His gaze settled on Trent, who was just coming around.

When he saw Seagraves, he said, "Thank God, Roger."

Seagraves smiled. "Wrong deity, Albert." He fired, hitting Trent in the chest. The man gasped and slipped off the chair onto the floor. Seagraves aimed his other pistol at Stone and Reuben, who'd made a move toward him. "I don't think so." He leveled his other pistol at Chambers. "Your services are no longer needed either." As Chambers braced for the impact of the bullet, Stone stepped between him and Seagraves.

"I've already called the police, they're on their way. If you're planning to escape, now would be an excellent time."

"That's really touching; one Triple Six looking out for another?"

Stone stiffened slightly.

Seagraves smiled. "So it's true. Then you know the first rule of our business: never leave any witnesses. But I am curious, how did you end up working in a cemetery? That's a long fall for somebody like you."

"I actually considered it a promotion."

Seagraves shook his head. "I would have saved myself a lot of trouble by just killing you when I had the chance. You destroyed a great operation. But I've got enough cash to live very well."

Annabelle said, "If you get away."

"Oh, I'll get away."

"I wouldn't be too sure," Stone said as he started to ease his right hand toward his jacket pocket. "The Secret Service and the FBI are involved now."

"Whoa, that really scares me. And at the very least I need to collect a few items for my collection," Seagraves said. "Hold it!" he cried out, and Stone's hand froze where it was, his fingertips near his jacket pocket. "Hands up, old man!"

"What?" Stone said, appearing bewildered.

"Hands up, Triple Six, where I can see them! Now!"

Stone jerked both hands straight up in the air.

Seagraves gasped and staggered forward. Dropping his pistols, he attempted to pull the knife out of his throat. But the blade Stone had tossed while throwing his hands up had severed the man's carotid artery. The blood was pouring out so fast, Seagraves was already crumbling to his knees. Then he was on his belly. He slowly rolled over on his back. As the others watched horrified, Stone calmly walked over to Seagraves and pulled the knife free.

The last person he'd killed with the underhanded knife toss had been just like this man. He'd more than deserved it.

Milton looked away while Caleb turned pale and seemed wobbly on his feet. Annabelle's and Reuben's gazes were locked on the mortally wounded man.

Stone looked down at the dying man without a trace of pity. "If you're going to kill someone, kill him, don't have a conversation with him."

As Roger Seagraves quietly expired, they heard sirens in the distance. "I called Alex Ford when I realized that Chambers' house backed up to the bookshop," Stone explained.

"That's why I did this, you know," Chambers said, finally pulling his gaze away from the now dead Seagraves. "For books. To acquire them, keep them safe for the next generation. With the money I earned I've purchased some amazing specimens. I really have." He looked up to see them all staring at him in disgust.

Chambers slowly rose. "I have something to give you, Caleb."

A suspicious Stone followed him over to the counter. When he reached in a drawer, Stone grabbed his hand. "I'll do that."

"It's not a weapon," Chambers protested.

"We'll see, won't we?" Stone pulled out a small box, opened

it, glanced inside and closed it. He handed it over to Caleb. Inside was the first-edition *Bay Psalm Book.*

"Thank you, God!" Caleb screamed in relief. Then he looked at Chambers in amazement. "How did you get this? You didn't have the code or key to the vault."

"You recall that I felt ill as we were about to leave the vault and you offered to fetch me a glass of water from the bathroom down there? As soon as you left, I opened the small safe. I'd watched you unlock it and saw what the code was: the number of the reading room. I took the book and put it in my jacket. When you came back with the water, you closed up the vault and we left."

Reuben groaned. "You dork; you left him in the vault all by himself?"

Caleb snapped, "Well, I didn't expect him to steal the damn thing."

Chambers stared down at his hands. "It was just an impulse on my part. Once I'd taken it, I was both terrified and thrilled. I'd never done anything like that before; I'm scrupulously honest with my clients. But that book. To even hold it!" His eyes gleamed for an instant and then dulled just as fast. "At least I can say I had it, if only for a little while. I kept pushing you to get the book evaluated because I thought that would throw suspicion away from me when the loss was discovered."

Annabelle looked in the box. "Oh, *that* book! So he *did* keep it."

Caleb stared at her in disbelief. "What? You know about this?" he demanded.

"Oh, it's a long story," she said hastily.

CHAPTER

68

ALEX FORD AND AN ARMY OF agents arrived a minute later. Surprisingly, Albert Trent was still alive, though badly wounded. His bundle of travel documents inside his jacket pocket had partially blocked the bullet. He was taken away in an ambulance. Chambers gave a detailed statement to the police, recounting all that he had already told the others. As Chambers was being led away, he said to Caleb, "Please take care of the *Psalm Book*."

Caleb's reply surprised everyone, maybe himself most of all. "It's just a damn book, Monty or Vincent or whoever the hell you really are. I'd much prefer to have Jonathan alive and well over this lump of old paper." He held up the priceless *Psalm Book* before dropping it unceremoniously in the box.

As the story unfolded over time, most of the deductions made by Stone and the others proved correct. Bradley *was* killed because he was about to force Trent to leave the committee staff, making it impossible for him and Seagraves to continue their seemingly innocent relationship. And Behan *was* murdered because he'd uncovered that Jonathan had been killed using the CO_2 stolen from his company.

They also learned from Chambers' account that one of Trent's men, who had gotten a job at Fire Control, Inc., had gone into the reading room vault and placed a small camera in the air duct under the pretense of adjusting the gas nozzle located there. Annabelle and Caleb hadn't seen this on the tape they'd reviewed because it occurred on a Saturday, when the room was closed, and the tape machine wasn't turned on. Yet they, of course, had seen something even more critical: Jewell English's sleight of hand with the glasses, which had ultimately led them to the truth.

A man had been posted in the basement halon storage room waiting for DeHaven to draw into the kill zone. On the second day he unfortunately had, and his life ended before he told anyone what he'd seen. Chambers had admitted to having gone into the vault later and retrieving the camera.

Milton had given the coded letters to representatives from the NSA, and they had already decrypted it. From the little Stone and the others learned, the code was based on a centuries-old encryption formula. It was easily breakable by modern-day decryption techniques with their massive computing power, but Seagraves had no doubt assumed that no one would ever suspect Monty Chambers, Norman Janklow and Jewell English of being spies. And modern-day ciphertexts were all electronically generated, requiring keys consisting of massively long numbers to remain secure against brute-force assaults and other attacks by computers, which would have been impossible to replicate in an old book.

Trent had recovered from his wounds and was busily talking, especially when he learned that the government was trying mightily to pin the death penalty on him. This information included Roger Seagraves' prominent role as the head of the spy ring. Now that they knew of Seagraves' involvement, the FBI was investigating everyone remotely connected to him; other arrests seemed imminent.

They'd also searched Seagraves' house and found his "collection" room. While they hadn't quite figured out what these items represented yet, when they eventually did, things would really get complicated, since many of them belonged to victims killed by Seagraves as part of his past CIA duties.

Stone had met at length with Ford, members of the FBI and the same two D.C. detectives who'd confronted Caleb at the library.

An FBI agent said, "We knew there was a spy ring operating in the city, but we could never run it down to its source. We certainly never figured the Library of Congress to be involved."

Stone said, "Well, we had an asset you didn't."

The agent looked surprised. "What was that?"

Alex Ford answered, "A highly skilled librarian named Caleb Shaw, that's who."

One of the D.C. detectives' eyes twinkled. "Right, Shaw. Good, is he? He struck me as a little, uh, nervous."

Stone replied, "Let's just say his lack of personal courage is more than outweighed by his—"

The detective cut in, "Dumb luck?"

"Attention to detail."

They'd thanked Stone for his help and left the door open for future cooperation.

"You ever need any help, just let us know," one of the FBI agents had said, handing Stone a card with a phone number on it.

Stone put the card in his pocket thinking, *I hope to God I never need help that badly.*

After things had calmed somewhat, they all met at Stone's cottage. And that's when Caleb had held up the *Psalm Book* and demanded that Annabelle tell him the truth.

She took a deep breath and started explaining. "I knew how much Jonathan loved books, and one day I asked him that if he could have any book in the world, which one would it be? He said the *Bay Psalm Book*. Well, I read up on it and found that all of them were in institutions, but one seemed the best choice to hit."

"Let me guess, Old South Church in Boston?" Caleb prompted.

"How'd you know?"

"Easier to crack than the Library of Congress or Yale, at least I hope."

"Anyway, I went up there with a friend of mine and told them we were college students doing a paper on famous books."

"And they let you look at it," Caleb said.

"Yes. And take pictures of it, all that. Then I had another friend who was really good at making bad pa—I mean, good at making things."

"So he *forged* a *Bay Psalm Book*?" Caleb exclaimed.

"It was great, you couldn't tell them apart." Annabelle's excitement faded when she saw the furious look on his face. "Well, anyway, we went back up there and did a little switcheroo."

"You did a little switcheroo?" Caleb said, his face turning very red. "With one of the rarest books in the history of this country you did a little *switcheroo*?"

"Why didn't you just give DeHaven the excellent copy?" Stone asked.

"Give a *fake* book to the man I loved? I don't think so."

Caleb collapsed into a chair. "I don't believe what I'm hearing."

Before he got more wound up, she hurried on with her story. "When I gave him the book, Jonathan was stunned. But of course, I told him it was just a copy I'd had made for him. I don't know if he believed that or not. I think he might have called around to different places to check. And I believe he'd concluded that what I did for a living wasn't exactly on the up-and-up."

"*Really?* What a *stunner* that must've been," Caleb snapped.

She ignored him. "But since the church didn't know their book was a fake and no *Psalm Books* were missing, I guess Jonathan finally assumed I was telling the truth. It made him so happy. And it was just an old book."

"Just an old book!" Caleb was really about to erupt when Stone put a hand on his shoulder. "Let's not beat a dead horse, Caleb."

"A dead horse?" Caleb sputtered.

"I'll put it back," Annabelle offered.

"Excuse me?" Caleb said.

"I'll take the book back and do another switcheroo."

"You can't be serious."

"I'm completely serious. I switched it once, I can switch it again."

"What if they catch you?"

She looked at Caleb with pity. "I'm a lot better now than I was back then." She looked over at Milton. "Want to help me do it?"

"Sure!" Milton exclaimed enthusiastically.

Caleb looked apoplectic. "I absolutely forbid your participation in a felony!"

Milton exclaimed, "Will you loosen up, Caleb? And it's not a felony if we're putting the real book *back*, now is it?"

Caleb started to say something and then rapidly calmed. "No, I guess it isn't."

"I'll take care of the details," Annabelle said. "I'll just need the book from you, Caleb." She reached out for it.

He immediately clutched it to his chest. "Can't I keep it until you really need it?" he asked, his hand lightly running over the cover.

"You told Monty Chambers it was just a dumb book," Reuben reminded him.

Caleb looked miserable. "I know. I haven't slept a wink since I said it. I think the book fairies have cursed me," he added glumly.

"Okay," she said. "You can keep it for now."

Reuben looked at Annabelle hopefully. "Okay, now that all the fun's over, would you like to go out with me sometime? Like maybe tonight?"

She smiled. "Can I take a rain check, Reuben? But I appreciate the offer."

"It won't be the last one, may-dam." He kissed her hand.

After the others had left, Annabelle joined Stone, who'd gone to work in the cemetery.

As he washed off a tombstone, she gathered weeds in a plastic bag.

"You don't have to stay and help me," he said. "Working in a cemetery isn't exactly the life I'd picture for someone like you."

She put her hands on her hips. "So what *do* you picture for someone like me?"

"Husband, kids, nice house in the suburbs, PTO board, maybe a dog."

"You're kidding, right?"

"I'm kidding. So what now?"

"Well, I have to return the book so Caleb will get off my back."

"And after that?"

She shrugged. "I'm not one who looks that far ahead." She grabbed another sponge, knelt down and started helping Stone clean off the grave marker. Later, after they'd eaten a dinner that Annabelle prepared, they sat on the porch and talked.

"I'm glad I came back," she said, glancing at Stone.

Stone said, "I am too, Annabelle."

She smiled at his use of her real name. "That Seagraves guy, he called you a Triple Six. What's that about?"

"That was *about* thirty years ago," Stone said.

"Fair enough. We all have secrets. So you ever think about going someplace other than here?" she asked him.

He shook his head. "*Here* tends to grow on you," he said simply.

Maybe it will, Annabelle thought. They sat in silence, staring up at the full moon.

A four-hour drive north, Jerry Bagger stood looking out his window at the same moon overhead. He'd called in every favor he'd ever earned, threatened and beaten up more people than he could remember, loving every minute of it. The result was he was closing in as her defenses and covers started falling away. Very soon it would be his turn. And what he'd done to Tony Wallace would pale next to what he had planned for the lady. The image of her slow destruction at his hands never failed to curl his lips into a smile. He was back in control. Bagger puffed contentedly on his cigar and sipped a finger of his bourbon.

Get ready, Annabelle Conroy. Here comes big, bad Jerry.

ACKNOWLEDGMENTS

To Michelle, the one who really makes it all work.

To Colin Fox, thanks for a great editing job. Here's to many books together.

To Aaron Priest, the master, enough said.

To Maureen, Jamie, Jimmy and all the rest at Hachette Book Group USA, for being great friends and business partners.

To Lucy Childs and Lisa Erbach Vance, for all you do for me.

To Dr. John Y. Cole at the Library of Congress, for making the Library come alive.

To Mark Dimunation and Daniel DeSimone at the Library of Congress, for showing me the gem that is the LOC Rare Book Reading Room.

To Diane van der Reyden at the Library of Congress, for making the rounds of your department with me. I hope I got it mostly right.

To Dr. Monica Smiddy, thank you for the detailed and thoughtful medical advice.

To Bob Schule, my eagle reader and world-class consultant.

To Deborah, who helps keep me sane and on schedule.

To Rosemary Bustamante, for your foreign language skills, and for being a great friend.

To Maria Rejt, for making it better from across the pond.

To Cornelius Behen, for the use of your name. Hope you liked the character.

And finally, to the memory of Robert (Bob) Bradley, who never got to see his name in the book but who lives in the hearts and minds of the Bradley and Hope families and all his friends.